THE
CHANGELING

Victor LaValle is the author of six previous works of fiction. He has been the recipient of a Guggenheim Fellowship, an American Book Award, the Shirley Jackson Award and the Key to Southeast Queens. He lives in New York with his wife and children and teaches at Columbia University.

@victorlavalle

victorlavalle.com

'I say this without exaggeration: it's a masterpiece'
MAT JOHNSON

'Absolutely compelling, completely thrilling, *The Changeling* overflows with menace, wonder and beauty'
KELLY LINK

'[A] bewitching masterpiece' USA TODAY

by victor lavalle

FICTION

The Ecstatic
Big Machine
The Devil in Silver
The Changeling

NOVELLAS

The Ballad of Black Tom
Lucretia and the Kroons

SHORT STORY COLLECTION

Slapboxing with Jesus

THE
CHANGELING
VICTOR LAVALLE

CANONGATE

First published in Great Britain in 2018 by Canongate Books Ltd,
14 High Street, Edinburgh EH1 1TE

canongate.co.uk

1

First published in the United States by Spiegel & Grau, an imprint of
Random House, a division of Penguin Random House LLC, New York

The moral right of the author has been asserted

British Library Cataloguing-in-Publication Data
A catalogue record for this book is available on
request from the British Library

ISBN 978 1 78689 382 6

Printed and bound in Great Britain by Clays Ltd, St Ives plc.

For Emily, Geronimo, and Delilah.
My Supreme Team.

1
FIRST COMES LOVE

THIS FAIRY TALE begins in 1968 during a garbage strike. In February New York City's sanitation workers refused to pick up trash for eight straight days. One hundred thousand tons of garbage filled the sidewalks, spilled into the streets. Rats ran laps alongside morning joggers. Rubbish fires boiled the air. The five boroughs had been given up for dead. Still, there was some cracked magic in the air because that was when Lillian and Brian met. Each had journeyed from far-flung lands to find one another in Queens. Neither could've guessed the wildness that falling in love would unleash.

Lillian Kagwa emigrated from Uganda while Brian West arrived from the only slightly less foreign territory of Syracuse. This daughter of East Africa and son of upstate New York met at a cut-rate modeling agency on Northern Boulevard. Neither was a client.

The week of the garbage strike Lillian got hired as a secretary at the agency, greeting guests at the front desk. A pleasant sight for folks strolling sidewalks saddled with week-old waste. Brian, a parole officer, had been paying occasional visits to the agency's founder, Pavel Aresenyev, one of his parolees, who'd spent four years in prison for fraud. Brian didn't believe Pavel had gone legit. But that week Brian became focused less on Mr. Aresenyev and more on the new secretary who greeted him when he arrived. Meeting her felt like finding a rose growing in a landfill. Brian dropped by the modeling agency four times that week.

Despite his immediate attraction, Brian had a habit of mispronouncing Lillian Kagwa's last name, and Lillian kept mistaking Brian for other white men. Hardly kismet. Still Brian West—short, stocky, and persistent—simply wouldn't quit. And on the days when he didn't show up, Lillian, to her own surprise, found she missed him.

Lillian Kagwa had come from Jinja, the second-largest city in Uganda, where she'd lived through the country's emancipation from Britain and its eventual homegrown rule by Milton Obote. Obote used the army and his secret police, the General Service Unit, to rule the land. They spread wickedness wherever they went.

In 1967 Lillian and three cousins were traveling to the capital, Kampala, when they were pulled over by three men claiming to be agents of the GSU. The four cousins sat quietly as the agents inspected their identification, then demanded the only male cousin—Arthur—come out and open the trunk. Arthur didn't want to leave Lillian and his sisters and hesitated. In that moment, one agent leaned in and casually shot Arthur in the stomach.

Lillian and her cousins were temporarily deafened by the sound, blinded by the muzzle flash, but Lillian still sensed the agent who'd fired the gun pawing inside the car to pull out the keys. Lillian, at the wheel, shifted the car into drive and shot off before her senses had returned to her, weaving across the two-lane road like a drunk. The agents fired at the car but couldn't pursue it; their own vehicle had run out of gas. They'd set up the checkpoint to steal a suitable vehicle and would have to wait for another.

Lillian reached Kampala in half an hour, speeding the whole way. Arthur died long before that. An incident like this hardly counted as newsworthy. Uganda, as a whole, was going buckwild, and Lillian Kagwa wanted out. One year later Lillian secured a visa to the United States.

In 1968 Lillian came to New York. She was twenty-five and knew no one, but because of Uganda's British rule, she already spoke the king's English, and this made her transition easier. One of the reason's Mr. Aresenyev hired her at the modeling agency was because her command of

English was so much better than his. She made the business sound serious, legitimate, though Brian West's suspicions were right: the whole thing was a scam. Lillian didn't know this when she accepted the work. All she knew was the job paid twice the state minimum wage, three bucks an hour. Back in Uganda, she hadn't been able to find work of any kind, so she cherished the gig. And what was a garbage strike compared with state-sanctioned murder?

The agency, Glamour Time, was run out of a windowless second-floor office near Queensboro Plaza, remote from any hub of high fashion but centrally located for soaking the aspiring models of working-class Queens. Potential clients could join the agency as long as they had headshots. Luckily, Mr. Aresenyev had a small studio right there at the agency and could snap the shots himself for a fee. For certain young women, he offered to take the shots after hours, just the two of them. The streets of New York were overrun with uncollected garbage, but Glamour Time carried its own stink. The only honest aspect of the business was the East African woman answering phones out front.

Mr. Aresenyev's business might've run just fine for quite a while, soaking hopeful young women for years, except his damn parole officer had made the front office into his second home. How were you going to run a decent fraud when a cop was stopping by every other morning? Brian West was bad for business. And since he was smitten with Lillian that meant Lillian Kagwa was bad for business. So Mr. Aresenyev fired her. Not the smartest plan, but Mr. Aresenyev wasn't bright. Now Brian pursued Pavel relentlessly, an Inspector Javert from Onondaga County. Charging for the headshots wasn't illegal, but running a photo studio without a permit was enough to count as a violation of parole. Pavel Aresenyev went back to jail. Brian West got a commendation. Lillian Kagwa needed a new job.

She worked as an administrative secretary at a law firm in midtown Manhattan. The new job paid less. She moved into a smaller apartment. She cut off all communications with Brian. He'd cost her a good job, and the commute to midtown added a half hour of travel time each way, so no, she did not want to get dinner and a movie with Brian, thank you. Anyway, she was young, and it was New York City, where a lot more fun was to be had than back in Jinja. They met in 1968 but didn't go on their first real date until eight years later.

Brian West gave Lillian room, backed off by a borough; he rented a place on Staten Island, but he couldn't stop thinking of her. Why? What was it about Lillian? He couldn't quite explain. It was as if she'd cast a spell.

Brian West had been the only child of two wildly unromantic drunks. At twelve Brian had a job selling candy at the Elmwood Theatre. He made the mistake of proudly displaying his earnings to his father, Frank. He expected a pat on the shoulder, words of congratulations; instead the boy endured a strong-arm robbery right in his own living room. His dad bought a case of Genesee beer with the money. Mom and Dad finished it before bedtime. A household like that will either break you or toughen you up. Maybe both. What was waiting on a woman to forgive you compared with having your father beat you up and steal your first paycheck?

Late in 1976 it finally happened. Brian West and Lillian Kagwa went on a date. They'd both been twenty-five when they first met during the week of the garbage strike, but now they were thirty-three. Lillian had met a lot of men during those intervening years, and Brian benefited from the comparison. He worked hard, didn't drink, saved his money, and paid his debts. Funny how much she valued such qualities now. The only hiccup came at dinner, when Brian talked about how much he wanted children, the chance to be a husband and a father. As soon as he'd seen her at Glamour Time he'd sensed she would be a wonderful mother. When he finished talking she reminded him, gently, that this was their first date. Maybe they could wait to make wedding plans until after the movie at least? To Brian's credit, he didn't act wounded or angry—he laughed. He didn't know it, but it was at this moment that Lillian truly fell for him.

He took her to see *Rocky*. It wouldn't have been Lillian's choice, but halfway through the movie, she started to enjoy herself. She even saw herself on the screen. A fierce dreamer. That's what this movie was about. And wasn't that her? She liked to think so. Maybe that was why Brian brought her to see this picture. To show her something about himself that he could never put into words. He'd told her the story of being robbed by his father, and she'd told him about Arthur getting gutshot in the car, and now here they both were in a darkened Times Square theater. Together. A pair of survivors. It seemed so unlikely—all the life that had led them here—as improbable as myth. In the dark she held his hand. Though they wouldn't have sex for another three hours, it would be accurate to say their first child—their only child—was conceived right then. A thought, an idea, a shared dream; parenthood is a story two people start telling together.

By April 1977 Lillian was showing. Brian found them a two-bedroom apartment in Jackson Heights. Their son came in September. Brian thought it would be weird to name a half-black kid Rocky, so instead they named him Apollo. Brian liked to carry the newborn in the crook of one arm, cooing to him, "You are the god, Apollo. Good night, my little sun." And they lived happily ever after. At least for a few years.

By Apollo's fourth birthday Brian West was gone.

Brian hadn't run off with another woman or skipped town to move back to Syracuse. The man might as well have been erased from existence. He couldn't be found because he'd left no trail, neither breadcrumbs nor credit card receipts. Gone. Disappeared. Vanished.

When Apollo was born, Brian and Lillian thought they'd reached the end of the story, but they'd been wrong. The wildness had only begun.

RIGHT AFTER BRIAN went missing, the boy began having a recurring dream. Since he was only four, Lillian couldn't make much sense of the details. Most of it came in the long hurried babble of a scared child in the night, but she pieced it together. There was a man knocking at the front door. When Apollo unlocked it, the man pushed his way in. He knelt down in front of Apollo. He had a face, but he took off that face. The face underneath was the face of his daddy. Brian West opened his mouth, and a cloud spilled from his mouth. Apollo watched the fog roll out from his father's throat and began to cry. The mist filled the apartment until the boy could hardly see. His daddy picked him up. Now the sound of rushing water, loud as a waterfall, filled the apartment. Apollo's father carried him through the fog. His father finally spoke to him. Right about then Apollo would wake up screaming.

This nightmare came to the kid night after night for weeks. Apollo no longer wanted to sleep, and Lillian couldn't shut her eyes because she knew, at some point, her four-year-old boy would be in terror.

You're coming with me.

That's what Brian told Apollo in the dream.

While trying to console him, Lillian asked why those words made him wake with such fear. His answer cut her down through flesh and bone. It wasn't fear that made him cry out. It was longing.

"Why didn't he take me with him?" Apollo said.

Eventually the nightmare passed, or at least, Apollo stopped talking about it. This let life reset to its new normal: Lillian, a single mother who worked full time, taking classes on Saturdays to become a legal secretary, and raising her child alone, a life both grueling and rewarding. Apollo, a bookish child, growing up to be self-contained and watchful.

They stumbled along like this for eight more years. By the time Apollo turned twelve, they never spoke of Brian West and neither expected to make him a topic of conversation for the rest of their days, but then one afternoon Apollo received a message from the man. A gift.

THIS WAS IN the fall of 1989, and Apollo Kagwa was a junior high school student at IS 237 in Flushing. With Brian gone Lillian reverted to her maiden name and she damn sure did the same for her son. He became a Kagwa by legal decree. They erased the West from their lives.

Even a self-contained and watchful kid like Apollo could end up running with a crew. He had two best friends and did well in American history with Mr. Perrault. Lillian had passed her classes to become a legal secretary and found a better job at a law firm in midtown Manhattan. But the work had her keeping even longer hours, not getting home until eight o'clock sometimes. *Latchkey kid* was the term. Adults lamented this new reality on the *Donahue* show. They scolded working mothers who were damaging their poor kids by their need to make a living.

Apollo spent that afternoon as kids do when they don't have to be home right away: dipping into the nearby diner to play a few quarters' worth of Galaga, then off to the bodega for quarter waters and chips, looping around the corner to Colden Street, where a game of running bases had popped off. He played for an hour or three, then headed upstairs. It had been—in all honesty—a day or two since he'd had a shower, and the game worked up a funk even he couldn't ignore. Apollo turned on the shower and had stripped halfway down when he heard heavy knocking coming from the far end of the apartment. When he ignored it—probably just a neighbor looking for his mom—the pounding only got louder. The hot water in the shower started to form steam. When Apollo walked out of the bathroom, it looked as if he'd stepped out of a cloud.

He'd made it halfway across the apartment before a prickly feeling ran across his neck. The knocking at the door continued, but he looked behind him to find the steam in the bathroom flowing out into the hall, as if it was following him. Apollo felt woozy just then. As if, without knowing it, he'd taken a step into someone's dream. His own dream. He felt jolted by the realization. He'd had this dream, night after night, when he was young. How young? Three or four? There had been knocking at the door, and the sound of running water, the apartment dense with fog and . . .

He ran for the front door. As soon as he got close, the knocking stopped abruptly.

"Wait for me," he whispered. He felt stupid when he said it. Even stupider when he repeated it.

His father was not on the other side of the door. His father was not on the other side of the door. His father was not.

And still Apollo snapped the locks open. He felt as if he was shrinking. How had he opened the door in that dream? How had he reached the top lock when he was only a small child? Anything was possible in a dream. How about now then? Maybe he'd fallen asleep in the bathroom, sitting in the tub, and some random firing of electricity in his brain had helped this fantasy resurface. Apollo decided not to care. There was a certain freedom in knowing you were in a dream. If nothing else, he might open the door and see his father and be reminded of the man's features. He couldn't remember them anymore. But when he opened the door, his father wasn't there.

Instead a box sat on the threshold.

Apollo leaned out, as if he'd catch a glimpse of his dream father, maybe farther down the hall. Nobody there. He looked back down at the box. Heavy cardboard, one word written on the lid in black marker.

Improbabilia.

Apollo went down on a knee. He picked up the box—it wasn't heavy—and brought it inside with him. The contents of the box shifted and thumped. He sat on the carpet in the living room. He opened the lid.

"THAT WAS YOUR father's box," Lillian said.

Apollo didn't notice the sun had set, didn't hear his mother enter the apartment. It was only when she touched the back of his neck that he became aware of anything else at all.

She dropped her purse and crouched beside him. "Where did you find all this?" she asked.

"Someone left it at the door," he said.

Apollo had spread the contents out on the living room carpet. A pair of movie ticket stubs, the headshot of some young white woman, the rental agreement to an apartment in Jackson Heights, the bill for an overnight stay at a hotel on Ninth Avenue, right near Times Square, a small stack of receipts for takeout food, a marriage certificate for Brian West and Lillian Kagwa, and one children's book.

"What are you talking about?" Lillian whispered as she scanned the collection. "My God," she said even more softly.

Apollo turned to look at her, and she reared back, standing straight, trying to recover. "Tell me the truth," she said. "Was this in my closet? Did you go through my things?"

Apollo pointed to the front door. "There was a lot of knocking. I thought—" He stopped himself. "I didn't know who it was. I was about to take a shower."

This was when Apollo registered the running water, still going. He got to his feet and sped to the bathroom. Because of the slow drain in their apartment, the tub had overflowed, and the bathroom floor showed puddles all over.

"Apollo!" Lillian shouted when she found the mess. She pushed past her son and turned off the water. She pulled towels down from the rack and laid them on the floor. "I have to go check with Mrs. Ortiz and make sure we didn't leak through her ceiling."

Despite this impossible box in the living room, there were some concerns no parent could ignore; for instance, did her son just cause a major accident for their downstairs neighbor, a kind old woman who used to babysit this thoughtless child? And how much might it cost her to fix Mrs. Ortiz's ceiling?

Lillian left the bathroom, and Apollo followed her. On her way to the door, she glanced back to the box, the items on the carpet, and quickly returned to them. She leaned over and snatched up one piece of paper, turned, and left the apartment. Apollo returned to living room. Lillian had taken the receipt for the overnight stay near Times Square. She thought she was hiding something, but it didn't matter. In the time that he'd been sitting there, he'd basically committed all of it to memory and tried to connect the items to the stories he knew about his mother and father. One of the things he hadn't been sure of was the bit his mother just confirmed.

How could a man who held on to all these things just abandon his wife and child? And how had all this evidence ended up at Apollo's front door? He looked at the lid of the box again and read the word etched across the top. *Improbabilia*.

His mother would have to explain what most of the items signified, but one seemed easier to grasp. The children's book, *Outside Over There* by Maurice Sendak. Apollo opened it. He'd been hoping to find a special note, a dedication of some kind, from father to son, even just evidence of his dad's handwriting. None of that, but the pages were well worn, the upper-right corner of each page faintly smudged, the spine of the book showed cracks. This wasn't for display; this book had been read many times. Apollo imagined Brian West—maybe sitting on this very couch—

reading the book aloud to his child. Now he read the first page aloud to himself.

" 'When Papa was away at sea,' " he began.

His mother wasn't a reader. For all her good qualities, this just wasn't one of them. Lillian worked like a beast, and at night she had the energy to sit with him and watch television, that's all. Many nights she fell asleep right there. Apollo didn't mind. But once she'd knocked out, he'd take off her shoes, slip off her wig, turn off the television, and go into his room to read. He'd been like this ever since he could sound out words. The book in his hand allowed him to imagine there was a time when he wasn't the only reader in the home. He liked to believe he'd inherited a taste for texts. Maybe this book had been only the first of many his father planned to share. Apollo's appetite for reading only grew after he found the box.

Apollo read in bed and while using the bathroom. He took books to the park. He read paperbacks while he played right field. He lost books, spilled soda on them, and splotches of melted chocolate fingerprints appeared inside. Even the kindest librarians had to start charging replacement fees. So Lillian began a practice of bringing books and magazines home from her law office. *Reader's Digest* and *People*, *Consumer Reports* and *Bon Appétit*. He went through all of them and still wanted more. She befriended secretaries on other floors of the building and even convinced a few to start subscribing to magazines that differed from the ones at her firm. A dentist's office across the street kept mass-market paperbacks for its clients, and she convinced the woman at the front desk to give the old copies to her rather than throw them away. These were romances and thrillers, mostly; true crime thrived. Lillian Kagwa didn't vet the volumes, just plopped them into a plastic bag and took them home on the 7 train. So Apollo read Ann Rule's *The Stranger Beside Me*, *The Wayward Heiress* by Blanche Chenier, and *Dragon* by Clive Cussler when he was way too young to understand them. Nevertheless, he finished each one. Unsupervised reading is a blessing for a certain kind of child.

Lillian didn't fully grasp the kind of child her son was until a Saturday in early October when their neighbor, Mrs. Ortiz from downstairs, came to the apartment. Mrs. Ortiz was there to see not Lillian but her son. Lillian's immediate guess was that Apollo had done something wrong, but Mrs. Ortiz only waved a dollar bill in the air saying Apollo had promised her the issue of *People* magazine with that sweet Julia Roberts girl on the cover, but he hadn't come by with it yet. After a few minutes Lillian sorted through her confusion, and consternation, to understand that her son had been selling off the books and magazines she'd been bringing home. She felt so aggravated that she went into Apollo's room, found the issue amid one of the stacks on the floor, and gave it to Mrs. Ortiz for free. She tried to throw in a more recent issue with Barbara Bush on the cover, but Mrs. Ortiz didn't know who that was.

Apollo returned home right around sundown. New York had been going through a warm spell so the day had been only in the mid-seventies. He and his friends had been at Flushing Meadows Park playing two-hand touch until the temperature finally cooled. He showed up grimy but glowing. Lillian let him find her in the kitchen. She'd spent the late afternoon putting all the magazines and mass-market paperbacks into garbage bags. Those bags were on the small kitchen table instead of dinner. Before Apollo could ask why, Lillian told him about the visit from Mrs. Ortiz.

"I went through the trouble of getting those things for you because I thought you were going to read them," Lillian said. Now she lifted one bag, grunting with the weight. "But if not, we can just drop all these down to the incinerator."

Apollo untied one of the bags and peeked inside. "I do read them," he said. "All of them. But after I'm done, what should I do?"

"Throw them away, Apollo. What else?" She tied the bag closed again.

"But Mrs. Ortiz likes reading *People*, so . . ."

"So why not charge an old woman?"

"She pays me a quarter. Cover price is $1.95. That's a great deal for her, and she doesn't care if it's a few weeks old. What's wrong with that?"

Lillian opened her mouth to answer him but found she didn't have a ready reply. She scanned the bags. "You sell all of it?"

"The stuff I can't sell, I throw away, but I do pretty good around the neighborhood."

"You're twelve," Lillian said, sitting down with a plop. "Where did you learn to do this?"

Apollo remained silent a moment, then smiled widely. "You, Mom. I learned it by watching you."

"What does that mean?"

"You work so hard. I see that. And I'm your son. It's in my blood."

Lillian pointed to the chair beside her, and Apollo sat there. She watched him for a long count.

"If you're going to run a business, you should have business cards," she said. "Your name should be on them, and a phone number. I guess we could put the home phone there. I'll get them made for you. I can get them for free through my office."

Lillian rose from her chair and returned a moment later with a sheet of typing paper and a pen. She drew a large rectangle and scribbled in a few lines:

Apollo Kagwa
Used Books & Magazines

She crossed out that second line and wrote in another.

Affordable Books & Magazines.

Under that she wrote their phone number.

Then she set the tip of her pen at the top of the rectangle, right above Apollo's name. "You'll need a name for the business." She waited on him, pen poised.

He slipped the pen from her hand and wrote it in himself.

Improbabilia.

APOLLO KAGWA MIGHT'VE gone to college if it wasn't for a man named Carlton Lake. Apollo was a senior at John Bowne High School, and based on his grades, he qualified as absolutely average. Bs and Cs straight down the report card. It had been that way since ninth grade. A surprise to some of his teachers since the kid could be counted on for brains and even study, but school wasn't his true enthusiasm. All Apollo Kagwa cared about was his business.

By the age of seventeen, he'd turned Improbabilia into a thriving concern. The kid was known in Queens, Manhattan, and the Bronx. Rare and used book dealers learned of him because he would call a shop cold and ask if he could stop by, a fellow dealer who happened to be near and wanted to make a courtesy visit. Sure, they'd say, baffled by the decorum. These guys weren't generally known for their Emily Post. And soon enough some fifteen-year-old black kid clomps in, he's got a pack on his back that would make a mule buckle, and he introduces himself as Apollo. The kid's glasses are so large, they should have windshield wipers.

He enters their stores and tries selling off weathered issues of magazines like *The Connoisseur* and *Highlights*. The combination of entrepreneurial spirit and absolute naïveté was enough to make some of those old booksellers fall hard for that fifteen-year-old. Through them he got the education he craved. They taught him how to value a book, how to navigate estate sales, and the best spots to set up a table at antique shows.

Other booksellers were far less welcoming. When he shared his stock, trying to sell, they accused him of having stolen the merchandise. Maybe he'd broken into a storefront and looted whatever he could. A few stores—the higher-end spots in Manhattan—had buzzer entry at the doors. This was the era of Bernhard Goetz shooting black boys on the subway and many white folks in the city cheering him on. Every kid with excess melanin became a superpredator, even a black boy with glasses and a backpack full of books. He might be standing at the entrance for fifteen minutes while the clerks pretended not to notice him.

To make things worse, Apollo would find himself wondering if he actually was frightening, a monster, the kind that would drive his own father away. That conviction flared brightest at moments like this, when the world seemed to corroborate his monstrousness. If he wasn't careful, he'd be consumed. To endure these humiliations, these supernovas of self-loathing, Apollo dreamed up a mantra—or maybe the words came to him from some old memory—one he'd repeat to himself while he stood there being judged. *I am the god, Apollo. I am the god, Apollo. I am the god, Apollo.* He'd chant it enough that he soon felt downright divine. But that didn't mean those store owners let him in.

In 1995, senior year of high school, he got accepted to Queens College, but the summer before school started, one of the dealers who mentored Apollo gave him his graduation gift, *Confessions of a Literary Archaeologist* by a man named Carlton Lake.

Lake gives a history of his life as a collector of rare and valuable books, manuscripts, music scores, and even letters from the era of Napoleon. While the collector, and his collection, apparently became quite famous, the early part of the book details how he came to love these materials. He'd been a big reader and browser of secondhand bookstores. When it came time to start truly collecting books, the kind that cost more than a couple of quarters, Lake mentions he was "abetted by an indulgent grandmother." In other words, Grandma bankrolled him. And quickly enough Carlton Lake was collecting the great nineteenth-century French poets:

Baudelaire, Verlaine, Rimbaud, Mallarmé. Soon he had his moment of revelation, "illumination" he calls it, when he made his first great purchase at an auction in New York. He bought a copy of Baudelaire's *Les Fleurs du Mal—Flowers of Evil—*and inside found corrections written in the margins by Baudelaire himself. With this find, he became a literary archaeologist. For Lake this was the start of his true calling. He had become a book man.

By the time Apollo Kagwa finished reading that anecdote, he knew he wouldn't be attending Queens College in the fall. Though he didn't have a grandmother bankrolling his purchases, and despite the reality that he didn't yet know the difference between Baudelaire and Beatrix Potter, he still felt sure he was also a book man. If Carlton Lake could do this shit why couldn't he? The son of two fierce dreamers had become one, too.

"**E**STATE SALE" SOUNDS posh, but for Apollo it might mean traveling all the way to New Rochelle to inspect one garbage bag full of water-damaged books in the basement of some Victorian Colonial. Then again he might find four bookshelves of perfectly preserved first editions at a townhouse in Sugar Hill. The suspense, the surprise, mattered nearly as much as the profit.

Apollo had found his calling early, but his first great find in the field—his Baudelaire moment—didn't happen till he was thirty-four. He'd moved out of Lillian's apartment at nineteen and found a studio in Jackson Heights, the place so crammed with books he hardly had room for a twin bed. He crossed the country on his book hunts. Occasionally he looked up from the frontispieces and margins to take in the sights, date a woman, but after a few good moments he always got back to work.

The big day, though, was at an estate sale in the basement of a Bronx apartment building, forty-two containers of books—from sneaker boxes to an old orange milk crate scavenged from a supermarket. In them were some of the rarest books on magic and the occult that Apollo had ever seen. A loving couple, Mr. and Mrs. D'Agostino, died within months of each other and left behind a collection that creeped out their four children and eleven grandchildren. He found a snapshot of the old duo tucked in the pages of a grimoire. They looked like the old man and wife from that movie *Up*, but this version of Carl and Ellie Fredrickson had been stockpiling volumes of sorcery. The homely photo and the otherworldly collection were so incongruous, Apollo had to fight hard not to laugh in front of the family.

He made a lowball offer right there, and because he'd been the first dealer willing to come out to the South Bronx, he got the sale. He rented a van that afternoon and took the stuff home. It took a week to catalog everything and upload the relevant info for the books. As he leafed through them, he found scribbled notes here and there in the margins, in two different kinds of handwriting.

As he examined a third edition folio of a lighthearted little book called *Witch Hunter Manual of the Blood Council*, out slipped a postcard addressed to the D'Agostinos. The plain postcard hadn't yellowed as much as he would've expected since the date stamped on it read 1945. The addresser's name, his signature absolutely clear, was Aleister Crowley. A quick check online verified Crowley had been a famed occultist in the early 1900s, called "the wickedest man in history." Accused of Satanism. A recreational drug user and sexual adventurer back when such a thing was scandalous rather than just a part of one's online dating profile. Ozzy Osbourne wrote a song about the guy in 1981. And apparently Domenico and Eliana D'Agostino had received a postcard from him. Apollo read Aleister Crowley's note to the couple.

Some men are born sodomites, some achieve sodomy, and some have sodomy thrust upon them.

Thinking of you both.

Well, how did you like that? The D'Agostinos had been certified freaks!

Even before the postcard this haul had been Apollo's best. Now, if he could authenticate the card, this find could become legendary. Carlton Lake got Baudelaire's corrected texts; Apollo Kagwa got a horny postcard from Aleister Crowley. He read the card again and laughed. He held it up to share the joke with someone else—but he sat alone in the living room. The find of his life, and no one there to share the news. Now he felt surprised, overcome, with a different emotion.

Apollo Kagwa felt fucking lonely.

He looked again at the books he'd bought from the family; he scanned the postcard. Mr. and Mrs. D'Agostino had been up to some wild stuff, it seemed, but the two of them had been on their occult adventure together. The handwriting in the margins, two different styles, suggested husband and wife both spent time studying these tomes, exchanging marginalia, an ongoing conversation that spanned decades. Apollo suddenly understood all these books as more than just an excellent payday. They were the evidence of two lives intertwined.

At three in the morning, in his one-bedroom apartment, surrounded by a small library of occult texts, Apollo Kagwa, thirty-four years old, realized his biological clock had gone off.

A POLLO HIT LIBRARY sales less regularly than estate sales, or used bookstores, but he'd been in Washington Heights anyway—for a fruitless estate sale—so he stopped at the Fort Washington branch of the NYPL.

Library sales were usually a mix of old books the branch hoped to sell off rather than recycle and books that locals had donated. You weren't going to find something like the D'Agostino haul at a library, but you could buy a book for fifty cents, then sell it for five dollars. Almost any small business succeeded or failed by such margins. It wasn't romantic, but reality rarely is. Apollo tended to come to library sales for things like large print editions of crime novels, the kind of stuff he sold to retirees who'd found his website and wanted the stuff shipped. Selling those books reminded him of his first business model—*People* magazine to Mrs. Ortiz in apartment C23.

The Fort Washington branch stood three stories tall, but the sale was being held in the basement, in a nook off the reading room. One of the librarians had to cover both the sale and her desk. Apollo reached the basement to find her helping a mother with two kids pick through shelves of well-worn picture books. The younger kid had taken on the vital task of pulling every third book to the floor. The mother didn't seem to notice, or had decided not to notice, so the librarian now had a third job—cleanup crew. Then, from the reading room, a man's voice called out loudly. Because the space had been so quiet, it sounded as if he was using a megaphone.

"Hello! Hello! I am in distress!"

The librarian shuttled from the book sale back into the reading room, where an enormous man stood at her desk. He wore a bulky old backpack and carried crammed shopping bags in each hand. A one-man pack mule.

"This is dire!" he shouted. "I am in need of a toilet!"

The librarian made her way around the man, and his bags, to the other side of her desk. She stood narrow at the shoulders, fuller at the hips. The man had a good two feet on her. From a distance you'd have thought you were watching an ogre and an elf square off.

The other patrons, mostly elderly, looked up from their newspapers and magazines but seemed wary of doing more. Apollo moved closer, ten more steps, and he'd be there to help.

"Listen to my voice," the librarian said to the big man. "Can you hear me?" The librarian smiled when she said this, but her volume and her posture suggested something more commanding.

"I got ears, don't I?" He leaned forward, as if he was going to throw himself across the desk, right at her.

"Well you see, I have ears too," she said, not stepping back. "So why are you yelling?"

The man wobbled, as if the bags in his hands had become heavier. Or maybe he just felt confused. A man that size isn't used to being barked at. Least of all from a woman who stood only an inch or two taller than five feet.

The librarian opened a desk drawer and revealed a wooden two-foot ruler with a single key attached by a string at one end.

"I need a piece of ID before I give you the bathroom key," she said.

The woman never dropped her smile, but by now everyone—even the big man—could tell this lady was no joke. Slim as a crowbar and just as solid. Maybe a woman that small had to learn how to assert herself early, a survival technique to keep from being overrun or ignored. It worked. Everyone in the basement had been spellbound.

"I don't have ID," he said, now sheepish.

The librarian used the ruler as a pointer. "Leave all your bags here with me. I know you'll come back for them."

Instead of setting the loads down, he clutched them close, a pair of oversize purses. "These contain secrets."

She nodded, opened the drawer again, dropped the ruler inside, pushed the drawer closed, crossed her arms, craned her head back, and looked the man directly in the eye.

Apollo made it to a count of ten before the man set the bags down. He looked hypnotized. "The backpack too?" he asked.

"All the bags," the librarian said.

At that moment, if she'd gestured to Apollo, he would've handed over his bag as well. The big man set the large pack down with the others, and the librarian opened the drawer, handed him the key.

"Thank you," he said softly.

"My pleasure," she said, smiling warmly this time.

The whole reading room waited in silence, listening for the key fumbling in the lock, the squeak as the wooden bathroom door opened. When it slammed shut, everyone in the reading room shuddered as if they were waking up from a dream. All except the librarian, who'd already come around the desk, moved past Apollo, and returned to the mother with two kids. They bought four books for a dollar.

The librarian then turned to Apollo, who'd been standing there dumbstruck.

"Do you need something?" she asked.

Apollo pointed toward the man's bags, gathered by her desk. "I was going to help you with that guy."

The librarian looked at the bags, then back to Apollo.

"But you handled it yourself," he said.

"That's my job," she said.

He asked her to dinner, and as she rang up his three books, she politely declined. The library sales in the basement nook were held every Friday, so Apollo returned the week after, and the week after that. Eventually she told him her name. Emma Valentine.

Five months after they met, she finally agreed to go out on a date.

T RYING TO IMPRESS, Apollo took Emma to a tiny sushi place on Thompson Street, where they had to wait outside on a line. The season—late fall—made waiting on the sidewalk feel like standing inside a fridge, so they were shivering by the time they got seated. They downed a bottle of hot sake before any food came.

He learned she'd been raised in Virginia, a tiny town called Boones Mill. She had a sister, Kim, eleven years older. Her parents had died when she was only five, but she wouldn't say any more about it than that.

Kim became Emma's legal guardian when she turned eighteen, got work locally, and raised her sister instead of going to Jefferson College of Health Sciences in Roanoke, where she'd been accepted. It wasn't until Emma graduated high school—and matriculated at UVA—that Kim finally went to Jefferson, for nursing. Emma remembered her life after her parents died as time spent in only three places: home, school, and the South County Library, twenty minutes away in Roanoke.

"My favorite librarian there was a woman named Ms. Rook," Emma said. "She helped raise me almost as much as Kim."

They were halfway through dinner, onto their second bottle of hot sake, and leaning toward each other across the small wooden tabletop. The customers crowded close all around, and the waiters had so little room to move that Apollo got bumped every time they passed by, but he hardly noticed. He only listened to her.

"Ms. Rook used to sit me down with a movie if Kim was late coming for me. That way she could start closing up. I watched everything they had for kids. Then one day, when I was twelve, I picked up something almost at random. I just liked the picture on the front. A couple of black people half naked and carrying spears."

"That made you want to watch it?" Apollo asked.

"It was the only movie in the entire library that had black people on the cover. Of course I wanted to watch it! The movie was called *Quilombo*. A Brazilian film. Ms. Rook even came to check on me. She saw the movie playing, saw that I was occupied, and went on her way."

Emma had become tipsy by then, laughing loudly.

"There's no way Ms. Rook could've known it was a movie about the slave uprisings in Brazil. Or that the movie would show tons of Portuguese people getting killed by those slaves! She was such a sweet lady, I never told her what the movie was about. I knew she'd be mortified, and I was too polite to say anything. But I really liked it. It became the only thing I wanted to see."

Here Emma tilted her head to the side and watched the ceiling, grinning.

"It was in Portuguese with English subtitles. I loved the way the language sounded. It took awhile, but I got Ms. Rook to order a few more Brazilian movies after that. *Bye Bye Brasil, Subway to the Stars, Os Trapalhões e o Rei do Futebol.* Finally, Ms. Rook had to stop buying them because one girl's love of Brazil wasn't enough to justify the costs of the tapes. But she'd done enough for me. I realized how big the world was. Bigger than Boones Mill. And I wanted to see it."

"One of your eyes is bigger than the other," Apollo said. He'd only just noticed it. The difference was hardly noticeable, but it made her seem to be peering at the world more deeply than most. Or maybe Apollo was just falling for her.

Emma lowered her head and covered the larger eye. Maybe she'd taken his observation as an insult. He doubted he could say anything to make it better now, so instead he said the first thing on his mind.

"I never cared if I had a boy or a girl, you know? I just want to be a good father to whatever kids I have."

Even as he said it, he understood how nutty that sounded. *Great topic of first date conversation, Apollo! Why not ask if she'd like to sign a thirty-year fixed-rate mortgage with you, too?*

Emma lowered her hand and poured herself a little more sake. She drank it in a slow sip, set down the cup, then spoke. "I want to explain why I said no when you asked me out that first time."

"And the next five times," Apollo added.

"And the next five times," Emma agreed.

Now Emma sat back in her chair while Apollo hunched forward.

"I said no because I'm moving to Brazil. Already bought my tickets. I'm going to Salvador do Bahia, in the north."

"For how long?" Apollo asked.

"I don't know," she said.

Apollo drank straight from the ceramic sake bottle to finish off the booze.

"Then why did you say yes to me now?" he asked.

She looked at the table and grinned. "I found myself looking forward to Friday sales because I hoped you'd be back." She raised her eyes to meet his. "I missed you."

As he led her back out onto the street, he took her hand. She squeezed it tightly when he did.

"Now about this trip to Brazil," Apollo said.

I am the god, Apollo, he told himself. *I am the god, Apollo.*

"Are you sure I can't convince you to stay?"

Emma Valentine smiled at him crookedly, intoxicated as they kissed.

Four weeks later she left for Brazil.

TRY DATING OTHER women after a night like that. Apollo certainly did. But his heart wouldn't buy it. It was Emma Valentine or bust. How long could she stay in Brazil, anyway? They wrote each other, but Emma couldn't rely on an Internet connection. She left Salvador after a few months and moved to Manaus, then Fortaleza. Eventually she'd hit Rio and São Paulo, but not yet. Apollo found himself reading news from Brazil online. He got a DVD of *Quilombo*, and though the movie was serious business—African slaves battling the vicious Portuguese—he laughed when he imagined a twelve-year-old Emma watching it again and again in a public library in Roanoke. In Emma's absence, he only fell more in love with her.

Apollo sold off the entire D'Agostino library, piecemeal. He put the Crowley postcard up on his site, and fourteen hours later he had five bids, finally selling it for three thousand dollars. In late 2003, he helped Lillian put a down payment on a house, a neat single-family home out in Springfield Gardens, Queens. She refused his help until they sat down together and calculated how much she'd save if she could put 30 percent down on the house instead of 20. This kind of thing helped occupy Apollo's time and mind. After a year Emma wrote to say she was coming back to the United States. Her flight wouldn't arrive until late at night, she wrote, and he might not even be interested in seeing her anymore, but if he did want to see her, she'd love for his face to be the first one she found at arrivals.

The plane, meant to arrive at ten o'clock, got delayed twice. Apollo ended up spending the night at JFK. The families and friends in the arrivals area sat, slumped, shuffled, and shrugged, and some fought. The longer the delays, the more everyone settled in, Apollo among them. Sometime after midnight he slipped into sleep.

At intervals one delayed plane or another arrived, and its sluggish passengers appeared, greeted by similarly sluggish loved ones. The grand windows of the international arrivals terminal let in the dawn light when Emma's plane finally landed.

Her hair had grown longer, curlier; the brown showed a faintly reddish tinge now. Her skin was darker, and her clothes bright, fabric thin, all wrong for the cool spring season. She hadn't brought back her suitcase, only a backpack slung on one arm. She'd left with more and returned with less. She moved slowly, seeming weary but also unrushed, and she saw him before he saw her.

"You stayed?" she asked as he took her pack.

It might've been exhaustion, but her eyes grew wet and trembled.

"You stayed," she said again, quietly.

They sat in the food court to enjoy the best Dunkin' Donuts had to offer.

"Welcome to America," Apollo said as they unwrapped their egg and cheese sandwiches. He lifted his. "I'll take you somewhere nicer soon."

She pulled the sleeves of her shirt up slightly. "*Fique tranquilo*," she said. She smiled. "I won't keep doing that."

Apollo went to the counter for a knife because the sandwich hadn't been cut all the way through. He watched Emma raise the sandwich to her mouth to eat. He stayed by the counter to marvel that she'd returned. Around her wrist she wore a thin red string. Why did the sight of it make him stiffen? It had a sentimental appearance, the kind of thing some beautiful Brazilian boy tied around an American woman's wrist because he could afford nothing more. She'd been gone a year. Why couldn't she have fallen in love with someone else? Maybe she'd come back with fewer belongings because she was planning to return.

Thinking in this way, he came back to the table with a plastic knife and a belly full of anxiety. He pushed the egg and cheese sandwich around but had no appetite. Emma remained quiet as well, until she'd finished her whole meal. Then she raised her arm, the one with the red string, so he could see it clearly. The string had gone a bit stiff. It was dirty. It had been on her wrist a long time.

"When I got to Salvador, I stayed with a family in a neighborhood called Itapuã. There they have a lagoon called Lagoa do Abaete. You remember, at our dinner, you told me about the old married Satanists? I thought of you when I saw the lagoon because it's supposed to be haunted. There was a washerwoman there who I came to know after my Portuguese got stronger. My host family tried to keep me away from the woman, they told me she was a witch, but I liked her. I wasn't scared of her. She made me think of my mother, who she might be if she were still alive. Tough and funny, and she didn't give a damn about other people's opinion of her. I found myself sneaking out of their house just to sit by the lagoon with her while she did her washing. Before I left for Manaus, she told me to make three wishes for my life, and then after I did, she tied this string around my wrist."

Emma turned her hand clockwise, then counterclockwise, watching the red fabric.

"I must let it come apart, she said, and when it fell off my wrist, those wishes would come true. I could not cut it off. *Nao corta-la.* I thought it was fun for a while, a little bit mystical, but this thing has been on my skin for more than six months! It looks ratty, but I want my wishes to come true. Don't look at me like that! I guess I believe in magic."

Apollo took her hand and pulled it toward him.

I am the god, Apollo, he thought. *I am the god, Apollo.*

He picked up the plastic knife on the table, and with one move he cut the red string off her wrist. It fell onto the plastic tabletop. Emma shivered. He held on to her hand.

"I promise you," he said. "With me, all three of your wishes will come true."

In this moment Emma Valentine faced a choice. She could see this moment as proof that Apollo Kagwa was an arrogant dick, or she could decide he was bold and worthy. He'd made his move, and now she must make her decision.

2

THEN COMES
MARRIAGE

ARLY EVENING BY the time Apollo arrived at the two-story row house in Ridgewood, Queens. As he scuffed up the front stairs, he laughed at how, when he lived in the two-bedroom in Flushing with Lillian, these sorts of places—not apartments but actual homes—had seemed so high-toned. He'd ask her why they didn't live in one, and she'd say, *Those are for owning not renting.* Even now that he and Emma had an apartment of their own—on the island of Manhattan—he couldn't stop himself from admiring the row house, gawping at the second-floor windows, the rain gutter running along the roof. Apollo Kagwa, thirty-seven now, but he still felt like that little boy.

When Apollo rang the bell, he heard a woman calling from inside, and then the locks clicked and the curtains of the first-floor window slid aside a few inches so he could be seen there on the stoop by someone he couldn't see. Then another voice, deeper, male, and the door stopped being unlocked. Apollo felt thrown back to the days when he'd been left waiting outside some nervous bookseller's storefront, or all the times the owner of a private residence refused to let him in. *I am the god, Apollo,* he thought. *I am the god, Apollo.* These days the mantra came automatically, as commonplace as breathing. He took out his cellphone while he waited and sent Emma a text. He wondered if she'd already made it to the restaurant.

Will be late for dinner, but I'll be there.

"Hold on!" a woman shouted from the other side. "I'm here!"

The door shook in its frame, locks clacked then clicked, then clacked back again.

"Come help," the woman growled. "Don't you see me?"

The curtain in the front window fluttered, another set of footsteps, heavier and faster. Two clicks, and the knob turned, the door opened. A man in his early thirties stood in the doorway, and behind him was a small, much older woman. White folks, they looked like a pair out of some old central European woodcut. Those gaunt, lined faces and stiff postures.

"It's that easy!" the man said, shouting at her over his shoulder. He seemed too old to sound so childish.

The woman pulled at the man's arm so he'd move.

"Mrs. Grabowski?" Apollo asked.

"You're the book man?" she asked.

"I'm the book man."

Apollo held out his card for her, but the man snatched it fast, then retreated into the house. Apollo decided to call the man Igor, no matter what his real name turned out to be. The old woman, Mrs. Grabowski, smiled tightly and waved Apollo in.

They entered a dining room where six cardboard boxes were laid out on the dining table. There was a sectional couch in the adjoining room, a large flatscreen television on a stand, and little else.

"You said your husband died," Apollo began.

"Ex-husband," Mrs. Grabowski said. She looked around the dining room. There was a dining table here, but no chairs. The off-white walls so dusty, they appeared gray. Black garbage bags were heaped in one corner of the dining room. One of them lay open, and a few dingy sport coats, weathered slacks, spilled out. Mr. Grabowski had succumbed to bachelorhood in his old age.

"My son and I have lived around the corner in recent years."

"At least you stayed close," Apollo said.

Mrs. Grabowski shrugged. "This is Little Ukraine. Where else could we go? Now we have to clear it out by the end of the week. The owners want to rent to someone else."

She had an accent, though she might've been living in the United States for twenty years. Lillian never lost that faint British lilt that had got her hired by Glamour Time over forty years ago. Apollo used to get such a laugh out of hearing his mother pronounce *aluminum* like a Brit. Al-loo-min-ee-um.

Igor waggled the business card as if he was a bouncer checking ID.

"Did you go to school to do this?" Igor asked.

"Those are the books?" Apollo said, pointing to the boxes on the table. He didn't wait for her to answer—he just wanted to clear some space between himself and Igor. Keep it moving, Igor.

"He enjoyed reading," Mrs. Grabowski said as Apollo opened the flaps of the first box. "But his eyes became worse with age."

Igor didn't like being ignored. He raised his voice. "You heard of Bauman's?" he demanded.

His mother looked at him. "Please don't be foolish," she said.

Apollo didn't even have to peek inside the box to be sure this one was worthless. The scent of mildew—water damage—rose into the air like a specter. He moved on to the next box, but the same smell greeted him.

"Bauman's Rare Books," Igor said. "They have already made an offer for my father's collection."

The old woman turned now and slapped her son's arm. She spoke in their native tongue, and as Apollo moved on to the third box, he felt himself shrinking. He'd come all the way out here for what would no doubt turn out to be six boxes of stained, curled, and torn books.

He did this instead of going straight to the dinner with Emma. One of her oldest friends, Nichelle, was visiting town and made reservations for them at Bouley. Just say that name with the proper French accent to guess how much the meal would cost. And here he was in Ridgewood, listening to a Ukrainian family bicker in Ukrainian. Or were they speaking Russian? He had traveled all this way so this twit Igor could try and tell him that Bauman's Rare Books made an offer on Mr. Grabowski's collection of sour-smelling paperbacks. He had come all this way to have his authority and experience questioned by a man who assumed superiority as a kind of birthright. But a good book man never turns down the chance at some rare find.

Especially not a book man with a child on the way.

Igor took out his cellphone, and as he tapped at the screen, he spoke in English again. "I've got the direct line for the Baumans," he said.

Apollo reached the sixth box. Hardcovers this time, and a quick sniff suggested mildew hadn't been introduced to the batch. This time he reached in and checked the books.

"Which Bauman?" Apollo asked. "David or Natalie?"

A few works of nonfiction about Vietnam. Some of these books even had their book jackets. If he hadn't been on his way to dinner, he might've offered twenty bucks for the box just so he could sift through it all at home.

Mrs. Grabowski swung at her son again. "I told you not to lie!" she shouted.

She hit his cellphone this time, and it soared out of his hand, into the den, skittering across the hardwood floor and under the couch.

"Mama!" He ran for the device, and Apollo's card fluttered to the floor.

The old woman turned back to Apollo. "Do you like to buy these books?"

"Well," Apollo said, looking into the sixth box again. How to be nice about this? "It's obvious your husband got a lot of enjoyment out of them."

She dropped her head, trembling with desperation. When she did, he came across a book that made him stiffen. A novel called *Fields of Fire* by James Webb. No discoloration to the book jacket, and the book itself showed no fading to the board edges, no rubbing, and when he turned to the copyright page, he saw it was a true first edition. Nothing like the Crowley postcard of course, but he had a regular customer in Virginia, a history hound, who might pay two hundred and fifty for this book.

Apollo scanned the house again. Old clothes in garbage bags, a decaying sectional couch. The kitchen, visible from the dining room, looked like a graveyard for pots and appliances. Apollo doubted Mrs. Grabowski's ex-husband had left her anything worth a damn. She'd even said this house was only a rental. She'd inherited a messy house that she had to clear quickly, and her only help was feckless Igor.

And yet she'd retained dignity, hadn't she? She'd refused to go along with her son's stupid plan. Even as much as she no doubt needed money, any money, she hadn't been willing to lie to Apollo to get it. He imagined her working some job during the day, then coming out to Ridgewood each evening to sweep up after her dead, no doubt equally feckless husband. Though she was Ukrainian, she reminded him of his mother. Someone who worked like hell and still didn't get all the good luck she deserved. If he paid her what this book was actually worth, it would be a kindness. Even half its value, even a hundred bucks, might make a difference: a week's worth of groceries, a month's Con Ed bill.

From the other room, Igor shouted, "You better not have cracked the screen, Mama!"

She looked over her shoulder at her son, on his knees, pawing for the device under the couch. He looked like a toddler scrambling for his toy. Mrs. Grabowski visibly deflated. Apollo felt his sympathies flare across his face like a rash.

But quickly Apollo reminded himself why he'd come out to Ridgewood tonight: because it had been six years since the D'Agostino haul and nothing worth even as much as the Webb novel had come his way since then. Because Emma's job at the library had been reduced from full time to part time. Because Apollo Kagwa and Emma Valentine were expecting their first child in two weeks.

When Mrs. Grabowski looked back, Apollo held two hardcovers out to her. "I missed these when I first looked," he said.

She peeked at the covers and mouthed the titles to herself. "They're valuable?" she asked. She watched his face closely.

"A little," he finally said.

If he'd tried to buy only one book, Mrs. Grabowski would've felt sure it was valuable, but the second book—a ratty copy of an unremarkable thriller—acted as a kind of camouflage for *Fields of Fire*. Apollo learned this trick from the old dealers long ago. He hated doing all this, and so he decided, deep in the well of his mind, that he was doing it for his unborn child. *It's for the kid*, he told himself. The words soothed his conscience, like applying aloe to a light burn.

"I'll give you fifty dollars," Apollo said softly.

"Each?" Mrs. Grabowski asked, her voice rising.

Apollo went to his wallet. "For both," he said.

He waited until she nodded and took the cash.

Igor returned from the other room, his phone gripped tight in one hand. "You're proud of yourself?" he asked. "Cheating an old widow?"

Mrs. Grabowski folded the bills into her fist, then hit Igor with her closed hand. "Don't talk like that! This is more money than your father gave me in years."

Igor ignored the attack and her words. "You know it's true," he said, grinning at Apollo. "And I know it's true."

Apollo tucked both books under his arm. Mrs. Grabowski walked him back toward the front door, Igor trailing behind them.

Apollo crossed the threshold and walked down to the sidewalk. He turned back to find Igor in the doorway. Behind him Mrs. Grabowski counted the money in her hand. Apollo couldn't tell if she looked satisfied or suspicious.

"It's business," Apollo said. "I'm just doing business here."

"The devil likes to hide behind a cross," Igor said, then shut the front door.

ENTERING BOULEY RESTAURANT felt like stepping inside a gingerbread house. Outside he'd been on Duane Street, a tony block in Manhattan but still just downtown NYC. The exterior of the building, an understated apricot, and a simple wooden door with glass panels suggested Nichelle had picked a pleasant enough place. But when he opened the door and stepped into the foyer, he found himself surrounded by apples. Shelves had been built into the wall, running as high as the ceiling; rows of fresh red apples and their scent enveloped him. The door to Duane Street shut behind him, and Apollo felt as if he'd stumbled into a small cottage off an overgrown path in a dark wood. He stayed there in the perfume of the apple room inhaling the scent. If he'd brought the stain of his interaction with Mrs. Grabowski downtown with him, then this room made him feel cleansed.

Another door led from the foyer into a waiting room, a long narrow hall with padded chairs and tiny tables. Six small chandeliers hung from the wooden rafters but offered little light. The curtains covering the windows looked as lush as bridal gowns. The waiting room sat shrouded in an elegant gloom like the little parlor of a storied mansion.

Immediately, instinctively, Apollo checked to see if he was wearing sneakers or shoes. He shifted his messenger bag so it hung behind him. A few people were waiting to be seated, but Emma and Nichelle weren't among them. There was a dark wooden station, and behind it the maître d'—a tall man in a tailored blue suit—gazed down into a screen that lit his sharp face strangely. When he looked up to greet Apollo, the man's eyes were lost in a shadow. Since his mouth stayed shrouded in darkness too, it was impossible to see his lips. He looked more ghoulish than gallant.

"Forty regular?"

Not what Apollo expected. He set his bag down and presented his empty hands. If they were turning him away, this had to be the strangest rejection he'd ever heard.

"Nichelle Murray?" Apollo replied.

The maître d' nodded quickly and stepped away from his station, then retreated to a door behind him. Apollo looked at the guests in the waiting room—mere silhouettes in leather chairs. In a moment the maître d' reappeared with a sport coat. He helped Apollo slip it on.

He waved Apollo forward, a menu under one arm, led him through the waiting room and past the other customers. The dining room's vaulted ceilings had been laid with eighteen-karat gold leaf sheets, and on top of that a twelve-karat white gold varnish, so the ceiling seemed as supple as suede. The floors were Burgundy stone, overlaid by Persian rugs. If the foyer felt like a woodland cottage and the waiting area a haunted parlor, the dining room became an ancient castle's great hall. This only added to the fantastical atmosphere of the restaurant. Apollo felt as if he was trekking through realms rather than rooms. If there had been men in full armor posted as sentries, it wouldn't have surprised him. And in fact, when the maître d' reached the right table, there was a queen waiting there. Emma Valentine, too pregnant to stand. Apollo leaned close and kissed her.

Nichelle rose from her seat and hugged Apollo. "Here he is then," she said. "Father of the bride."

Emma grinned, she rocked forward in her seat. "You're a mess, Nichelle."

Nichelle still hadn't let go of Apollo, clinging to his left arm, and he realized it was because Nichelle was drunk. Zooted. An open bottle of white wine stood on the table, half done. Another bottle of Perrier stood before Emma's plate, two-thirds down. Three small plates of appetizers were laid out: oysters, mushrooms, and a third thing he couldn't recognize. The tablecloth looked as mussed as a slept-in bed.

"Am I that late?" Apollo asked.

"We got here early," Emma told him.

Nichelle pointed at Emma. "Best way to get seated fast is bring a woman who's nine months pregnant."

"Thirty-eight weeks!" Emma said.

Nichelle waved one hand dismissively. "That math doesn't mean anything to normal people. You are nine months pregnant."

Apollo sat across from Nichelle and next to Emma. Even before he'd settled into the chair, a waiter came to the table and poured some of the wine into his glass, topped Nichelle's glass off, then refilled Emma's cup of sparkling water. He didn't ask if they wanted another bottle of wine, merely raised the empty one slightly, and Nichelle pointed at him.

Apollo set the messenger bag between the legs of his and Emma's chairs. She'd set herself down at an angle so her belly wouldn't bump the table and she could stretch her legs out. She looked down at the bag quickly, then up at Apollo.

"Ridgewood," Apollo said. "Nothing great."

Emma patted his leg. "Good to try."

Thirty-eight weeks pregnant, and she looked like a hummingbird that had swallowed an emu egg. And yet she moved in this body with a kind of exhausted authority. She seemed to take some pleasure in being, temporarily, larger. When the waiter arrived with the new bottle of white wine, she had her legs extended, feet out, and ankles crossed. Any other time in her life, even an earlier stage of the pregnancy, she would've tucked her feet in to accommodate the waiter. But not now. Let the world accommodate her a little. Her feet stayed stuck out, and the waiter went around them.

The waiter poured another round for Nichelle, then topped Apollo off though he'd only taken two sips. The diners at the other tables gave off a distinctly different air from theirs. The median age of these customers was billionaire. Even the busboys in this place were white.

"How is Los Angeles treating you?" Apollo said. "Does that town ever change?"

"Time goes slower when you're happy," Nichelle said. "And I'm happy there."

Emma stabbed at an empty oyster on the table, then moved on to forage the last mushroom from another plate. "She writes for *The Witching Hour*," she said, pride playing in her voice like a musical note.

"Hey, we watch that show," Apollo said. He pulled at the wine and felt himself relaxing into the seat, the conversation.

"Why do you think we started?" Emma asked, leaning into his arm. "Got to support my girl!"

"Long way from Boones Mill," Apollo said, raising his glass.

Nichelle looked to Emma, raised her glass. "For both of us."

After a sip she pooched her lips toward Emma's belly. "But I hear you two are going to the planet of 'natural childbirth' next. I'm sorry, but that's too far for me."

These natural childbirth conversations weren't ever meant for Apollo, even if he was in the room, at the table. When they'd told Lillian about the plan, she'd practically short-circuited from fear. "Concern" is what Lillian called it. And so on with most of the women in Emma's life. Only her older sister, Kim, supported the plan, but she had good reason: Kim Valentine was their midwife.

While Nichelle told Emma all her concerns about natural childbirth, Apollo made the mistake of finally looking down at his menu. There were three appetizers on the table, already finished. The oysters cost thirty-two dollars. The mushrooms were forty-two. Forty-two motherfucking dollars for a small plate of mushrooms. He couldn't guess what the hell the last plate had been—there was only a white soup dish with some broth in it now—so he couldn't figure what the price might be. But why not be conservative and guess twenty-two? Twenty-two dollars for a dish of broth might not even be a joke in a place like this. That meant this meal already cost nearly one hundred dollars. He and Emma were down fifty bucks, and he hadn't even eaten anything yet.

Apollo finished the wine to calm himself; an exquisite Chablis. How much could it have cost? The wine list hadn't been left at the table. If he'd known, just then, that this Chablis Grand Plus cost three hundred and seventy-five dollars per bottle, what would he have done? Run screaming, probably. His thirty-eight-weeks-pregnant wife up on his shoulders.

Writing for television sure had to pay better than an independent bookseller and a part-time librarian ever made. At least Emma, his beautiful and thoughtful wife, drank only water tonight.

Perrier, he corrected himself. Not tap water. And just how much in sweet black Jesus did Bouley Restaurant charge for sparkling mineral water? Did they infuse it with fucking diamond dust before they served it? The women turned their attention to Apollo only when he audibly whimpered in his seat.

Emma leaned close and touched his back gently. "I know you're hungry," she said. "Let's get the waiter over here."

Nichelle ordered the Organic Long Island Duck (forty-five dollars). Emma the Organic Colorado Lamb (fifty-three dollars). The waiter then faced Apollo.

Apollo handed over the menu. He pointed at the empty little basket in the middle of the table. "I'll just have more bread."

BY THE TIME the second bottle of Chablis had been finished, Nichelle practically levitated from her chair. She'd cycled from tipsy to tornado. She spoke loudly enough now that Mrs. Grabowski and her son might've heard her out in Queens. The surest sign that she'd become truly drunk was neither her slurred words nor her lack of bodily control—though there was a little of both—but the way she'd stopped listening to the others at the table. Tipsy people are chatty, drunks harangue.

This wasn't so bad, though, because by ten o'clock both Emma and Apollo had lost their ability to make conversation. Emma, hardly napping at all these days, had drifted into the half sleep of her long nights. She "slept" propped partway up with pillows in their bed, so it wasn't all that different to drift in her seat at Bouley. Apollo, meanwhile, had ingested nothing but tap water and the restaurant bread. While the bread tasted magnificent, it wasn't enough. By dessert, Apollo and Emma had low batteries, but Nichelle seemed wired to a generator.

"*Limbo? Coolimbo?* I can't remember what the damn thing was called," Nichelle said. She'd ordered port to go along with her Hot Caramelized Anjou Pear. Emma asked for the Amaretto Flan, though she swore she wanted only one bite. Apollo didn't know what either cost because by then his vision had gone fuzzy. He couldn't have read the menu if he tried. He only hoped there wasn't such a thing as a "second dessert" or a "digestif tasting menu" or some other high-tone shit that might require him to go into their savings just to pay for it.

"This girl tried to get me to watch a movie about a slave uprising when I was busy trying to figure out how to marry that boy out of New Edition." Before Apollo could say anything, she waved her hand dismissively. "No, not Ralph or Bobby. I liked Michael Bivens. He could ball."

A pause during which neither Apollo nor Emma seemed to blink or breathe.

"*Quilombo!*" Nichelle said, slapping the table hard enough to knock over her port. "Oh damn," she muttered, then looked to the waiter and signaled for another, though, really, there had hardly been enough left in the glass to make a spot the size of a nickel.

"I watched that movie one time with her and about ten minutes in I'm like, 'What the hell kind of English is this?' Emma says it's Portuguese. I took the headphones off and left her right there by the VCRs."

Emma finally took a fork to her dessert. "You liked *Bye Bye Brasil*."

"Betty Faria," Nichelle said, puckering her lips and shutting her eyes.

The new glass of port arrived. Emma bit into her flan. Despite his exhaustion and his terror of the upcoming bill, Apollo felt a blush of happiness. He liked to think of these two women as girls in Boones Mill, Virginia, lucky enough to find each other, to love each other.

He'd made a friend, a fellow book dealer, not too long ago. Patrice Green, an army vet who'd gone into the trade when he came back to the States. Usually they were the only two black book men at local estate sales. They might as well be two unicorns that happened into the same field. Of course they'd become close. Thank God for friendships, that's what he sat there thinking. Nichelle and Emma, Apollo and Patrice. Before he could talk himself out of the gesture, he raised his hand for the waiter and ordered a glass of bourbon.

By the time the drink arrived, Emma huffed quietly beside him. Apollo worried for a moment, but she was touching her throat, not her belly.

"That flan wants to come back up," Emma said quietly. Nichelle suggested water, but that would only make it worse. "I'll find the bathroom," she said.

Apollo helped her up and watched her shuffle toward their waiter. The waiter nodded quickly and led her out of the dining room. When she'd disappeared, Apollo looked back to Nichelle and found her watching him with an unnerving seriousness. It was as if her drunkenness had all been playacting, and now she had dropped the play.

"There's a nude photo of your wife in an art gallery in Amsterdam," Nichelle said.

Is there a proper response to such a revelation? "Color or black and white?" Apollo asked. It was the best he could do.

"You know she went to Brazil. She told me how you waited for her at the airport when she came back. Very sweet. Big points for you. While she was down there, she had a few adventures. I'm sure she told you about some of them."

"The red string. She told me about that one."

"Three wishes!" Nichelle shouted, as if someone had just brought out a birthday cake. "Yes. That was a bold move you made, Apollo, let me tell you. I liked that."

"I kept the string," Apollo said. "So I wouldn't forget my promise." Right then it was tucked flat inside his wallet, right behind his driver's license.

Nichelle nodded, but he couldn't be sure she was listening. Too drunk, but still she smiled playfully. "By the way, you should be proud. You've given her two of those wishes already. She never told you what they were. Bad luck. But I guess it's okay now."

Nichelle lifted her right hand in a fist and raised the pointer finger. "A good husband," she said.

She raised the middle finger. "A healthy child. That reminds me. Do you know the sex? Emma said you all didn't want to find out, but come on, you can tell me."

"We really don't know," Apollo said. "We want to find out together, right when it happens."

Nichelle shook her head. "I never met black hippies. I didn't even know there were black hippies, but I guess there's at least two."

Nichelle still hadn't lowered her hand. Apollo stared at the third finger, Nichelle's ring finger. It trembled as if about to rise and reveal the third wish, but then Nichelle opened her hand wide, all five fingers out in display.

"About a month before she came back to the United States, Emma met this Dutch photographer down there in Brazil. It's while she was in Salvador."

Apollo's bourbon matched the color of his sudden mood. He instantly forgot about the third wish.

Dutch photographer?

Dutch fucking photographer?

"Emma and this photographer get on real well, and the two of them start going around Salvador together taking pictures of everything. The photographer keeps trying to get Emma into the photos, but she doesn't want to do that. She wants to learn how to shoot the photos, not how to be in them.

"One trip they take is to some abandoned factory that looks kind of romantic and decayed. They spend most of the day there. But at some point the photographer has to go and pee, so Emma's alone with the equipment, and this is when she decides to finally be in a photo. But it's one she's going to take herself. By herself. This is high-grade camera work, so it's not just digital shit with your phone. Emma's smart, though, and she's learned enough by now to set up the shot on a timer.

"She makes the shot in front of a wall that's been half torn down so you can see she's standing inside a man-made building that's gone to the dogs, but over her right shoulder you can see the forest that surrounds this factory. Two worlds at once. Crumbling civilization and an explosion of the natural world.

"Emma walks into the shot, and just before the shutter clicks, she pulls off her dress and takes that photo nude!"

Apollo found himself nodding, though he couldn't say why. Nichelle hadn't said anything that required agreement. Instead it was as if he was testing to be sure his head remained on his neck. Apparently it was there, but Apollo still didn't quite believe it. Better down all this bourbon to be sure.

"She didn't even tell the photographer she'd done it. It would get de-veloped later, in a darkroom, and the fate of the picture had nothing to do with her. The point was just that Emma Valentine had done it. You see? She has always been like that, ever since she was a girl. If she sets her will on something it is going to happen, believe me. You like to think you chose to wait for her at the airport when her plane arrived late, but I'm telling you different. She was on that plane, like, willing you not to leave. You couldn't have gone home if you tried. I know how that sounds, but I believe it."

Nichelle nodded for a few moments longer than necessary, enjoying the movement more than anything else. Then she jumped back into the story of Emma and the photo.

"Well, that Dutch photographer didn't even develop the film until returning to Amsterdam. But it was clear that shot was worth keeping. Had it framed and included in a show, and the gallery owner bought it and never took it down. I've never been to Amsterdam, but Emma showed me the JPEG. I think the owner even included the shot in the gallery's catalogs."

"And?" Apollo asked, his throat too dry to say more.

He scanned the corner where his wife had gone to use the bathroom. How different would she seem when she reappeared because of this story Nichelle decided to share? And why had she shared it? Just because she was drunk?

"Emma has never been a big girl, you know? But down in Brazil she looked lean, not weak. Muscle and bone and those big eyes of hers, that's all she was. Wiry and fierce, naked and unashamed. She's looking into that camera lens like she can see you, whoever you are, wherever you are. She looks like a fucking sorceress, Apollo. It was one of the most beautiful things I've ever seen."

Nichelle stopped there and looked at the port glass in her hand with surprise. She gulped it all and chonked the glass onto the table, upside down.

"And the Dutch guy?" Apollo asked. "What was his name?"

Nichelle watched him quietly for seconds. She narrowed her eyes when she spoke. "I'm trying to tell you something important, and you are focused on bullshit."

"If it's bullshit, then you can just tell me about him," Apollo said.

Now Nichelle reached across the table and dug her nails into the backs of both his hands. "I'm trying to tell you about Emma's third wish," Nichelle said. "In a way that won't break her trust. Because it's the only wish that hasn't come true yet."

At this Apollo felt hit, hurt. He fell back into his chair as if Nichelle had kicked him. "Okay. I'm listening."

But before anything more could be spoken, by either of them, their waiter appeared. The man had been sprinting. He reached the table. He didn't speak—he roared.

"Your wife!" he said. "Your wife needs you!"

THE QUESTION NICHELLE never got to ask Emma and Apollo—though she'd been trying, in her way, to lead to it earlier in the night—was why? Why on earth had Apollo and Emma decided to do a home birth when they seemed like such sane people? They weren't third-world peasants. They weren't wealthy white folks or anti-hospital-industry kooks. So what the hell happened?

The concern felt truly pressing as Nichelle settled the bill with the waiter. She'd been signing the credit card receipt when Apollo appeared again holding Emma under one arm. Emma looked so red and exhausted that Nichelle had her phone out to call 911 as the waiter took the check away. Emma told Nichelle to stop dialing, and Apollo tried to give her money for the bill. She told Apollo she'd been planning to cover the tab ever since she'd made the reservation—told Emma as much when they first sat down—and simply forgot to repeat the news when Apollo arrived. He could've eaten! As it was, the only stuff in his stomach was bread and bourbon. He'd never expected to be tipsy during the birth of his first child.

Harder for Nichelle to handle was the fact that Emma didn't want an ambulance called. As they left Bouley—rushing as fast as a nine-months-pregnant woman could move—Emma reminded Nichelle they were having this baby at home. Ambulances weren't some private car service, they would take her to a hospital, not her apartment. In the apple room Nichelle offered to at least hail a cab, request a Lyft, but this offer too was denied. They were way downtown, on Duane Street, on a Friday night. The best a car could do was hit the West Side Highway. There they'd find the kind of traffic only Beijing or Mumbai would recognize. An hourlong trip by car to Washington Heights from here, maybe longer.

Meanwhile the Chambers Street station lay only four blocks away. They could catch an A train and be home in thirty-five.

Nichelle walked alongside them to the corner of Church Street. She couldn't contain her vexation. "Why are you doing this?" she shouted on the street. All the liquor had loosened her volume knob. "What is wrong with you!"

As they crossed Reade Street, Emma spoke. "Call Kim," she said.

Apollo already had the phone out. Older sister; trained midwife. Kim Valentine on the speed dial. "Kim!" Apollo shouted in a moment. "Emma's having contractions."

On the other end of the line, Kim spoke so quietly, the street traffic made her impossible to hear. Why was she whispering? Emma walked slowly but soldiered forward. Nichelle trailed them by half a block shouting words so slurred they became an invented language. Pregnancy is hard on women, and it can be tough on their friends, too.

"Stop shouting," Kim whispered on the phone. "I'm in a movie. Hold on."

They reached the train station. Apollo wondered, for no good reason, what movie Kim had been watching. "It's a little early," he said.

They were at the top of the station stairs. Nichelle caught up and clutched at Emma in a sloppy hug. "She's only thirty-eight weeks!" he said, sounding as if he was pleading with Kim to put the labor on hold.

"Stop shouting," Kim said. "Maybe it's a false labor. Could be Braxton Hicks."

Apollo looked to Emma, who'd collapsed onto Nichelle, heavy breathing into her old friend's neck. They looked like some sloppy prom couple. Apollo didn't care if this would turn out to be a false labor, just a test run. He wanted Kim to leave her movie and get her car. She kept her birthing equipment in the trunk at all times. He wanted her driving north no matter the traffic. They might get to the apartment before her, but soon enough she'd be there. She could mock them all she wanted if this whole thing went in the Braxton Hicks direction. He'd endure the taunting to ensure her arrival. Imagine him and Emma birthing this baby in their apartment alone. Kim had prepared them for this possibility, but that didn't mean he ever expected it to actually happen. The idea was so laughable, it almost made him scream right there on the street.

"We'll meet you at home," Apollo said, hoping he sounded assured and not panicked. "Get your car."

"I love you," Nichelle said as she clutched at Emma. "I love you."

Emma touched Nichelle's head and stroked her hair. "We'll be fine, Nichelle. I promise you. We'll be fine."

"You shouldn't be comforting me!" Nichelle cried, then sort of laughed.

"Your hotel's very close," Emma whispered though the words came out pinched. "Can you make it there?"

The Bradley Method classes had taught Apollo that if Emma could carry on conversation, then she wasn't in true labor yet. This eased him slightly. Even as Nichelle hugged him goodbye and he led Emma down the stairs into the station, he was thinking ahead to the steps awaiting him at home. Inflating the plastic tub rapidly with the electric air pump, putting the plastic liner in, attaching the hose. Apollo knew every step, had practiced each half a dozen times in the last month. He knew his job, and that calmed him.

Apollo hadn't hung up his cellphone yet. Kim could be heard shouting from the receiver. He tapped the speakerphone. Emma clung to the handrails as they descended.

"We're going down," Apollo said.

Kim, caught midsentence, stopped shouting to register his words.

"I'm on speaker?" she asked. She didn't wait for confirmation. "Emma!" she shouted. "I'm on my way. Stay strong! You can handle this!"

Reception died after that.

And there, finally, was the reason that Apollo and Emma were having their baby at home. Kim Valentine had switched from being a pediatric nurse to a midwife in a kind of midlife conversion. Like most converts, she proselytized hard. Kim called on friends and old co-workers, cousins and random women riding in elevators. She'd even accept calls from telemarketers just so she could chat them up about home births. So when her sister got pregnant, it was without question that Kim would be the midwife and this delivery would happen at home. Kim had never had children of her own, but she'd raised Emma since the age of five. That had to count. Becoming an aunty would be one hell of a milestone for her. Natural childbirth for Emma; Kim as midwife. That was that, the decision clear. They informed Apollo over brunch at the diner on Fort Washington Avenue. He had questions, but it was only curiosity, not resistance. By the end of the day, he'd been on the computer researching inflatable birthing pools. Kim promised she could get him a discount.

Apollo and Emma reached the bottom of the staircase, then pushed through the turnstiles. They didn't have long to wait. The A arrived in record time. They boarded at Chambers Street feeling downright blessed.

E MMA AND APOLLO boarded the A train so flustered that they
didn't even notice the other passengers. Couldn't have told you
if there were other passengers. Emma wanted to stay standing.
She held on to one of the poles in the train car, and Apollo stood
behind her so she could lean her weight back into him. The train doors
shut, the hiss of the car going into motion, then they heard a young man
shout.

"Showtime, ladies and gentlemen, showtime! What time is it?"

Three more voices answered. "Showtime!"

Emma groaned. Apollo couldn't be sure if it was from the labor pains
or because she'd seen the four boys who'd started dancing on the train.
These crews—boys between fifteen and nineteen mostly—worked New
York City subways like carnies in the Midwest. One manned the radio,
blasting a beat loud enough that it drowned out the subway wheels grind-
ing the rails, while the other three did breakdancing routines that had
been modified to fit a subway car. These kids tended to do good business
on the A train but never this far downtown. Usually they worked the ex-
press ride from 59th Street to 125th, a long enough trip for every member
of the crew to do a routine and work up some tips from the passengers. But
now they were down here at Chambers Street, in the middle of the night,
right when Apollo and Emma most needed a little peace. The boys had

their backs to Apollo and Emma, huddled together at the far end of the car. They didn't even seem to be putting on an actual show, but practicing their routines.

"I can't stand here," Emma said as the train rattled toward the next stop, Canal Street.

"I'll get them to stop the music," Apollo said, but as soon as he took a step away from Emma, she reached out and pulled him back.

"I'm going to throw up if I keep standing," she said. The train left the tunnels and pulled into the Canal Street station. For the first time, Apollo actually looked around the car. Not more than ten people in here, including the four dancers.

"If your man can't do this . . ." one of the dancers called out coolly, like an actor going over his lines.

"Leave him at home!" the other three replied.

They'd never have time to get out of this car and back into the next before the doors closed again. He certainly wasn't going to try and maneuver her between the cars while she was in labor. They would have to endure the routine until it ended.

"Black guys stripping?" called the leader of the boys.

"Just flipping!" the others answered back.

Emma swayed where she stood, and her cheeks puffed out, and she brought one hand over her lips. He braced his body around hers trying to keep her as steady as possible. He wasn't sure what they'd do if she vomited. Who would the remaining few passengers in the car hate more at that point—the dancers or the couple covered in puke? Ah, New York.

At West 4th Street, Apollo set Emma down onto the gray plastic corner seat gently. But as soon as she sat—her full weight going down on her tailbone—she lurched forward again, her face tight with concentration. It hurt to sit, but if she stood she'd throw up, and they had ten more stops to go.

Emma looked at him, her eyes slightly vacant. "Why did you eat nothing but bread?" she asked. "Do you know how good that food was?"

Jokes were good. No one ever told a funny in true labor. Apollo took off his coat. He rolled it into a ball and set it under Emma. Across the platform the C train, a local, pulled in. The doors opened, and passengers scrambled over to the A. The car that had been so empty suddenly became half full.

Just before the doors shut, three more passengers slipped on, a mother with two children. One was a young girl, maybe nine. The younger child lay asleep in a stroller. The mother saw Apollo and Emma—two sweaty, panting adults—and quickly scanned the rest of the car.

"Showtime, ladies and gentlemen, showtime!" the boys called out.

The mother buckled in defeat. The dancers had moved to the middle of the train car, and their radio had, somehow, become even louder. Most on the train acted as though nothing at all was happening in the middle of the car, as if the music weren't playing, as if four young men weren't pulling off incredible feats of acrobatic flair; a few filed audible complaints, and the train began to move.

The mother pushed her stroller to the seats opposite Apollo and Emma. She called to the nine-year-old in Spanish, and the nine-year-old followed. The girl took a seat and pulled a book out of her bag. Apollo wondered, just for a moment, if this could've been the same mother and children who'd been at the Fort Washington library on the day he'd met Emma. Impossible, improbable, but he felt an urge to snatch the book out of the girl's hand and see if it had the Fort Washington branch's stamp somewhere inside.

The kid didn't pay attention to the dancers or to Apollo and Emma. She had that book and seemed satisfied. The toddler in the stroller stayed sleeping, but now, from this angle, the mother seemed to understand Apollo and Emma differently. Maybe, because of the sweating and huffing, she'd thought they were addicts tweaking out on the A train, but it was impossible to ignore Emma's belly from here. Now the woman watched Emma quietly, and for a few moments the two locked eyes.

Emma scooched up off her butt as the A train picked up speed, rattling like a roller coaster. As soon as the A train rocked, she was sent falling back into the seat, and that hurt Emma even more. She pressed her face to Apollo's shoulder when he held her, and through his shirt, his skin felt wet. He looked down to see Emma wiping her chin across him, pinching her lips as tight as she could.

They reached 14th Street, and the boys slapped their radio off when two NYPD officers got on the train. The cops knew what the boys had been doing, but deterrence seemed like enough right then. The ride from 14th all the way to 42nd Street, without the radio playing, seemed as quiet as a cave.

Emma worked on her breathing, two little breaths in and one big breath out. She found her way to a meditative state.

"We can't wait to meet you," Apollo whispered to her.

She couldn't acknowledge what he was saying because she was concentrating on her breathing. The pain she felt in her hips, in her lower back, it became a white light that drew her close one moment and pushed her further away the next.

"We can't wait to meet you," Apollo whispered again.

They'd come up with this mantra in the Bradley Method class. Their teacher Tonya suggested coming up with a saying the father could repeat to the mother when she began labor. A mantra of a kind. Apollo and Emma had decided they'd say something to the baby. A simple welcome that summarized their excitement, their anticipation. Focus on that rather than the pain.

"We can't wait to meet you."

Who'd said it that time, Apollo or Emma? She couldn't be sure, and frankly, neither could he. They were on that A train, pulling into the 59th Street station, but they were not there. They were in their apartment, both of them in the tub, Kim by their side. They were already greeting their child. They only had to catch up to that moment in the future, and all would be fine.

The train stopped, and the car cleared out. It became almost as empty as it had been down by Chambers Street. When the car doors closed again, there were only a few passengers left: Apollo and Emma, the mother with her children, and the dancers counting the little money they'd made before the cops got on. Nine souls. One more on the way.

The A train left 59th Street. The next leg of the trip would be the toughest. From here the A train wouldn't stop until 125th. The single longest uninterrupted ride in the entire New York City subway system. The A train would never go any faster than it did here. Apollo, anticipating the jerking and jumping to come, tried to wrap his arms around Emma like a living seatbelt, but as the train passed 79th Street, 81st, 86th, it didn't seem to matter. The only solace was that Emma had gone into a kind of trance. The breathing worked. She didn't talk anymore. She approached true labor, but luckily they were nearly home.

The A passed 103rd Street, the weak light in the station hardly seeming to reach their train car before they were back in the tunnel again.

And then the wheels of the train creaked as the train suddenly slowed.

No problem at all, a common occurrence. The motorman had been chugging at high speeds, and it was normal for the train to start coasting. This way they'd simply glide into the 125th Street station. Totally normal.

Then the squeal of the train's brakes as they came to a full stop.

Apollo looked out the car's windows but couldn't see anything out there in the dark. A squawk played over the car's speakers, just a stab of feedback. The speakers went silent again. And a moment after that, the lights in all the cars of the A train went out. Apollo and Emma and the mother and her kids and the four dancers sat in total darkness.

I N THE BRADLEY method class their teacher taught them that the majority of women had been having babies without the aid of modern hospitals, obstetricians, crash teams, pediatric nurses, and—most of all, Pitocin—for, well, always. The female body knew exactly how to deliver a child, just as all living things do, and the job of the midwife was basically just to get the twenty-first-century out of the way. Apollo and Emma hadn't been as adamant about home birth as others: if they truly needed to go to a hospital, they agreed they would. Emma had even packed a small suitcase for just such a contingency. They kept it under their bed. Nonetheless, Tonya explained, these Bradley Method classes were designed, in part, so that even the fathers could do the job of assisting with the delivery if needed. Apollo had believed this, had—with a degree of arrogance—repeated all this to Patrice when they were out on an estate sale together. But let's be clear, Apollo Kagwa had been a staunch believer in the idea that he could deliver a baby because he was absolutely sure he would never, ever actually have to do that.

But there they were, on the stalled A train, no midwives in sight.

Maybe the nine-year-old girl, no longer able to read her book in the dark, might also be an accredited doula? Or could the four-man crew of dancers please also be a team of traveling obstetricians? At least the toddler in the stroller hadn't woken up. How was this possible? Maybe the mom had dosed the kid with Night Time Triaminic.

"Ohhhhhhhhh." Emma made the sound, and Apollo, in his fear, almost clamped a hand over her mouth. He was worried not about decorum but about what that sound indicated. They'd practiced this moan in class. When the woman couldn't simply breathe through the pain anymore, she was supposed to release exactly this moan.

"Ohhhhhhhhh." Emma did it again.

In class one of the other expectant mothers had asked when she should make that call, when she should tell herself to begin. But Tonya—mother of two—had smiled kindly and said, *When you're in true labor, you can't help but do it.*

"Ohhhhhhhhh."

When you're in true labor.

"Why you hurting your girl?"

Apollo looked up to find the four dancers crowding close. One of them held his phone up, using it like a flashlight, which wasn't really necessary—their eyes were already adjusting to the dim glow coming from the LED bulbs and signal lights in the tunnel. Being this near, he realized how young they were. Their leader, the oldest, couldn't have been more than fifteen. He stood over Apollo, already making a fist.

"Why you hurting your girl?" he said again.

Apollo actually laughed at them. They thought they were coming to Emma's aid, but once they looked at her instead of Apollo, all four boys lost their courage.

"Yo! She's pregnant!"

Emma corrected them. "I'm starting labor."

He felt surprised by how calm she sounded, and these four boys seemed shocked as well. The kid in front, their leader—his closed fists loosened. When his mouth went slack, he looked as young as the toddler in the stroller.

"We need some help," Apollo said. "Could one of you run up and find the conductor?"

None of them moved. The other three had actually stepped back, shrunk behind the oldest. Twelve or thirteen, the others couldn't have been older than that. They peeked around the oldest one's muscled arms. Emma had to make the same request.

"One of you run and find the conductor," she said, locking eyes with them.

"I'll go," the youngest of them said. He pulled open the car door and sprinted.

"Ohhhhhhhh."

Apollo stood up, and the other three boys moved away. The woman across from them watched only Emma. The girl leaned her head against her mother's shoulder, her book now facedown on her knees. She watched Emma, too.

"I need to get her on her feet," Apollo said.

"But she's having a kid," the oldest said quietly. "She's supposed to lie down, right?"

"What's your name?" Apollo asked.

"I'm Cowboy," the boy said. "I used to live in Dallas, like ten years back, then we came up here with my parents so everybody calls me Cowboy, but my real name is—"

"Cowboy," Apollo said, and the kid looked up at him. "That's a good name. Can we call you that?"

Cowboy took a breath, spoke slower. "I want to help," he said.

"The best way to help my wife is to get her on her feet," Apollo said. "Two of you hold her hands and pull while I lift her hips. Yeah?"

Cowboy nodded and looked to the kid on his left. They positioned themselves in front of Emma and grabbed her fingers.

"Wait," Emma said. "Don't hold my fingers. Hold my wrists."

The boys watched her quietly and didn't move.

Emma smiled softly at both of them. "You're doing great," she said. "You're brave boys."

When they rose, as one mass, they nearly crashed into the stroller. The mother pulled it to the side just in time.

"Now walk me to the closest pole," Emma said.

It was only three steps. It took four minutes. When Emma reached the pole, Apollo, who'd been behind her, his arms around her middle, reminded her of the next step.

"Darlin', you have to grab hold."

Emma held the pole.

"Any of you have something to drink?"

The boys looked through their book bags. "Red Bull?" one offered.

"No," Emma said firmly.

Apollo turned to the mother. Between the nine-year-old and the tod-dler, this woman had to have a juice box or something.

"*Agua?*" Emma said.

The mother reached into the back of the stroller, found a pouch, and revealed a red and black sippy cup. Apollo didn't have hands free, so he looked to the only boy who hadn't been given a job yet. The kid almost looked grateful for the simple task. He brought it back and set it down on the floor.

"Ohhhhhhhhh!"

Emma's hands slipped off the pole. They were already too sweaty to hold on.

"Hands and knees," Emma said to Apollo. "I have to be on my hands and knees. Get me down."

"Fellas," Apollo said. "I'm going to need you to hold her up a little longer."

"Where you going?" Cowboy asked, panicked, stricken.

"I'm going over there to get my coat."

"I don't need the coat!" Emma shouted.

But Apollo couldn't stop himself. He got the coat. He laid it flat. It wasn't much. It wasn't much. He wished he'd kept the loaner jacket they'd given him at Bouley. He leaned in close to Emma again. "I'm going to have to take down your tights," he said apologetically.

"Well get on with it," Emma growled.

Then the rumbling roll of the car door opening. The fourth boy re-turned with the conductor, who looked almost as young as the dancers.

"God damn," the conductor said.

"Any chance we're going to move soon?" Apollo asked.

"God damn," the conductor repeated.

The mother reached over her son's stroller and pinched the conductor on the leg.

"Lost power to the third rail," the conductor explained, coming back to himself as he rubbed his thigh. "This train ain't moving. I'll go back and radio this in. They'll send EMTs. But even that's going to take awhile."

"Ohhhhhhhh."

Apollo told him to make the call, but knew no one could arrive in time. The only help Emma would get was already in this train car. The conductor left, and when the door of the next car rolled shut again, the glass filled with faces. Spectators. Folks who'd figured out something big was happening in this car. At the other end people in the next car were gathering, too. Now they had a viewing public. Even worse, Apollo could already see the light of cellphones held up to record the event.

"Cowboy! Could you and your team keep all those people out of this car? Block the windows?"

The kid looked to both ends. "We could do that easy."

There were a lot of folks at both doors, and many more behind them. "You sure?" Apollo asked.

The one who'd run to the conductor laughed. "Most of these people shrink up as soon as we step on a train." He clutched his hands to his chest and shivered. *"Those black boys are so intimidating!"* The others laughed.

"We'll keep them out," Cowboy said, smiling.

And with that they broke off, two boys to a side.

"*No* showtime for you, ladies and gentlemen!" Cowboy shouted.

"*No* showtime for you!" the other three called back.

Apollo got down on his hands and knees and crawled around close to Emma's face. Her head was down, hair like a shroud and matted flat from perspiration. He brought the sippy cup of water closer and lifted her head. He tilted the cup and let her have two sips.

Apollo set the bottle down. He didn't know how he could post up behind Emma to receive the baby but also keep giving her sips of water, keep up reassuring contact. He looked over Emma. The mother watched them. When they'd first boarded the train, she and Emma had seemed to share a powerful moment, locking eyes to communicate something Apollo knew he could never understand. He gazed at her, pleading. After a moment the woman patted her daughter and rose from the seat. She pushed the stroller closer to the little girl, who peeked in on her brother.

The mother took the sippy cup and spoke quietly, in Spanish, to Emma. The woman's tone seemed soothing, and maybe that was all Emma needed. Emma even leaned forward and touched her forehead to the woman's shoulder, intimacy so acute it appeared mystical.

Now Apollo looked over his shoulder, the boys had their backs to the scene, their arms up and flailing to reject all attempts at a shot. He pulled off Emma's shoes. He slipped her tights down to her knees. He brought his hands to either side of her hips and pressed gently, something that soothed her in the third trimester. He spoke now not to his wife but to their baby.

"We can't wait to meet you," he said.

16

THERE IN A stalled A train in the bowels of the earth, Emma bled and bore down. Apollo called out the two commands Kim had told him were always appropriate, *Slow down. Just breathe.* Apollo focused on nothing but his wife and their child. When Emma arched her back and grunted, he pressed his thumbs into the small of her back, just above the tailbone, until her back went straight again. When she bled and pushed harder, he pressed her thigh and said, *Slow down. Just breathe.* When he saw the baby crowning, he had a moment of confusion. There was the baby's head, but it looked like it was wrapped in bubble tape. The amniotic sac hadn't burst yet, and it served now as a thin layer between the baby and Emma's pelvic bone. For all the agony she might be feeling, this little miracle—that her water didn't break right away—was what spared her just enough pain to survive this.

Apollo watched his hands stretched out now, ready to catch their child. He felt like a witness and a participant. Their child teetered between his mother and the world; in one place and another; alive and in that ether of the womb. Apollo felt as though he, too, balanced on this threshold. Its head nearly out but body still hidden, his child seemed like an emissary of the divine.

"Can you see his head?" Emma asked.

Apollo tried to answer but only stammered.

Then Emma's water broke, and she cooed with relief, and their child slipped right out, and Apollo Kagwa caught the baby before it touched the floor of the train.

"It's a boy," Apollo said.

"A boy," Emma whispered.

Emma leaned forward into the woman. The woman kissed Emma on the top of her head. Emma had to stay on her knees for a few minutes more until the placenta passed.

This meant that for a short while Apollo remained alone with his son. Apollo unbuttoned his shirt so he could hold the boy directly against his skin. The baby didn't cry, didn't flutter his eyes yet, only opened and closed his tiny mouth. Apollo watched his son take his gasping, first breaths. He watched that little face for what seemed like quite a while, an hour or an eternity.

"Can we call him Brian?" Apollo croaked. He hadn't meant to ask that right now, at the moment of birth, hadn't thought he'd ever want to name his son after his missing father. The question, the desire, simply slipped out; it was as if it had been hiding—biding time on his tongue for years.

"I like that name," Emma finally said, turning now, hands open for her child.

Apollo brought his cheek to the baby's.

"Hello, Brian," he whispered. "I'm so happy to meet you."

3

THEN COMES BABY IN
A BABY CARRIAGE

THE BABY CAME on Friday night. The EMTs arrived twenty-two minutes after Apollo and Emma met the kid. As Emma predicted, they took her directly to Harlem Hospital, where she and the baby were kept under observation for two days. Though they assured Apollo he could go home without them, he spent both nights upright in a chair in Emma's room. By Monday morning, they were home in a taxi, and Apollo got them both into bed. He'd already given the boy his first name, and now he suggested a middle name.

"His middle name is not going to be Cowboy," Emma said as she prepared herself for the climb into their bed. Apollo held Brian as if the boy were made of Baccarat crystal. His eyes were open. He looked at nothing and everything.

"Give him," Emma said. She'd propped pillows behind her. Apollo handed her their child, and she leaned close to his face and blew gently on his head.

Brian came out totally bald. He had a faint overbite and a small chin. He looked like a turtle. In the full light of the hospital room, they'd both seen it, laughed about it.

"Brer Turtle," Apollo said. "I'm going to get your mother some food."

Emma brought her breast to the baby's face. She stroked his cheek, as she'd been taught to do, but when the baby opened his mouth, she stuffed so much of her breast inside that he coughed and turned away. Emma curled forward and stroked Brian's cheek and tried again, but it was another failure to latch. Emma had been trying to get this since late Friday night. At the hospital every nurse, and both doctors, had offered differing opinions about what she was doing wrong.

In the kitchen Apollo found the breakfast dishes they'd left before going out for work on Friday morning. He'd been expecting to wash them after dinner with Nichelle. They'd been a family of two just that recently. He already had a hard time remembering that ancient age, Before Brian.

He washed the dishes. Lillian and Kim were both scheduled to arrive this morning. Maybe while they were here, he could make a supermarket run. Lillian and Kim had both come to the hospital, but the visits weren't long. Even Nichelle made it on Sunday morning, though she had a flight back to Los Angeles in the afternoon. She'd entered the room horrified, as if Emma were still down in that subway car giving birth. She couldn't stop asking what it smelled like down there. Neither of them remembered. The birth even made the news for a day. The *Post*, the *Daily News*, even a mention on NY1. It might've become more of a story if someone had been able to capture clean video of the birth, but Cowboy had been as good as his word. Cellphone footage from that night showed four black kids waving and smiling and looking gleeful, and generally speaking news outlets don't find that sort of thing worth sharing.

Apollo checked the back room. A couch and a television and four filled bookshelves were in here. So was the Moses basket they'd be using with Brian for the next few weeks as they slept him in their bedroom. Before Brian this had been their lounge; after Brian it would be his room. Apollo scanned the space, imagining what they'd need: a crib, plush toys, a dresser for the blankets and clothes, a Diaper Genie, a few crates of diapers, and much more stuff than he could currently guess. They should've made all these purchases long ago. In fact, Emma had created a list, but then her job went to half time, with the possibility of losing the work altogether, and with that they had to wait a little longer and plan a little better for exactly what they needed first. The Moses basket, newborn diapers, one-piece sleepers, baby wash and washcloths, those were the only things to make the initial cut. But now Apollo couldn't help wanting to give his son more. He closed his eyes and kissed the doorframe.

How long had he stood there before the buzzer rang? It's entirely possible he'd fallen asleep upright. Kim and Lillian appeared in a cluster at the door. Both women carried large bags. Kim made a supermarket run for them, basic ingredients, and Lillian brought meals she'd prepared at home. Four cartons of red bean soup, meatloaf and mashed potatoes, lasagna and samosas, two quiches, and oxtail soup. He set all their things down in the kitchen, then led both women into the bedroom, where Emma tried to disguise the tears of frustration she'd been shedding as she still tried to get Brian to latch.

Kim slipped Brian from Emma's hands. A chance for the midwife to check the baby, for an aunt to hug her nephew. As Kim undressed the baby, Lillian moved close to Emma and kissed her head.

"I had the same trouble with Apollo," Lillian said softly. "I didn't know what to do, and my mother wasn't with me."

Emma nodded. She understood that problem.

"I didn't think I'd ever get it," Lillian said. "But it just took time."

Now Emma leaned into Lillian and breathed deeply. Lillian held her close.

Kim turned a now naked Brian onto his stomach. "I love that little blue butt!" she shouted.

"Let me see what you're doing," Lillian said to Emma. "Maybe I can help."

Kim returned Brian to his mother. Emma brought him close and stroked his cheek. The baby's eyes waggled and swam, and his mouth opened to pucker.

"Wait," Lillian said. Now she examined Emma's breasts like a jeweler. She nodded gently, then sighed. "It's too bad your breasts are the wrong shape," she finally said.

"Mom!" Apollo shouted. He yoked his own mother to get her out of the bedroom. Kim stepped in between Emma and Lillian, showing Lillian her back. Emma didn't even cry out or sob at what Lillian had said. She just returned to lining her nipple up with the baby's mouth.

Apollo enlisted Lillian in unpacking the food and supplies, and once that was finished, he took her out to get coffee. She didn't understand what she'd said wrong. Apollo tried to explain three times but gave up. Eventually he thanked her, sincerely, for the food and walked her back to the A train.

On the way to the apartment, his cellphone vibrated with a text message from Patrice: *Estate Sale Today. Come with me. You got mouths to feed!*

He wrote back: *Too soon.*

Patrice wrote again: *Your family can't live with us when you get evicted.*

Apollo laughed as he slipped his phone away. He missed Patrice. Also, he knew he couldn't wait more than a week before he had to get back on his grind.

Kim already had on her shoes and jacket when Apollo returned. He let her out and came back to the bedroom. He closed the curtains, and the place went dim. He climbed in beside them.

"'I had a rooster, my rooster pleased me,'" Emma sang. "'I held my rooster by the old willow tree.'"

Apollo moved closer to his wife, his son.

"'My little rooster sang cock-a-doodle-doo.'"

She sang, and each of them fell asleep in turn. First Apollo, then Emma. The baby kept his eyes open the longest but soon enough joined his mother and father.

At one point, well after midnight, Apollo woke and crept out of the bedroom. He found his bag, the one he'd been wearing the night Brian was born. He opened it to find the copy of *Fields of Fire* inside. In the kitchen he opened his laptop and sent an email to that collector in Virginia. He attached a photo of the cover. The glow of the screen lit his face.

"I am the god, Apollo," he whispered as the god got to work.

He fell asleep at the table within half an hour.

18

PATRICE SENT WORD of an estate sale in the Bronx. Close enough to Washington Heights that Apollo had to get on the road, no excuses and no more delays. And he had to bring Brian with him. Six weeks was the most time Emma could take off from work before her salary vanished. In the United States this counted as generous.

Going out the door that morning, she'd cried worse than when she'd been in labor. Apollo promised to be careful with the boy, but that wasn't what crushed Emma. Of course she trusted Apollo, but leaving her baby so soon after birth felt like stepping out of an airlock without a space suit, no source of oxygen. How would she breathe? Nevertheless, she had to do it. They couldn't afford for her to lose her job.

Apollo rented a Zipcar for the trip, something sturdy, a Honda Odyssey. The company gave each car a name. This one's was Suave. He admired that level of self-delusion. He strapped the boy into his rear-facing car seat and arranged the armful of pillows he'd brought along on the floor and around the car seat. The baby lay surrounded by padding, and still Apollo never drove faster than fifteen miles per hour along the Henry Hudson Parkway. Other drivers beeped and cursed as they swerved around him. This bothered Apollo not a bit. The pair crept all the way to the

Riverdale section of the Bronx. The twenty-minute trip took almost an hour. At one point, on Dodgewood Road, a street sweeper passed them.

This pocket of the Bronx turned suburban, nearly rural, with uneven single-lane streets and two-story homes sitting on large grassy plots. On Dodgewood Road, Apollo found the place: a large single-family house with a driveway and two-car garage. A familiar car by the curb, a red 2001 Toyota Echo. Its bumper sticker read LIBRARIAN OF ALEXANDRIA.

Patrice Green had beat him here, and that man lived in southeastern Queens.

Apollo turned off the car and arched himself over the front seat so he could see his son. Brian Kagwa watched the bright sky through the passenger window, mouth opening and closing as if he was actually feeding on the sunlight.

"Let's go hunt some books," Apollo said.

Apollo came around and unlatched his son. Wind rattled the property, and Brian seemed to focus on the quaking limbs of a tree. Apollo looped on his BabyBjörn baby carrier and strapped his son in. Daddy's heartbeat would be mood music for the kid.

Apollo went through the baby bag, cross-checking like a pilot about to take flight. Bottle, three diapers, wipes, burp cloth, set of plastic keys for rattling, and finally, a small, fluffy blanket.

"Flight attendants take your seat," Apollo whispered. "We are prepared for takeoff."

As he rolled the minivan's door shut, a man's voice came from the garage.

"I didn't have that much gear on when I was fighting in Fallujah."

Patrice stepped into the daylight, so tall his head nearly clipped the raised door. Patrice had a face like a catfish, with an overhanging upper lip and errant mustache hairs. Eyes a little too small for his head.

"You were never near Fallujah," Apollo said.

Patrice shrugged. "Closer than you ever got."

Apollo raised his diaper bag. "Now I'm in my own dirty war."

Patrice Green had never fought in Fallujah, but he did serve in the army from 2003 to 2004, during Operation Iraqi Freedom, in the 62nd Air Defense Artillery Regiment. He'd spent much of his time doing counter-

IED operations along a supply route in Iskandariyah, Iraq, a city twenty-five miles south of Baghdad, not far from the Euphrates River. He'd done that work and then returned to the United States. He'd been the manager of an AMC movie theater on 34th Street. He'd been a graduate student at Queens College, in library studies, for five months. And eventually he became a used and rare bookseller.

The garage behind Patrice looked bigger than Apollo and Emma's apartment, filled now with fifty cardboard boxes of books. The top flaps of every box lay open, a treasure room already plundered.

"Grandmother," Patrice said. "She died four months ago. Family finally got all the old lady's books into boxes and put out the ad. Son-in-law let me into the garage. Other than that, he's stayed out of my way."

"He's cool?" Apollo said, bouncing in place lightly, for Brian's benefit.

"I asked to use their bathroom, and the dude wouldn't let me in the house. Motherfucker said they didn't have a bathroom." Patrice gestured at the two-story structure. "Four-bedroom home but no bathrooms. Imagine that."

"You'd think they would've checked before buying the place."

Apollo laughed with Patrice just to keep from crying. Now Apollo looked inside the garage, scanning the open boxes as Brian wriggled against his chest. If Patrice had already been through all these, then he'd found everything worth anything.

"Grandma liked books," Apollo said. "She have good taste?"

"I found a few winners," Patrice said.

No doubt he'd already set those books aside, but look how full the boxes in the garage remained. That meant most of them were nearly worthless, the kind of stuff that would turn a profit only on the shipping. He'd rented the minivan to keep his son safe, but at least it had plenty of storage space.

"There's a few more in the basement," Patrice said, pointing to a door, slightly open, near the back of the main house.

"You haven't been down there yet," Apollo said.

For the first time since he'd stepped out of the garage Patrice Green shrank. "Nah. Thought I'd leave something for you."

Patrice Green, big man and expert bookseller, counter-IED specialist and child raised in the roughest part of Roxbury, did not like basements. He'd returned from Iskandariyah uninjured but not unharmed. He had never explained his fear, but Apollo intuited it and, most importantly, never asked about it directly. A fair number of estate sales in New York City took place in the basements of various apartment buildings, and Patrice Green never set foot in one of them.

"You hear that, Brian?" Apollo said as he let the front flap of the Baby-Björn fall loose and pulled his son free, turned him around. "Uncle Patrice is letting us take point."

"But we split whatever you find," Patrice said, looking over the baby's head. "Sixty-forty. That's the deal."

Apollo lifted the boy higher. He'd expected Patrice to say something about the baby from the moment he'd shown up, but instead they'd gone on about the books. This was the first time his best friend had met his child—shouldn't that merit at least one comment? Apollo felt surprised by how much this moment bothered him.

"Look into his eyes," Apollo said, trying to act playful.

"What am I supposed to say to him?" Patrice asked.

Apollo raised his voice to a child's register. "Tell me what happened in Iskandariyah, Uncle Patrice."

Patrice leaned close to the baby. "Tell your daddy I said, Fuck you."

"I haven't mastered language yet."

Patrice grinned. "I'll teach you the gesture."

Now Apollo had to smile. "You're going to be a bad influence on me."

"No worse than your daddy's going to be."

Apollo smooshed Brian right up against Patrice's face. "Can you spell PTSD?"

Then Apollo turned and moved to the basement door with the baby.

Patrice shouted after him. "I understand why your pops abandoned you!"

19

THE BASEMENT FELT warmer than the garage. Down the Kagwa boys went. The basement sat as one grand open plane. In the far corner stood the boiler—a large white cylinder with a blue control panel, copper pipes running up into the ceiling and a silver tube running outside through the wall. It looked like something from the set of James Whale's *Frankenstein*. The boiler rumbled now as if reanimating life.

In the opposite corner sat the washing machine and the dryer, and beside the two machines lay cleaning materials, shovels and rakes, and paint cans showing rust. The third corner of the basement was cluttered with children's toys that had been sitting down here for a decade or four. Plastic dolls gone nearly gray and their dresses threadbare. Toy trucks overturned or dismantled. Teddy Ruxpin looked like he'd died in hibernation.

In the corner closest to the basement steps lay seven cardboard boxes. Maybe the garage had been too full to accommodate them. Apollo went down on one knee. He sniffed his son's head. Didn't even realize he'd done it until the smell made him smile. A moment later Brian wriggled and squirmed.

The fluffy blanket came out of the diaper bag. Apollo spread it out right beside the boxes of books. He set Brian down on his stomach, and the boy lay there, eyes wide, opening and closing his mouth, small gasps trickling out. Brian's feet wriggled, and his hands swam over the blanket. In a moment he set his hands out flat and with a push he raised his head.

"Tummy time!" Apollo shouted, as if Brian had just successfully piloted an airplane.

A moment later Brian dropped his head back down onto the blanket. Apollo rolled him onto his back, and the baby looked up at the boards of the ceiling. Apollo left him to it and scooted forward to the first of the cardboard boxes. As he opened the flaps, he looked back at Brian.

"My father, your grandfather, disappeared when I was four years old. I used to have a nightmare about him leaving. His name was Brian West. We named you after him."

Brian wriggled his head from side to side and threw his hands out wide.

"I didn't hear anything about him, nothing from him, until I turned twelve years old. Then, out of nowhere, he left a box at my front door. It had the tickets to the movie he and Grandma saw on their first date. The headshot of the woman who testified against the shady businessman Grandma worked for. The thing was like a time capsule."

Brian lifted his chubby legs, then dropped them back down. He rocked his body slightly and looked like that turtle once more, trapped on its back and trying to turn over.

"I always wondered why he did it. Why'd he leave the box and then disappear again?"

Apollo helped roll Brian back onto his belly.

"Now that you're in my life, I understand. He wanted me to know how much I'd meant to him. He didn't want me to go my whole life thinking I just didn't matter. I don't know what kind of situation he was in at the time, I don't even know if the man is still alive, but I don't think he could have been all that different from me. And I'm so happy with you already, little man. If I was trapped on Saturn, I'd still find a way to send a message and let you know you were loved."

Apollo stopped moving, even breathing, and watched his baby boy labor to his lift his head. This small act, working to develop the muscles of his neck, would someday lead to sitting up, crawling, stumbling, sprinting. All that began here and now, in this basement of a Riverdale home. Apollo felt so fortunate to witness it. With the baby only two months old, Apollo was a mess of raw nerves. He got back to work just to keep from crying.

The books in the first box were worthless, so Apollo moved on to the second. The second box had as little to offer as the first. The third box, too.

"Brian left a book behind. A children's book that he used to read to me. It's called *Outside Over There*. I know it from memory by now."

The fourth box had nothing good in it and neither did the fifth. Brian's head lowered, the muscles exhausted, so Apollo turned him over again. The baby whimpered there on his back, so Apollo came closer to check him. After pulling off socks and shoes and pants, undoing the snaps on the onesie, he found the cause. As he changed Brian's diaper, he spoke to his son again.

"'When Papa was away at sea,'" Apollo recited. "That's how the book begins. That's the first page. Papa is gone and Mama sits out in an arbor. I had no idea what an arbor was. It's basically a small wooden structure people put out in their gardens, like a trellis. She sits on a bench underneath the arbor. So dad is far away and mom is outside in the garden."

He wrapped the boy back up, slipped the piss diaper into the special pouch provided in the diaper bag, and put away the wipes and the tube of coconut oil.

"But inside the house there's a little girl named Ida. She's very young, but she's left to take care of her baby sister all on her own. She plays a horn for the baby to try and help it sleep. But she's looking out the window while she makes music. She's in the same room, but even she's not watching the baby. And that's when the goblins sneak in."

Brian fell asleep. Apollo scooted backward quietly. Two more boxes to go. When he opened the sixth, a cloud of fungus funk entered the air. Every book in this one, all hardcovers, showed black spots on the endpapers. Worthless. Ruined. Only one box left.

Brian sighed in his slumber. It looked like contentedness, comfort. The seventh box could wait. Apollo took out his phone. Emma would want to see Brian like this, the holy vulnerability of their sleeping infant. He snapped eleven pictures and sent all of them to Emma's phone, even the blurry ones. He couldn't bear to erase even those. Then he went on Facebook and posted all eleven again. Lillian joined Facebook the day

Brian was born, and she always wanted more images of the kid. This is how he justified what he did even as he knew what kind of parent he'd become, the kind that used to make him gag as recently as two months ago. The ones who blithely assumed their online friends were gluttons for punishment. *Here's my baby lying on his back! And here's my baby also lying on his back! And how about this one: blurry baby on his back!* Good God, the vanity of it all, the epic self-centeredness. He knew all this, and still he uploaded eleven pictures of Brian. Decorum be damned, he was in love. Then he hit "post."

While Brian slept, Apollo turned back to the last box in the basement. He decided he'd go slow with this one. At the very least it would save him from checking too quickly for likes on all Brian's photos.

A SCREAMING COMES INTO the apartment. It has happened before, but there is nothing to compare it to now. This time it's the loudest Emma Valentine has ever heard. It's Apollo, practically howling, as he unlocks the front door and rushes the living room with their son wriggling in the BabyBjörn. At first she thinks maybe Brian has been hurt, but Apollo's holding a book out in front of him like a shield. To make the moment more chaotic, Emma has the television on and the breast pump running. Their apartment sounds as loud as a rocket attack during World War II.

"I got it, I got it, I got it!" Apollo shouted, as he had been shouting since, well, since he'd strapped Brian back into his rear-facing car seat and drove the Honda Odyssey home. He'd been chanting those three words all along the Henry Hudson Parkway, then when he got pulled over by the police and was given a ticket for driving "less than the normal speed of traffic."

Apollo had incredibly important news to share with his wife, the kind of thing that would bear no interruption. Or so he thought. Now he lowered the book in his left hand slightly, and with his free hand he pointed at his wife's chest.

"What are you wearing?"

Emma Valentine looked down at her chest. She wore a beige nursing bra, and a pair of suction cups were attached to the nipples. Those cups fed into a pair of small plastic bottles collecting her breast milk. A pair of clear tubes, each thinner than a straw, ran from the cups toward a breast pump on the floor. The pump remained on, generating a repetitive sucking noise like something a mechanical squid would make as it thrust itself through the sea. Emma stooped and turned off the machine. She stood again.

"How have I never seen you using that thing?"

"You've seen me use the breast pump," she said.

"But not with that bra attachment. It's like hands-free milking."

"I don't want you to call it 'milking.' I'm 'pumping.'"

She mimed a soft slap in his face, then pulled at the BabyBjörn so she could look at Brian. She didn't wait for Apollo to unstrap the kid but did it for him with one hand. With the other she detached the cups from her bra and brought Brian to her chest. He sniffed the air, an animal out to root, and attempted to latch. It took two tries but Emma remained patient and sure until they were connected.

"How was the first day?" Apollo asked.

She might've answered him, but Brian's face captured her attention, and she went quiet watching him. "I missed you," she whispered. "I missed you." She contorted her neck so she could kiss the boy's head even as he suckled.

The television remained the only thing making noise now. It showed a home improvement show.

"I'm just not sure we'll get this whole project done in five weeks," a man on the screen said, speaking directly to the camera.

"We'll blow our budget if we don't," the woman beside him said.

Emma picked up the remote and muted the screen. She settled onto the couch, never once looking away from Brian.

On the television the man and woman who'd been fretting about budgets and timetables wore clear goggles and swung sledgehammers at the walls of an ugly kitchen.

"That part looks like fun," Apollo said.

"I like to watch the demolition," Emma said, smelling Brian's ears as she sat on the couch.

Sitting together, Apollo finally revealed the object he'd been holding when he entered the apartment screaming.

"*To Kill a Mockingbird*," Emma read aloud.

Apollo opened the book, flipping to the copyright page. "A true first edition of *To Kill a Mockingbird*," he said. "With the original cover. The whole thing in Fine condition. That alone would make this worth five thousand dollars. When she dies, that'll at least double the price."

Emma winced.

"Did he bite you?"

"No. What you said was morbid."

"Sorry."

Emma leaned against Apollo, shifting Brian so he tucked closer against her ribs.

"You know Harper Lee never does interviews or anything, but she also never signs books." Apollo opened to the title page. "Well, she signed this one."

Emma lifted her head. "Wow. And she signed it to someone. Pip. Who's Pip?"

"Oh, Pip?" Apollo asked, enjoying the buildup. "That's her best friend from childhood. He turned out to be a writer you might've heard of, too."

Emma, a well-versed librarian, gripped Apollo's leg so tight it hurt. "Truman Capote," she whispered. She looked at the book with a new reverence, grasping the kind of difference this one little item might make in their lives.

"You know they put out that second novel of hers this summer? The one where Atticus Finch is all racist and crabby? Seems like nobody liked it. They didn't want to see Atticus in that light. It was too honest. I think Ms. Lee knew the deal even back when she signed this book decades ago. Check out what she wrote to Truman," Apollo said. "That's the cherry on the cherry on the banana split."

Emma leaned closer so she could read it, and Brian twisted in her grip. Milk dribbled from his lips, and her breast released a faint spray that dappled his cheek.

"'Here's to the Daddy of our dreams.'"

Apollo closed the book. This would outdo the D'Agostino haul by a factor of ten, maybe more. With that signature and dedication, this find could end up being national news. They could buy an apartment with the loot it would bring. Or at least put a nice down payment. Not a huge place—this was still New York City—but it would be theirs.

Apollo had understood exactly how fortunate he'd been when he brought this book out of the basement in Riverdale. When he knocked on the side door and called out for the old woman's son, he'd tried hard to sound calm. The man didn't even let Apollo into the house. Suggested they finish the transaction out there in the driveway. Apollo offered fifty dollars, trying not to choke on the lowball offer. He let the guy talk him up to one hundred so he would feel like he got one over on Apollo. The whole time the man kept checking his phone. He even stopped talking midsentence to return a text. Apollo paid cash and practically levitated back to the minivan.

Apollo left Emma and Brian on the couch. Home improvement shows were in heavy rotation, and Emma enjoyed vegging out to the next one with her son clutched tight. Apollo went into the back room, the former den and Brian's future bedroom. There he found a footstool and pawed at the highest shelf in the closet. He found the box and set it on the floor.

Improbabilia.

How long had it been since he'd opened this lid, pawed through the contents? Years. But tonight he felt ready to add to the time capsule. He opened the lid. The only thing he removed was the children's book. He thought he might start reading it to his son just as his father had once done to him. From his wallet he fished out Emma's red string. It had gone bunchy and tight so he pulled it straight. Four or five inches of frayed red thread, and yet, he had to admit, the fabric seemed to warm to his touch, as if it still burned with sentimental magic. He set it down inside the box.

He went to the bookshelf in the room and found the second book he'd bought at Mrs. Grabowski's, the one he'd used as camouflage for *Fields of Fire*. He scanned the cover. *Once Upon a Die*. That didn't even make sense. He leafed through the worn-down thriller. A few pages were falling out. He couldn't sell this piece of hot garbage if he tried. But every time he looked at it, the book would remind him of the night his son had been born. He laid it in the box.

Stuffed in his front pocket, he even found the ticket he'd been given on the drive home this evening. That too? Why not? When Brian grew old enough, he'd sit with him and tell him the story behind it. He planned to be here to explain everything.

Last Apollo placed the copy of *To Kill a Mockingbird* inside. What better place for a find like that than in a magic box? Apollo closed the lid, climbed back up on the footstool, and hid Improbabilia in the dark.

B RIAN LET THEM sleep in the next morning, didn't wake until
five A.M. A new record. Apollo had been awake since three.
The old record. His body anticipated Brian's wake-up, and he
couldn't convince his nervous system to rest again. Anyway, he
had all the book excitement brewing, too.

Though it should be a wholly unnecessary step, he decided to hire an
appraiser through the American Society of Appraisers so he'd have outside
certification of the book's authenticity. Big outfits like Bauman's had their
reputations for quality and rare books, but a guy like Apollo might need
some outside body to assure potential buyers.

By five, Emma's breasts were so full, they hurt her. They'd become
used to the three o'clock wake-up, too. Apollo brought Brian to her. She
fed him lying on her side, feeding and cuddling him while still largely
asleep. When she finished, she forced herself up to change his diaper.

"I'll take him to the park," Apollo whispered.

Emma nodded and grinned appreciatively and tried to kiss her husband but didn't have the energy to stay upright, so she fell back into bed
and rolled the blankets around her until she looked like an enormous
enchilada. Today would be Emma's second day back to work, and another
two hours of sleep might mean the difference between showing up incredibly tired instead of utterly drained. Apollo kitted up, dressed the baby and

himself warmly, slipped Brian into the Björn, and they were out by five-thirty.

Apollo had become one of those men. The New Dads. So much better than the Old Dads of the past. New Dads wear their children. New Dads change the baby's diaper three times a night. New Dads do the dishes and the laundry. New Dads cook the meals. New Dads read the infant development books and do more research online. New Dads apply coconut oil to the baby's crotch to avoid diaper rash. New Dads bake sweet potatoes, then grind them in the blender once the baby is old enough for solid foods. New Dads carry the diaper bag—really a big old purse—without awareness of shame. New Dads are emotionally available. New Dads do half the housework (really more like 35 percent, but that's still so much better than zero). New Dads fix all the mistakes the Old Dads made. New Dads are the future, or at least they plan to be, but since they're making all this shit up as they go along, New Dads are also scared as hell.

Five-thirty in the morning, and the parents were already out at Bennett Park. There were moms in a huddle at one end of the playground, over by the swings. Apollo sought out the other New Dads. Four of them already there, by the padded play squares. Apollo made five. Most of them in their thirties or early forties. One guy might be fifty, or just in terrible shape.

Apollo greeted the other fathers, and they greeted him. He didn't remember their names. They didn't remember his. They knew the names of each other's children, and that mattered more.

"Brian!" the men called, one by one, as Apollo unhooked the Björn.

Apollo greeted the other kids, Meaghan and Imogen, Isaac and Shoji. The children weren't required to respond. The greetings had been for each parent to hear.

Apollo set Brian on his belly on the black rubber padding while the other kids tore around the play equipment. At two months old, Brian remained, by far, the youngest. Meaghan and Imogen flickered with interest at the sight of the baby. Isaac and Shoji completely ignored him. While on his belly, Brian puckered his lips and basically kissed the ground a few times before Apollo rolled him onto his back. Brian reached out, and Apollo slipped a set of large, plastic toy keys into the baby's hand. Brian gripped and yanked and stared at the keys. He shook them wildly. His face practiced expressions, squinting at the keys, pursing his lips as if he were suspicious of them.

The other dads crowded closer and asked after Brian's development like coaches eyeballing a rival player. Had Brian rolled over on his own yet? Transferred objects from one hand to the other? Raked up Cheerios by himself? The fathers bandied these questions about, half curious and half competitive, but Apollo didn't mind. In fact, he enjoyed it just as much as them. He said nothing of the tremendous book he'd found the day before. Why would he? None of these men talked about their jobs, or their hopes and dreams, not when there were children to discuss. Apollo took out his phone and snapped a dozen pictures of Brian there on the rubber matting. The post from yesterday—the pictures of Brian in the Riverdale basement—had been a hit, at least the first few. Apollo logged onto Facebook and, just to be thorough, uploaded the images he'd just taken. All twelve.

22

THE DAY BEFORE, on Emma's first morning back to work, she woke up alone, the two boys already off on a book hunt in Riverdale. After taking a piss, she ran the shower. Half an hour under the water, and Apollo never walked in to shit, Brian didn't cry to be changed or fed or held. She'd never want a life without those two, but thirty minutes?

Yes, please.

Emma shaved her legs in the shower, though this had to be done slowly because it hurt to bend over. She washed her hair. She applied makeup in the mirror after the steam dissipated and felt surprised by her own face. How could she feel so different and look, largely, the same?

First day back to work. She surprised herself with how eager she felt to get there. Only part-time, but she retained her health insurance. That alone made the job worth having. Apollo never had health insurance. Once she'd been cut from full-time, he made more money, but her health insurance made a big difference. For instance, Kim would still be paid for her work as their midwife. Though, sadly, they were refusing to pay her for the delivery because, technically, she hadn't been the one to do it.

Before getting dressed, Emma went to the freezer and found her store-house of pads doused in witch hazel. She slipped one inside her panties and enjoyed the cold relief. Before leaving, she found her phone, tapped it on to find the message from Apollo. Eleven pictures of Brian deep asleep. She laughed at the sight, and her face flushed with love. She texted back: *Why is my baby sleeping in a basement?*

Then she left for work.

Emma passed Holyrood Episcopal Church on the corner of Fort Washington and 179th. Maybe they'd have Brian baptized there. Only two months, and already Lillian, raised Episcopalian in Uganda, had been hinting about the need. Emma's family had been Catholic, rare birds in Boones Mill. But after her parents died, there hadn't been much church-going for Emma and Kim. People were kind to them, invited them to worship all over the place, but the Valentine girls became a congregation of two.

Emma headed east, passing a worn-down Papa John's branch and the new pharmacy that had replaced a butcher's shop. St. Spyridon Greek Orthodox Church on Wadsworth Avenue, then 24-Hour Dental Lab, N&C Brokerage, and New Age Financial, all in a close row on the next block. At this hour the sidewalks were blurry with working people headed to their jobs and swarms of teenagers buzzing toward school. Emma announced herself as a problem to all those around her because she moved slowly. People muttered, even growled, as they sped around her, but she didn't give a shit about them. Worse was the growing pain she felt the farther she moved from her apartment. A strange sort of swelling filled her chest, her throat.

She missed her son.

The feeling, nearly like grief, forced her to stop at one corner and lean on a mailbox. She cried quietly while the light went from green to yellow to red. She missed Brian, and now her breasts swelled, both filling with a stabbing pain. She'd brought her breast pump in her bag, planning to empty them during lunch, but she couldn't wait that long. She sobbed softly and felt the distance from her child as surely as the ache in a phantom limb. Passersby noticed her, then ignored her. She caught her breath, straightened up, and made her way to work.

The three-story limestone building, built in 1914, had been funded by Andrew Carnegie, and the list of former locals it once served included Marianne Moore and Maria Callas, Ralph Ellison and Lou Gehrig. But

Emma preferred to think of all the kids, anonymous and important, who'd been served at this branch, by women like her, for a hundred years. She hoped to be for each of them what Ms. Rook had been for her, a low-key liberator, a safeguard and a salve. Emma loved being a librarian.

Emma reached work at 8:35 and let herself into the building to find her colleagues—her friends—had strung up a sign that read WELCOME BACK in gold letters. Sheryl bought a cake from Carrot Top, best carrot cake in New York City. Carlotta had already brewed a fresh pot of coffee. Yurina, the youngest librarian, was the one who'd bought and hung the sign.

"I missed you," Emma said as she hugged each woman.

Carlotta, overcome, kissed Emma on the forehead. It felt like a blessing from a high priest. They asked to see pictures of Brian, and Emma happily obliged. They cooed about his beautiful big eyes, the shape of his darling ears. Carlotta and Sheryl, mothers themselves long ago, gave unsolicited advice and made Emma promise to "cherish every moment because it all goes so fast." Oh, the clichés of parenting! She knew that someday she'd be saying them to new parents, too, and so what? Really, all of it was lovely, and Emma couldn't have asked for a better return. She ate cake and sipped tea. The older ladies crowed with praise when they heard Apollo had taken Brian to work with him. Then the librarians prepped for the day.

Emma grabbed the books in the book drop bin, then got the newspapers from outside. Down to the basement—the adult reading room level—where she replaced yesterday's editions with today's. Carlotta had already begun unpacking the new arrival books and checking them against the packing lists. Sheryl would be on the second floor today, the children's section, though the branch was so small that all of them traded floors, and jobs, a few times a day. At the front desk Yurina powered up the two computers, and Emma checked that the four loaner laptops were fully charged. Then it was ten o'clock, and they opened.

Just then her phone rattled in her bag. When she took it out, she found another photo blast from Apollo. Father and son in the driveway of a large home. Apollo is leaning into the minivan he'd rented, either loading or unloading bags. Meanwhile Brian is lying on a blanket in the driveway staring up at the trees. Before she could do more than glance, a group of daycare kids entered the branch, and Emma found herself fully occupied.

Emma made it all the way to noon with the feeling she had something stuck between two of her back teeth, that kind of irritation. It didn't let up until the end of her day, returning home at three P.M., when she realized the problem. That second photo sent to her phone this morning. The shot of Apollo and Brian in the driveway. Her first thought was, *Why the hell are you letting my son lie down in a driveway?* But then a second thought came to her: *Who took the picture?*

She found her phone in her purse and spent the next ten minutes on 179th Street trying to find the picture to confirm her memory, but it had disappeared. It wasn't in her texts, her downloads, her photo gallery. Just gone. As if the person who'd sent it had snatched it away.

"I'M GLAD YOU brought the kid."

Apollo and Brian made their morning meet-up with Patrice downtown on Avenue B. Patrice waited outside a tiny computer shop. At about this same time, Emma was opening the Fort Washington branch on her second day of work.

"Check out this rig," Patrice said, turning his phone screen toward Apollo. It showed the photo of a desktop computer with two monitors, four speakers, and more. "I'm going to build me an even better one than this."

Apollo was wearing Brian turned 'round in the BabyBjörn, so the kid faced Patrice. He lifted the baby slightly higher as if to show off his own rig.

"You know who you look like?" Patrice asked. "Master Blaster."

"Who runs Bartertown?" Apollo said.

Patrice sneered, "Master Blaster runs Bartertown."

Apollo and Patrice hugged each other as best two men could with an eight-week-old dangling between them.

"Really though," Apollo said. "Master Blaster had the little guy on the back. Me and Brian are more like Kuato and his brother."

Patrice held open the door to the computer shop. "You going to compare your baby to motherfucking Kuato?"

Apollo rested his hand gently on his son's head. "The Martians love Kuato," Apollo said. "They think he's fucking George Washington."

Patrice ushered them into the store. "You're a weird dude, my man. Just know that."

Five customers were in the store. With Patrice, Apollo, and Brian inside, the place now reached maximum capacity. The woman behind the counter looked up from her conversation, took in the new bodies, then returned to her sale. Brian wriggled in his carrier and mewled softly. This caused an almost allergic reaction throughout the room. Every adult besides Apollo hunched forward as if protecting their ears with their shoulders. Two of the men scanned backward, straight-up scowling. The woman behind the counter sighed loudly.

Apollo hardly registered the reactions. He made himself busy getting his bag off his back, setting it down, then unstrapping Brian. He went down on a knee, undid Brian's onesie, and pulled back the lip of his diaper. Brian kicked both legs out and mewled louder. Soiled. Apollo pulled out the changing pad and laid it flat on the floor and pulled back one of the diaper straps—that adhesive crackle.

Only then did he look up to find seven horrified expressions focused on him and the now half-naked and soiled baby.

"Problem?" he asked.

A moment passed, and all five customers stampeded out of the store. Even the guy in the middle of a sale joined the exodus.

Now Patrice grinned. "I'm real glad you brought the kid," he said. He turned to the woman behind the counter, instantly first in line for service. "I've got a long list."

Apollo shrugged and finished up with Brian.

Patrice left the store with a half-dozen bags in hand while Apollo carried only a rolled-up dirty diaper.

"You and Dana should think about having a kid," Apollo said as they walked down the block.

He'd regretted it right after the words left his lips. It was a dick thing to say. He knew it. Didn't he hate it when people on the streets offered unsolicited advice about how he should be caring for Brian? Old women scolded him for not covering him up, and others demanded he be uncovered. Old men jabbered about how best to burp or bounce or feed the child. Didn't he loathe even those with the best intentions? But then he'd done something like it to Patrice. Maybe having a child was like being drunk. You couldn't gauge when you went from being charming to being an asshole.

"You're right about that," Patrice said. "If we don't have kids, how will I ever know the joy of carrying a handful of shit?"

They weren't far from the Strand, just a walk crosstown. They headed that way without making a conscious decision. The store's motto was "18 miles of books." Apollo couldn't think of the last time he'd found a book worth serious money there—the stacks were picked over by thousands of readers every day—but they couldn't be downtown and refuse to visit. It would be like snubbing a beloved uncle.

Manhattan air, in early winter, gets as crisp as a fresh apple. As they walked, Apollo turned Brian around so he wouldn't face the cool wind. Turning him inward made Brian look up into his father's face, or perhaps just up at the blue sky between buildings. The boy puckered his lips, and his tiny nostrils flared as Apollo and Patrice walked quietly toward the Strand.

As a matter of routine, they pawed through the wheeled carrels that lined the front of the store. These were the worn-down paperbacks, the Signet Classics of *Frankenstein* and *Jane Eyre*; beat-up textbooks and cookbooks. Patrice and Apollo weren't looking for anything worthwhile—it was just part of the ritual.

"So I had to leave before you came out of the basement in Riverdale," Patrice said.

"You should've come downstairs and said goodbye," Apollo teased.

Patrice cleared his throat and ignored the taunt. "You find anything good?"

Apollo cradled the back of Brian's head as he leaned forward to read the paperback spines. He inhaled his son's scent and considered the question. Did he find anything good? A book he'd be willing to split profits with Patrice over? Brian rubbed his head against the small patch of his father's skin he could reach. Did he find anything good?

"No," Apollo said. "Nothing good. It was a bust."

APOLLO AND BRIAN returned home in the late afternoon but found the apartment as dark as nighttime. The curtains had been pulled shut in the living room. When he went to pull them open, he found a safety pin holding the two panels together. The same in their bedroom. The blinds in the kitchen were pulled down. Apollo found Emma in Brian's bedroom, up on a short ladder, with a drill in one hand. The room's curtains were in a small pile on the floor.

She remained so immersed in her task that she hadn't even heard them come in. Apollo watched her quietly from the doorway. Brian didn't even struggle in his carrier, as if he too were taking in the strange sight. Emma raised the drill to the top of the window frame and pulled the trigger, then sank the spinning drill bit into the wood until it disappeared. When she pulled it back out, dust fell across her and to the floor.

"What are you doing?" Apollo asked.

Emma turned so fast, she nearly fell off the ladder. She brought the drill out like a pistol, pointed straight at him.

"How was work?" he said.

"Blackout curtains," Emma said, then turned back to the window frame and drilled a second hole. The noise finally made Brian stir. He hadn't been sleeping, but at least he'd been calm.

"I thought we weren't going to start sleep training yet," Apollo said.

Emma came down the ladder and set the drill on the floor. She took something out of a box that had been hidden under the piled curtains. She climbed back up the ladder, pulled a screwdriver from her pocket, and installed the blackout curtain's frame.

"We're not starting that yet," she said as she worked.

"Then why are you putting those up?" he asked. "And why are all the windows covered up?"

"I found a good message board for moms," she said. "They told me these were best blackout curtains around."

"How much did they cost?"

Emma didn't answer him. She finished and came back down the ladder.

"Why did you lay Brian down in that driveway?"

Apollo practically clutched his pearls. "I was packing up the car. I tried to do it while I was wearing him, but I had to lean over too far. He cried. So I put him down. But it was just for a few minutes. Anyway, how did you know?"

"You sent me a damn picture," Emma said.

Apollo stepped back. "I did?"

Emma held out one hand. "Let me see your phone."

She scrolled through a few screens, then shut off Apollo's phone with a grunt. Together they went into the kitchen. Apollo asked to see her phone now. She held hers up and said the picture was gone.

"Well, why did you erase it?" he asked as he handed Brian to her.

"Did I say I erased it?" she asked. "Why would I erase it?"

She sat at the kitchen table with Brian, pulled up her top, and snapped open her nursing bra. Brian attached without error.

Apollo opened the fridge and took out ingredients for a quick dinner. "Sometimes you think you've sent me a message, but it's just sitting in drafts," he said. "It's possible you still have it. Let me look."

Emma almost leaped up from the chair but caught herself. If she hadn't been feeding the baby, she might've pounced right on Apollo's back.

"I'm trying to tell you I got a disturbing photo, and all you can do is accuse me of making a mistake."

Apollo brought a frying pan to the stove, poured a capful of olive oil, set the fire, and quickly chopped an onion and garlic clove. He paid inordinate attention to the process in an effort to keep his mouth closed. Behind him Emma cooed at Brian, whispering sweetly, in a way that suggested she too was trying her best to change the mood.

By the time they were eating dinner, they'd calmed enough to talk about the photo again. Emma explained what she'd seen and when it arrived, and now Apollo scrolled through his phone with the thoroughness of a detective. Brian had been set on the kitchen floor in a baby bouncer. As Apollo checked Emma's phone, she used one foot to move Brian in a gentle up-and-down motion. The boy stared at the ceiling light, but his eyelids quivered. With the potential of his sleep so near, Apollo and Emma began to whisper. Then they were nearly drowned out by the steam pipe right behind Apollo's chair. At night the radiators would rattle to life, but hopefully Brian would be deep asleep by then.

"I'm going to fix the door to his room," Apollo said. From his chair he could look directly into the back. There actually wasn't a door at all. It had been that way since they moved in. He'd needed some kind of motivation to go ahead and do the job. "I'll go to the super and see if he has one. I'll give him some money to install it."

New Dads didn't know how to do serious home repair. But they could pay for it.

Emma nodded and laughed quietly. Nice to see her smile.

They ate quietly, and Brian fell asleep. The offer to fix the door to Brian's room didn't have one damn thing to do with the text she'd received, but it provided a service much like when she'd hung the blackout curtains. Fortify the nest.

When they finished dinner, they rose and quietly set their plates in the sink. They moved around the baby as they would a bear trap. They tiptoed out of the kitchen. Apollo turned out the light. Was it wrong to let their infant sleep in a bouncy seat on the kitchen floor? What could be the harm? He'd been born on a stalled A train, after all. They went into their bedroom, leaving the door open so they'd hear Brian if he cried.

"This is the farthest he's slept from us since he was born," Apollo said.

They climbed onto the bed, and Emma turned on her side so she faced the baby. Apollo spooned behind her, brought his arm around her belly. He kissed her neck, and she turned and kissed him back. Within minutes both Emma and Apollo passed out. As the entire Kagwa clan slept, Emma's phone lit up on the kitchen table, a new message sent. It was as if one bright eye opened in the dark apartment, then shut again.

25

LILLIAN ARRIVED EARLY. Meant to come to the apartment at seven but was there by six-thirty instead. She buzzed downstairs, and Apollo rang her in, then scrambled to figure out how he might do three months of cleaning in the three minutes it would take his mother to get upstairs. Messy kitchen, messy living room, messy bedroom, bathroom, too. Emma was in the shower, and Apollo had just been. He almost forgot where Brian might be until he remembered he was carrying the child. If nothing else, his left arm had become stronger. Then the doorbell rang, and Apollo opened the door, and there was Lillian.

While Emma dressed, Lillian showed Apollo her new cellphone. Brian sat in her lap, and he grabbed at it. Lillian let him hold it—try to hold it—but then Emma came out of the bedroom, practically sprinting, and slipped the cellphone from her son.

"He's too young for that," Apollo said.

Emma handed it back to Lillian. "We just don't want him getting used to it already."

Lillian set it down on the arm of the couch. "He's too young for it, and I'm too old for it. So instead we'll spend the whole night playing games and hugging."

Emma leaned close and kissed Lillian on the cheek. "Thank you, Mom."

"Don't thank me. Spending time with my grandson is a gift." Lillian turned the baby so he faced her. How much did Apollo love to see his mother holding his son? More than he could say, so instead he took out his phone and snapped fifteen pictures quickly.

"He's not wobbling his head anymore," Apollo said from the other side of the phone.

"I see that! He's getting stronger. And he still looks like a turtle." Lillian turned Brian again and kissed the baby six or seven times, right on his weak chin. "How's the sleep?"

"There's a rumor he should start going six or seven hours in a row soon," Apollo said. "I'll believe it when I sleep it."

Lillian smiled at Apollo. "You got a haircut."

"Date night," Apollo said.

Emma reappeared from the bedroom. She wore yellow teardrop earrings, and her lips showed a faint reddish blush. Lillian nodded and cooed at her daughter-in-law. Apollo took her hand.

They traveled downtown to see a movie at Film Forum. It might've been Terrence Malick's *Tree of Life*, back in the theater after its initial release. They picked the flick because its showing time fit their date night plan and they wanted to eat downtown. As soon as they sat down, they felt comfortingly, surprisingly, like adults again. Not mother and father but husband and wife. This lasted for all of eighteen minutes. Previews began, and both of them fell asleep. When they woke up, about an hour into the film, Brad Pitt was being a mean father, why exactly they couldn't tell. It seemed unlikely to let up. Apollo and Emma looked at each other, faces illuminated by the screen, and agreed to get the hell out of there.

Next they headed to the sushi place on Thompson Street, site of their first date. They'd been feeling vaguely nostalgic and were already going to be downtown, so why not? But with the weather turning temperate, the line outside went halfway down the block. Instead they went around the corner to Arturo's for the coal-oven pizza. The place had a piano right next to the bar, and a man sat at the bench, not exactly playing but draping himself across the keys in a way that occasionally produced a tune. Emma let herself have one glass of red wine. She'd pump tonight and toss the milk. Apollo let himself have the other three or four that came out of the bottle. He hoped he appeared as handsome to her as she appeared beautiful to him.

When they left the restaurant, they hurried to reach the train, sure they'd been out till midnight. But when Emma checked her watch, she had to laugh, it was only quarter to ten.

"Let's do one more thing," she said.

Apollo waggled his head there on the corner of Houston and MacDougal Street.

"How about a great escape?"

"As long as we're home by twelve," she said. "Your mom's going to be tired."

Apollo pushed his wife out into the street. "Hail us a taxi, my love."

Emma got one on her second try. It stopped, and Apollo scurried into the car behind her. "Wall Street," Apollo said, leaning too close to the divider. "Pier 11."

When they reached the pier, they were just in time for the last Water Taxi tour of the night. A one-hour cruise on the East River, passing the Statue of Liberty and Governors Island, threading under the Brooklyn Bridge. Tourist shit, but so what? Being a new parent in New York demotes you to tourist status. Worse, actually. At least tourists go out at night.

Though spring would soon turn to summer, the weather hadn't become truly warm, so most of the passengers huddled inside the main cabin the whole ride. Apollo and Emma stayed out there longer, leaning at the railing and tucked up against each other.

"I'm glad we went out," Emma said quietly, watching the skyline of Manhattan. "Date night." She sounded as if she were practicing a phrase in a new language.

THERE WAS A man at the front door. Apollo heard him knocking from the living room. Apollo walked to the door, as the knocking grew louder. He reached his hand in the air and turned all three locks of the apartment door. A man stood in the hallway. His face looked blue. He had no nose or mouth, only eyes. He pushed his way inside. The man knelt down in front of Apollo and pulled off his blue skin. Underneath it was his daddy's face. Apollo smiled and hugged him. Apollo's daddy held him, and he heard the sound of crashing water. Apollo's daddy opened his mouth, and a white fog rolled up from his throat. It spilled out past his lips, and Apollo tried to turn away, but his father held him tight and made him watch. The apartment filled with cloud smoke, and the sound of rushing water grew louder, wilder. Apollo's daddy picked him up. Apollo's daddy walked him into the mist.

Daddy said, *You're coming with me.*

Apollo woke up with a start. He expected to be back in his apartment in Queens. A boy again. But his wife and son were there in the bed with him. She breastfed the baby with her eyes half-closed. Apollo turned his back to them and failed to fall back asleep.

27

Six months without much sleep is very different from three months without sleep. The mind gets swampy. The body goes sluggish and soft, gears grind down. Kim knew all this but still felt caught by surprise when she arrived at Emma's place and found her sister looking so torn down. It was one thing in a client but quite another in your sister. Kim had had to ring the doorbell for what seemed like ten minutes before one of the walking dead answered it.

"Emma?" Kim asked in the doorway. She set down her medical bag and her purse. She stopped herself from embracing Emma but couldn't say why.

"What are you doing here?" Emma asked, in a tone so affectless, she sounded like someone muttering in her sleep.

"I've been calling and texting for a week," Kim said. "Six-month checkup for you and Brian."

Emma looked back into the apartment. Early morning, but the interior stayed so dark. "Brian is with Apollo," she said. "And I've got to go somewhere."

That did it. Kim stopped being the concerned midwife and once again became the older child. "You understand these are medical guideposts. I have a job to do."

Emma shrugged and nothing more.

Kim felt herself about to argue and blame, but why? Plenty of mothers ignored her texts, needed to reschedule checkups, forgot them entirely, and slept no matter how long she rang the bell. She closed her eyes and calmed herself. "Can I come with you on your errands?" she asked.

Emma finally looked at Kim now.

Kim wanted to brush her sister's hair, pull it back, and tie it up. She wanted to wash her sister's face and feed her lunch and put her to bed. She raised a hand but caught herself. Emma had always had an asymmetry to her eyes, the right a little larger than the left, but somehow the discrepancy had grown more pronounced. Or at least it seemed that way. Emma's right eye almost looked dilated. Kim left her medical bag inside the doorway, then waited as Emma locked the door.

"So where are we going?" Kim asked as they walked downstairs.

"If you're coming, then you'll see," Emma said.

They walked north along Fort Washington Avenue. At mid-morning the rush-hour crowds had disappeared. The elderly and the parents of the very young were out in force. Emma improved outdoors. At least she swatted her hair out of her eyes and in a few minutes she even spoke. "I stopped checking my phone," she said. "That's why I didn't realize you were coming."

"Stopped when?"

"Maybe a month ago."

Emma didn't wait for the light at 181st Street. She glided right through the intersection and put up one hand. Cars trying to turn stopped short.

Kim played catch-up. The drivers didn't honk at Emma, but they sure got loud with Kim.

As they continued up Fort Washington, they passed Bennett Park. "Apollo brings the baby here every morning now," Emma said. "He doesn't sleep much anymore."

"Brian isn't sleeping?"

"Apollo," Emma said. "He started having nightmares."

"If he takes Brian out, then at least that gives you time to rest in the morning."

Emma trouped along. "I don't sleep while they're out," she said. "I don't sleep at all. We're a mess."

Kim made note of this as she felt her worry rise again. She switched into her professional mode, taking refuge in expertise. "You could try Benadryl, or there's something called Tranquil Sleep," she said. "They're both safe to use while breastfeeding. Are you drinking coffee? The caffeine can stay in your system longer than you'd think."

Emma nodded, but lowered her head as she walked. A curtain seemed drawn between them.

Kim tried to figure out how she'd part it again.

They reached a building on the corner of 190th Street, and Emma turned without any warning and entered the lobby. By the time Kim got inside, she'd already rung the buzzer and the lobby rattled as someone upstairs let her in. If Kim hadn't rushed close, she felt sure Emma would've let the door shut behind her.

As they waited for the elevator, Kim tried pure honesty. "I'm worried about you, Emma. I see you, and I feel worried."

"I'll tell you something," Emma said as she walked into the elevator. "I'm worried, too."

The elevator crept upward slowly. Kim felt her throat tighten as she waited for Emma to say more, to explain, but Emma didn't say a word.

The elevator reached the sixth floor, finally. Emma walked to an apartment door, rang once, and put her hands behind her back to wait.

"This is the place?" Kim asked. "What is this place?"

"Just try to trust me for once in your damn life," Emma said.

Kim felt cold shock at the words, her cheeks tingling as if she'd been hit. Soon the door's peephole went dark as someone inside watched them. A woman's voice from the other side.

"Can I help you?" An accent to the voice.

"I heard about you on the message board," Emma said. "You were told I'd come."

"Who sent you?" the woman asked.

"Cal sent me," Emma said.

The door opened a moment afterward. The woman inside looked much younger than Kim or Emma but wore the same signs of exhaustion that new mothers come to bear. Her skin sallow and her eyes a waxy red.

She handed a large tote bag through the door, something heavy inside, the sound of metal shifting and clinking.

"I hope these are useful," the woman said. She looked at Kim quickly, then shut the door.

Emma made for the elevator with Kim close by her side.

"Let's go up to Fort Tryon Park," Kim offered. The determination with which Emma moved made Kim fear her sister would get outside and sprint back to the apartment and lock Kim out.

"No," Emma said.

Kim watched her sister, the way she clutched the bag with two hands and still had trouble carrying it.

Kim reached for the bag. "What the hell is in there?" She yanked it from Emma. Her sister put up surprisingly little fight.

Kim looked inside the bag. "Chains?" Kim said, so surprised she lost her breath.

Emma didn't acknowledge the question. She slipped the tote back from her sister's fingers, picked it up with a huff, then tired of waiting on the elevator, she made for the stairs.

"Chains," Kim said again, but no one else was there.

28

KIM VALENTINE CHASED her sister out the building and followed her farther north. Not hard to find a thirty-three-year-old woman hauling a tote bag full of chains. And she became even more conspicuous in a playground. Kim watched Emma slip into Jacob Javits Playground and considered calling Apollo, but what would she tell him? Your wife is acting strange? She loved her brother-in-law, but this would seem like a betrayal. Since their parents died, no one had ever come between the two sisters, not truly, and Kim wasn't about to break the tradition now. Also, maybe Emma needed the chains because they'd bought new bikes. There had been a U-lock in the bag, after all. Kim tried to get herself to believe this, but had a hard time feeling convinced.

Two mothers pushed their daughters in swings, and a couple helped their son climb the ladder of a jungle gym. An older girl, maybe eight, sat by herself in a tire hung from chains and spun it around and around to make herself dizzy. The girl's grandmother sat at a nearby bench watching her but hardly seeing her, a distracted air, deeply tired.

And there was Emma walking the perimeter of the play area. She moved quietly, like a soldier on sentry duty, hefting the heavy bag alongside her; at times it slapped the ground making the chains rattle. It sounded like old Jacob Marley had come to haunt the kids.

Kim reached Emma, and they moved together quietly. Emma's body gave off such tense energy that Kim's own back stiffened and her shoulders locked until her posture matched her younger sister's. It would not do to ask about the chains directly, about the woman at the door, about the kind of message board where coils of chain were advertised. Kim couldn't expect to reach Emma with direct questions so instead she told her sister a story.

"April 14, 1988. You don't remember the day as well as I do."

Emma lost a step, nearly tripped. "I remember what you've told me before," she said, then resumed her march.

"Oh yeah? Tell me what that was."

"You and me came back from school, and the fire trucks were already there. The house was on fire, and we watched it burn for a long time. Mom and Dad got caught inside. The firemen tried to take us away, so we wouldn't see, but we fought them, and they took us to the hospital. I never understood why they took us to the hospital, though."

"That's what I told you for years," Kim said. "But that's not what happened. Today I'm going to tell you what happened."

One of the girls in the swing wanted to keep being pushed while the other decided she wanted out. Her mother tried to accommodate, but the girl wouldn't leave without her friend. The one in the swing gripped its chains tightly and wouldn't move. The mother, caught between the two, gave one a push and the other a hug.

"We were in the house," Kim said. "I never went to school that day."

"I don't remember that," Emma said, resting the bag of chains on the ground.

"You were five," Kim said. "You've forgotten it all. Mom told us we could skip and stay home until Daddy got back from the overnight. We watched TV and ate Cap'n Crunch, ate Cap'n Crunch and watched TV. When Daddy got home and saw us there, he went into the kitchen and screamed at Mom about why the hell we were home making noise when he needed to sleep. And you might remember this about Mom; she screamed right back at him, *I want them close!* After an hour Daddy gave up on the fighting and went into their bedroom, straight to bed.

"Mom came out to sit with us. She did your hair while we watched

Card Sharks and *The Price Is Right.* Then she tried to do my hair, but I was sixteen years old. We weren't . . . friendly. She almost got in a fight with me about it. That, and the fact that she let us stay home, should've been enough to tell me the day was all wrong. But I couldn't think that far ahead. We were home, and after lunch I figured I'd go out and find my friend Shelby, break her out for the afternoon. After *The Price Is Right* we watched *The Young and the Restless.* Mom made me sit on the couch with her, and she had you in her lap."

"In her lap," Emma repeated.

They'd stopped walking. Emma and Kim had their backs to the girls in the swings. A peace had been reached. The girl who wanted to keep going had been promised a treat if she came down. Now the two girls held hands and ran from their mothers, toward the jungle gym.

"Mom made us lunch after the soap ended. Soup. It's funny, but I can never remember the kind it was. It tasted terrible, that's the most I know. Mom said I had to have it anyway. We ate it in the living room, right on the couch, and that was the third strange thing about the day. We weren't even allowed to bring a drink into the living room, and now we're slurping up soup during *The Bold and the Beautiful.*"

"We sure watched a lot of television," Emma said.

"Yeah," Kim said. "We finished that soup, as much as we could, and then I'm at a loss for time. Next I know Daddy is standing over you and me on the couch and the house is hot. It's full of smoke. *House on fire.* That's what Daddy says to me, so tired he sounds calm about it. *Better get up.*"

"We were in the house?" Emma said.

The mothers of the girls greeted the parents of the boy, and the adults became a quartet while the kids tested diplomacy. The girls were interested in whether the boy wanted to go down the slide with them. The boy, who hadn't acquired language yet, clapped and smiled at them. At the tire swing, the eight-year-old finally flopped free onto the rubber mat, and now she moved toward the younger kids, wobbly and curious.

"We were in the house," Kim said. "I remember the soup bowl was right in my lap, turned over, like I'd spilled it and fell right to sleep. Next thing was Daddy standing over me. *House on fire. Better get up.* I remember that part perfectly. But I couldn't get up. Too foggy. Daddy had to do it. Small as that man was, skinny as a matchstick, but he picked you and me up at the same time, one over each shoulder.

"Once he had me up, I could see what he meant about the house. Burning all over. I couldn't see anything. I started choking on the smoke. Daddy took us into the kitchen. And Mom was in there."

"Did he try to carry her too?"

"Mom set the goddamn fire."

Kim grabbed Emma's elbow and squeezed it so hard the tote bag fell from her hand.

The parents by the jungle gym looked up at once. Even the grandmother on the bench leaned forward to see. The parents made a quick scan of Kim and Emma, the bag, then another sweep of the playground. Which kids belonged to these two women? Why would these women be here without kids? Kim could see both questions occur to the three mothers and the dad. Two black women in the kids' park. Were they nannies?

"Daddy brought us into the kitchen," Kim continued. "And Mom was there, at the kitchen table. She had a bowl of soup in front of her, half finished. She shouted at Daddy when he moved toward the kitchen door with us. She grabbed you and pulled you off his shoulder, pulled you into her lap. She held you so tight, I thought you were going to choke, but you were so calm. That was wild. I started crying like a crazy woman, and you just sat there calm as could be. I understand now you must've been in shock. Daddy shouted at her. It was like they were just having the same fight as they had that morning, except now the house was on fire, and we were all fit to die."

"How did we get out?" Emma whispered.

"Well, Daddy had me already. He yelled for Mom to let you go. I started begging too, but I doubt I made any sense at all. Mom cried. She said she didn't want to leave us girls as orphans. Better if we died with her. What kind of mother would leave her girls to deal with this cruel world alone? She gripped you close."

"But here I am," Emma said. "Here we are."

"And it was you that saved us. You helped, at least."

"Me? I was five."

"Me and Daddy and Mom are screaming and crying, and the house is burning down, and you turn to Mom and you said two words. *Let go.* Just like that, didn't even shout it, but we all heard it. I can't explain that part. It was like we could hear you, I don't know, inside our heads. And Mom opened her arms, and you climbed down and walked over and took Daddy's hand. He took us outside. Last thing I saw was Mom with her head down and her hands in her lap. She looked so alone."

"But he died," Emma said. "In the fire, too. Didn't he?"

Kim spoke barely louder than a whisper, as if she was the same young woman witnessing the old horror anew.

"He went back in. I thought he was going to get Mom out, but when he reached the door, he looked back at me. I saw his face. I always dreamed he was trying to tell me something, like from his mind to mine. Maybe I just wish it was true. I saw his face, and he looked beat. He grabbed the handle of the kitchen door. It must've been so hot, I can't understand how he could hold it. But he grabbed the handle, and he went back inside with her."

Kim and Emma sat on one of the benches. When Kim looked up, she discovered they were alone in the park. The parents must've taken their children and fled. Did the two of them look so monstrous? Maybe so.

"EMTs took us to the hospital to treat us for smoke inhalation," Kim said. "We were in there for five days. Then we were in foster care until I turned eighteen. We lived with a nice couple, Nathan and Pauleen. You remember them?"

"Pauleen made the best oatmeal cookies," Emma whispered.

"Yes, she did.

"I turned eighteen and applied to be your guardian, and that's how we rolled until you finished high school."

"Why didn't you tell me any of this before?"

Kim leaned back against the bench, crossing her arms. "I wasn't ever going to tell you. I know how that sounds, but I made an executive decision long ago. You didn't seem to remember, so why would I remind you? I'm not saying that's right, but it was the choice I made. I thought I was protecting you."

Emma leaned forward, elbows on her knees. "So why'd you change your mind?"

Kim rested a hand on her sister's back. "Because you're scaring me. You've got a look on your face that's like Mom on that morning, and I—"

"Sometimes I look at Brian, and I don't think he's my son," Emma interrupted.

"What do you mean?" Kim asked, patting Emma's back lightly.

"Maybe it's his eyes," Emma said. "Or the way he puckers his lips? He looks like the Brian I gave birth to, but it's like he's someone else. When I hold him with my eyes closed I can almost feel the difference." Now she sobbed softly. "I know how I sound. I understand."

Kim leaned close to Emma. "Let me tell you what I understand, Emma. You're exhausted. You had to go back to work way too soon. And when you were a baby, your mother and father were taken from you. It doesn't surprise me at all that you might start to worry that you're going to lose the person you love most in the whole world."

Emma sat upright and leaned against her sister's shoulder. She pointed at the bag. "Brian's room is the one with the fire escape. We have a security gate, but it doesn't feel like enough. I wanted to wrap these chains around the gate, too. It would just make me feel better, but I'm afraid Apollo won't let me do it. He'll argue with me."

Kim squeezed Emma and looked down at the bag. "Let's tell him it was doctor's orders. I'll even help you put them on."

Emma grinned. "You're a good sister," she said.

Soon enough they rose. Kim took one handle of the bag, and Emma took the other. Together they carried the chains home.

KIM VALENTINE LOVED and supported her sister. She also suggested she go on an antidepressant. Zoloft. One of the potential side effects was rapid weight gain, but somehow it went the complete opposite for Emma. She stopped eating and lost six pounds in two weeks. Most mornings Apollo made oatmeal for breakfast—quick and easy and filling—but only he and Brian ever finished it. This morning Emma offered to make the meal. A small act of kindness. Apollo appreciated it.

The Harper Lee book had been sitting with the appraiser for weeks by now. Apollo used a guy off in Connecticut because he had a strong reputation among rare book dealers, but the guy's high standards caused him to work slowly. *Carefully*, he'd say whenever Apollo called to check his progress. The kind of thing Apollo might've appreciated if his mind hadn't already been worn thin. Some nights Apollo felt sure the guy had designs to cheat him out of the find and sell it off—fuck over the small-time black businessman. But that had been the whole point of going to this dude, his reputation for scrupulousness and honesty. Fine, fine, but Apollo Kagwa wore the tension like a lead apron.

Brian could sit up now, roll from his back to his stomach. Whether on his back or sitting up on his butt, the kid liked to laugh. Nearly everything made him smile, things that were actually funny and things that were simply new to him. For instance, shoes. Boy, did he find shoes hilarious. Didn't matter if it was Apollo's or Emma's. Set a shoe down in front him, and watch him grin. Apollo would sit there trying to guess what exactly made footwear so pleasing to Brian. Could a six-month-old have a foot fetish? Although, technically, this would be a footwear fetish. To make things even stranger, Brian would smile at the shoe but then call out the only word he knew:

"Bus!"

Like a gunslinger, Apollo found his phone, tapped the camera, and held his finger down so the lens would snap ten quick shots in a row. Apollo uploaded all of them to Facebook right away. This practice became a running joke on Apollo's page. Those who still commented (only two or three) would bet on how many versions of the same shot Apollo would post the next time. Twelve almost always won, though Lillian had guessed twenty-four one time and turned out right. Lillian regularly wrote him to ask for more photos. Patrice regularly wrote him to ask for fewer. ("You used to have outside interests, my man.")

Brian might be six months old, but Apollo felt as if he'd aged five years. He sat in the same chair as always, back to the nearby steam pipe, tucked into the kitchen corner in raggedy underwear and a threadbare T-shirt. He'd showered recently, hadn't he? Maybe weariness had an actual smell. Emma stooped over her bowl of cold oatmeal and didn't look up at her husband or her son. Was the Zoloft making her sluggish, or was that due to some deeper cause? She'd fallen asleep in the clothes she wore yesterday, the jeans so loose on her they dangled around her waist when she stood up again.

Say something about this photo . . . Facebook demanded.

Apollo dutifully typed: OUR HOUSE IS FULL OF SUNSHINE!

"I want to get the baby baptized," Emma said. She didn't even look up when she spoke, so at first he didn't realize she'd said anything to him.

"Brian?" Apollo said. "You mean Brian?"

Now she looked up from the bowl. "Your mother's been asking ever since he was born. I thought we should finally do it."

Apollo sat back in his chair. Brian reached for the shoe in front of him, batted at it. Apollo scooped a spoonful of oatmeal into Brian's mouth. Brian swallowed, then opened his mouth for more.

"He's got such a good appetite these days," Apollo said. "I think a growth spurt is coming."

"The church around the corner," Emma said. "Holyrood. That's where we could do it. I made an appointment with the priest. Father Hagen. He seems nice."

"When?" Apollo asked.

She looked at the clock in the microwave. "Today," she said. "In an hour."

"I'm glad you gave me some notice."

"You don't have to be there. I can take him on my own."

"You're not taking my son anywhere without me," Apollo said. He stood and cleared their bowls just to get up from the table, just to move. He set them on the counter in case Brian had room for a little more, picked up the pot to scrape out the last of the oatmeal, took it to the garbage, and opened the lid with his foot.

"Why is your phone in the garbage?" Apollo let the lid close and looked at his wife.

She turned in her chair. "I got another text last night. A photo of you and the baby in a Zipcar. He was in the backseat, in a car seat. It looked like you were stopped at a red light. The photo was taken through the passenger window. As if someone crept right up next to the baby."

"Brian!" Apollo shouted. "His name is Brian!"

He raised the pot into the air and didn't know what he was about to do with it so he dropped it into the sink to get it out of his hands. A sharp, metal clang filled the kitchen. Brian startled.

Apollo rushed to him and picked him up. "I'm sorry little man," he said, kissing the boy, holding him so tightly he squirmed to be free. "I know that was loud."

Emma spoke over him. "GOT HIM. That's what the text said. Right under the picture. GOT HIM."

Apollo moved to the garbage again, stepped on the lever, and reached inside. "Show me that on this phone. Show me just one of these texts."

Emma crossed her arms and leaned forward, looking as if she would throw up. "They're gone," she said. "You know that. They're always gone."

"They were never there," Apollo said.

Emma looked up to the microwave clock again. "Let's just go, let's get ready."

Apollo looked into Brian's face, then back at her. "We are not going to church with you. You probably told this priest you wanted an exorcism instead of a baptism."

Emma shot up in her chair. She held on to her pants with one hand. "That's not it. I just want to talk with someone else around. You and me are not talking to each other. On the message board, they suggested therapy or church. And we can't afford therapy."

"On the message board? I'm so happy a bunch of stir-crazy mothers offered suggestions about fixing our family. But the answer is simple. You're what's wrong with our family, Emma. You. Are. The. Problem. Go take another pill."

Emma left the kitchen and went to their bedroom. Apollo stayed in the kitchen with Brian, trying to give him another spoonful of oatmeal even though the boy had already had his fill. He just felt too angry to enter the bedroom and speak calmly with his wife.

Emma reappeared. She'd thrown a coat over her shapeless clothing. It shrank her, tidied her slightly. Apollo couldn't ignore how small she'd become. He felt himself wobble slightly. He scooped Brian up and held the baby while Emma opened the front door.

"You don't see," she said. "But you will."

As she left, she slammed the door. Apollo saw she'd left her keys hanging on the wall. Instinctively he thought to give them to her, but he stopped himself. Instead he locked her out. He held Brian up and looked into his son's eyes.

"No matter what happens," Apollo whispered, "you're coming with me."

SOMEONE IN THE apartment was screaming. Had been screaming for a while now. Was it him? No. He didn't think so. How could he scream underwater? Underwater was how he felt. Sunk. Waterlogged. Drowned. He couldn't see. Felt nothing. But he could hear. That goddamn screaming. Wailing. And it wouldn't stop.

In a way this was good. If he couldn't hear that high-pitched voice, he'd be lost in this darkness at the bottom of the sea. But the screams were like a light, flickering at the surface of the waters. He could move toward it. Hone in on the howls. Did he really want to? Better than being left down here. He could hardly breathe.

He kicked his legs. He was a strong swimmer. He tried to use his arms, but for some reason they wouldn't move. They'd gone so numb that he couldn't even be sure they were attached to him anymore. There was only this deep chill in his shoulders. An arctic stab in both sockets. This was because his arms were chained behind him. They'd been that way for hours now.

He didn't open his mouth for fear of swallowing water. He wasn't in a river. Nor in the ocean. But that's how he felt. Submerged.

He was in an apartment in New York City. His apartment. Where he'd lived with his family for two years. Being guided back to clarity, to consciousness, by the lead line of another person's agony. In a way, he had to be grateful for this stranger's pain. If not for that screaming, he'd only flail aimlessly in this darkness. Lost.

When he finally opened his eyes, once he blinked away the seawater of stupefaction, he saw he was in a kitchen. His kitchen. Sitting in one of the white IKEA chairs Emma had ordered for them six months ago. He was backed into a corner. Was saturated not by seawater but by sweat. There was vomit across his chest, on his pants. Still moist. The color of a crème brûlée. He couldn't smell it, not yet, because he was too confused.

He kicked his legs again, like when he'd been swimming, and his feet rattled. He shrugged his pinched shoulders and heard another rattle. He tried to look down, but when he did, his neck got squeezed so tightly, he had to open his mouth to gasp. He was in his own kitchen. Chained to one of his chairs. A bike lock, a U-lock, had been looped around his throat. It held him tight to the steam pipe that ran from the kitchen floor into the ceiling. Because winter had lasted so long, the steam pipe was on. When he pulled forward and gasped, the lock resisted, and he slumped backward. As soon as he did, the back of his exposed neck touched the steam pipe like a pork cutlet pressed against a hot skillet. He hissed, the same sound as frying meat, and lurched forward but got yoked in the throat yet again. He had to sit in one position, exactly straight, to keep himself from being choked or burned.

The whole room felt tropical. Heat in the high nineties filled the place. The steam pipe was partly to blame, yes, but he could also hear now, from the other rooms in the apartment, the rattle and fizzle of the radiators. All were on. The apartment might as well be melting. His face, his exposed arms, his bare feet. His skin puckered all over from this heat.

And then there was the screaming. Which still hadn't stopped.

He could turn his head if he did it carefully. He could look around the kitchen if he mastered the natural panic. He scanned the kitchen, panning like a security camera. There was a claw hammer on the counter. A carving knife on the windowsill. And the wooden floor was littered with hundreds of tiny green pellets. This was rat poison. They'd found a box of the stuff under the kitchen sink when they moved in and just left it there. He'd meant to get rid of it now that Brian was crawling, but there had been so many other things to handle that he'd forgotten. Now the pellets were sprayed across the kitchen floor like buckshot.

Upturned on the floor, right near his feet, lay a bowl. His bowl. Morning breakfast. Oatmeal spread in a burst.

And there on the oven, finally, he found the source of all that screaming.

Not a person, but a kettle.

The flame was turned high, and the water inside was on the boil. The kettle wailed and spewed a plume of smoke from its snout. A little dragon. It had been sitting on the fire for so long, the water inside roiling, that it jiggled and jumped on the stovetop. The kettle couldn't wait to pounce.

But at least it was only a kettle. Not a person in pain after all. The only one in danger was him. For a moment, this even relieved him. Take a breath. But then his body shook all over, the legs and arms clanging in their chains. All this was for him? He was surprised to be alive. The burning kettle wailed a wet threat: his current condition would not last.

His mouth opened then, and he called out hoarsely. It was a woman's name, but you wouldn't know it. A slurred sound, that's all it was.

He tried a second time. "Em?"

If he'd been a boy, he would have called for his mother. Since he was a man, he called to his wife.

"Emma?" he tried again, but who could hear him over the kettle? He barely heard himself. And after that third try, a spasm of pain shot up from his left foot, through his thigh, and into the small of his back. So bad it made him twist, which teased the bike lock, and in retaliation it choked him backward again. This time it was the back of his head, not his neck, that glanced against the steam pipe. It burned right through his short hair, but he controlled himself this time. He didn't lurch too far forward, so he was spared another squeeze around the throat. He panted in the kitchen. Out of breath and out of ideas.

"Brian," he whispered.

Emma and Brian. His family. He forgot his chains, his pains, the instruments of violence scattered across the room. Where was his family? Were they safe? Despite the months of distance between Apollo and Emma, in this moment he drew her back to his heart, as close as his son, instantly. She'd gone out that morning. She'd left her keys. He'd locked her out. At least she wasn't here then. But that left only him and Brian. Now the kettle's screeching seemed like the voice of his newer fear. Not for himself but for the boy.

And just then, he heard the creak of the floorboards in the next room.

From his chair, in the corner, he could look out of the kitchen and see the back room. Its off-white door was shut. Good as his word, he'd paid the super to hang the door in Brian's room, and now he couldn't regret the improvement more. If they hadn't hung the fucking door, he wouldn't have to sit here looking at it, nauseous with fear. If the door hadn't been there, at least he could have seen who was in the back room rather than waiting for the monster to be revealed. Unlike pain, the ache of anticipation gets so deep inside you, it can't be soothed by adrenaline or shock. It's a torture to the nervous system. As he watched the door of the back room, his nerves were being shocked in wave after wave.

The door creaked as it swung back. The kettle insisted that it not be ignored. The left side of his face almost seemed to burn from the high-pitched screeching. A figure stood in the doorway.

Apollo felt a child's terror, overwhelming and immense.

The back room was completely dark even though he could see, through the kitchen window, that it was light out. A sunny day. This was happening under pleasant skies. The blackout curtains were down in Brian's room. They were meant to keep the room as dark as a cave. And they did. But now that darkness hid the person stepping out, and whatever he had done inside it.

"Just . . ." he groaned.

Just what? What sentence was he trying to shape? *Just leave? Just let me free?* No. *Just let my son go.* That's what he was trying to say. And even he was surprised to realize those were the words he meant. Surprised because a person never really knows how he or she will react at those worst moments, do they? Each of us hopes to be brave, to be kind, to be heroic. But how often do we get the chance to find out which it'll be? But in this moment the thing he was willing to beg for was the life of his son. He would've done it for Emma, too.

The bottom of the teakettle must've been scorched black by the high flame by now. The water inside nearly as hot as the surface of the sun. Let this attacker pour it over his scalp, let his skin bubble and burst, let his eyes melt right out of his skull. Okay, okay. He would scream and die. All right. But put Brian out in the hall first. At least then he'd have a chance of being found by a neighbor, of being safe. Maybe Emma had even taken a seat out there, perched in the hallway right now. *Give Brian to her, and do whatever you want with me.*

The floorboards in the little hallway between the back room and kitchen creaked just as loudly as the ones in the back room had done. It was an old apartment. Every board was brittle. Now they creaked and popped, here and there, as the figure stomped into view.

Smaller than expected. Short and thin.

How had this little man overpowered him? Apollo wondered. There was a throb in his stomach. He couldn't even remember how this guy had gotten into the apartment. They had a security gate over the window in Brian's room. They were on the fourth floor. Too high to scale the side of the building and slip in through an unguarded window. Too low to drop down from the roof on the sixth floor. Maybe this was the man who'd been sending pictures to Emma. If he could send her pictures then snatch them away, maybe slipping into a locked apartment proved no trouble at all. Oh God, Apollo was willing to believe Emma now. Much too late. Much too late.

The stranger, this creature, brought along something else. A low noise. Even in his chair Apollo could make the sound out through the noise of the teakettle's trill. Grumbling. Mumbling. The monster was talking to itself. He couldn't understand the words, but the bass of the voice rumbled, something seismic about it. He felt it below his feet.

The monster's hair was long and hung over its face. The locks were ratty and dry. It slumped as it moved forward, which only made it seem more ghoulish. It stepped into the kitchen, brushed past him. So close. Only inches. He shot forward. The chair underneath him rose, and its legs banged against the floor. Despite the chains around his shins, the ones around his wrists, he would've crashed into this little man, this thug, with so much force that it would've gone through the fridge.

But that bike lock wasn't playing.

Apollo lurched forward like that and choked himself so badly that he almost passed out. Not so surprising. He'd been close to unconsciousness moments ago. Maybe he'd been floating up and down, from the depths to the shallows, for much longer than he realized. Maybe he and this monster had gone back and forth like this a few times already. The claw hammer on the counter, the carving knife on the windowsill. Maybe he'd been stabbed and bludgeoned already and just couldn't see his body well enough to tell from this angle. Maybe the kitchen floor right beneath him had already been restained by his lost blood. The stabbing chills throughout his body made it impossible to distinguish between a cut and a crack and a mortal wound.

Meanwhile his home invader didn't even seem to notice him. Walked right past the grown man choking in the corner, went to the oven, and finally turned off the flame. The teakettle yelped for another few seconds. The water bubbled inside the little cauldron.

But why didn't that make the screaming stop?

Without the distraction of the steaming kettle, he could hear, distinctly, from the back room . . .

It wasn't. It wasn't. He tried to calm himself, but it was so much harder now. A child was crying in the back room. Who else's child could it be?

Apollo's body seemed to lose all shape. He felt larger, like the size of a star, the sun. A burning gaseous form. Too enormous for the small kitchen of a two-bedroom apartment. Why weren't walls disintegrating? How soon before the floor and ceiling singed into dust? Why hadn't the world been burned to ashes instantly? His terror flared hotter than the star at the center of our solar system. *I am the god, Apollo! I am the god, Apollo!* He rose in his chair. If the bike lock choked him, he couldn't feel it.

What had been done to his child?

He found his voice, but not his words. He growled at the little man in his kitchen. The one holding the kettle of scalding water. What threat could that pose now? He bellowed at the home invader while in the other room his son squealed. The figure in the kitchen stood in place. It was holding the teakettle not by the handle but in its palm. Its flesh must've been burning, but the hand didn't quiver. The invader finally held his gaze. The creature saw him there, chained in the corner, spitting and raving and rattling his chains.

And now the man in chains could see his attacker clearly.

"Emma?"

In the back room his son's cries turned into hiccuping shrieks. Brian was six months, but these were the cries of a newborn. That special sense-less yelping. They ride one on top of the other, the next one begun before the first has even finished. Not only pain. Also confusion. And such naked weakness. The cries that make a new parent panic right inside the bones.

Emma Valentine had come out of that room.

"*Emma*," he tried. "What did you do?"

Maybe nothing yet. Maybe Brian was only terrified and not hurt badly. The weapons were all here in the kitchen, weren't they? Even in this nightmarish moment, he fussed at a thorn of hope.

She watched him.

The steaming kettle sitting on her palm made her look like a waiter, about to bring a tray to a table. How could she not feel the pain? He could *see* her palm had turned red. Despite his son's screams, he could even hear the flesh of her hand roasting. The air smelled like burned charcoal now. And yet his wife registered none of it. She stood in the room, but she wasn't there.

"It's been hard on you, Emma," he began. "I've been hard on you."

He set back on the chair because his vision had been going blurry, and he realized the bike lock could still hurt him even if he couldn't feel it now.

"You've been so broken down, and everything seems to make life feel worse."

She watched him. She didn't speak. How could this be his wife? She looked drained, as if her whole soul had been siphoned out. She looked almost green. A likeness of his wife carved out of slate. She stayed there, silent. He thought maybe, deep inside, she wanted him to talk her out of whatever she had planned.

"You're not the only one. It happens to mothers all the time. Emma, it's not just you. Kim told us that before you went on the meds. I can hear

Brian in there. He still sounds . . . *strong*. There's nothing that happened here that we can't fix."

She shuffled and looked away from him. For the first time her hand and the kettle wobbled, as if she finally felt the pain. As if she was coming back to herself.

"Just let me loose. We'll check on Brian."

Hearing her son's name seemed to work on her like some post-hypnotic suggestion. Her head tilted backward as if she'd gone into a trance. Her eyes became electrified. There was his wife. He had her. Appeal to that woman. The mother of Brian. Sister of Kim. Friend of Nichelle. Professional librarian. The woman who'd lived in Brazil. The girl from Boones Mill. His wife. All these versions of her were women who would never willingly hurt her only child.

But Apollo was wrong. He didn't have her.

With her free hand, Emma grabbed the claw hammer off the counter. She stepped toward Apollo with one fluid motion and drove the hammer's face into the side of his head. Apollo's cheekbone cracked. He heard the bone chipping, the sound played loudly inside his skull. And suddenly the right side of his mouth wouldn't open as easily. His vision shifted, the bottom half going dark, as if his eyeball had just slipped out of its housing. Through the left side of his mouth he pleaded, even as Emma, his wife of five years, dropped the hammer to the floor.

She walked past him now. He rose from the chair again. What pain could compare to what Brian would go through? Nothing. Not one damned thing. He rose in the chair, and the bike lock barked him back down. His weight crashed with such force that one chair leg broke right through the thin wooden floorboard. So now his chair went back down at a new angle, and his throat caught on the bike lock yet again. But this time good posture wouldn't help. He was like a ship listing to port. He was sinking. The bike lock became a noose. He was going down.

"Don't hurt Brian," he pleaded.

His wife walked out of the kitchen.

In the hallway, just before the back room, she turned to him. She raised the kettle of scalding water.

"Don't hurt my son."

The child wept and choked and coughed and cried.

"Please don't hurt my baby," he begged.

As she stepped back into the darkened room, he sank into a darkness of his own.

Spots appeared in his eyes, and still he strained so hard that blood coughed out of his mouth.

Emma spoke then, clearly and directly.

"It's not a baby," she said.

4

SHIT, DAMN, MOTHERFUCKER

RECOVERY.

The word defined as "the regaining of, or possibility of regaining, something lost or taken away." Economic recovery. Data recovery. Asset recovery. Common enough terms these days. A plausible matter with information once held on a computer or funds siphoned out of some savings account. Even the human body will validate the noun. For instance, a fractured cheekbone, the result of a hammer shattering it, can be repaired with surgery. A zygomatic orbital fracture (a secondary result of the fractured cheekbone) will require a slight realignment of the eye, but once the eye has been lifted, set back in its proper place, the zygomatic rim can be reconstructed. Within weeks recovery will be noted. Bruising to wrists and elbows and even the throat will not last. Burst blood vessels heal. Topical treatments containing vitamin K applied to the skin are suggested. Bodies recover.

But what about the soul?

How long would it take for Apollo to "regain" what had been "lost or taken away?" A son. A wife he'd thought he'd known. A marriage. Three lives.

Apollo had time to consider all this as he waited with 149 other men in cells, the prisoners called them bullpens, as they were prepared for release from Rikers Island. The men were so tightly packed against one another that two had already fainted where they stood. Apollo, and the other men, had been in the bullpen for eleven hours already as the guards ran through whatever mysterious procedures demanded a half day to get done. Anyway, Apollo had been quite lucky compared to some of the other men here. On Rikers Island for only two months. And he'd been held in Taylor, filled mostly with short-timers. It had been as calm a bid as a man could hope for. Apollo was processed—his clothes and belongings handed to him in a brown paper bag—the only prisoner leaving who didn't want to be released.

Four blue and white buses filled up, and the atmosphere bubbled. The men on Apollo's bus ranged in age from seventeen to fifty-eight, but every one of them bounced in his seat like a child off to sleepaway camp. One of the guards on the bus occasionally growled for the prisoners to be quiet. *You're grown-ass men!* he'd say, but he was wrong. They were kids again.

Kids up early. Prisoners released from Rikers Island were driven from the jail out to Queensboro Plaza before dawn. Dropped off with their bag of possessions and an envelope containing just enough money for one ride on the subway and a grande cup of coffee. Apollo sat by the window and watched the bus cross the bridge into Queens. He hadn't been scared for even a moment in prison. He followed orders, he never made a phone call, he always wore his ID and kept his shirt tucked into his pants. An untucked shirt could send certain guards into an unfathomable rage. He made an impression on no one and liked it that way. The story of Emma Valentine and Baby Brian, as their son came to be known, made the news. Baby Brian killed by his mother; Emma Valentine disappeared and on the run. His family had become the cast in a horror movie. Was it any wonder he wanted to become invisible in jail?

The act that landed Apollo in prison, using a shotgun to hold three people hostage, that was its own story, too. There hadn't been much sympathy for him inside Rikers. No veteran prisoner wanted to help keep his spirits up. Everyone had their own problems. They were on Rikers, after all. Apollo considered this a relief. He existed in a state of suspended animation. A body compelled to move here or there, eat on schedule, shower once a day, but there was nothing more to him. Apollo became convinced his heart had failed, or been removed, when he'd been in surgery for his eye. It made sense that he felt no fear in jail because he wasn't actually alive. He died when Brian died.

But as the bus approached Queensboro Plaza, he felt revived, revitalized. This wasn't a good thing. His heart pulsed in his chest, and he felt invaded by some alien presence. The men around him were joking about how quickly they'd cop once they arrived. Before the plaza had been made over, there was a Twin Donut where prostitutes waited for the newly released men to get out. They'd be stuffed up together, four women to a booth, quite aware of how desperate these men would be for their service. An old-timer shared this information in nostalgic tones.

"They still there," another man said. "They wait at the spot on Twenty-seventh Street now. Panini Grill."

"What the fuck is a panini?" the old convict asked.

One of the youngest laughed. "Things change, old head. You can't fight that."

Apollo's heart beat louder with each block they passed. For most men leaving Rikers, the Queensboro Plaza drop counted as a remote location. So many of them were from Brooklyn or the Bronx or Uptown, and the trip home from here would take hours, easy for the plaza to feel like one last fuck you from the Department of Corrections. But Apollo knew Queensboro Plaza well. Had a good idea of exactly how long it would take to get him back to Washington Heights.

He hadn't been home since the morning Brian died. Not once. He'd been discovered by the super who called the paramedics, and they took him to New York Presbyterian Hospital. He stayed there until after the surgery to repair his eye. Upon release, he went to Lillian's to recover. While there he met with detectives from the NYPD and agents from the FBI. Brian had been dead three weeks by the time Apollo returned to Washington Heights.

He didn't go home though. Instead, he showed up at the Fort Washington branch of the New York Public Library wielding a semiautomatic shotgun. He took three hostages, Emma's co-workers. Basically, he'd lost his mind—he wanted them to tell him where Emma had gone. He wouldn't believe they didn't know. The police had to be called in. There was a standoff that lasted six and a half hours. Despite all this, Emma's co-workers refused to press charges and even testified on his behalf when he appeared in court. Apollo spent two months on Rikers Island. And now, as the hint of dawn appeared in the sky, Apollo Kagwa was free again. He hadn't told Lillian he'd be arriving, hadn't spoken to Patrice since he'd gone to jail. No one else left. Remarkable to think his inner circle consisted of only four human beings.

The men departed the bus like soldiers on leave. Maybe Rikers released the men in such a remote location, at a time so early, because they wanted to risk as little collateral damage as possible. Like the thinking behind doing atomic testing in the desert or on some distant isle. Though there were always casualties in those cases, weren't there? The land of the Bikini Atoll remained uninhabitable to this day. Apollo felt as if he glowed with grief, poisoned with mourning instead of radiation. He couldn't go home. He could not be in that place. Not yet. This was why he might've been the only man on the bus who didn't want to board it. Everyone else wanted to get back home, but Apollo Kagwa had no home anymore.

APOLLO ARRIVED AT Bennett Park and didn't even realize how he got there. It had been five-thirty in the morning by the time he reached Washington Heights. His body had become used to hitting the park with Brian at that hour, so even after months away, that's where his body took him. He had an appointment downtown at eleven, but that was a long time from now.

He entered the park and saw the tops of four men's heads, gathered in a semicircle by the play structures, and he came out of his hazy state and nearly turned away. He'd been meaning to go to the apartment, hadn't he? But then they saw him, just a quick glance from two of the New Dads, and Apollo didn't know what to do. How much weirder would it look if he ran away? So instead he moved toward them. They were his friends—of course he should say hello.

He quickened his pace and almost fell as he reached the playground gate. When he entered the gated area, the four men turned and watched him. To a man, all of them scanned him and abruptly looked away with embarrassment. Apollo saw this but tried to unsee it. The mothers were nearby, at the swings with their kids, exactly as they had been three months ago. Except today his hands were empty. He carried nothing. He had no child. He moved toward the other fathers, and probably for the first time ever, he shook each man's hand. Then he turned to the play equipment.

"Hi, Meaghan," he said. "Hi, Imogen. Good morning, Shoji. Good morning, Isaac."

Apollo grinned at the other dads as the four kids ignored him.

"Imogen is walking so well," Apollo said.

Normally her father would've taken the opportunity to explain exactly when she'd made the progress. More than likely he had a video—ten videos—of the early tries. He should've already had his phone out for the other dads to see, but this morning he didn't do any of that. He registered Apollo's words with a nod, but then merely blinked at his daughter, looked dazed.

All four of the men looked stunned, in fact. Disoriented. They stole the quickest of glances at Apollo, then immediately looked away, at the children or the trees or Fort Washington Avenue, anywhere but back at him.

Apollo understood this was happening, but he felt addled, too. He didn't know why he'd come, and now that he was here, he didn't know what to do with his hands, didn't know what to say. Should he keep commenting on the kids and their progress, or should he explain where he'd been? Did they want to know about the bullpens on Rikers Island? About his morning shifts on the grounds crew? Of course not, of course not, but what should he talk about instead? He should leave. They talked about only one thing here on the playground, and he didn't want to talk about that, he couldn't, but before he turned to go, it came up anyway.

"Apollo," Isaac's father said quietly. "We all felt terrible when we saw the news."

The other three fathers nodded but still refused to look at Apollo.

"We wanted to get in touch somehow, but none of us ever traded numbers with you."

Apollo almost melted with relief. He took out his phone, but it had no charge. Rikers Island wasn't in the habit of sending prisoners home with a full battery. It was just an automatic gesture. "I'd like that," he said.

None of the New Dads spoke. Instead, Isaac's father put a hand on Apollo's shoulder and patted it gently. Then he moved so he stood beside Apollo. Shoji's father then moved alongside Isaac's, and in an instant the semicircle of fathers formed a barrier that blocked any view of their children.

"You shouldn't be here," Imogen's father said. The man opened and closed his hands, the fingers turning tense as claws.

"You're mad at me?" Apollo said. His heart beat more rapidly than it had even on his first night at Rikers. "You're mad at me?" he said again.

"No one's angry," Isaac's father whispered.

"I'm angry," Imogen's father said. "I'm angry you came around our kids."

Apollo tried to speak but only stammered. He had the impulse to smash his phone into the side of this man's face. "I would never hurt your children," he whispered.

Shoji's father looked over his shoulder, catching some movement with his practiced parent's eye. "Did you snatch that from Meaghan?" he asked. "Give it back. Give it back."

Meaghan snatched back whatever "that" had been, and Shoji grabbed at it, too. The pair of them screeched as they scrapped. The fathers of both kids turned and rushed in, a tactical support team.

This left only two of the fathers with Apollo. They watched him nervously.

"You're scared of me," Apollo said.

"You went into that library with a gun!" Imogen's father shouted. It sounded that much louder because of the earliness of the morning.

"I was trying to—" Apollo began, but stopped himself.

"We're really sorry about Brian," Isaac's father said. "I can't tell you how sorry."

Hearing his son's name uttered out loud made Apollo's stomach quake. He hadn't spoken the name since being handcuffed by the police sixty days ago, but in his mind, his heart, he'd been repeating it a thousand times an hour. It sounded strange in the other man's mouth. Apollo had the urge to tear out his tongue.

"We're just trying to be good dads here," Isaac's father said.

"I was, too," Apollo said.

He turned to leave Bennett Park. Six in the morning, and no choice left but to go back home.

33

"Y OU GOT TO wake up. You can't sleep here."

Had Apollo fallen asleep? Surprising. He'd only meant to sit here in the basement of his building, in the laundry room, for a little while. He'd figured he could wait the time out until his appointment down here. He'd entered the elevator and planned to go up, but instead of pressing the button for the fourth floor, he went down.

And promptly dozed off, it seemed.

"Get up," the man standing over him said. "You heard me? How'd you get in this building?"

Not only had Apollo gone to sleep, he'd bedded down on the laundry room couch, nuzzled into it like a tick. He'd curled up on the cushions, his back to the man now jabbing him with a broom handle. He rolled over and sat up.

"It's you."

The super of the building, the man who'd hung the door in Apollo's apartment, stepped back and gawped at him. He held a broom in one hand and had a length of green garden hose coiled on his left shoulder. He had the air of a sherpa, experienced and impossible to ruffle. His name was Fabian. A man in his late fifties, born in Puerto Rico, keeping this building running since long before Apollo and Emma moved in. He lowered into a crouch and tilted his head as he watched Apollo.

"They did a real good job on your eye," Fabian said.

Apollo reached up to pat the cheekbone that had been reconstructed. It would've been better to leave the damage visible, at least then his outside would match his inside.

"When I found you, it was all . . . not good," he said, tapping his own cheek.

"I never got to thank you for that," Apollo said, hand still on his face.

"Your mother thanked me," he said. Then he heard how it sounded, like a joke boys play with each other. "I mean, I seen her around here while you was locked up. She stopped me and gave me a hug. Bought me a tall boy, too."

"My mother's been here?" Apollo asked. "My mother bought you beer?"

Fabian rose and with his free hand helped Apollo up.

"You got out fast," Fabian said. "Rikers likes to hold on to people."

"My mother got me a lawyer," Apollo said.

"Good mothers are a gift," Fabian said, tapping the bristles of the broom against the basement floor. Then he looked up, face flushed. "Sorry. I didn't mean . . . sorry."

"What time is it?" Apollo asked, just to talk about something else.

"Ten o'clock," Fabian said. "You got your keys? You need me to let you in? I still got my set."

Apollo pointed to the brown paper bag on the floor by the couch. "My things are in there. I can get in."

But he wouldn't have to. He had an appointment at eleven, downtown, with his parole officer. Another strange thing to be thankful for, but still it was how he felt. Was he supposed to wear a suit to his first meeting with his PO? Would it matter if he wore the clothes he'd slept in, clothes he'd been arrested in?

Fabian nodded and turned away. He had an office down the hallway, past the washers and dryers. He made it five feet before Apollo called out to him.

"How did you know?" Apollo asked.

"Know what?"

"How did you know to come into our apartment?"

Fabian turned back but didn't move closer. He adjusted his shoulder so the hose wouldn't slip down his arm. "The man in number forty-seven called me," he said. "There was a smell." He shook his head. "It was a very bad smell. I never smelled nothing like it."

Apollo placed a hand against the couch for balance. "A smell," he repeated.

"I thought I would need my keys, but the door wasn't locked. It was real hot inside. I shouted a few times before I came all the way in, but I had a bad feeling, too."

He lowered his head and scanned the floor rather than meeting Apollo's eye.

"I found you first. I thought you was dead. For real. Your eye was hanging out." Fabian made a fist and dangled it by his cheek. "Then I went in the back, and I found the baby."

The building's boiler, far off in another corner of the basement, rumbled. Apollo and Fabian remained quiet. Apollo wanted to ask Fabian what he'd seen in that room. No matter how horrible it might've been, this man had been in there with Brian. Apollo didn't want to know a single detail, and he wanted to know all of them. Both feelings at once. But how could he ask? What would he ask? What might he say that wouldn't seem awful and ugly and perverse? He felt the gaze of the New Dads even from here, and his body flamed with shame.

"I said a prayer right there," Fabian said. "When I saw him. I say a prayer for him every week at church."

Apollo nodded. "Thank you for that."

"I say them for you, too." Fabian pointed toward his office. "I gotta go," he said, though the words were choked.

34

APOLLO REACHED EAST 79th Street slightly early. The building sat on the kind of block made for movies about Manhattan. On a broad street with a grand view running west all the way to the Hudson River. Apartment buildings only twenty or thirty stories high, small and homey by the standards of the island. It took a lot of money to make Manhattan feel quaint. And amid all this sat the Yorkville branch of the New York Public Library, an elegant townhouse and a New York City landmark.

Apollo stood in the middle of the sidewalk staring up at the building like the worst sort of tourist. Old men gave him their elbows on purpose. Mothers used their strollers as steamrollers. He couldn't believe he had to be here at all, but the Manhattan district court mandated his visit as a "vital aspect of his parole."

The event space at the Yorkville branch, in the basement, was billed as big enough to seat seventy-two. But capacity wouldn't be tested this evening. Twelve men and women sat in chairs that had been placed in a circle. Only one of them noticed Apollo approaching, a tall woman who waved him closer. She had the casual authority of a school crossing guard, used to helping the vulnerable and confused reach safety.

"This way," she called. "We've already begun."

He reached the circle. The others looked at him as he sat.

"I want to welcome you to the Survivors," said the tall woman as she took her seat. "That's what we call ourselves."

Apollo looked from one person to the next. Court-ordered group therapy. That had been a condition of his parole. *Thank our progressive new mayor*, the judge had told Apollo, unable to disguise his disdain.

Apollo stayed quiet as the other Survivors spoke. It felt a lot like an AA meeting, or what he'd seen of AA meetings on television and in the movies, and more than half of these folks seemed to be struggling with some kind of drug. But instead of stories about the excessive and ugly things they'd done under the influence of this or that, these people were caught in a loop of tragedy. *Something terrible happened, but for some reason I'm still here.* That might as well have been the subtitle of every conversation. Soon it seemed strange to call this group the Survivors. They were here, but none of them had survived.

"I'm still wearing my wedding ring," Apollo said, sounding surprised. He looked up at the dozen others in the seats. Now they stared at his hand, too, and he held the ring finger up. "I'm sorry," he said. "I didn't mean to say that out loud."

Alice, the tall woman, leaned forward. "That's fine. Don't worry."

"My wife was a librarian," Apollo said.

Why was he talking? What was he saying?

An older guy with a graying beard nodded. "I saw that in the news."

Apollo sat upright. "You knew about that? Why didn't you say anything when I sat down?"

The old guy crossed his arms. "I had a few problems of my own to talk about, you know."

Apollo actually laughed, a quick, sharp sound.

"But now the floor is yours," he added softly, more kindly.

"This is my first time here," Apollo said. "I got released from Rikers Island before the sun came up this morning. I met my parole officer this afternoon. I had to wait two hours before he saw me. And now I'm here."

They watched him quietly. He found each one as inscrutable as a statue of the Buddha. Alice said, "Your parole officer made you come here on the same day you were released?"

His parole officer actually encouraged him to go home, take a shower, and get some rest. But Apollo asked for help finding a meeting right away. He'd do anything to avoid stepping back into that apartment. But how could he explain all that?

"Yes," Apollo said. "He's an asshole."

A few of the Survivors tutted and clucked. The guy with the graying beard gave Apollo a faint nod that he interpreted as *fuck the police*.

Then a younger woman spoke, haltingly. "Why did she do it? Did she explain?"

Apollo turned to her, startled. Had they all known who he was when he appeared?

It's not a baby.

"No," Apollo said. "She didn't explain."

"But why did you do it?" Alice asked this question, the pleasant air of the crossing guard having dissipated.

"You're talking about the library?" Apollo asked.

"Yes, I am," she said, leaning backward slightly, crossing her arms.

"I lost my mind," Apollo said. "I didn't understand what Emma had done until I came out of surgery at the hospital. I was lying in my bed and watching it on the news. That's how I found out.

"The apartment was still considered a crime scene, so I wasn't allowed in. I stayed at my mother's place after I was released. When I felt strong enough, I went directly to the Fort Washington branch of the New York Public Library, where my wife worked. It was a Thursday. They didn't open until noon. I got there by eleven, when I knew the other librarians would be inside preparing for the day. As you probably also heard in the news, I had a shotgun with me."

He had been forced to recite the events of that morning with his lawyer, a few times, and then in front of the judge and the prosecutor as well. He'd never stood before a jury, though he felt as if he was doing so now.

"I had her work keys, and I let myself in. I found two of the three librarians on the first floor. We had to wait for the third to come from using the bathroom."

"Were they scared?" Alice asked.

"Of course they were," Apollo said.

Now she looked down into her lap.

"I don't think I was making much sense," Apollo said. "It took awhile for me to speak clearly. To tell them why I was there. That early part of the day was when I shot the ceiling by mistake. Somebody outside heard it. Which was how the police got called. Then me and the three librarians went down into the basement. I took them down there. We spent the rest of the time locked in the reading room."

One woman got out of her seat and left the circle. She practically sprinted from the basement.

"When I came out of the hospital, the big story was already about the hunt for Emma Valentine. The FBI and NYPD were on the case. They'd both come to me and asked for information that might help catch her. Maybe they'd already been to the library and spoken with all three of those women. But the women obviously hadn't told them what they knew, what I thought they knew, about Emma. Who else would she have spoken to? Those librarians were her family. Her own parents were dead, and her husband and child meant nothing to her. I couldn't get hold of her sister. So I showed up to ask my own questions. I was sure Emma had told them something that would help me track her down."

"And had she?" the guy with the gray beard asked, leaning forward in his chair.

"No," Apollo said. "They swore to it again and again, but it still took me six and a half hours to believe them. At the end I gave the shotgun to Carlotta. Ms. Price. I turned myself over to the police. All three women testified on my behalf. They refused to file any charges against me. That's one reason I got out as quickly as I did. It was incredibly forgiving of them."

The younger woman, who'd first spoken, said, "Do you think your wife is still alive?"

"I hope not." He looked at her, then realized how he must sound. "I mean, the FBI and NYPD haven't found her yet," Apollo said. "So I don't know."

"But what were you planning to do anyway?" the young woman continued. "If the librarians had information. If you had found your wife."

"She killed my son," Apollo said. "If I'd found her, I would've killed her. Then myself."

Apollo couldn't think of what else there was to say, so he said nothing. The Survivors sat in silence.

"Okay," Alice finally said. "Thank you all for coming. Time's up."

H E STAYED AT the Yorkville branch until they closed their
doors at seven o'clock. He spent those remaining hours on
the main floor, in a chair near the checkout desk with a magazine in his lap. It hadn't been comfortable to tell the Survivors about what he'd done, but right after the group session he felt even
worse. At least down in the basement he'd been among others like himself. The guy with the gray beard had been on his phone—texting—when
he'd rolled into an intersection, and his car got smashed by a moving
truck. His fiancée was dead before their car stopped spinning. But after all
of you have shared, shouted, or cried, then what? Then it's just Wednesday evening, and you're back on your own. Six months of that? No fucking
thanks. But if he didn't go, he'd be on a bus back to Rikers, and there'd be
no quick release date to secure. So he sat in that chair for hours trying to
talk himself into tolerance, tenacity, and recovery. Finally he had to face
it. He had to go to the apartment.

Still, as he reached his block, as he approached the building, as he
entered the elevator, he kept expecting someone to leap out and stop him.
No one did. He reached the front door of his apartment and hesitated. He
slid the keys into their locks.

Apollo opened the front door.

Had he expected noise when he walked inside? Not really. But then why did he feel so surprised by the silence? Maybe because it had been so loud the last time he'd been in here. Three months ago. Only three months.

He entered the apartment and shut the door behind him. He stood in the darkness and slowed his breath. Even with the lights out, he could see the wooden floors were clean. Supple and almost wet looking.

He walked into the living room and stood in the silence. More space, more quiet, no life in here at all. But there was the couch, where it had always been, under the living room windows. The lamp in the corner, the low bookcase, the radiator. Even the radiator didn't make any noise. It must've been shut off. The bedroom he'd once shared with Emma lay to the left, the kitchen to the right.

He went to the bedroom door and opened it, half expecting to find Emma there, a fugitive hiding in plain sight. But of course he found only their bed, the sheets made, the floor just as clearly swept and mopped. The curtains had been left open, and he looked down to the street below. He watched a man trying to park his car in a space that was obviously too small. When Apollo left the window, the man still hadn't figured that out.

He entered the kitchen. When he looked at the floor, he saw the pellets of rat poison. When he looked at the counter, he saw the claw hammer. When he looked at the oven, he saw the kettle, the fire underneath it making the bottom glow, steam spraying from the spout. He saw it there, but he couldn't hear it. It rattled on the stovetop, but there was no clatter. He brought his hand to the cloud of steam but felt no heat.

He backed away from the phantom teapot and shuffled his feet to avoid the pellets he thought were still on the floor. But when he moved to the kitchen table, when he looked down at the chair where he'd been chained, he saw no ghostly repetition of the scene. No chains. No blood. He pulled the chair from the corner. The hole in the floor had been repaired. He got down on his knees to check.

Lillian had done all this. Who else would have bothered?

It was in this position—still on his knees—that he turned to face the back room. The door had been shut. A neon green sticker was affixed to the door, about a foot above the handle, half on the door and half on the doorframe. He crawled closer; his legs trembled too much for him to stand.

"These premises have been sealed by the NYC Police Dept. pursuant to Section 435, Administrative Code. All persons are forbidden to enter unless authorized by the police department or public administrator."

Even now, in his mind, this remained Brian's room. He put his hands to the walls to press himself up. He didn't want Brian to see his father crawling. Eventually this room would have to be opened, too, but not tonight. He thought that being here—in this place, at this door—would cause an instant avalanche of emotions, but instead he felt quite the opposite. He felt nothing. He couldn't even tell if his heart was beating in his chest.

Apollo lumbered into the bathroom. He hadn't taken a shower alone in sixty days. He ran the water and removed his clothes. He spent half an hour under the spray before he even started cleaning himself. When he finished, he made it to the bedroom. He hadn't slept on a good mattress in ninety days—the one in the hospital had given him an ache in his lower back. But he couldn't make himself lie down in the bed he'd shared with Emma. He stripped off the comforter and top sheet and went back into the living room. He plugged in his phone, then lay down on the couch. He looked up at the night sky through the windows here. No stars.

"What now?" he asked.

He fell asleep long before his phone rattled and lit up. In the dark it shone brighter than a star. Then, after a moment, all went black again.

36

ATRICE STOOD IN the doorway of his basement apartment in southeastern Queens. The owner of a two-story home had decided to make a little extra income, something to help cover the mortgage. She'd had the basement converted into an apartment and rented it on the sly for $1,300 a month. Two bedrooms, a kitchen and bathroom, a private entrance at the back of the house. Patrice lived here with Dana, the woman he'd met after he returned from Iraq and his marriage fell apart.

Patrice leaned out the doorway and sniffed at Apollo. "It's the Bird Man of Alcatraz. You're late."

"I had to take a train and a bus to get here," Apollo said. "I forgot that Queens was this far from New York."

Patrice waved one big paw. "We started eating without you."

"I brought wine," Apollo said, lifting a brown bag.

"You brought wine from a place that doesn't even give out plastic bags?"

Apollo had to smile. It felt good to see this guy again.

Behind Patrice a woman, Dana, called out. "Why don't you let him in rather than standing out there putting all our business on the street?"

Patrice looked over his shoulder. "Baby, our entrance is on the side of the house. Most we're doing is letting the neighbors get a look."

"Come inside!"

The ceiling down in the basement felt low to Apollo, and Patrice had to be six inches taller than him. The wood-paneled walls sucked up the ceiling lights and made the whole room darker. The kitchen and the stove both had to be ten years old. Older. The best item in the kitchen was the dining table, beamed in from a Crate & Barrel. Aspirational furniture that took up too much room in the cramped kitchen.

Dana had set the table elegantly, a red gingham check tablecloth and rattan placemats; blue gingham check napkins and white porcelain plates with silver trim. As Apollo entered the kitchen, Dana was already setting out the exact same arrangement for him. Once Patrice shut the door, a passerby would never know—or probably even imagine—that inside a basement apartment in southeastern Queens there lay such a beautifully appointed dinner table. It was like catching a glimpse of the glittering soul inside a rumpled passenger on a subway train. Apollo lost his breath for a beat.

Dana took down two wineglasses after Apollo revealed his bottle. They owned only two wineglasses. She gave Patrice a coffee mug for his wine.

"I'm sorry I'm late," Apollo said.

Dana poured the wine. "Nobody wants to come this far out into Queens. We're just glad you made it."

Dana hugged Apollo. She had big arms, big legs, and a broad back—a perfect body for hugs. Where Patrice's hold had been wary, Dana's offered only warmth. The baby's funeral had happened while Apollo sat on Rikers Island. Both Patrice and Dana had attended the ceremony. The way she held him now, the long slow warmth of it, conveyed her condolences better than words ever would.

"You sit," Patrice said to both of them. "I'll serve."

Dana patted Patrice's belly before she took her seat. "He acts like he's being gallant," she told Apollo. "But he just wants to be sure you know who made the meal."

Dana worked for the Port Authority as a senior toll collector at the Bayonne Bridge in Staten Island. It was an hour's drive from their place in Queens. On the days when Patrice went on book buys in New Jersey, he'd drive her out and pick her up again in the afternoon. They had a good thing together, and both seemed to know it.

Patrice slipped a ladle from a drawer. "Crockpot chicken," he began. "Chicken legs and breasts, half a jar of pitted olives, three teaspoons of olive brine, one lemon cut into slices, one teaspoon of Herbes de Provence, a cup of chicken broth, half a teaspoon of salt, an eighth of a teaspoon of pepper." Patrice dipped the ladle into the white crockpot on the kitchen counter, and the rich smell of brine and lemons made Apollo lean forward as if the food was already in front of him.

"And one bay leaf," Patrice added as he filled the first bowl. With the low ceiling and the close walls, he looked like a brown bear doing a cooking show inside a cage.

"I can't believe you're living in a basement," Apollo said.

Dana sucked her teeth. "What's wrong with living in a basement? I found this place for us."

Apollo looked at her and smiled. "But Patrice is terrified of—" And caught himself. He looked back at Patrice, who'd stopped moving mid-serve. Apollo could see Patrice watching him even as he pretended to be playing host. Dana clearly hadn't been told that basements made Patrice quiver, but—just as much of a surprise—Patrice really thought he'd kept this secret from Apollo, too. Once he would've passed this off as the normal way of life. People tell little lies to get by. That goes for marriage and friendships, too. But now Apollo couldn't brush off these untruths as benign. If our relationships are made of many small lies, they become something larger, a prison of falsehoods.

"Patrice is terrified of commitment," Apollo offered. An old chestnut, a truism about men, an idea so blandly conventional that to say it was like casting a kind of sleep spell. They were no longer sinking into the depths of the issue but merely skating across a slick, thick surface. Chatter. Sitcom humor.

Dana visibly relaxed in her chair. "Maybe before, but then he met me."

And just like that, the moment passed. Patrice brought the bowl to Dana and kissed her forehead as he set it down. He looked at Apollo quickly and then went back to the counter for Apollo's bowl.

After they finished the food, Dana and Patrice cleared the bowls, the utensils. Apollo pushed back from the table. "I want to show you something," he said.

He opened his bag, set down his phone. Lillian had been trying him since yesterday, must've been fifteen phone messages from her. She wanted to take him out to Brian's gravesite. He should see his son's final resting place. But when Apollo woke up on the couch that morning, after his first night home, he'd also found a text message waiting. Right after he read it, he called Patrice and Dana and asked if he could come over that night.

Out of his bag, he brought a smaller gift bag, one bought at the Duane Reade on 181st. Dana and Patrice had cleared the table. Dana wiped down the surface with a wet cloth before Apollo laid out the present.

"Take a look," Apollo said.

Patrice opened it while Dana went on her toes to see.

"*To Kill a Mockingbird*," Patrice read. He opened it, scanning through it like a pro. "Book jacket is Fine. Boards, too. Endpapers clean. And . . . it's a first. Shit! You found an estate sale on Rikers Island?"

Dana reached for the book, but Patrice closed the cover and held it tight.

"Look at the title page," Apollo said.

Both read quietly. Dana nudged Patrice. "Who's Pip?"

Patrice shook his head, but couldn't bring himself to say he didn't know. He tapped the bottom of the page, by the author's signature. "I do know who this is, though."

"I drove up to Connecticut today to pick this up," Apollo said. "The guy sent me a text to let me know it was ready. He'd been writing me for weeks. I guess he doesn't watch the news. The appraisal certificate is folded in there."

"This is some shit you retire on," Patrice said. "Or at least go on a damn good vacation. Where'd you find it?"

Apollo swayed a bit but set his hands on the kitchen table.

"It doesn't matter," he said. "I found it, and I want you to have it." He didn't let them interrupt. "I planned to sell that thing and have enough money to buy a place for me, Emma, and Brian. But that's done now. All done. I don't care about the money. I wouldn't use it. I'm—"

He stopped speaking here, his throat clutching. He didn't want to finish the sentence in front of them. Dana put up one hand and said, "We'll take it."

Apollo and Patrice both gawped at her with surprise. Her eyes were wide, and she seemed just as taken aback. She slipped the book from Patrice's hands.

"It's generous of you," she said softly. "And we appreciate it."

Then she turned and left the kitchen. Escaped to the back room, their bedroom, and shut the door. Patrice watched after Dana as if trying to catch up on an equation she'd already solved, but sighed as he failed.

"I guess that's good night?" Apollo said.

When they were outside, climbing the back stairs, Patrice said, "You know why I always liked you? Why we became friends?"

"I'm a better bookseller," Apollo said. "You wanted to learn from the best."

Patrice raised his eyebrows. "Even you can't believe that. First time I met you, I think it was at the West End Bar, back before it closed. Rich Chalfin had a bunch of buyers out for drinks. I told you I was just back from Iraq, just like I'd told everyone at the table at one time or another, and you know what you said?"

Apollo gently tapped the aluminum siding of the house. "'There's an estate sale in Pennsylvania. You in?'"

Patrice shook his head at the memory. "You never said any of that thank-you-for-your-service shit. You never asked me if I was against the war. Never asked me who I killed. You basically acted like you didn't give a fuck. And I liked that. Right then I knew you were a dude I could be normal with. Not some vet. Just Patrice."

He slapped Apollo's leg once so Apollo would look at him. "So I'm going to break protocol and talk straight as I ever have with you."

"Okay."

"If you go off and kill yourself tonight, I'm going to soak that valuable fucking book you gave me in the toilet. Then I'm going to piss on it. And worse. That will be my revenge against you. I will ruin that book."

"What are you even talking about?" Apollo said, not very loudly.

Patrice put a big mitt on Apollo's shoulder, then lowered his head so they faced each other square. "I've seen that look before."

"What look?"

Patrice watched Apollo. "This one. The one staring back at me right now. I have seen that look, and I know." He squeezed Apollo's shoulder tightly. "I know."

Apollo yelped and pulled free. He hadn't been planning anything like that. *Had he?* Now he took two steps backward and turned. *Had he?*

He walked around the side of the house and toward the front gate. He heard Patrice behind him.

"You're a book man," Patrice said at the gate. "So tonight I'm going to put that book online, and if you're not around, you will never find out exactly how much someone would've paid for it. You. Will. Never. Know."

Patrice stood at the fence, him on one side and Apollo on the other, clearly calculating whether he should tackle his best friend and put him on suicide watch.

"You're a motherfucker," Apollo said. "But I do want to know what it's worth."

Patrice pointed at him. "My man. I'll be calling you as soon as I hear. You be alive to pick up."

37

POLLO RETURNED TO the apartment after midnight, and when he opened the front door, he heard someone in the kitchen, the hiss and *tick tick tick* of an oven burner being lit, and he had to grip the front door's handle so he wouldn't fall to the floor. The kitchen light had been turned on, the rest of the apartment stayed dark. He listened to a pot being pulled from a cabinet, water rushing from the tap. He almost turned and ran, but instead he closed the door behind him as quietly as he could. He slipped his shoes off and moved his socked feet across the floor. She was back. Maybe she'd been coming back to the apartment for all the months he'd been on Rikers. Maybe it had really been she who'd cleaned the place up just to clear away evidence. Maybe she felt so guilty, she just couldn't help herself.

Apollo slipped into the living room. He could hear the quality of the oven's flame change as the pot—or kettle?—was placed on the burner. He smelled, faintly, ginger in the air. In the darkness of the living room, he could almost see his breath as a faint cloud of blue electricity. Every sense became more finely tuned as he approached the threshold of the kitchen. Emma would be in there reenacting her crime, and this time he would find her, and they wouldn't speak with each other. They would tear each other apart, down to the atomic level, a little nuclear fission in the kitchen, nothing left of them but the silhouettes of who they used to be burned into the wall.

"Apollo? Is that you?"

"Mom?" he said. He walked into the kitchen swatting the air, his confusion swarming him like flies.

Lillian Kagwa stood at the open fridge, holding a quart of skim milk. "I'm making tea," she said.

Apollo looked at the oven to find a small pot of milk bubbling up. The tea leaves were already inside, and small strips of ginger, too. They boiled, and the level rose toward the lip, and Apollo did just as he'd learned when he was a boy, turned off the flame before the potion spilled over. With the heat off, the tea settled again, steaming, spinning, a rich brown color.

"Well done," Lillian said, standing beside him. She had a teacup on the counter, and a sieve. She strained the tea, set the pot back on the oven, picked up her cup, and took one long sip.

"Why are you here?" Apollo asked. "It's the middle of the night." He pulled out a chair and sat because he felt unbalanced by his confusion.

"It's twelve-twenty," she said, standing over him. She'd always liked to have her tea on her feet, the habit of a woman who had to rush to work in the morning. "How was dinner with Dana and Patrice?" she asked.

Apollo looked up to the ceiling light. "Dana called you," Apollo said. "She went into the bedroom and called you."

"I was surprised that you'd been out to see them before you saw me."

Apollo shook his head and laughed. "Please tell me you're not guilting me right now, Mom."

She sipped her tea. "What guilt? Do you feel guilty? Why didn't you call me to pick you up, though?"

"Too early," Apollo said. "I didn't want to wake you."

Lillian took down a second mug and poured Apollo a cup of tea like hers. "Four in the morning," she said. "That's criminal. Let me make you something to eat."

"I just had dinner with Patrice and Dana," Apollo said.

In the time it took him to complete the sentence, Lillian had already opened the fridge and removed a half-carton of eggs, an onion, a block of cheddar cheese, sour cream, and a bag of semisweet chocolate chips. A selection strange enough that Apollo wanted to make a joke, but as she removed more items from the fridge—tangerines and cherry tomatoes— he realized how anxious she must be. They'd seen each other at his trial but hadn't been allowed to talk. He'd called her from Rikers once, but this was the first time they'd been in the same room since then.

"I'm happy you're here," Apollo said. "I'm happy to see you."

He stood and shut the fridge door gently. The two of them stood close and looked at the things she'd laid out.

"What was I planning to cook?" she asked.

"Let's just have the tea," Apollo said, guiding her to the chair he'd vacated.

He sat next to her, and neither spoke as they sipped. He felt sure he looked older than her. It seemed important to comfort her, to soothe any fears she could have. In a way it felt good to have someone to care for.

"You need to sleep," Apollo said. "And I do, too."

She brought a hand to her chest and patted it softly. "I was asleep when Dana called me. I go to bed so early most nights."

"You were in Springfield Gardens?" he said. "How did you get here before me?"

Lillian gave a smile. Her purse sat on the table. She reached for it, unzipped the top, took out her phone, and swiped once on the screen. She held the phone toward him.

"I called an Uber," she said.

"How much did that cost you?" He'd taken that scolding tone adults do with their elderly parents.

Lillian's face flushed, and she set the phone down. "I called an Uber," she said. "And now I'm here. Let's leave it at that."

They finished their tea and put the food back into the fridge. None of this stuff looked rotten, so Apollo realized Lillian must have brought it all recently, restocking his fridge for his return. *Good mothers are a gift*, he thought to himself.

"I called the police once a week until they finally told me it was okay to enter your place," Lillian said. "Your super, Fabian, he let me use his keys. The police dug through everything, went through all the closets and dresser drawers. I didn't want you to come back and find the place a mess. Not with everything else."

Lillian washed the cups and cleaned the pot. Apollo told her to take his bed. When she protested, he explained he couldn't sleep in it anyway.

"I'd offer to buy you a new bed," she said. "But that Uber ride took most of my savings."

Apollo laughed, and the sound turned a valve in Lillian, so she laughed, too.

They went into the bedroom, and he pulled back the sheets as if he was about to tuck his mother into bed for the night, but she grabbed his hand and shook it. "Tomorrow morning," she said. "I want you to come see Brian's grave. We can bring flowers."

Brian's grave.

Two words, and suddenly Apollo felt like the one in need of tucking in.

"Nassau Knolls," she said. "It's in Port Washington. It's a beautiful location."

"Mom," he whispered, "I'm not ready for that."

She pulled him down next to her on the bed. She held his hand in both of hers.

"Let me tell you a story," she said.

Apollo pulled his hand away. "You're not going to tell me about Arthur getting shot again, are you? Ugandan dictatorship. You drove like crazy, but he still bled to death. You came to the United States. Immigrants are so amazing. You make America great. I got it."

Lillian rubbed her thighs. "That's not what I was going to say."

"What then?"

"Something else!" Lillian stood up, slipped her shoes off, and set them by the bed. She gestured to the door, and Apollo was dismissed. She closed the door, and Apollo remained on the other side until he saw the light go out under the door. Did he want to apologize? No he did not. He wanted to say more, to say much worse. He wanted to do something worse. Not to her, to himself. Patrice had been right. If his friend hadn't said something, who knew where he'd have gone next? The George Washington Bridge was a block from this apartment. Every 3.5 days somebody attempted to jump the waist-high handrail. Maybe tonight it would've been him.

Apollo thought giving Patrice and Dana the book had been a selfless gesture, but it's possible he couldn't be trusted to understand himself right now. What would he have done if Lillian hadn't been here? He didn't know, and that surprised him. Who was he now? What might he become? He'd always been so sure—a book man, a husband, a father—but now none of those roles seemed his to fill.

A POLLO HAD TO saw through the neon green sticker the police had affixed to Brian's bedroom door. He'd probably dulled the blade of his bread knife by the time he cut through. Then he stood in the hallway listening for Lillian. Had he woken her? He held the knife in one hand and the door handle in the other. Was he really standing out here straining to hear his mother, or did he just want to avoid going inside? He turned on the light in the hallway and then pushed.

There were footprints in the room. All over the floor. Big shoes. Cops and EMTs; gray dust on the dark wooden floor, the space looking like a square-dancing diagram. Even in the dark he could see this much. Here he found the one room Lillian hadn't been able to clean. One of the blackout curtains was half down, moonlight coming through the bottom. The other was completely pulled up.

A large piece of wooden board had been put in to replace the broken window that led to the fire escape. When Fabian entered the bedroom, after he'd seen the baby but before he called the police, he'd found the security gate open and this window smashed. The glass had been on the sill and the fire escape, not inside the room. Emma had escaped this way. No one had been able to explain how—without keys, with the front door locked—Emma Valentine had gotten in that morning.

The glass had all been gathered and taken by the police forensics team. The hope had been to find blood on the fragments, and indeed, blood had been found. The blood of Emma Valentine. No revelation there, just corroboration.

Apollo stepped inside but hesitated to turn on the light. His mind returned, of all places, to the night Emma had given birth to Brian on the A train. Not to the dinner with Nichelle, nor to the bargaining with the dancers, but to the moment when his son's head—still protected by the amniotic sac—had pressed against Apollo's open palm. That moment just before his son slipped out and the sac burst all over his hands and the dirty floor. That slow time when their child had existed in two worlds at once— reality and eternity—and because Apollo and Emma were both in contact with the boy right then, they too, in a sense, had slipped between the two. The entire family had been Here and There. Together. A fairy tale moment, the old kind, when such stories were meant for adults, not kids. Apollo stood in the semidarkness of this room and felt much the same. If he reached out now, he thought he'd even feel the thin membrane in the air like a curtain he might part. Here and There.

What would he find on the other side? What would find him?

Then Lillian turned on the light.

"I'm sorry," she said when he turned back to look at her. "I woke up and had the worst feeling that you had disappeared."

With the light on, the room returned to reality, became merely monstrous again. What a relief the police had taken the crib as well as the shards of glass. Somehow pictures of the crib had been leaked online. Who'd done that? One of the police? Someone in the lab? Apollo had been in the hospital when the images of it played on the local news. By the time he understood what he was seeing, a nurse turned the television off.

Brian's room felt fifteen degrees colder than the rest of the apartment. The wooden board in the window hardly kept out the chill. There were bugs in the room, flies. Some flew around lazily, while others climbed on the walls. Lillian left and returned with a yellow flyswatter.

Apollo left and returned with the broom and dustpan. He wanted those footprints out of the room, to erase all those strangers who'd stomped through. There were bookshelves that had been used to store Improbabilia's stock before Brian was born. After Brian the books had gone into storage in the basement, and the shelves carried all the hand-me-downs and children's toys and infant supplies. A case of day diapers and a pack of night diapers—both size two—sat on a shelf.

Emma had bought plastic drawers for the clothes even before the baby was born and spent hours sorting them all. Here lay the proof. Bins labeled "Onesies 0–6 mos," "Sweatpants 0–6 mos," and "Jeans 0–6 mos." Another series of the same for clothes six-to-twelve months. "Sweaters," "Socks," "Hats & Scarves," "Bibs," "Washcloths." An old yellow and orange coffee can from Café du Monde held a dozen pacifiers they'd never used because Brian soothed himself to sleep by sucking his thumb. Next to the can on the shelf sat a book about how and when to wean thumb sucking. Emma had arranged all this. She'd nested with the best of them, prepared such a welcome for the boy. How had that same woman turned this room into a crime scene?

The copy of Outside Over There also stood on the shelf, right beside the book on thumb sucking. Apollo took it down. He'd planned to read this book to the boy every night, but how many times had he actually done it? Zero. He'd recited it from memory that morning in the Riverdale basement, but there'd been a different magic to the idea of reading to him. Teaching his child to love a book. Turning the pages until Brian became old enough to do it for himself. Reading the words aloud until Brian needed no help. Sitting alongside his son, the two of them lost in their stories. He'd daydreamed it from the day they brought the baby home, and yet in six months, he'd been so tired and worn out that it hadn't happened once. But then, it didn't make sense to read to a six-month-old. *There would be time. There would be time.* He'd always assumed. Apollo opened the book and leafed through it.

Behind him Lillian slapped the flyswatter against the wall, making a faint cracking sound.

"'You're coming with me,'" Apollo said.

Behind him Lillian stopped swatting.

"What did you just say?" Lillian asked. The wooden floor croaked as she stepped toward him.

He turned away from the closet. "That's the last thing I ever said to Brian."

"Why did you say that to him?" Lillian asked.

"I started having the dream again," Apollo said. "That old one, do you remember? Right after Brian was born."

"I didn't know that. Why didn't you tell me?"

"Why would I tell you? It's just an old nightmare."

His mother began to cry. "I guess I have something to tell you," Lillian said.

APOLLO KAGWA NEEDED a mop and bucket. Though it was nearly two in the morning, he needed to clean the wooden floors in Brian's room *tout de suite*. He left the bedroom before Lillian could say any more. Went to the kitchen and found the mop in the closet and a bucket under the sink, even a bottle of Seventh Generation Wood Cleaner, half full. He moved from the kitchen into the bathroom, dropped the bucket into the tub. He'd run away from his mother. He didn't know why, but he'd sensed that whatever she had to tell him was something he didn't want to hear. But where could he go?

Lillian caught up with him as he sat on the edge of the tub. She stood in the hall, watching him through the doorway, arms crossed and head down.

"I'd been working at Lubbick and Weiss for only about eleven months," she began. She cleared her throat and spoke louder. "They had a very good dental plan. You just turned four, and it was past time for you to start seeing a dentist. And they had an excellent eye care plan. Grandma had glaucoma when she was only forty, so I worried something like that could happen to me. I felt very happy to be at the job. They were in midtown so I could just take the seven straight there and walk six blocks to the office."

Apollo turned on the warm water and let it fill the bucket.

"But one of the lawyers, a man named Charles Blackwood, he started to spend a lot of time at my desk. I knew what that meant. And a few of the other girls warned me he was persistent. I would say he was relentless. He reminded me of your father except without the sweetness. He gave us tickets to see a show once. Do you remember that? At Shea Stadium. The Police and . . . who was it? Joan Jett and the Blackhearts. That was it."

Apollo said nothing, only watched the bucket fill.

"Why would he think I would even enjoy that music? I didn't know who those people were. All I really remember anymore is that it was loud. There were so many white people. And all of them were drinking. I think he meant for me to go with him, but I took you instead. We both had a bad night's sleep that night."

As the water ran, Apollo grabbed the wood cleaner and read its list of ingredients. Laureth-6 and organic cocos, nucifera oil, and caprylyl/decyl glucoside. He kept reading though the list of ingredients became less and less pronounceable. Lillian Kagwa might feel compelled to tell him this story, but that didn't mean he had to listen. Why was he so sure he didn't want to listen?

"I tried to be nice about saying no to Charles, but some men, you can't be nice to them. If you're polite, they think it means you're undecided. They hear your tone and ignore your words. It makes life a lot harder for the woman, but I don't think a man like that notices.

"At a certain point I had to tell him, clearly, that I would not go out with him. I didn't actually put it that way. I said I had a boyfriend. I wish I'd just said no, but it was hard to be that direct. I said I had a boyfriend and that was why I couldn't go out with him. And do you know what he did? He made me start coming into the office on Saturday mornings. He wasn't even there when I came in. It wasn't like he wanted to see me. He wanted to punish me. And what could I do? Working there less than a year? I needed the job."

The water reached the rim of the bucket, but Apollo didn't shut it off. He'd turned back toward Lillian and lowered the bottle of wood cleaner. She dropped her arms and raised her head, meeting Apollo's eyes. She stepped one foot into the bathroom but stopped there.

"For three weekends I was able to leave you with one of the other mothers in the building. Usually MJ and Petey's family. You all liked each other, so that was easy. But one weekend I couldn't get anyone to watch you. Just a lot of bad luck all at the same time. I called in and explained to the service, but Charles Blackwood called me personally soon afterward, from his home in Connecticut. He said if I didn't go in, he'd let the partners know. He didn't even come out and say he'd get me fired, but he reminded me of how much the partners liked discipline in the staff. I argued with him. I couldn't argue for myself, but I felt I was arguing for you, and then I was fearless. Finally I talked him down to a half day. I'd come in from ten to one. He wouldn't accept less. I got off the phone, and I felt completely lost. I tried everyone I knew. Either they weren't home to answer the phone, or who knows what. Lots of people didn't have answering machines back then, you couldn't even leave a message. Anyway, I had no help. What could I do? The longer I tried to think of something, the later it got. So finally. Finally. I left you at home."

The water splashed over the bucket, into the tub, running to the drain. Apollo hardly heard it. He stood now, facing Lillian, the two like rival gunslingers.

"In the living room, I set out a sippy cup of milk and two sippy cups with water. I set out toast with peanut butter, a bag of popcorn, and a bowl full of grapes, I think. You were potty-trained by then, but I put you in an overnight diaper, and you didn't like that. You kept tearing it off, so finally I brought in two plastic buckets and left them on the far side of the couch. That's the thing that made you scared. Not when I told you I was leaving for a while, but the fact that you'd be doing number one and number two in the living room. Then I turned the television on. You paid no attention to me after that. Your fears disappeared once I found your shows. *The Smurfs*. I said you could watch TV until I came back. You kissed me. I remember. You kissed me. I probably kissed your head fifty times. I shut the front door and locked it. I went to work. You were four."

Lillian took two more steps into the bathroom, her eyes on the bathtub faucet. She watched the water overflow rather than turn it off. Apollo had turned only the hot water handle, and steam rose from the bucket. Lillian stared into the steam.

"When I got home, you were asleep. The popcorn and the milk and one of the waters was finished. The grapes were finished. The peanut butter toast was facedown on the carpet. One of the buckets had pee in it, and the TV was on. *American Bandstand*. You'd passed out on the couch. You were all right. I never felt more relieved in all my life.

"But then when next Saturday came around, and MJ and Petey were visiting family in New Jersey, I set things up the same way, with you in the living room, and I went in to work for a half day. When I got back, things were exactly like the first time. You were so good! It worked well, so it became the routine. I worked half days on Saturdays, and that seemed like enough to satisfy Charles Blackwood. I even felt proud of you for being so self-sufficient. At least that's how I justified it to myself."

Lillian sat on the edge of the tub, looking at the steaming water flowing into the bucket. She reached out and turned off the water, watched as the last droplets fell from the spout. Apollo, still standing, leaned against the wall, beside the towel rack.

"But then things changed. You started waking up with nightmares. You screamed that your daddy was at the front door. You said he had come here to get you but then left you behind. Why did he have to leave you behind? That about killed me."

Apollo sat on the toilet so he'd be level with his mother. "Are you telling me my father really was at the apartment?"

"Yes." She said this so quietly that he practically had to read her lips.

"It was a memory, not a dream."

"Yes," Lillian said, even more softly.

They both remained quiet. Excess water gurgled as it drained from the tub.

"So what happened?" Apollo asked, his volume matching hers.

"One afternoon I came home and found him there," Lillian said. "I couldn't believe it. I sent him away."

"Why?"

Lillian opened her left hand and pressed her ring finger. "I filed for divorce. I was leaving him."

Apollo lunged for the bucket of water, spilling almost half as he pulled it from the tub. He grabbed the sponge mop, too, and left the bathroom.

He returned to Brian's room and set the bucket down. He felt outside himself, watching himself. He held the sponge mop with two hands, the head a full foot off the floor.

Lillian crept into the room carrying the wood cleaner. She brought the bottle to Apollo and offered it up.

"Why did you want a divorce?" Apollo asked.

She lowered her hand, bumping the bottle of wood cleaner against her thigh. "Your father was a good man. You saw how he saved everything, movie tickets, a headshot, that book. He could be a real romantic, and that was fun for a while. But I had to put you in daycare at two months old so I could go back to work. After a long day I pick you up, and your father is sitting on the couch watching television and asking me when dinner will be ready. The same at breakfast. Every damn day. Then he lost his job and it got even worse. He was around the house all day, but still was no help. It's like I was married to two children. That's what I came to America for? To be a servant?"

"So it was me," Apollo said. "I made it too tough for you to stay together." He held the mop handle with two hands and swayed faintly on his legs.

Lillian set the bottle of wood cleaner on the floor. She stepped closer to her son. She put a hand to his back and patted him lightly.

"You're the reason we stayed together as long as we did," she said. "And you're the best thing to come out of that love. It was a choice I had to make. Leaving Brian was what I needed to do just to keep afloat."

"What about me, though?" Apollo asked. "I needed both of you."

"I know," Lillian whispered.

"My whole life I'm just trying to figure out how to be a good man, and now you tell me you left one behind. When it was time for me to be a father, I didn't have any example. A model. One I could learn from, compare myself to. So I'm stuck making it all up as I go along, feeling like I'm inventing everything and doing it badly. And look how fucked up it got. Because of some choice you made more than thirty years ago."

Lillian left the bedroom. Apollo followed her, still gripping the sponge mop so tightly it seemed fused to his hands. "I tried my best," she said. "That's all I could do." She walked through the kitchen, into the living room, and into Apollo and Emma's bedroom. She slipped on her shoes. She walked back into the living room and found her purse by the couch. She took her coat from the front closet. She opened the front door, then looked back at him as if she might still be offered a reprieve.

"Why couldn't you let him be a part of my life at least?" Apollo asked. "He could've picked me up every other week and dropped me off again. You two didn't even have to speak to each other. Lots of my friends had families like that, and I envied them every day!"

"I couldn't do that," Lillian said.

"I'm not talking about you! I thought I was a monster. Like something must be wrong with me."

"How could you ever think that?"

"My father left me without looking back. That's what I thought. Why else would he leave unless I was worthless? And now I found out it's just because you made some choice that was good for you? Maybe he wasn't much help around the house because he lost his job. You couldn't give him a little while to get back on his feet? Jesus."

Lillian nodded softly, then stepped into the hallway. She unzipped her purse, found a card, and wrote quickly on the back. "This is the address for Nassau Knolls," she said. "You don't have to go there with me, but you should go to Brian's grave."

Apollo didn't move, so she set the card on the floor. He shut the door and locked it. He double-checked that he'd done this. Triple-checked. He looked through the peephole to see Lillian on her phone, ordering a car back to Springfield Gardens. She stayed in the hallway, on the other side of his door, and he watched her until the phone bleeped that her ride had arrived. Apollo went to the windows in his bedroom and watched her get inside. The time was two-thirty in the morning.

OLYROOD. AN EPISCOPAL church in the Gothic style. Opened in 1914, all steeples and sound planning. It sat in the shadow of the George Washington Bridge bus terminal. This was the church where Emma had wanted to baptize Brian.

The front doors of the church were open, but despite the daylight the interior stayed dark. Apollo entered slowly. Three women sat in the last pew praying quietly. A tall, slim man stood at a table of flyers and stacked hymnals. He held a small flip phone, jabbing at it angrily.

"Father Hagen?" Apollo asked.

The man's face had gone red. He looked to be in his sixties. His eyes were vital, his hair thinning. He looked up at Apollo, exasperated. He shut the phone with a snap.

"Call me Jim," he said. He waved the cellphone. "I was just trying to call you, but I couldn't find your number. I'm no good with these things."

He shrugged as if used to playing the role of the slightly befuddled old man. His wily grin suggested he was only playacting.

"Did you have any trouble finding us?" Father Hagen asked. The three women in the pew looked up from their silent prayers and Father Hagen raised a hand of apology. He waved for Apollo to follow, then led him through the nave and through a door leading down into the basement.

"I live around the corner," Apollo said. "It wasn't hard to find you."

"Yes," the priest said, as if this wasn't a surprise. Apollo watched the old man cautiously. Father Hagen stopped him on the stairs and brought a hand to his shoulder.

"This is where I confess," he said. "I know who you are."

"Because of the news," Apollo said.

Father Hagen dropped his hand. "Because of your wife."

"Emma?"

"She came here," he said. "She wanted to plan a baptism for your son. She made an appointment for her to come back with you. And with Brian."

Apollo leaned back against the railing of the stairs but felt as if he might flip backward and fall to the bottom. "I remember that," he said.

Father Hagen watched Apollo. The priest had the look of a basset hound, that drawn face and sense of sadness in the eyes. "She seemed to be having trouble," he said. "But I never would've guessed that . . . I would've tried to help if I'd understood."

Now it was Apollo who touched Father Hagen's shoulder. "It's not your fault."

Father Hagen tapped his forehead lightly and grinned. "I wish I could've helped her. That's all."

Each man stood with arms crossed, hovering between the church and its basement. Apollo found himself choking down a surge of anger. He wished he could've helped her? All the people to sympathize with in Apollo's family and he chose Emma? But okay, fine fine fine, no point in arguing with the man. Just get on with life.

Apollo took a folded sheet of paper from his pocket. "I'm going to need you to sign this," he said. "For my parole."

Father Hagen took the sheet and scanned it. "I'll be happy to, but why don't we do it after the meeting?"

Father Hagen moved to the bottom of the stairs. "We host the Survivors at least four or five times a year, so I've become friends with Alice. As we were planning when they'd come through again, she mentioned you'd been at the last meeting at the library. I begged her to come here this week, even though I think they had plans to meet downtown. I wanted to meet you face-to-face and say again how sorry I am that I couldn't have been more help to your family."

Now Father Hagen opened a heavy door and waved Apollo through.

They entered a large community room. Holyrood served coffee and snacks after mass down here. Birthday parties and communion parties were held, and voting machines were brought in for local and national elections. On Tuesday and Thursday mornings they ran a soup kitchen in the basement—the line ran out the door and partway down the block. But this afternoon it was reserved for the Survivors. More than a dozen chairs, more than a dozen Survivors this time. Fifteen. Sixteen now that Apollo had arrived.

As Father Hagen entered the room, a small older woman approached him, whispering.

"We'll talk about that later," he said softly. "I promise."

Alice caught Apollo's eye and waved him toward an empty chair. The old guy with the graying beard was there. His name was Julian, and he lived in the Bronx. Apollo recognized a few others, but not all of them. It didn't matter. He'd been new last week, and now it was their turn.

"I want to welcome all the new arrivals," Alice said when they finally began. "I'm happy you were able to find us today. I know I changed the location pretty last minute."

A middle-aged woman—new arrival—sitting two places away from Apollo raised her hand slightly. "I found out from the Facebook page," she said. "My therapist told me about the group."

"Oh good," Alice said. "Have you become a member? Or is it a fan? When I put together the page, I think I did it wrong. Who wants to be a fan of the Survivors?"

Julian raised one hand. "I'm a fan."

Alice smiled. "Thanks, Julian. I'm a fan, too." Then she looked around the room. "I'm Alice, by the way. I forgot to introduce myself. And . . . sir?"

Another new arrival, paunchy guy in his fifties, had slipped his phone out of his pants, his eyes glazed as he tapped the screen. He looked up at Alice.

"No phones during meeting," she said coolly.

He showed her the screen. "Sorry! I figured I'd become a fan right now." He looked around at the group. "If I don't do it right away I'll forget." He tapped the screen once more, then slipped the phone back into his pocket. "Sorry."

Alice leaned toward him. "Thanks for doing that. I appreciate it. Why don't we go around the room now and introduce ourselves? You don't have to speak, but we'd love to get to know you. If you're here, then you're a Survivor, too."

The middle-aged woman spoke again, more of a mumble that wasn't heard. "Since my daughter went off I've been having a hard time."

"My father used to read to me when I was a baby," Apollo said.

What was he talking about? What did this have to do with Emma's crime? His recovery?

"'When Papa was away at sea,'" Apollo recited. He went on from there, reciting the words up until Ida had her back to the baby and the goblins—small, faceless creatures wearing purple cloaks—sneak in through an open window.

He stopped here for a moment, because he'd lost his breath. In his pocket his phone vibrated twice. He didn't bother checking it. He looked around the group. They'd been down here talking for fifty minutes.

"It's a Maurice Sendak book," Apollo said.

"*Where the Wild Things Are?*" Julian asked. "That guy?"

"That's him. But this one isn't as sweet. It's called *Outside Over There.*"

"Why'd he read you that one?" Alice asked. "Even the little bit you recited sounds frightening. No one is watching the baby."

The whole room took on a certain stillness then. Maybe they were all considering the implications of what Alice had just said. Apollo certainly did.

No one is watching the baby.

Each person in the room had his or her own sadness to inhabit. The group fell into a meditative state, silence and prayers.

Then Apollo's phone rattled again in his pocket, and he shot up straight even though he had the sound off. He looked around, damn near stricken, but no one seemed to notice. The phone rumbled again. And again. Not a phone call but a series of texts. Apollo looked at Alice, whose eyes were shut, as she did some kind of breathing exercise in her chair.

While he watched her, Apollo slipped his phone from his pocket. He held it in the palm of his hand, down by his thigh. Four texts appeared on the screen, one after the next:

Already found buyer for book!

Wanted to talk price in person.

Told him you were at church.

Make the sale.

Apollo didn't have time to wonder how the hell Patrice knew he'd be here. Now he scanned the room trying to figure out if one of these people was this buyer. He hoped not. Imagine talking so much personal history before trying to make a sale. He wished Patrice had just done the haggling himself. But if Dana called Lillian over to keep Apollo alive, then this must've been Patrice's way of doing the same. The meeting had gone on for fifty-five minutes at this point. Five more and they'd be finished, and then he could call Patrice back.

"I saw my daughter in the computer."

Talk about whiplash. The voice, and the sentence, caused everyone in the room to make a sharp turn. Apollo felt so surprised, he dropped his phone right there. It landed on its face with a clop. He quickly looked at Alice, who saw it, then glared at him, then looked to see who'd spoken, all within about five seconds.

"I turned on my laptop, and there she was. My baby girl. A picture of her, out in the park with her grandparents."

The middle-aged woman who'd spoken earlier, the one who'd mentioned the Survivors' Facebook page, that's who talked now. She sat two seats away from Apollo, but he hadn't really looked at her until now. The woman was so narrow, she looked as if she hadn't eaten in aeons. Her hair had been pulled back into a haphazard ponytail, and her face showed creases along the forehead and the sides her mouth, the edges of her eyes, yet she might've been younger than Apollo. Her face wasn't aged but agonized. As she spoke, she turned to Apollo.

"But who took the picture?" She seemed to be asking him directly.

She reached into her pocket, and instinctively, any number of the people in the group curled in their chairs as if she was about to pull a gun. Instead she retrieved a sheet of paper, bunched into a ball.

Father Hagen looked to Apollo quickly, then back to the woman. When he spoke, he sounded utterly, impossibly, casual. Like a man more than used to cracked characters.

"I once opened my Gmail account," Father Hagen said to her, "and saw an ad running along the side of the page. This ad addressed me by name. It said, 'Jim, we think you deserve a vacation in Costa Rica.' And I wondered how they knew I liked to be called Jim because my given name is Francis. James is my middle name."

The woman turned her head from Apollo to Father Hagen. A quick baffled look crossed her face, as if Father Hagen were the one who sounded nuts. She unrolled the paper, so wrinkled and creased that it looked more like a piece of cloth.

"The photo is from across the street, some apartment window," the woman said softly. She wasn't showing the page to them—she looked at it herself. "Who would be taking pictures of my child from up there? We don't even live across from that park. My mom and dad took her there to play."

Apollo felt himself shudder. The other people in the room seemed to be moving at half time, the whole world in slow motion. Alice, Julian, Father Hagen, the rest—were they all looking at him, or did he only feel that way?

"There were more pictures," the woman continued. "Other places and days, but whenever I tried to show one to Gary, they were always gone. Deleted. Erased from my emails. Who could do that? I had the sense to hit print as soon as I saw this one. It's the only proof I've got."

She leaned forward now, staring at the page as if she might dive in.

"But when I looked at it long enough, I realized something else. That girl in the picture. That's not my daughter. That's not Monique."

Father Hagen came alongside her. He put a hand to the person in the chair next to her. The priest pulled this man up and out of the way, but he didn't touch the woman. He sat beside her and spoke in a voice too soft for Apollo to hear.

"I told Gary all this, and do you know what he said?" The woman looked up from the paper, back to Apollo again. "He told me to go on medication. They took my daughter, and he called me a crazy bitch."

Apollo needed to leave. Hit the escape pod. A sense of suffocation threatened him. He reached down for his phone but had to paw around because the woman's gaze had captured him.

"I had to find my own help," she said. "No surprise, I found it with the mothers. The wise ones. Cal told me how to get my daughter back. Cal told me what to do." Her eyes dropped, and she leaned forward. "But I don't know if I can do it."

Apollo stood, pointing. "That woman is going to kill her baby."

Father Hagen looked up at him.

Apollo pointed directly at the priest now. "If you don't call the police on her, she's going to go home and kill her baby. You can't say you didn't know this time."

His words had the force of revelation. He couldn't stay in this room, this church. He moved toward the basement doors. Behind him the woman sobbed.

"It's not a baby," she muttered.

"DON'T MAKE ME chase you!"

Apollo scurried down the block like a city rat. He didn't look back until he'd reached Amsterdam Avenue. He couldn't flee any farther east. The island of Manhattan was at an end. Across the Harlem River the Bronx came into view. The big, broad evening sky shrank that borough until its skyline of high-rises looked quaint. He wondered if he could make the swim.

"Don't make me chase you!"

Apollo heard the voice a second time and, this time, realized it was a man and not that woman. He stopped on the corner of Amsterdam and 179th and let the man catch up. He recognized him. He'd been at Holyrood, too. It was the paunchy guy, the one who'd been caught using his cellphone.

"You're fast," he said, when he finally caught up, "and I'm old. I'm William." The man didn't extend his right hand for a shake because it held his cellphone. His left quivered as he held it against his rising and falling belly. "William Wheeler," he said more loudly. "Patrice sent me. Patrice Green? I want to buy the book."

Buy the book.

Despite what he and Patrice had discussed last night, no sentence in the English language seemed stupider right now.

"So buy the fucking book," Apollo said. "Why did you need to come see me?"

This man—William Wheeler—clutched his neck as if he wore a string of pearls. "Well, I didn't insist. I mean, I'm sorry, but it was Patrice who told me to come here. If you're going to curse at someone, you should give him a call, but I certainly don't deserve it." He dropped the hand and slipped his phone back into his pocket, hitched his pants, and straightened his posture. He turned away from Apollo, and Apollo watched him go. The man made it about five steps before he stopped and looked back.

"But I really would like that book," he said with a bashful smile.

Half a block from Holyrood, and they could see the ambulance lights. Apollo stopped and watched, and William Wheeler went quiet, too. Apollo recognized some of the Survivors standing in a small cluster on the sidewalk, talking to one another and gesturing toward the church's basement doors. Eventually Father Hagen appeared, following two paramedics and two police officers. Hidden between the four uniforms was one wiry woman. She'd been handcuffed, hands in front. All these men led her to the ambulance and helped her inside.

"I didn't think they'd really call anyone," Apollo said.

"It was a pretty bad scene," William whispered back.

Wheeler offered to buy Apollo dinner, but Apollo suggested coffee instead. They crossed the street and walked toward Broadway—there was a Dunkin' Donuts on 178th. As they moved, Alice looked up. Did she see him? She gave a faint wave, but maybe she was just stretching an arm. Julian stood beside her; they talked and looked around. Maybe they were wondering about him, where he'd gone. He'd write them later, on the Facebook page. For now he'd forge Father Hagen's signature or Alice's—he knew what hers looked like. Why hadn't he thought of doing that right from the start? As long as he showed up with the signed paper, his PO would be fine. The man had a hundred other ex-cons to shepherd anyway. So Apollo went with William. For Apollo, getting back to business was the best way to survive.

Inside the Dunkin' Donuts, most of the chairs were already occupied. Loners mostly. Almost all of them men. At night the place had the aura of a holding cell. Much less crowded than the ones on Rikers. They found the last empty table. Wheeler sat down and scanned the room like a CCTV camera. The workers behind the counter—all Bengalis—chatted with one another loudly, casually, but their puffy, glassy eyes betrayed their exhaustion. Finally Wheeler turned back to Apollo. "I've never been this far uptown in Manhattan."

"Best roast chicken in New York is right on 175th," Apollo said. "At Malecon."

Wheeler nodded and grinned as one does when learning about something one will never try. He asked if Apollo wanted coffee, and before Apollo could answer, Wheeler had gone up to the counter to buy for both of them. He chatted with the cashier, who watched his lips move with great concentration as she translated and tried to make change.

"So I spent awhile on the phone with Patrice this morning," Wheeler said when he returned with their coffees. "He served in Iraq, you know."

"Yes," Apollo said.

"Of course I thanked him for his service," Wheeler said.

"He loves that," Apollo said, trying not to laugh.

"Well, I certainly meant it," Wheeler said earnestly, and Apollo's laughter curdled. The man was sincere, and Apollo didn't want to mock him for it.

"So you must really love Harper Lee," Apollo said.

Wheeler nodded faintly, took two sips of his coffee, nodded again. "I'll be totally honest with you," he said. "*To Kill a Mockingbird* is one of the two books I've ever read for pleasure." He leaned back in his chair. "That must sound pretty stupid to a man in your business."

Apollo tapped the side of his coffee cup absently. "You'd be surprised how many book men aren't readers. It's not romantic to say this, but for a lot of the guys, the books are just things to sell. I've known some who go into fits talking about the condition of a book. What kind of endpapers it has. Whether it's bound or just cased. Whether it has an *insert* or an *inset*. But if you ask what the book is actually about? Six out of ten have no idea and act like you're stupid for thinking it matters."

Wheeler brought his coffee cup to the side of his head and bumped it against his temple. "Boom," he said. "You just blew my mind."

They spoke like this for some time. Wheeler turned out to be a curious man. He found the book trade endlessly fascinating. And Apollo felt happy to talk about something, anything, that didn't revolve around his grief. You could even say Apollo was having a good time with him.

"We had a drink with each other," Wheeler said. "That's a sign of trust."

Apollo looked around the Dunkin' Donuts. Wheeler had spoken so loudly, so lacking in any self-consciousness, that he seemed childlike. Apollo peeked at the lone men who still sat by the windows and caught two of them giving Wheeler a glance. Was Apollo being paranoid to think Wheeler had suddenly made himself seem like an easy victim? The kind of person they might follow outside and rob of his phone and wallet? Probably it was paranoia, and yet Apollo made sure that all of those men saw Apollo scoping *them*. Telling each, silently, *He's with me.*

"Tell me where you found the book, would you?" Wheeler said, gulping down more coffee. "Tell me how it all came about."

They'd been sitting for half an hour by now. Where else did Apollo have to be? He told him about the house in Riverdale.

"Imagine if you had given up after six boxes," Wheeler said, sitting back in his chair and shaking his head in wonder.

"I wouldn't have given up," Apollo said. "Not with a child to feed."

Here Apollo stopped speaking and reared up straight. Thirty minutes had passed without a direct thought about Brian. A new record. It had been a relief, he realized, but maybe also a betrayal. Why should he ever be without that pain? What gave him the right to enjoy anything?

Wheeler misread the moment, though. He grinned as he set his phone on the tabletop. "I have two daughters, so believe me, I understand."

He opened his phone, found the gallery app. A limitless supply of photos of two no doubt lovely—and living—children was about to be revealed. Wheeler's naïveté, his sweetness, were about to turn into tone deafness. Hadn't the man heard Apollo talking in group therapy? Hadn't he seen Apollo's story all over the news?

In an instant Apollo tracked back over the way Wheeler had been speaking to him all this time. No sense of trepidation, no tone of grave concern or condolences. With a short sigh, Apollo realized this guy might not know who the hell he was. In group therapy he'd talked about the children's book that Brian West used to read to him. Maybe Wheeler thought Apollo was just a guy with serious daddy issues. Which was also true. But this only made him like Wheeler more. He didn't know a damn thing about Apollo's story, or at least he didn't care all that much. He only wanted to buy a rare book. Maybe this was what Patrice meant when he said he liked Apollo because he didn't give a damn about his military service. Every human being is a series of stories; it's nice when someone wants to hear a new one.

"I saw my daughter in the computer." Wheeler shook his phone. "Oh damn it," he said. He hadn't brought up photos of his healthy children—instead he'd tapped the newest file in the gallery, a video. Made only an hour ago. "I turned on my laptop and there she was. My baby girl. A picture of her, out in the park with her grandparents."

"I'm sorry!" Wheeler said, shaking his phone.

Wheeler moved to tap the screen, turn off the phone, but Apollo reached out and brushed his hand aside. He pulled the phone down so Wheeler had to lay it flat on the table. The image hardly registered, just blurs. Wheeler must've been making the video with the phone by his leg. Apollo had already forgotten nearly everything that woman had said. All but those last four words. *It's not a baby.* Now he felt a morbid fascination growing as he waited to hear her say them again.

Another shift of the camera as Wheeler rose from his chair and moved back into a corner, and now the camera caught the scene: Father Hagen moving toward the woman. The other Survivors staring in shock. *I once opened my Gmail account,* he began.

"I don't know why I taped this," Wheeler said. "It's a bad habit, I know. First thing I do when something strange happens is reach for my phone. I'm sorry. Let me delete it."

Wheeler's words drowned out Father Hagen's Gmail anecdote.

"Wait," Apollo said, and leaned closer to the phone. Wheeler did, too.

I had to find my own help. No surprise, I found it with the mothers. The wise ones. Cal told me how to get my daughter back. Cal told me what to do. But I don't know if I can do it.

Suddenly Apollo tapped the screen to stop the video. This was the moment when he jumped up. *That woman is going to kill her baby.* He didn't want to see himself saying the words. It would've felt too much like he was talking about Emma.

Wheeler, seeing Apollo's pain, flipped the phone over so the screen faced the table. "It's a stupid habit," he said. "I'm sorry. I'm sorry."

Apollo slumped in his chair.

Wheeler sipped his coffee quietly. "Who's Cal?"

"I don't know," Apollo answered.

They both sat quietly for a minute longer. Apollo replayed the woman's words in his head another time.

"'The wise ones,'" Apollo said. "You ever heard of that?"

Wheeler took up his phone and tapped at it with concentration. A handful of seconds passed, his eyes moved across the screen. "Oh," he said softly. He looked up from the phone, caught Apollo's stare, and looked back down, almost embarrassed.

"You found something?" Apollo asked. "Tell me."

"'In the villages were invariably found one or two "wise ones."'" William looked up. "This is from a book."

"But does it say what 'wise ones' means?"

Wheeler opened his mouth and closed it. He squeezed his lips together, then turned the phone toward Apollo.

Apollo took the phone and read the screen. "Come on," he said. "Is this for real?"

Wheeler looked away, as if he'd stumbled across someone else's mess and felt too embarrassed to mention it.

Apollo stared at the screen and read the words again.

"Wise Ones."

Witches.

5
THE WISE ONES

WELL, THAT'S JUST some bullshit. You know that, right?"
Patrice and Apollo stood together on a platform at
the Long Island Rail Road's Jamaica station. They were
waiting for a train to Long Beach in Nassau County,
due in six more minutes.

"He said he wanted us to bring the book to him," Apollo explained.
"And when a man has agreed to pay seventy thousand dollars for a book,
you best believe I'll take a train ride to get it to him." He raised his eyebrows at Patrice. "And you will, too."

Patrice waggled his head. Though he was the bigger man, his movement made him seem smaller, younger. From a distance they panto-
mimed a parent and scolded child.

"I feel like we're two drug dealers out to make a sale."

"Drug dealers don't gift wrap," Apollo said.

Apollo opened the case that carried the book and slid it out. The book
was wrapped perfectly in paper that had been silkscreened with an ornate
gold medallion pattern. Apollo had even applied a bow.

"That's some fruity shit," Patrice said, waving the package away. Then
he leaned closer and touched the wrapping paper gently. "Is it from Kate's
Paperie?"

"Hell yeah. It's called Yuzen Paper, Gold Medallions."

Patrice nodded. "That shit is tight." Now he looked in either direction. "But put it away before someone sees two grown men talking about wrapping paper."

Apollo felt the temptation to hold the wrapped book in the air and run up and down the platform calling out Patrice's full name and address. With his luck, though, he'd play that prank and stumble, and the book would fly out of his hands and fall onto the train tracks, where it would be crushed by an arriving train. He slipped the book back into the bag. Now the two of them returned to silence on the platform. Apollo hadn't mentioned anything about the woman at the church or Cal or the Wise Ones to Patrice. What would he say about it? He didn't even know what to think about it.

The Jamaica station had been renovated in 2006. New train platforms, elevators from the street level, and brand-new escalators. A pedestrian bridge linked the station with the newly complete AirTrain to John F. Kennedy Airport. A steel and glass canopy rose over the train platforms, allowing riders to be protected from bad weather but still enjoy the open air. There was a slightly European railway feel after renovations, a distinct difference from the Jamaica station as Apollo remembered it from the 1980s. Dresden after the bombing and Dresden today. That's how drastic the change.

But when he looked around, he could still see the old platforms, and down on the street level, the old Jamaica, Queens. If his mother had been with him, would she have seen a third Jamaica, the one she first encountered when she was a young immigrant in the United States? How many Jamaicas might there be? If you were a thousand years old, you'd remember when all this was marshland, and Jamaica Avenue was the Old Rockaway Trail used by the Rockaway and Canarsie Indians. And before that? In the 1800s city workers dredging the bottom of nearby Baisley Pond found the remains of an American mastodon. A mastodon sculpture had been raised in Sutphin Playground. All those tales were told right here, one after the next, each informing the one that came after. History isn't a tale told once, it's a series of revisions.

Would it be so surprising if once there had been witches here, too?

The train car was nearly empty. Few were headed out to Long Beach at one in the afternoon on a Wednesday. Outside, Queens whipped by.

"I'm all for this sale," Patrice said. "But think about if we waited until this lady was dead. We could double what this dude is paying."

"It's 2015," Apollo said. "She might not die for another ten years. Meanwhile this guy wants to buy it now. For seventy thousand dollars. I bought this book for a hundred bucks. Think about how much of a markup that is already."

Patrice crossed his arms, looking out the window. "If you're going to make rational arguments, I'm not going to keep talking with you. But she might die, like, next year and then I'm going to be pissed we sold it too soon."

Apollo patted his friend's shoulder. "That won't happen."

"You're going to have a quick turnaround," Patrice said casually. "You got another meeting tonight, right?"

Patrice was right. Despite running off for coffee with William Wheeler last week, Apollo did plan to attend tonight's meeting of the Survivors. He missed them. Plus his parole officer had looked at his sign-in sheet pretty funny. He hadn't come out and accused Apollo of forging Alice's signature, but the man stared at the sheet cockeyed before filing it. There was a warning in the gesture, and Apollo decided he wouldn't risk it again. So yes, he'd be back with the Survivors. He even checked in on the Facebook page, saying he'd be coming in case the PO sniffed around his online trail.

Patrice scanned his phone. "'The Survivors Club,'" Patrice read. "'Meeting at The Chinese Community Center of Flushing.' You want the address?"

"You're a member?" Apollo asked, so dumbfounded, the bag slid right off his lap and onto the floor. He didn't even notice.

Patrice reached down and scooped the bag. "No," he said. "But when you checked in, it popped up on the tribute page."

Apollo felt as if his head had been dunked underwater. "What in the fuck are you talking about?"

"The tribute page," Patrice said softly. "To Brian." He tapped his phone, then handed it to Apollo.

"'Tribute to Baby Brian,'" Apollo read.

There was a Facebook page dedicated to Brian Kagwa.

It had sixteen thousand fans.

The page used the same photo of Brian that had been in all the news reports. The one Apollo had taken down in the basement of the home in Riverdale. Who'd snatched that picture from his personal page first? Which news outlet? And now it was here, too. Apollo's fingertips felt hotter, as if the phone were burning him.

Patrice spoke softly. "I'm a fan," he said. Then heard himself and put up his hands. "Not a fan. You know what I mean. I'm going to shut up now."

Apollo scrolled down, reading through many, many posts. He had a lot of nicknames on the "Tribute to Baby Brian" Facebook page.

The Hanging Husband.

The Prisoner of Apt. 43.

Strangled Dad.

Failed Father.

Mr. My-Son-Is-Dead.

There were kinder ones, of course, but some were even worse. Quite a few blamed him for what had happened. Men and women, members from every race and region of the United States, international contributors, too—all of them had opinions. A segment of every population you could imagine hated him. Many more loathed Emma. Almost all of them spent at least a line condemning her to some kind of hell. *The only innocent in all this was the child.* And though it hurt, Apollo couldn't argue with that.

Apollo scrolled back up the page. It had been started while he'd been in the hospital. When he and Emma and Brian had been breaking news. In all likelihood, someone had started the page with good intentions, but then his or her own life got busy, and this person stopped keeping track. Soon no one was driving the train, and everyone was driving the train. Some folks posted messages of love addressing Brian directly, prayers from more holy books than Apollo recognized. There were images of angels holding a baby that looked vaguely like Brian, and others of angels with Brian's little face scanned directly onto the body. Pictures of Emma, and sometimes Apollo, scanned onto monsters from movies or myth, *Medea* a mainstay. The image of a tombstone with Emma's name and the phrase "Rest in Piss."

For a while, early on, there were people having ongoing arguments about the case, about Emma's disappearance, about the inability of law enforcement to find her; various conspiracy theories about how Apollo had killed them both and got away with the crime. Posts condemning the misogyny and misandry surfaced throughout. Some threads turned into parenting forums, of a sort, where people discussed the ways Apollo and Emma had parented badly from the beginning. What evidence any of them had about Apollo and Emma's parenting style was unclear and obviously didn't matter. They'd been helicopter parents, and that was what went wrong. They'd been a household with two working parents, and that had started the whole mess. A few wrote of their empathy for Emma, saying she'd clearly suffered from severe postpartum depression. Some suggested, one might say gloated, that this kind of thing was incredibly common in black households. *They live in hell, these people. So they act like devils.*

"I can't believe this," Apollo whispered, but he couldn't stop reading.

All this time—while he'd been in the hospital, in Rikers, and even now, struggling through some sort of recovery—he'd been discussed, dissected, and denounced. He felt as if he'd just been told he'd been walking around with his ass hanging out, so utterly exposed. Was it better that he hadn't known this page existed, or was that worse?

And then there was the person who'd started the page. The administrator. He went by the name *Green Hair Harry*. His own page was clearly just a placeholder. The profile photo showed the Grinch grinning. Only one piece of personal information provided (Hometown: Mount Crumpit).

"Why would this guy do this?" Apollo asked, looking up from the phone.

Patrice stared back, his mouth hanging open. "I thought you knew about the page, my man. I never would have . . . I got a note there was activity on the page. When I went there, I saw that you'd checked in with the Survivors. I figured if you were posting on the Baby Brian page, that meant you knew."

"I didn't do that," Apollo said. "Not on purpose at least. I was just trying to cover my ass with my parole officer."

Apollo had to stop talking. Going over the technical details about posts and alert notifications made him want to crack Patrice's phone against the side of Patrice's head. Speaking of Patrice, why would he even join such a page?

Patrice slipped his phone from Apollo's hand and placed it facedown on his thigh.

Apollo leaned away from Patrice until his shoulder touched the window. Outside, they'd left Queens and reached Long Island. The yards of the homes were slightly larger, the commercial buildings no more than two stories tall.

Sixteen thousand people had joined that page? For what? As the train sped past these residential homes, Apollo wondered if he might be seeing places where many of them lived. Maybe Green Hair Harry lived in that brick Tudor home right there. Or the next one. Apollo felt his breath leaving him, dizziness so severe he might black out. What had he been worrying about twenty minutes earlier? Fucking witches? Why worry over witches when the Internet could conjure so much worse?

THE LONG BEACH station's depot had a red-clay-tiled roof and white walls with brown accents at the corners, making it look more like a Mediterranean bungalow than the last stop on the Long Island Rail Road. It was even more incongruous in midwinter when cold winds from Reynolds Channel to the north and the Atlantic Ocean to the south made the building shiver.

"That's our guy?" Patrice asked.

In the parking lot, William Wheeler stood in front of a green 2003 Subaru Outback. His arms were crossed, and he watched the asphalt as if reading tea leaves. For a moment, Patrice and Apollo stood inside the station and watched him. Wheeler uncrossed his arms and walked around the Subaru. He opened the driver's side door and pulled out a plastic supermarket bag. It was tied at the top, and William untied it with urgency.

The waiting area of the Long Beach station was soundtracked by a low fuzzy buzz; the ticket agent left his microphone on while he stepped away from his chair at the booth. The room practically throbbed as Wheeler reached into the plastic bag. He pulled out a sixty-four-ounce bottle of soda.

Tab.

"It's 2015," Patrice said quietly. "Who the fuck still drinks Tab?"

A forty-ounce of beer would've been problematic, a liter of gin downright troubling, but a sixty-four-ounce bottle of Tab? Ridiculous. The bottle's pink wrapper had faded to the color of fiberglass insulation. Wheeler walked back to the front of the Subaru and rested against the hood. He lifted the jug to his mouth and chugged.

"You know what that is?" Patrice said. "That's your future."

Apollo was mesmerized by the sight of Wheeler's Adam's apple rising and falling, rising and falling, his belly expanding and contracting as he gorged himself on Tab. Patrice pulled Apollo by the shoulder.

"That's a man who's lived without a woman for a long time," Patrice explained. He placed an arm around Apollo and squeezed to make his point. "Not months but years. Decades. A man who lives alone for that long forgets what it's like to be civilized. He starts walking around his house in nothing but ratty underwear. Then one day he steps out to get the mail in that underwear and doesn't even notice. Then he's out on his porch in some saggy-ass boxer shorts and no T-shirt and is surprised when people think he looks like a troll."

Wheeler lowered the bottle, took a breath through his nose, and raised it again. He drank with such gusto, a little seeped from his mouth and ran down his neck. His throat expanded like a snake swallowing a mouse.

"Living without a woman in your life is how you see these fat dudes wearing 'interesting' facial hair and posting angry videos about how everyone else in the world is stupid for not appreciating them. 'Women only like jerks.' That's the mantra of dudes who have made themselves undateable but aren't willing to take the blame. These motherfuckers are so backed up sexually, it creeps into their brains and rots out the skull. That's how you end up being a grown man publicly guzzling a bottle of goddamn *Tab* in a parking lot on Long Island."

Apollo nodded, but the only thing he felt right then was pity for William Wheeler. He'd invited Apollo and Patrice out here and offered to pick them up, all so he could have the privilege of writing them a five-figure check. And for this generosity, Patrice paid him back with scorn.

As he and his partner walked out of the station, Wheeler waved to them with his free hand. He set the bottle of Tab on the car hood. He took two steps, and the bottle teetered forward, went flat on the hood, and rolled right off the car and onto the ground. Brown fizz streaked the hood. Wheeler spun around and crouched, plucking up the soda as if it was a fallen child. His slacks hugged him too tightly, and his jacket rode up, exposing the fleshy waist.

"I'm starting to think this dude has never been with a woman," Patrice said.

Apollo didn't feel compelled to bring up the two daughters Wheeler mentioned. What for? Besides, the wind rushing across the parking lot felt good to Apollo. Maybe it was also seeing Wheeler again. Even a moment this embarrassing reminded Apollo of that evening in the Dunkin' Donuts, and Apollo understood—as he couldn't consciously then—that Wheeler had helped, in some small way, to save Apollo's life. Walking out of that church, after that woman's words, well, maybe Apollo had been close to cracking up. Then this middle-aged guy wanted to sit, have coffee, and do some business, and weirdly, that was enough to keep Apollo's mind intact.

"I know one more thing this guy hasn't done," Apollo said, turning to Patrice. "As much as you make fun of him, I know he's never joined a fucking Tribute to Baby Brian Facebook page."

Patrice actually stopped walking, stopped blinking, stopped breathing. It was as if his whole central nervous system had gone on the fritz. Meanwhile Apollo moved on. He waved at Wheeler and, when he got close, shook the man's hand.

The inside of the Subaru smelled surprisingly sweet. The cause became clear quickly—two car fresheners hanging from the rearview. Strawberries. From the backseat, Patrice leaned forward and tapped at them with one long finger.

"Those are from my daughters," Wheeler said. He looked more sheepish about the fresheners than he had been about the Tab.

"Daughters," Patrice repeated.

"And one wife," Wheeler added as he started the car.

Apollo didn't look back at Patrice to grin or gloat. In fact, he avoided eye contact with the big man for the rest of the drive.

As Wheeler drove out of the parking lot, he said, "I used to call each one a little strawberry. When they get mad, their faces all go so red." He smiled at the memory as he merged onto East Park Avenue. "I thought we'd go out and talk on the water," he said, continuing east. "Does that sound like a good time for you two?"

"Like on a ferry or something, Mr. Wheeler?" Patrice asked. He looked a bit thrown off. His usual manner of leaning into, leaning over, every conversation had been forgotten. Now he sat back and spoke softly, still chastened from what Apollo had said.

"Not a ferry," Wheeler said, enjoying holding on to the mystery.

At the light, he made a left on Long Beach Boulevard, then drove on a small bridge over Wreck Lead Channel. Finally they reached a single-lane drive. Wheeler parked in front of a two-story colonial home with a shingle hanging over the front door that read ISLAND PARK YACHT CLUB. He pointed toward a series of docks where five small boats were in the water.

"'You ever been in a cockpit before, Joey?'" Wheeler asked.

Apollo knew the quote but couldn't bring himself to laugh, or even grin politely. In the backseat Patrice had taken out his phone and tapped at the screen.

Wheeler flicked at the two strawberry air fresheners, making them bump and swing. "I'm old," he said and laughed. "Just ignore me. But can I ask you guys a favor? Can you please call me William?"

He guided Apollo and Patrice to a forty-one-foot Hunter sloop. It bobbled faintly in the water, brushing two inches closer to the dock, then two inches away. William stepped onto the boat easily, but it took Apollo and Patrice a fair bit longer. Baby steps for them.

Meanwhile William opened a doorway and went below. The gray-green waters of Wreck Lead Channel slapped against the hull. The boat had been christened *Child's Play.*

"Come down," William shouted. "I've got beer."

"Let's make some money," Patrice said to Apollo, trying to sound upbeat.

Apollo didn't answer as he went first below deck.

44

WHEN SOMEONE INVITES you onto his boat, what do you imagine? That probably depends on how common boat ownership is in your life. In Apollo's case, he wasn't expecting things to be so . . . tight. There was booth seating, but the table at the center was about the size of a chessboard. The seating had been upholstered in red faux leather, making it look like a couch you'd get at Rent-A-Center. There was a galley kitchen—a sink, microwave, hotplate, and coffee machine—but the space itself was about as big as a closet and almost as dark. And the bathroom? Well, it made you envy the roominess and comfort of an airplane toilet. William's boat was a bit underwhelming.

And yet how many damn boats did Apollo Kagwa own? Exactly none. So as he sat at the little table with Patrice and William, he lifted his beer and said, "You've got a lovely boat."

William sipped his beer and smiled. "I'm going to just admit something to you because I'm not any good at keeping secrets."

"You stole this boat?" Patrice said. He'd already finished one beer, downing the whole thing in two gulps, and was on to the next. Two six-packs sat on the table. The bottles sweated their chill.

William barked out laughter. "I didn't steal it! But it's not mine."

Here he leaned back as best he could in the tight squeeze of the seating and slipped out his phone. He set it on the table. Patrice leaned forward to gaze at the screen. The boat rose and fell faintly. An icon of a small dinghy in splashing waters glowed on the phone.

"This is called Afloat. It's like Airbnb, but for boats." He tapped the app, and it bloomed like a flower. A picture of *Child's Play* appeared on the screen and, beneath that, a timer. "I rented the boat for two hours."

Why bother with all this? Apollo wondered. Making them take the train out here. Driving them out to a boat. The theatrics played against William's low-key suburban dad style, but maybe some people just liked putting on a show.

"You planning to take us somewhere?" Apollo asked. "Because I have to be back in Flushing by five."

William picked up his phone and put it back into his pocket. "I don't even know how to drive a boat," he said.

"So why rent it at all?" Patrice asked, on to his third beer. Maybe guilt was making him throw them down.

"It's my app," William said. "I wrote it. If I don't use it, who will? Besides, I don't get much company these days."

"How many boats do you have signed up?" Apollo asked.

William patted the table. "One," he said. "So far."

"You're a coder," Patrice said. Then he reached into his pocket and took out his phone. He opened to a photo and held it toward William. "Check out this rig."

William cooed. "You built it yourself, didn't you?"

"If I'd bought it, they'd charge me eight times the price!"

"I built my older daughter's first laptop," William said.

"You have pictures?" Patrice asked, warming to William for the first time.

Apollo couldn't guess if Patrice wanted to see photos of the child or the laptop. William scrolled through his phone, then held the screen toward Patrice.

"Beautiful," Patrice said.

"Put a Core i5 processor in her," William cooed.

Apollo warmed to both these tech geeks but knew he'd better change the subject quickly or they'd spend the next two hours exactly like this.

Apollo pulled the book out of its bag. That worked. William looked away from Patrice.

"You wrapped it? That's nice. It was meant to be a gift anyway." William picked it up after drying his hands on his pants. He brought the wrapped book so close to his face, Apollo thought the guy would sniff it.

"I guess I hoped to see it before I bought it," William said. He looked from Apollo to Patrice. "But that's okay. I feel like I can trust you guys."

"Give that to me," Apollo said. He took the book and laid it flat.

"No, no," William said. "It's okay."

Patrice finished his beer and reached for his fourth but stopped himself. No matter how guilty he might feel, he was not going to risk having an open beer near a book meant to sell for so much money. A few droplets along the page edge, and William could cut the offering price by ten thousand dollars.

"You are about to pay us seventy thousand dollars for this thing," Apollo said. "I want you to be able to say you saw it first." He set the book down and worked the tape up with the tip of his mailbox key.

"You said it was a gift," Patrice slurred.

"It's for my wife," William said. He watched Apollo work.

"It's her birthday or something?" Patrice asked. He held on to that fourth beer, squeezed it tight.

William dropped his head. "We're estranged." He stopped and sighed. "My wife moved back to her parents in Bay Shore. I've been on my own for eleven months."

Apollo lifted the book. "Here it is."

William took the book and held it close to his face. He opened the covers. He read the inscription on the first page.

"This is perfect," he whispered.

A look of relief passed across William's ruddy face. A few tears gathered in the corners of his eyes. From just the littlest bit of information—an estranged wife, the family moved out—Apollo saw the outlines of a moving story forming.

"Gretta's father used to read this book with her when she was little," William said. "That's my wife. Gretta Strickland. Her father was Forrest Strickland. They were from Alabama, just like in the book. A city called

Opelika." He spoke so softly that the waters slapping against the hull nearly drowned him out. Apollo had to lean closer so he could hear.

William closed the book and looked at the cover. "It's just a story about a good father, right?" he continued. "Nobody could live up to it, not in real life, but I think her dad used to read it to her just to give her a model, something to strive for, you know? She never forgot it. And then she married me, but I wasn't Atticus Finch."

"Neither was he!" Patrice said, much too loudly. William looked to him quickly, but then back to Apollo. "You know," Patrice muttered. "Because of the other book."

William spoke to Apollo directly. "I'm about ten years older than you, I think. I was one of the last waves of men who thought all you had to do was work, work, work and that made you a great dad. Provide. Provide. Provide.

"But you know what happens when you do it like that? You look up after twenty or twenty-five years, and your wife doesn't know you. Your kids might respect you—might—but that other thing, the happiness, you aren't close enough with them to share it. You understand? Your wife doesn't know you, and neither do your kids.

"Then guys your age get a whole new data set. It's not enough to make the money, and besides you *can't* make enough to cover everything, not on your own. Your wife might want to work or she might not, but it doesn't matter—she has to work. When I was starting out, you got by on one income, and that was enough, but these days you've got to be poor or rich to survive on one income. You want to stay afloat in the middle, and you both are hitting that nine to five."

William returned the book to Apollo, who rewrapped it with a new reverence. It was not simply an expensive sale anymore—it was soon to play a part in one family's history.

"'New Dads,'" William said. "I know people make fun. But I see those guys pushing babies in a stroller on the way to work, or the ones with their kids at the park at six in the morning, and I feel like I missed the good part. I know it's a lot of work, but it's the good stuff. And I didn't even know I was missing it. No one ever told me it was the stuff to covet. My dad certainly didn't make it a priority. Anyway, it's not like doing things the old way left me rich. I worked my ass off to barely stay afloat. It's costing me most of what I have saved to try and win Gretta back. With this."

William pointed at the book, then gulped the last of his beer. Apollo finished the wrapping and lightly ran his pointer finger along the edges one more time.

"If I could just get my wife back into the house, I could do better. Now I know what matters. I love my daughters so much, but I never said it. I thought it was obvious, or should have been obvious, because of the things I did for them. But people need to hear the words, you know? I didn't realize that for twenty-five years."

William accepted the book from Apollo. He clutched it to his stomach as if to protect it.

"When I saw your listing for the book, I figured maybe it could convince Gretta I was serious. She read this to the girls just like her father did with her. I used to call my wife Mockingbird when we were young. Like a pet name. I don't remember when I stopped. It was after the kids came, I know that much. Couple of years ago I finally figured out what I was doing wrong. I tried to go back to the old days. Go back to the way things used to be. But maybe it was too late. Or she didn't want to go back in time. Not with me. She left me because we were absolute strangers. I never hit her or cheated on her. We barely even argued.

"I mean, I've been a programmer for nineteen years. Nights and weekends are when you catch up on the work you didn't get done from nine to five! I bet I spent more time on code than I did on my marriage. I know I did. I turned into a ghost to her, and maybe she was a ghost to me. You think this could work, though? What's your feeling, guys?"

Patrice lifted one of the empty bottles and placed it back into the case. He did the same with the others, his and theirs. He stopped looking tipsy. It was as if William's earnestness, his honesty, had sobered the big man.

"You tell her all that stuff you just told us," Patrice said. "I bet she'd at least consider it."

William nodded faintly. He reached into his pocket for his phone again.

"I can write you both a check if you want," he said. "But it would be even quicker if I just sent the funds to an account electronically. Do you want to do that?"

Apollo gave William his routing number and the account number. He and Patrice would split the profits after the money cleared.

William refreshed his phone's browser and stared at the number in his savings account, all zeros. "That's it then," he said softly. "If this doesn't get them back, I'm all tapped out." He set down the phone and held the wrapped book. "This paper is a nice touch."

Then, right there on the boat, William took one hiccupping breath and cried. After the surprise of it passed, both Apollo and Patrice brought a hand to William's back and patted him as he let his tears out.

FIRST THING YOU do when you get some money is pay off old debts. Don't buy anything new until your ledger is clear. Apollo learned that early in his career as a book man, and it remained a bit of gospel for him.

Which is how he ended up making plans to see Kim Valentine again.

The Mahayana Buddhist Temple is one of the most famous sights for tourists to visit in all of Chinatown. Two golden lions guard the red front doors, and inside sits the largest Buddha statue in all of New York City. Before it became the Mahayana Buddhist Temple, it had been the Rosemary Theater, a place that showed a steady rotation of kung fu movies and porn films.

In 2011 Kim asked Apollo and Emma to meet her at this temple when they'd agreed to take her on as their midwife. None of them were Buddhists, and when they arrived they were treated—appropriately—like any of the other million tourists who wandered through to gawk at the red and gold designs inside. They stood under the great golden Buddha, sixteen feet tall and perched on a lotus flower, his head ringed by a blue halo fashioned from neon tubing. They hadn't known if they were supposed to get on their knees, bow their heads, or what. Apollo, out of a very old habit, even made the sign of the cross.

Kim finally had to admit that meeting clients at a Buddhist temple just seemed kind of "holy" in a way that promised to offend none of her clients, all of them Westerners. Emma and Apollo had been the first ones to even question the meeting place. Feeling silly, they all went out to eat at a spot nearby called Tasty Dumpling, on Mulberry Street, the best dumpling spot in Chinatown. A good meal together felt even holier than the temple visit.

It was in this spirit—the warmth of those old times—that Apollo greeted Kim out in front of the temple. He stood next to one of the golden lions, making room for the tourists and actual practicing Buddhists moving in and out of the space. When Kim arrived, she seemed burned through, bone tired.

"I was up for two days," she admitted after they hugged. When she stepped back, she watched his face warily for a moment. "It's good to see you. Did you bring me here to yell at me?"

"I thought about it," Apollo said, trying to seem light but not sure if he quite pulled it off. "But I picked this place because it's a happy memory."

Kim leaned into him again, and the hug lasted longer this time.

"Do you want to go inside, or do you want to walk?" Apollo asked.

"It's kind of dark in there," Kim said. "I'm so tired I might fall asleep."

Apollo pointed over her shoulder toward the Manhattan Bridge. "Let's walk then," he said.

They crossed the street and stopped on the traffic island as five hundred cars took the on-ramp to the bridge. The grand arch and colonnade of the Manhattan Bridge appeared majestic even under decades of soot.

Kim looked pained for a moment before she spoke. "Triplets," she said, then caught herself and scanned Apollo. "Do you mind me talking about this?"

"It's okay."

"Triplets," she repeated. "Never had that many before. The couple used fertility treatments. It's kind of amazing how commonplace that kind of thing is now. I'm still amazed by it, and I see it all the time."

"Do you think it's a bad idea? Would you go back to the way it was?"

Kim opened her hands as if she held a baby in them now. "It means more life in the world," she said. "I'm a sucker for life."

"I wanted to pay you what we owed you." Apollo took out his wallet and found the check he'd written. "I'm sorry, it's postdated until Friday. That's when the money clears."

He held the check between two fingers, and it flapped there in the strong winds rolling off the East River. Kim couldn't have looked more confused. She shook her head, and her tired eyes turned even redder.

"In the end you didn't even need me. Emma did it herself. You did it together."

"Between you and that class, we were well trained," Apollo said. "And this is yours."

"Apollo," she said, but then seemed lost for anything more.

"I never found out her third wish," Apollo said, not really speaking to Kim.

Kim stepped toward him and put her arms around him. "I think you should know," she started. Her face stayed pressed close to his neck, and the traffic moved on and off the Manhattan Bridge. "It wasn't supposed to be like this," she said, crying openly now.

"But this is how it is."

They let go of each other. Apollo still held the check between his fingers, and finally Kim nodded and slipped it into her hand. She kissed his cheek once, and he watched her go.

"Goodbye, Valentines," Apollo whispered.

Apollo stayed there until long after Kim disappeared in the throngs of Canal Street. He turned back to the bridge. He liked the idea of walking it, crossing over water into Brooklyn. He jogged across the road and made it to the pedestrian footpath. He wasn't on it for two moments before his phone rattled in his pocket. After two more steps, the phone vibrated again. He stopped and looked down at the East River below him. For one moment he considered tossing the phone away, but then he succumbed to a much older technology, hardwired into the human brain: curiosity. He swiped his phone and found one new text message.

Emma Valentine is alive.

I can help you find her.

APOLLO STAYED THERE on the bridge for how long—twenty minutes, maybe more? He stared at the phone as if it would speak. Whose voice would he hear? He stayed there clutching at the phone and waiting while passersby skirted around him, huffing with aggravation because of the space he occupied. People on bikes rang their bells or shouted to let them pass, but Apollo only stared at his phone like a caveman who had just discovered fire. Then another text appeared.

Follow the map.

Just like that, a map opened on Apollo's screen. A grid appeared, and in a moment the contours of Chinatown were drawn in. A rendering of the Manhattan Bridge that mimicked an architectural plan, and on it a small blue dot that was Apollo's phone. Now a red blip appeared at the far edge of his screen.

Come to me.

At first Apollo thought the red dot marked a spot in Chinatown, but as his blue dot came closer to the red dot, the map on the phone rearranged the city, nudging the red dot farther north. Not Chinatown but Little Italy, not Little Italy but NoLita. Apollo held on to his phone, a hook reeling him toward the fisherman. He stepped into traffic four different times and received a chorus of horns. He slammed into countless people as he moved on the sidewalks, but if they cursed him, he never noticed. He left NoLita and entered the East Village. He walked west until he reached Washington Square Park. The blue dot and red dot nearly overlapped now.

The Washington Square Arch mirrored the arch at the Manhattan Bridge. But where the first had felt like the gateway to his escape— a chance to cross the waters—the Washington Square Arch only led him farther inland. As soon as he passed through the archway, the map on Apollo's phone closed. The application shut down, and he hadn't been the one to close it. Another text message.

I see you.

Apollo wondered if this would turn into torture. A scavenger hunt across all of Manhattan, led by some mastermind who'd reveal himself—or herself—only at the end of the long game. Apollo didn't have the patience for any bullshit like that.

Just tell me where the fuck you are or I'm leaving, he texted back.

The phone vibrated.

Sorry! I'm by the fountains.

An apologetic mastermind. That was a nice surprise.

47

ILLIAM WHEELER STOOD by the large old fountain waving his cellphone like a ramp service agent guiding a plane on the runway.

"William?" Apollo said once they were close enough to talk. He'd honestly been expecting it to be Kim, or maybe Patrice. Even Lillian, but not this near-stranger who'd recently paid an enormous sum of money for a book. What if this turned out to be some intricate, perverse way to request a refund? Another flash of showmanship on William's part.

"Mr. Kagwa," William said. "Apollo. I'm sorry to see you again like this."

It was too loud here, and too many people passed through. The mass of bodies bumping Apollo built a kinetic charge inside his body. Strange to be drawn all the way to the West Village by a cryptic message; even stranger to find William fucking Wheeler standing here, and now all these people kept bumping and tussling, and it made Apollo feel like he needed to do something epic and thoughtless. If they didn't move from this crowded park, Apollo realized he was going to hit William. He grabbed William at the elbow and shoved him through the crowd. He pushed him forward as if the man were a plow.

"Sorry," William muttered to people. "So sorry. My apologies!"

They crossed Washington Square North and stood by a block of beautifully maintained redbrick row houses that existed in almost direct opposition to the reality of Washington Square Park. Where the park practically seethed with vitality and chaos, the row houses were as ordered as rare books in a private library. Foot traffic fell off, too. Apollo's temper came under control.

He let go of William's arm, lifted his phone, and shook it at him. "What the fuck is this?" he asked.

William, for his part, seemed to be out of breath, or maybe just scared. He touched his elbow gingerly.

Apollo stepped closer. "What is with those texts," he asked, his tone stony.

"I know this has got to be pretty mysterious," William said. "I didn't mean to get cloak and dagger about it."

"Do you really know that Emma is alive?"

William leaned back against the low wrought-iron railing that protected the row houses from the sidewalk. "I do. I swear."

"Why didn't you tell me when we talked at the Dunkin' Donuts? Or on the boat?"

William shook his head. "I didn't know then. I only just found out. I only just wanted to find out."

"Why?"

"After meeting you," he said. "Talking with you. I mean, you go to those group meetings to deal with . . . what happened to you. That's hard enough, but then some woman jumps up and starts saying all sorts of crazy stuff to you? It's not right."

William spread his arms, hands extended, as if to show he carried no weapons, no malice. "I guess I thought I'd do what I could to help you."

"The FBI and NYPD couldn't find her," Apollo said. The phone in his hand felt as heavy as a brick.

William rose from the fence. He looked up and down the block as if scanning for eavesdroppers. "There was a time when the police were your only resource. If they couldn't find your wife, then no one could. But that's not true anymore, Apollo. A hundred people with a hundred computers across the country can cover as much ground. And if those hundred people really *care* about what happens? They'll work on it day and night.

They won't stop. And that's what they did when I told them I wanted to help you."

"You told other people about all this?"

"Only my friends," William said. "People I could trust. People who cared."

Apollo felt slightly dizzy. "So where is she then?" Had he asked the question out loud? Apollo couldn't be sure.

"She's on an island in the East River."

Suddenly, magically, Apollo was sitting on the sidewalk. He hadn't actually expected William to say anything so specific. Or for her to be so close. William put out his hand and helped Apollo up. A handful of people passed by but paid them no attention.

"How do I get there?" Apollo said.

"You need a boat," William said.

"I don't have a fucking boat."

William pulled out his phone. He swiped a screen, and another. He tapped the little icon of a dinghy. "There's an app for that."

"Let's go to the Bat Cave."

The Bat Cave was the spare bedroom in Patrice's basement apartment. The moment after Apollo separated from William Wheeler, he called Patrice and asked to come by. Again, it took almost two hours to get to the apartment. Dana let Apollo in. She seemed skittish, wouldn't meet his eyes.

"I'm glad you called my mom," Apollo told her. "I know you were trying to help."

As soon as he said this, she relaxed and offered to warm up some dinner for him, but Apollo had no appetite. Dana stared into Apollo's face—his furiously vibrant eyes—and understood something had come up, much bigger than a rare book. Then Patrice led them both to the Bat Cave.

Such a small room, this spare bedroom. It seemed even smaller because of the wood paneling. The dull walls ate the light, leaving the room in gloom. The shaggy brown carpeting didn't help. It was like being inside a Wookiee's armpit. And poor Patrice, the ceiling couldn't have been more than six and a half feet high. If he went on his tiptoes, his head would go through the ceiling panels. With Patrice, Dana, and Apollo all together in here, it felt like they were stuck in a broom closet.

Not to mention the other behemoth lined up against one wall.

"I give you Titan," Patrice said, with the reverence of a rabbi opening his synagogue's ark to reveal the Torah scrolls.

"Thirty-two gigabytes of DDR3-1866 RAM, 4.7 gigahertz processing speed, an Intel Core i7-3970x processor, storage capacity of two *terabytes*, a 16x Asus DVD-RW drive, three 27-inch display monitors, and I even got a mouse that's shaped like a grenade."

Dana went to a corner, under the room's one small window, where they had a space heater. She turned a knob on the edge, and the heater buzzed faintly, and then the coils inside glowed orange.

When Patrice turned the computer on, the three—three!—large monitors burned bright blue for just a moment as the system booted up. It felt as if Apollo was standing behind a military jet and its three engines were about to spit fire. He actually stepped backward.

Dana put one arm out and stopped him from moving any farther. "You don't want to set your pants on fire, do you?" she asked, pointing down at the space heater, the glowing coils. Then she reached out and took Apollo's left hand in hers. "What's this?" She touched his middle finger. A piece of red string had been tied around it.

"It was Emma's," Apollo said. "I had time after I called Patrice. I went home. I found this."

"And you put it on?" Dana asked.

"I tied it on and made a wish," Apollo told her. "Just one wish."

Dana scanned up from the finger to Apollo's eyes. "I don't want to know what you wished for."

"No," Apollo said, pulling his hand free. "You don't."

Patrice cleared his throat theatrically so Apollo would turn back to him and his computer.

"You and me are old enough to remember that *War Games* movie, right? Ferris Bueller was in it. This rack right here is more powerful than that whole fucking supercomputer. That shit was so big, they had to hide it in a mountain! Mine fits in the spare bedroom of a basement apartment in Queens."

On the center screen, a small box demanded a passcode. Patrice leaned over to type, but before he did, he blocked the keyboard from Apollo and Dana's view.

Apollo looked to Dana. She leaned close. "I know the password any-way."

"No you don't," Patrice snapped back. "I change it once a week."

Dana slapped him gently on the head. "But then you have to write it in your phone because you can't remember it because you change it every week."

Patrice sat up straight in his chair. "So you saying you go through my phone?"

Dana patted Apollo's arm. "Let's stay on topic here. Apollo needs our help."

Patrice sighed and turned back to the computer. This incredibly pow-erful system sat on a silver-powder-coated metal computer desk that cost $78.89 at Lowe's.

Dana got to her feet, holding a serving tray in one hand. She went to Patrice and touched his shoulder gently. He leaned back and puckered his lips; she leaned close and kissed him.

Patrice cleared his throat. "Now, did this dude have any actual proof Emma was alive?" He gestured to a metal folding chair leaning against a wall.

"He sent me a video," Apollo said, slipping his phone out of his pocket. "But my phone can't play it."

Patrice looked at the device with a grimace. "It's in Flash, I guess. You could download a Puffin Browser to get around that. Or you could just jailbreak your phone."

While Apollo knew that Patrice had just spoken three sentences in English, there was very little chance he'd understood even one of them. He lifted the phone higher, closer to Patrice's face. "My phone won't play it," he repeated.

"Just forward it to me."

Patrice watched as Apollo did this. Meanwhile Dana slipped the serv-ing tray under the space heater, a fireguard between the machine and the cheap carpet.

"The good news is that I did my due diligence on William Wheeler before we sold him the book."

Apollo looked up from his phone. "Like a background check?"

"We were about to sell him the most expensive book either of us will probably ever come across. Damn right I wanted to be sure he was at least using his real name!"

Apollo hit send on the phone. "And?"

"William Webster Wheeler. Owns a house in Forest Hills, on 86th Road. He served in the air force as a programming specialist for two years in the early eighties. After that he worked in Charleston for the Medical University of South Carolina until 1996. Then he started making his way back to the Northeast. He was born in Levittown. And he's been working as an application developer for a financial services company."

"Damn," Apollo said. "You really did snoop."

Patrice patted his belly with pride. "Want to know how much money he's got in his checking account?"

"You know that, too?"

"I'm just bullshitting. But if I wanted to find out, I could. Me and the Titan." He patted his keyboard as if it were a lion's paw. "But at least the dude is who he says he is. That means something these days. You sent me that video yet?"

Patrice didn't wait for an answer, just opened his browser.

"He'll get a boat for tomorrow night," Apollo said. "Promised to drive me out on the river and drop me off if we can find the right island. There are only nine in the East River, and I've already spent two months on one of them. So that leaves eight."

"But why is this guy helping you?" Dana asked, leaning against Patrice's shoulder. "What does it matter to him?"

The space heater's coiled rods glowed so brightly now, they almost looked red.

"That's why I wanted to come to Patrice before I went. Maybe Wheeler's sympathetic. Maybe he's out of his mind. Maybe he's planning to shoot me and dump my body in the water."

"Maybe all three," Dana said.

"But it doesn't matter. If she's alive, I want to find her." He held up his hand and brushed the red string with his thumb again. "I want to find her."

"And you'll bring her to the police?" Dana asked.

"No," Apollo said. "That's not what I'll do."

Patrice flashed a look at Apollo, then turned back, clicked on the email.

"This looks like camera footage from off the street," Patrice said. "Like NYPD surveillance shit. CCTV type of stuff. This dude's friends did some serious digging."

Patrice clicked play. He expanded the box until it filled about a quarter of the screen. The same screen played on all three monitors. Patrice, Dana, and Apollo crowded close to each other and watched.

APOLLO WATCHED A ghost on Patrice Green's computer
screen. Three months since he'd last seen her alive, and now
here she was.

The ghost of Emma Valentine walked freely down some
Manhattan avenue. Hard to say exactly where, much farther downtown
than Washington Heights, in the valley of skyscrapers, close to Wall Street.
She moved amid the foot traffic. If people saw her, they didn't act like it.
They moved around her as if she was a cloud of bad atmosphere. Apollo
could see people actually turning away as she moved by them. Looking
anywhere but at her. People pulled out their phones rather than putting
their eyes on her. Was this purposeful or just some natural allergy to Emma's haunted presence? In this way she walked unseen.

She wore a long winter jacket that came all the way down to her ankles. It really looked as though she glided down the sidewalks, across the
streets.

Was it the same day that she'd killed Brian?

When one camera lost her, another kicked in, from a new angle, farther down the block. This wasn't a continuous shot but a series of them,
cut together by William Wheeler and his hundred friends. At times Emma
had just left the shot, at times she hadn't quite entered. This gave the feeling that Apollo was stalking after her now. Like she might be walking this

route, in downtown New York City, right this minute. Only the time stamp in the corner of the screen reminded him this was old news.

The skyscrapers fell away as Emma approached open water. Now Apollo knew where she was. South Street Seaport. She walked to Pier 16, location of the New York Water Taxi. The location of their last date night as a happy couple. Apollo had been the one to take her there. Was this how she'd known where to find it, and how late at night it still ran? He felt punched in the throat. This was how she had escaped Manhattan Island? For the cost of an access pass? Thirty dollars to disappear.

But where would she even get the money? When she slammed a hammer into the side of his face, she hadn't seemed in the right mind to remember her wallet.

Emma waited on the pier. A mass of others, tourists, kids in their twenties, crowded the line for the next trip. And from out of the crowd appeared one woman. This woman walked up to Emma directly and put her arms around her, though Emma remained stiff in the embrace. When the water taxi arrived, the woman let go of Emma and led her to the end of the long line. They waited patiently until they reached the taxi. The woman flashed two passes, and then the pair climbed on board.

Apollo watched in awed humiliation as the water taxi pulled away from the pier.

Of course, he'd recognized the woman who helped Emma escape. He'd just been with her in Chinatown. That morning he'd given her a check for ten thousand dollars.

Patrice and Dana recognized Kim, too. Neither one of them would look at Apollo—they only dropped their heads.

Meanwhile Apollo took out his phone. He texted William.

I need that boat.

I want your help.

50

RIAN WEST WAS at the front door. Apollo heard him knocking from the living room. Apollo walked to the door, and the knocking only grew louder. He reached his hand in the air and turned all three locks of the apartment door. A man stood in the hallway. It wasn't Brian West yet. This man's face looked blue. He had no nose or mouth, only eyes. He pushed his way inside. The man knelt down in front of Apollo and pulled off his blue skin. Underneath it was his daddy's face. Apollo smiled and hugged Brian West. Brian West held his son tight. Brian West shut the door and locked it. Brian West walked through the apartment calling Lillian Kagwa's name. Brian West went into the bathroom and turned on the shower. Hot water ran in the tub. Apollo sat with his father on the couch in the living room and together they watched TV. *The Smurfs.*

On the television, an old man in a long black cloak cackled in his laboratory; a maroon cat perched on a tabletop snickered along. What were their names again? Gargamel and Azrael. They wanted to destroy the Smurfs.

The hot water ran in the bathroom for so long that steam filled the room. Soon the steam crept down the hallway. A fog filled the living room.

On the television the Smurfs sang together. They didn't see Gargamel and Azrael were hiding in the woods waiting to pounce.

Brian West stood and picked Apollo up. He held the boy tightly. He said, "You're coming with me."

He walked into the mist.

CHILD'S PLAY WAS docked at the Locust Point Yacht Club in the Bronx. Why was it in the Bronx instead of Long Island? Well, a round-trip rental turned into a one way, and then the card used for billing turned out to be a card reported stolen, and things only got messier from there. William didn't sound too pleased, but still he agreed to help Apollo. William thought they'd better travel under cover of night because their route might be too conspicuous to Coast Guard or NYPD boats during the day. William texted an address and meeting time and a smiley face emoji.

Apollo spent that whole day inside his place, and only a near-mythic level of self-restraint kept him from traveling out to Brooklyn to find Kim Valentine and burn her building to the ground. But if Kim could squirrel her sister away from the city just hours after Emma murdered her own child, then why wouldn't she warn Emma now? Even if he showed up with a phalanx of FBI agents and police, what would stop Kim from sending one last message to her sister? *RUN*. Apollo had to weigh the short-term satisfaction of confronting his sister-in-law against the chance of finding Emma on that island. Really there was no contest. So he stayed away from Kim. The only revenge he took was to call his bank and cancel the check he'd written her. Small consolation.

He tried watching movies, but he couldn't watch movies. He tried to eat but couldn't taste a damn thing. He checked online to find the next Survivors meeting—it would be at the JCC of Staten Island. He marked that he'd be attending. He'd claim there'd been some mix-up if his PO asked, but at least he'd have shown the intent to go. But being online, and with hours to wait until he met William, only led Apollo back to the "Tribute to Baby Brian" page. As soon as he got there, he told himself to log off. As he scrolled through the comments, he told himself to log off. He did not log off.

Which is how he came across a comment, posted just the day before, by a prolific poster who used the name Kinder Garten. Another obviously fake account. Really only Kinder Garten and Green Hair Harry posted with any regularity anymore. Kinder Garten wrote terrible shit. Cruel. The newest post might've been the worst one yet:

"Dinner plans tonight. A meal inspired by Baby Brian. BOILED VEGETABLES!"

That was it. That was enough.

Apollo logged off.

Locust Point Yacht Club sounds pretty damn fancy, but its members were not what some might expect. Mechanics and truck drivers; building supers and nurse technicians. The club sat behind a tall, rusted gate. The words LOCUST POINT YACHT CLUB were painted in red letters on the side of a gray railing just inside the fence line. The clubhouse looked like a crab shack. Weeds grew up through a boat hull that had been abandoned in the dirt. A series of old fishing boats bobbed and bopped in the water. William Wheeler stood on the deck of the *Child's Play*. He waved his cellphone, and in the dark the bright display glowed like a lantern. William helped Apollo onboard, and then he turned on the engines.

"There's a life jacket on top of the livewell," William said. When Apollo only watched him quietly, he pointed to the stern. "There at the back."

Apollo grabbed his life jacket, and the boat's engine guzzled and chugged. Apparently this was a good sound.

William returned to the console. "Now you're going to cast off the bow and stern lines. There and there. Untie them from the dock. Current's pushing us away from the dock, so that should be all we need to do."

William said it and it was so. The boat drifted as the engine idled. Once the boat had floated an arm's length from the dock, William shifted and slowly left the shoreline.

"You made that seem pretty easy," Apollo said.

William looked back and laughed softly. "You remember how hard it is for me to lie? Come here."

Apollo joined him at the console, an iPad perched beside the gauges. William let go of the throttle and tapped the screen. A video began. Silly synthesizer music played, then a woman in a striped black and white shirt appeared.

"Welcome and congratulations on joining the wonderful world of boating," she said. "I'm going to take you through the steps of casting off from a dock. First be sure . . ."

William tapped the screen, and the woman stopped midsentence. "I've been here since about noon," he said. "Teaching myself how to drive a boat."

"Thank you," Apollo said quietly. "Really. Thank you."

William waved off the words, half sheepish and half proud. He guided the sloop into Hammond Creek. They'd have to ride out past SUNY Maritime College, on the tip of the Bronx, then come back around, under the Throgs Neck Bridge to enter the East River. The lights of the Bronx receded behind them, and in the far distance Long Island's low-slung landmass appeared as a far shadow in the night. Apollo scanned that distance and thought he saw, for an instant, a green light, but he turned away from it, dismissing it as an illusion. He faced forward instead. The sound of their engine emptied into the dark, open sky.

"We could still turn back," William said. He sounded as if he hoped Apollo would say yes.

Apollo didn't speak to William. That's all the answer he would get. As they chugged forward, Apollo raised his left hand. He wore the red string on his middle finger and his wedding ring on the next. He turned his wedding ring twice, and then, with a twist, he pulled it off. He casually tossed the ring into the river. The red string his only vow now.

THE THROGS NECK Bridge lit up like a constellation, it loomed like a god. Both Apollo and William held their breath as they approached it. William cut the motor low. Apollo felt, viscerally, why ancient people stood in awe before mountains and glaciers. To strain your neck, looking up that high, and realize you weren't seeing all of it, couldn't see all of it. The instinct to worship overcame him, and he lowered his head until they'd passed under the bridge. Once they did, William kicked the motor higher, and they continued.

"Let me ask you something," William said. Wind made his hair fly back from his face, so Apollo could see his bright eyes. "Did you tell anyone we were coming here?"

"I told Patrice you were getting us a boat," Apollo admitted.

"You need to see something then," he said.

Still holding the steering wheel with one hand, William tapped at the iPad again. The server loaded slowly. Understandable since there wasn't much coverage on the East River. Eventually the Facebook app opened, right to the Baby Brian page.

So William did know about it. When had he found out?

William scrolled down. "There," he said, pointing to a new post.

Stay safe on them open waters! Our wish is that you come home safe.

The post had been left by Green Hair Harry.

"Patrice?" Apollo whispered.

"And then there's this," William said.

No words, just an image. A picture of a big ship sinking into the sea. The *Titanic*. This post left by Kinder Garten.

"You share some information with your friend," William said, pointing back at the Green Hair Harry post. "Then some stranger sees it, and he trolls you. I'm sure Mr. Green meant to show you support, but anyone on the page gets to see his post." He tapped at Kinder Garten's image of the sinking ship. "I'm out here with you, so I have a selfish reason for showing you this. We have to be careful. There are no secrets anymore. Vampires can't come into your house unless you invite them. Posting online is like leaving your front door open and telling any creature of the night it can enter."

Rikers Island is beautiful after the sun goes down. New York City's 413-acre jail complex, home to an inmate population of about twelve thousand prisoners, goes almost entirely dark at night. Only one building remains open for late-night intake, and all the rest of the island seems to shut down. Apollo remembered the lights out at nine o'clock. The prisoners sent to bed, but nobody sleeping. He expected the place to see him, sense him somehow, a dog sniffing out its old prey. Apollo watched the silhouette of the island as they passed. He might've missed it if the one building weren't lit up. It cast a weak, misty glow across the island. So strange to see it from here and know that only two weeks ago he'd been inside. As they moved closer, Apollo heard the shouts and cries of the inmates. The men were too far off for the words to be intelligible, so only a phantom howl carried across the water.

Now the surface of the water looked as supple as sculpted ice. Cold wind skipped across the river, and there was nothing in the boat to protect them. They were on the water for a while, but Apollo lost his sense of time. Apollo drew his hat low and hunched down in the stern of the boat where he could watch William, who stayed at the console.

Patrice Green was Green Hair Harry. He'd admitted to being a fan of the damn page but never mentioned he'd started it. No doubt he'd have some elaborate explanation as to why he'd kept this secret, but what did Apollo care? Everyone had a reason. Everyone had a disguise.

"There's an island," William shouted over the sound of the motor. He lowered the engine. "I did some research, but I don't think I read about this one."

Strange to call this an island, no more than one hundred feet by, maybe, two hundred. A pile of rocks with two or three bushes and what looked like a modest metal radio tower.

William leaned close to the iPad. "This must be U Thant Island. It's an artificial island. Well, how do you like that, it's named after a Burmese secretary general of the United Nations. Let me see what else it says here."

Apollo didn't want to listen to William reading some Wikipedia entry aloud. The only thing that mattered was that Emma wasn't there. Even in the deep of night, it was easy to tell. There was literally nowhere to hide but those two scraggly bushes.

"Let's move on," Apollo said.

"What's that?" William asked. "Oh, right. Right."

He powered the engine up, slightly, and they puttered off.

"There's not that many islands out here," William said. "Rikers we passed. U Thant, too. Roosevelt Island is residential, Randalls and Wards Islands are state parks, people use them all the time. I don't know if she'd hide out in any of them. Too risky."

"There," Apollo said. He spoke so softly William didn't hear him.

"We could try Mill Rock," William continued. "It's unpopulated, but the Parks Department uses it for events sometimes so I don't know. I think we must've been going up and down this river for longer than I realized. I'm pretty much lost, Apollo."

"There!" Apollo said, louder this time, standing despite the cold wind.

An island, draped in a shroud. Not fog but a shadow darker than even the night sky cloaked the land. No lights anywhere on the rock, hard to see more than the suggestion of a tree line even while staring directly at it.

"Oh my," William said, already lowering the engine. "I would've gone right past it. It's like it was hiding. Or hidden. How did you catch it, Apollo?"

"I wasn't staring at an iPad."

"I'll beach us," William said, sounding hurt but trying to hide it.

He brought the boat within ten feet of the beachhead, then cut the engine completely. The bow slowed as it lodged in the sand below the waterline. Apollo and William both crouched so they wouldn't fall overboard. With the boat beached, the engine off, Apollo heard the river dappling at the hull.

"I think I was supposed to stop farther out and pull the boat in the last few feet," William said. He walked to the front of the boat and hopped out. The water came up to his thigh. He walked backward until he was out of the water and stood on the small beach.

Behind him Apollo could now see clearly that the island thrived with plant life, a chaos of shrubs and trees. Apollo climbed down from the boat and waded into the cold water.

"Ready?" William asked, but his voice hardly reached a whisper.

"You don't have to come along," Apollo told him. "You've already done more for me than . . . anyone."

"Honestly," William said with a soft laugh. "I'm more scared of waiting out here on the boat alone."

"Okay," Apollo said. "All right then." He looked down at his left hand. The moonlight caught the red string. It seemed to throb against his skin, or maybe that was only his flushing blood. "Let's roll."

"I GREW UP WITH a guy who grew up to be a detective," William said.

Nighttime, Apollo and William were hardly a dozen steps into the fringe of the bush. Apollo could still hear the East River slapping at the hull of the sloop, though the brush was so tall he couldn't see the vessel anymore.

William moved as slowly as Apollo, no more sure of where to plant his feet, where to set his hands. The underbrush had grown so high, it looked as if they were wading. The trees huddled so close, William had to turn sideways and shuffle between them.

Then the trees cleared, as if they'd passed a fence line, and now William pointed at something growing about three feet out of the ground. In the starlight the thing looked like a giant mushroom covered in kudzu. If a caterpillar had been perched on it puffing a hookah, it wouldn't have seemed impossible. William pulled out his phone, adjusted his glasses, and found a flashlight app. He crouched and tapped the phone against the mushroom. There was a faint metallic clunk.

Apollo knelt beside William. "That's a fire hydrant," he said.

"I know where we are," William said. "This must be North Brother Island."

William didn't consult his device this time. He could recite the history from memory.

"North Brother Island remained uninhabited until 1885, when River-side Hospital was established to treat victims of smallpox. In time the hospital treated victims of other quarantinable diseases. After World War II, the island became housing for war veterans. And in the fifties it became a treatment center for drug addicts, though it eventually closed because of corruption among the staff."

William moved the phone's spotlight over the hydrant.

"In that time the hospital grew to include the original treatment center, a library, dorms for the staff, a chapel, a foundry, a stockhouse and a coal storage house, a doctor's cottage, a recreation center, and a morgue. It even had sidewalks and roads."

Apollo and William didn't realize it, but they were already walking on concrete, only inches below the overgrowth. North Brother Island housed a small town that had been reclaimed by the earth. If it had been daylight, they would've already spotted a few of the larger derelict buildings, but for now those were camouflaged by the night and vegetation. So they stayed by the fire hydrant, marveling at it as if they'd unearthed a spaceship.

William's phone beeped twice, faintly, and the flashlight app winked out to save power.

"You really did do your research," Apollo whispered in the dark.

"I told you, I was on the boat since noon," William said, straining a bit as he pushed himself up from a crouch. "I had time to read."

They walked again, using the overgrown hydrant as a sightline. In this way, with a fixed point behind him, Apollo hoped to save them from becoming lost.

Apollo's footing seemed surer now. He moved closer to William, walking in step but looking ahead.

"Why are you here really?" Apollo asked. "Don't give me this 'I just want to help' bullshit."

They kicked through the underbrush a few minutes more. Apollo felt himself still reeling from the recent revelations. Lillian, Kim, and now Patrice. If William was only tagging along so he could upload a video of his adventures to his YouTube channel, get a billion hits, and start making money from page views, then Apollo would rather just know it now instead of finding out when someone emailed him a link in a few weeks. At this point he felt so exhausted with people that he wouldn't even be angry about it. William had at least helped him get here.

"Gretta said no."

Apollo stopped moving. "Your wife?"

A long, deep sigh from William. "Maybe five years ago she might've been charmed. Ten years ago. But now? She told me to keep the book. She didn't want it." William went quiet. "If I wasn't here with you on this island, I'd be at home in my basement going nuts. At least this is something. It's insane, but at least I'm not alone."

Apollo stood beside William quietly for a minute or three.

"So can I come with you?" William asked.

"I'm going in here to fuck some shit up. You do whatever you want to do."

They walked again.

The immediate dangers they faced now were the little pockets of the modern world that had been introduced on the island. An open utility shaft, for instance, could send them falling twenty feet in the dark. A portion of a brick wall might choose that moment to collapse, hidden within creeping vines right up until it crushed them.

"You see lights over that way?" Apollo asked.

Firelight, not electric light. To the south and floating in the air.

"Will-o'-the-wisp," William said softly, watching them, too.

Apollo's eyes adjusted to the sight, and he realized he was seeing a small fire burning on the second floor of a two-story building. The entire wall facing Apollo had fallen away long ago, so it was like looking inside a diorama. He couldn't see anyone by the fire, but who else could have set it? Emma. Surviving alone on this island all this time. He never expected he'd actually find her. Nervous electricity shot down the back of his skull. If he was honest, it was the same charge he'd felt before their first date. In a moment William and Apollo were no longer walking together. Apollo Kagwa broke into a run.

B Y 1981 THE smallpox patients had been long gone from North Brother Island. The war veterans evacuated, the drug addicts no longer treated there. The island became known only as a nesting colony for the black-crowned night heron. Smallish, unassuming-looking birds that spend hours and hours clicking at each other, then stumble into asthmatic squawking when the mood hits. The night herons ruled the island for over twenty years, but in the early part of the twenty-first century, they abandoned it. The reason for their departure remained unknown, a bit of birder curiosity at best, nothing news making.

Tonight Apollo Kagwa discovered why the black-crowned night herons had left. They'd been displaced.

Women and children had returned to North Brother Island.

They weren't in the Tuberculosis Pavilion, the largest and still most structurally sound edifice on the island. Instead they'd moved into the Nurses' Residence, a four-story U-shaped Gothic Revival building large enough to house 125 nurses when it was completed in 1904. Natural forces destroyed the windows long ago, but the women and children had begun repairs. Apollo could see firelight licking and flickering against the clear plastic that had been thrown up in the window frames. The building he'd seen from a distance still carried that fire on the second floor, but now it looked more like a signal light than a dwelling, a fixed point that would help people make their way back to this place. Base camp.

Apollo stood at the edge of a cleared courtyard. Across it stood the Nurses' Residence, next to that the Doctor's Cottage, the building with a fallen facade. In the near-darkness, Apollo could make out some people. Women moved in pairs or alone between the two buildings. Here and there children peeked out at the night through the clear plastic window-panes. He might as well have stumbled across a village in the American wilderness back in 1607.

How could all this be happening so close to New York City? Apollo's apartment lay less than four miles from this exact spot. A short boat ride had landed him on the shores of an island out of a fairy tale. He watched these women and children with a sense of awe that bordered on terror.

Apollo didn't bother to consult William about what to do next. He didn't even consult himself. He walked out of the shadows and into the courtyard. He just stepped out into the open.

This isn't to say he was fearless. Actually he could hardly breathe because of the hiccupping breaths rising up in his constricted throat. To calm down, he talked to himself. The mantra. If he said it enough times he might believe it.

"I am the god, Apollo," he whispered.

He spoke so softly he hardly even heard himself.

"I am the god Apollo," he said, louder now.

He couldn't stop the volume from rising. He felt the wildness, a crazed energy, refusing to be contained. Another term for this is *panic*.

He reached the Nurses' Residence. The building had no front door. He climbed the front steps as quickly as his quaking legs allowed.

"I am the god Apollo!" he shouted this time. "And I want my revenge!"

Apollo had been spotted as soon as he stepped out from the overgrown kudzu. Four women appeared in the courtyard. Each one carried a chair leg that had been fashioned into a weapon, a club. The clubs had a leather strap looped through the base and the other end looped around their wrists. The women wore green cloaks that covered their heads and upper bodies like a chador. This camouflaged them perfectly in the green world of North Brother Island. As they moved around Apollo, it looked as if the woods had surrounded him. He didn't hear them approach, didn't notice as their clubs raised high.

Those four women beat the dog shit out of Apollo Kagwa.

55

KNOCKING SOMEONE UNCONSCIOUS is incredibly difficult. Apollo wished it was easier. Instead he found himself battered for a two-minute period that felt like twenty years, and he never passed out. The women attacking him were very good at their job. They weren't hitting him in the head because they didn't want to knock him out. Instead they were battering his arms and legs so he'd be incapacitated quickly. They didn't want him swinging wild or kicking at them, getting hold of a baton. If he'd brought a knife or a gun, he couldn't use it if both arms were numb. They hit him so hard, his arms and legs seemed to freeze, go cold with shock. Before he understood he'd been attacked, he'd already been defeated. He went to the ground as if he'd been tasered.

On his back he saw nothing. His eyes didn't work. He thought they might've beaten him until he'd gone blind. This confused him even more than the pain. He'd been beaten senseless. He was useless now, and the women knew it. He rolled off the stairs and down to the courtyard floor, where they left him on the ground like a rolled-up length of carpet.

The women set their clubs down on the ground. They brought the table legs together until they were in a rectangle shape, four right angles. The bottom of each leg slipped through the strap of the adjacent one until they formed a makeshift stretcher. They rolled Apollo over so he lay facedown on the stretcher. Then each woman grabbed the end of a chair leg, and with a collective grunt they lifted him. It was as if they were doing a fireman's carry but using the chair legs in place of their arms.

. The stretcher was just large enough to heft his torso. His arms and head dangled, and his legs dragged behind. The four-woman team took him away from the courtyard. All this took a minute and fifty seconds. They were a well-coordinated crew. The front windows of the Nurses' Residence filled with children's faces, and the Doctor's Cottage showed women watching, too. A third building overlooked the courtyard, a two-story brick building known, plainly, as the School. Only one room was lit in the School, and its glow was supplied by electricity. A figure stood at the windowsill and saw Apollo being carried away. She watched for far longer than anyone else.

The smell of wet dirt; the sound of insects in the trees; footfalls of the four women carrying him through the underbrush; the taste of blood in his mouth. Before Apollo's vision returned, his other senses helped him understand his situation.

"I'm here," he mumbled.

"Well, don't we know it?" one of the women answered. He couldn't say which one.

"He's *here*," another said. "I think he expects us to applaud."

How far had they come from the courtyard, from the little colony in the woods? The wild growth surrounded them, but the women walked him on a well-worn path. The kudzu and porcelain berry had been stamped down not cut.

"I'm here," Apollo said again, "for my wife."

"Are you here to apologize and beg forgiveness?" a third woman asked, sounding slightly winded and clearly sarcastic.

"Or did you mean to kill her?" asked the fourth, and when she said the words, his whole body tensed, and the women laughed together like people long hardened from a war.

"I want my revenge!" shouted the first.

"She took my child!" added the second.

"She made me suffer!" hissed the third.

"Her blood is owed to me!" came the fourth.

Now they didn't laugh but clucked their tongues. They seemed so unsurprised. Apollo wondered how many times these four women had made the same journey with a man who'd appeared on the island. Maybe this was how the path beneath them had come to be beaten down so well; back and forth with the bodies of the men. And where would this path end?

He tried to throw himself off the stretcher. The wooden beams were digging into his chest and stomach. A new sound came to him, the splash of the women's feet as they entered water. Cold water slapped his face and neck.

"Where are you taking me!" he shouted.

"We're here," one of them said matter-of-factly.

"Who was the last one?" another asked. "I forget."

"Kauffman?" said another, but she didn't sound entirely sure.

"Yeah. He's at the bottom of the East River with General Slocum's Gold."

They laughed together, as if they were discussing an old friend.

Before Apollo could really piece together the change from wilderness to water's edge, he felt his body being lowered, submerged; two hands on the back of his head pushed his face underwater, the cold another kind of attack. The water was even darker than the night sky had been. He felt the wooden clubs slip away, and his whole body went under. They were drowning him. He opened his mouth involuntarily and swallowed and, surprisingly, that saved his life.

His reaction to swallowing the water was so violent that it revitalized his entire body. He had no idea what he was doing, but he had the power of ten men with which to do it. Drowning someone is even tougher than knocking them out. He thrashed and flailed, and despite their best efforts, he struggled himself free. The pressure on the back of his head slipped away. He gasped and gasped. He shouted something, not words. He caught two breaths, and the women were on him again. They pushed him back under, but now he faced them, so he grabbed at two and dragged them down into the water as well. They surfaced, and he never let go. By saving themselves, they saved him. He didn't fight them, not really, but he clung to them ferociously. Apollo got his feet under him, felt cool air on his head and rushed for land.

They tackled him before he'd made it three feet, but it didn't matter. He'd made it far enough to grasp at gnarled roots in the dirt, and he wouldn't let go. The women's clothing had served as camouflage in the woods, but now the robes were wet and weighed the women down. Finally they just piled on top of him. Five people heaving and wheezing in the sand.

"How could you protect her?" Apollo asked when he had enough breath to speak. "Emma killed my baby! And you protect her!"

The pressure against his legs and back became lighter, little by little, as each woman rose. They turned him over. One of his hands stayed gripping a root in case they tried to pull him back into the water again. He looked up at them. They watched him silently. He couldn't make out their faces because the moonlight was behind them. Four faceless figures loomed over him in the dark.

"You're Emma's," one of them said.

A second looked up at the sky and groaned. "Of course he is. She was a pain in the ass. Why wouldn't her husband be one, too?"

"Quiet with that," the first one said sharply.

One of the others leaned close and pawed through Apollo's pockets. She came out with his keys. She turned and stepped into the water. The sounds of faint splashing could be heard, and then she returned.

"His wallet fell out in the river. Just a bunch of cards and stuff floating around."

"Bury them," the first one said. "What about his cellphone?"

"I didn't see it in the water."

"Check him again."

Two of the women lifted him, and a third checked every pocket and ran her hands along his legs, inside the waistband. No phone. Now the women let the chair legs dangle down from their wrists, gripped the handles, and stepped four paces back from him. He stood, at risk of tipping over, but they didn't help him.

"Cal will want to see you," one woman said. She pointed to the path they'd just come down. "You know the way."

Apollo wobbled as he walked, but none of them offered support. It was only on the trek back that he had the presence of mind, the calm, to look around and realize he was alone with these women. They'd caught him but not William. He felt as if he had one last card lying facedown on the table. One last card to play. What would William Wheeler do?

THEY LED APOLLO back but it took awhile. You don't just rebound from the kind of beating he'd taken. He looked as if he'd been flogged, which, in fact, he had. When they reached the courtyard, a deep silence met them. The fire that had been burning was extinguished; only the electric light in the School remained on. Apollo had the feeling that the entire Nurses' Residence had been emptied. The same with the Doctor's Cottage. He imagined the entire population had been ferried out while they'd been trying to murder him at the river. Maybe they had bomb shelter protocols, tornado basement procedures, places they went when a force of great destruction arrived. He imagined all those women and children tucked into some dark, airless bunker and wondered at the idea that they'd fled because of him. This didn't make him feel powerful. Instead it gave him a different perspective on what had just happened. A strange man showed up in the middle of the night screaming that he was a god, demanding vengeance on his wife. Why wouldn't these women and children be terrified?

Two of the women took him by the arms and guided him toward the School. The lighted room on the second floor looked even brighter now that there were no other signs of the living. Two of the women walked through the front entryway ahead of him, and the other two followed. They moved down a long hall whose walls slumped distinctly to the left.

The walls and the ceiling showed decaying, flaking white paint and underneath that graying drywall. The floors were covered in a layer of dust that showed their footprints as they moved. There were half a dozen rooms on this floor. Most of them looked like small, long-defunct offices. The sounds of their feet scuffing through the dust echoed up to the ceiling. As they climbed the stairs, the shuffling echoed, too.

Cal told me what to do. But I don't know if I can do it.

Apollo heard the woman from the church basement now, just as clearly as he had then. Maybe he reacted in some way to the memory, made some kind of sharp movement on the stairs, because one of the women behind him snapped him with her club on the right shoulder. He had to stop and catch his breath. The pain returned him to the moment and reminded him the guards were there.

At the top of the stairs they found another hallway that led off into another series of long-unused rooms. A bright light shone out of a room halfway down. The women led him to the room. This one had a door. Two words were stenciled there.

PRINCIPAL'S
OFFICE

A woman stood alone inside, her back to Apollo as he entered. She stooped over a long table covered with materials, varied blocks and shapes he couldn't make out. There was another desk, clearly salvaged, stacked high with papers and a very old word processor, a gray block that took up a third of the desktop. The plug for the processor ran down to a red 3,000-watt Honda Super Quiet Generator. The generator sat tucked up against one wall that had a large hole in it, and it chugged its exhaust out into the night air. Apollo hadn't heard the generator even when he'd been in the hallway. In here it sounded as if someone was running a small lawnmower far out in the courtyard.

Two standing lamps flanked the table where the woman stood, still with her back to him. Two of the corners of the room were left in darkness, but compared to the rest of the island, this might as well have been the Eiffel Tower lit up at night.

Apollo stepped into the room.

One of the women who'd led him here entered quickly, gingerly, and dropped his keys on the desk with the word processor. His cellphone lay on the table. Someone else had found it.

"How?"

The woman spoke without turning. "It fell in the courtyard when you caught him. One of the children found it and brought it to me. I thought I trained you to be careful."

"You did. I'm sorry."

"Sloppy," the woman replied.

The guard nodded, then returned to the others at the doorway. She left a faint trail of water dripping from her cloak. The four women who'd tried to drown him turned and left.

Now he was alone with her. She moved two steps to the right, picking up something from the table. She had the short, no-fuss haircut of many older women, and her hair was so gray, it looked nearly white. She wore slightly loose black leggings with an overlarge gray sweater that draped, elegantly, down to her thighs. She looked like an Eileen Fisher model. When she turned, the effect became even stranger. She wore a sock puppet on either hand.

"Which one's scarier?" she asked.

She smiled impishly, she knew exactly the wild effect she had, and this made her seem playful and powerful at once. Here she was alone with him, and it didn't seem to worry her one iota. He wasn't in any shape to do her harm—he couldn't lift his arms; and he felt his legs only because of the constant throbbing in his thighs.

"Hello?" she said, raising both hands higher. "They didn't cut out your tongue, did they?" She squinted at him. "No, they would've given it to me."

The puppet on her right hand was made of a dark green sock with a pair of googly eyes attached. It had a rainbow-colored horn for a nose. If not for the horn, it would've looked just like Kermit the Frog. The other sock was orange with three eyes spaced far apart; this made it look wall-eyed. Its nose was a sunflower decal.

"Neither one is scary," Apollo finally said.

The woman turned her hands so it looked as if she and the puppets were staring at one another. "I was afraid of that," she said.

"You're Cal."

She nodded and sighed as she watched the puppets a little longer. "That's me. It's short for Callisto. Come closer."

Apollo limped halfway across the room but still must've gone a little too fast for comfort. From the edge of his vision, he saw movement. The two darkened corners of the room seemed to shiver, tremble, then out from the darkness came two women draped in the familiar dark green robes. The shadows had hidden them, but now they wanted to be seen. Each was armed with a club, just like the women in the courtyard, except the tips of these clubs jutted with nails. Makeshift maces. Surprised, terrified of another beating, Apollo stumbled backward. He would've fallen except Cal was there and caught him.

"It's all right," Cal said. Apollo couldn't tell if she was talking to the guards or to him. She'd taken off the sock puppets, and her nails scraped his jacket. "They're very protective of me. But you're not going to do anything bad, are you?"

"No," Apollo said.

He felt the firmness of Cal's grip and realized she was actually holding his arms down by his side. If he'd fought back just then, he couldn't have broken free before those two imperial guards got close enough to drive a nail through his brain.

"I'm putting on a show for the kids tomorrow night," Cal said. "Why don't you help me make a good puppet?"

Cal walked back to the table, and from here Apollo could see the kinds of materials that were laid out. Bags of socks in every color, sticks of glue and a glue gun, piles and piles of felt in different colors, lengths of string in black, blue, red, yellow, and green, multicolored bundles of pipe cleaners, two adult scissors and a dozen smaller safety scissors, tiny hair ribbons and clip-on bows, miniature bow ties. There were two small "sets" on the table, too. A cardboard box that had been made into a cottage, and another, this one standing upright, with a single window cut out at the top.

"Can you guess which story I'm going to tell?" Cal asked, pointing to the shoeboxes.

Apollo watched the guards, who hadn't moved back into the shadows yet. Each clutched her mace in her left hand. Their narrow faces and high-set eyes made them look like a pair of pharaoh hounds, elegant but wary. They were quite tall, Patrice's height, and slim—this was clear even under their cloaks. Their stances were the same. They were twins. She waved them back. They moved three steps, and Cal waved them back farther. Finally they returned to the shadows, but Apollo could never unsee them.

"How about now?" Cal asked, pointing to the cardboard sets again. "Can you guess?"

She moved behind the upright box, pulled a new puppet onto one hand, and slipped it through the tower window. A pair of rough, raggedy orange braids fell from the scalp, so long they reached the table.

"Rapunzel," Apollo said.

"That's it," she said. "You probably think you know the fairy tale, but I'll bet you don't remember all of it. Can I practice it on you, before I do it for the kids?"

"AN OLD MAN and woman had long wished to have a child, but they had no luck. Every night they prayed and prayed for a change. One day the woman looked out her window into the garden nearby. There she saw a field of rapunzel, and she longed for it. She told her husband what she craved, and he wished to see her happy, so he decided to go and steal some rapunzel, even though that garden was the property of an enchantress, known and feared throughout the town.

"Nevertheless, he climbed into the garden and stole the rapunzel and made his wife a meal, and she enjoyed it. But because she was now with child, her cravings didn't go away, so her husband climbed into the garden a second time. This time when he plucked the rapunzel, the enchantress appeared.

"'How dare you!' she shouted. 'Thief! I will make you pay!'

"The old man pleaded for his life. He explained he stole only to feed his beloved wife, and this answer moved the enchantress. She agreed she wouldn't curse him and he could take as much rapunzel as he liked, but when the baby was born, he had to give it to her. The old man felt so terrified, he'd agree to anything just to save his life. And on that day when the baby came, the enchantress appeared and took the child and named it Rapunzel.

"The girl grew healthy and strong, but when she turned twelve, the enchantress took the girl and hid her away inside a tower that had no doors and only one window. The enchantress visited every morning and got in by calling, 'Rapunzel, Rapunzel, let down your hair.' The girl would drop her long braids through the window, and the enchantress would climb up.

"One day a prince rode by on his horse. He heard Rapunzel singing in her tower, and her voice was the most beautiful sound he'd ever heard. He found the tower but couldn't guess how to get in. He returned many times until one day he saw the enchantress call out, and the braids came down, and up the old woman went.

"The prince waited until the enchantress left at night. Then he went and called out, 'Rapunzel, Rapunzel, let down your hair.' When the hair came down, he climbed up, and Rapunzel was quite scared. He explained he'd heard her voice and had fallen in love with her. With time he soothed Rapunzel's fears. He returned to her each night after the enchantress had gone. When he asked her to marry him, she came up with a plan. Return each night with a handkerchief. When they had enough, she would make a rope and climb down with him, and they would run away.

"But one day while the enchantress was there, young, naïve Rapunzel asked why the enchantress had such a hard time climbing her hair when the young prince climbed up so easily. 'Ah-ha!' the enchantress shouted. 'You conniving girl!' She grabbed Rapunzel's braids and wrapped them around one hand, and with a pair of scissors she cut them off! Then she took Rapunzel from the tower and exiled her in the desert, where she would never be found.

"That night when the prince arrived, the enchantress let down the hair when he called. But when he climbed up, he found only the enchantress. 'The treasure you seek is gone! Now come so I can destroy you!' The prince, terrified, jumped from the tower to save his life. He landed in thorns at the bottom, and they gouged out his eyes. Blinded, he ran off and wandered the land for years.

"One day the prince heard a sound in the distance. A song he had not heard in a lifetime. He followed it until he stumbled before Rapunzel where she lived now, in the desert, with their two children. Rapunzel was so shocked to see him that she grabbed him and held him close. Her tears fell across his eyes and healed them. Now he could see! He led Rapunzel and their boy and girl back to his kingdom, where they lived happily ever after."

58

"Y OU'RE GOING TO tell that story to little children?"

They were still in the principal's office. Apollo remained standing and Cal behind the table, the Rapunzel puppet on her hand. She hadn't used it the whole time. Instead she'd become lost in the telling itself, as had Apollo. Even the guards had stepped out from the corners, hands down by their sides and heads tilted as they listened.

Cal pointed at Apollo. "Bingo! Fairy tales are not for children. They didn't used to be anyway. These were the stories peasants told to each other around the fire after a long day, not to their kids. This was how adults talked with each other. Fairy tales became stories for kids in the seventeen-hundreds. Around that time this weird new group started appearing in parts of Europe. The merchant class.

"Merchants were making money, and they wanted to live better than the lower classes did. This meant there were new rules about how to behave, both for the adults and for the kids. Fairy tales changed accordingly. Now they had to have a moral, something to train those children in the new rules. Which is when they started turning to shit. A bad fairy tale has some simple goddamn moral. A great fairy tale tells the truth."

Cal picked up a bag of socks and held it out to Apollo. She pointed to the sock puppets she'd been wearing when he arrived. "One of those was going to be the enchantress, but I can't make her scary enough. You give it a try."

He pulled out a gray sock. "Are you going to tell me about my wife? Is Emma here?"

To this there was no answer. It was as if he hadn't spoken at all.

"Your guards tried to kill me," he said as he laid the sock flat on the table.

Cal followed Apollo's example and took out a gray sock of her own. "Years ago one husband found us," she said. "This is long before we moved to this island. He brought two guns with him and so much rage. I made the mistake of trying to talk with him, to make him see, but it didn't work. He did a lot of damage. He killed three women and seven kids. Shot me twice but I came through. Since then I decided we had to protect ourselves. We left the world and came to this island. We armed ourselves the best we could. And if men showed up, we were more . . . proactive."

Apollo slipped the sock onto his right hand, then brought his thumb and fingers together until he saw the semblance of a face, his knuckles the top of a ridged skull.

"Exactly how many men have you killed here?" Apollo said.

"We're like the police," Cal said. "We don't track those numbers."

She walked around Apollo and plugged the glue gun into an extension cord that ran across the room and into the generator. Already he'd become used to the faint chug of the machine. When she plugged in the glue gun, the generator chugged slightly louder. She handed the glue gun to him.

"Can I get some of those cotton balls over there?" Apollo asked. He spoke to Cal but looked at the dark corners where the guards stood.

She picked up a stick of glue and tapped him gently on the nose. "That's the spirit."

Standing here, Apollo could look at the desk where the big word processor sat and beside that a small jumble of papers. They were children's drawings. The picture on top was of a tall, craggy mountain and at the bottom of the mountain a deep, black cave. Inside the cave two yellow eyes floated. He thought he saw the faint outline of an open mouth below the eyes. He felt mesmerized by the picture.

"Cotton balls," Cal said, pulling him from his trance, dropping a handful into his palm. "Will your enchantress have gray hair?"

She held up the glue gun and pulled its trigger gently until a teardrop of glue appeared. Apollo looked down at the cotton balls. For a moment, it seemed as if he held a cloud in one hand.

"How do we protect our children?" Cal said quietly.

Apollo watched the soft little shape in his palm. "Obviously I don't know."

"No," Cal said. "That's what Rapunzel is about. That's the question it's asking."

She brought the glue gun to the sock on her hand and dabbed twice. Then she affixed two googly eyes. She opened her hand flat inside the sock and squeezed out a few circles of glue. She pressed an oval of red felt to the spot, then brought her hand closed again so the red felt became the inside of a mouth.

"The old man and woman have the child," Cal said. "But they do nothing to protect it. They're completely hands off, and the baby gets snatched away."

Quickly, expertly, Cal took some green string from a pile and glued it to the top of the sock, locks of mossy-looking hair. She found small, precut bits of black felt and affixed them above the googly eyes. Eyebrows. Two small pieces of brown felt became ears.

"The enchantress hides the girl away in a tower. She won't let the child do anything in the world without her. She's a helicopter parent."

Two longer pieces of brown felt turned into a pair of arms.

"But the prince still finds a way inside, doesn't he? No matter what we do, the world finds its way in. So then how do we protect our children? Hundreds of years ago German peasants were asking one another this question. But rather than frame it as a question they turned it into a story that embodied the concern. How do we protect our children? It's 2015, and we're still trying to find an answer. The new fears are the old fears, and the old fears are ancient."

She held up the finished puppet.

"Now I know this isn't frightening," Cal said, grinning. "But when I do the show tomorrow night, the children will talk to this puppet as if she were as real as me. Actually, they'll think of this puppet as more real than me."

She held the puppet up close to Apollo's face until her own lost focus and disappeared. She didn't move her hand to pretend the puppet was speaking, and she used her normal speaking voice. She just let it hover there before him, and the longer he looked at it, the more it came to life.

"The Scottish called it *glamer*," Cal said. "Glamour. It's an old kind of magic. An illusion to make something appear different than it really is. A monster might look like a beautiful maiden. A ruined castle appears to be a golden palace. A baby is . . ." Her voice drifted off.

Apollo found himself speaking to the puppet just as Cal said the children would. "Not a baby," he whispered.

"What a smart boy," the puppet said.

"But this isn't a fairy tale," Apollo answered.

"Are you sure?"

"Best way to clear the air is to have it all out in the open!" A man's voice. Outside. In the courtyard.

Cal's fingers closed into a fist, and the puppet lost all animation. The mouth shut, and the eyes curled over—it was like watching a soul slip out of a body. Cal dropped the hand, and Apollo watched the guards move quickly to the two windows and look down.

One of them said, "Another man."

Cal looked back at Apollo with such fury, he thought she'd order the guards to tear his skull open right there.

"You didn't come alone," she hissed. "Why didn't you tell me?"

Apollo wanted to explain. He'd completely forgotten about William from the moment he'd stepped into this room.

"You never really understand a person until you consider things from his point of view," William Wheeler shouted in the courtyard. He sounded giddy. Or insane. "Until you climb into his skin and walk around in it!"

"Seclusion rooms," Cal ordered. "Both of them."

59

THE SECLUSION ROOMS were located in the Tuberculosis Pavilion. It was the largest, best-equipped building in the complex, four stories of red brick with enough bed space, in its prime, for three hundred patients. It was the one structure Cal declared out of bounds for the members of her community. The women had even designed makeshift barriers to keep the kids out, stacks of tattered furniture and rubble that would be tough for most young children to scale. The only area of the building ever put to use were these seclusion rooms, a makeshift prison.

Cal and her guards walked Apollo and William to the pavilion. While one twin pried away the boards tacked over the doorway, the other stood behind the prisoners, mace at the ready. This one held up William's phone.

"What was he doing when they found him?" Cal asked.

The pop of wooden boards sounded like gunshots.

"He was on the shoreline with the phone's light on. Just standing there waving it over his head, side to side."

"Did he have a signal?" Cal asked, taking the phone. "Could he make a call?"

"No," the guard said. "He was just waving the thing."

Apollo tried to catch William's eye, but it wasn't working. William looked at the night sky as if he was out strolling. He smiled faintly. If not for the location, you'd have thought he was a middle-aged man stargazing in his backyard.

Cal growled her next question. "Why the fuck haven't you destroyed this yet?"

"Thought you should see what else he has on the phone."

The last of the boards were freed from the entry door, and the other guard opened it. Apollo couldn't get any sense of the depth of the hallway or its width, the height of the ceiling. So dark inside, there might've been no floor beyond the threshold, just a bottomless pit.

"Oh God," Cal said quietly as she scrolled through the phone. "This is Gretta's husband?"

The guard behind Apollo pushed him forward, toward the shadowed hallway. Before he took a step, Cal smashed the phone into the back of William's head. He stumbled forward but didn't fall, so she hit him again. He barked, a real animal noise, but still he didn't go down. One of the twins kicked the backs of William's legs. He yelped and went to his hands and knees. His glasses flew off, and he scurried after them instantly, automatically. Cal brought the phone down five more times on William's back. William lay in the dirt, huffing. She dropped the phone on the ground right near William's head, and the guard who kicked him brought the mace down four times. It crunched and cracked. It died.

"We should tell her he's here," Cal said. "She'd want to be here when we kill him."

"You have her phone number?" William asked. "Can you share it with me?"

The guards kicked at him until he went flat in the dirt.

Now Apollo was pushed forward. He entered the dark doorway cautiously. Apollo heard William groaning. He must've been trying to rise. He spat and coughed. Eventually the twins had to drag him in.

The seclusion rooms were essentially mesh cages. There was a dead bolt to lock patients in. All this had been put in place back when it was an infectious disease hospital, and it was kept that way for the years when this place serviced juvenile addicts. Now Apollo and William were in them.

Two cages, side by side. They could see each other, talk with each other, though the mesh was too tightly woven for them to reach through.

"At least I got my glasses back," William said as he sat with his back to the cage door.

There were window frames in each room, the windows smashed out long ago. Mesh wiring lay across the frames, so escape was impossible, but moonlight entered and gave each cage a blue tint.

"They knew who you were," Apollo said. "Cal said your wife's name. You kept a few things from me." He stood at the window, looking outside.

"Well obviously," William said. He turned his glasses around as if he could catch his reflection in them. He smiled as if he was checking his teeth for stains. Then he slipped them on and looked at Apollo.

"They beat the shit out of me!" Apollo shouted. His thighs still hurt, his lower back, too.

"I'm sorry for that," William said. "Really. If I'm honest, I didn't think we'd make it this far. I've been going up and down the East River for months. Been on every island looking for Cal, but somehow I kept missing this place. Then you spotted it the first time through."

You don't see, but you will.

Apollo heard Emma's voice—the last words she ever spoke to him— and he shivered. He tugged at the red string on his middle finger. The knot held. Apollo looked up, slightly confused, overwhelmed, trying to make sense of so many things.

"If you've been going up and down this river for months, then you didn't learn how to drive a boat today," Apollo said.

"My father had me out on boats since I was a baby. We're Norwegians originally. Sailing is in our blood."

"But what's the point of all this?" Apollo said. "Why keep it from me?"

"Trust takes time. But I didn't pick your name out of a hat. I confess, I knew who you were."

"From the news," Apollo said, feeling so naïve for having ever believed otherwise.

"Not the news about what Emma did. I knew who you were long before that. I read about your wife giving birth on the A train."

"We never spoke to the press about that," Apollo said.

"You didn't," William agreed. "But the press covered it. Emma was brought to Harlem Hospital. They issued a birth certificate. You remember what I told you before I gave you that video of Emma? A person who has a computer connection and who really cares can dig up nearly anything."

Apollo kicked at the mesh wall between his cage and William's. "But why? Why do all that? I was just living my life, and you're in your house looking through some stranger's personal business?"

William walked closer to Apollo and patted the mesh wall gently. "Gretta had just left me. They were gone, and my home was empty. I was in a free fall. I wasn't thinking straight. I read about the stuff on the A train, and I just had so much time all of a sudden. And as good as I was at finding information, I couldn't find a damn thing out about Gretta. It was like she'd disappeared. And she had. She'd come here to be with Cal. I didn't know it then, though. So I had all this time, and I read your A-train story, and a mix of boredom and curiosity and just plain going nuts sent me down this path.

"I found Emma's name, but I also found out yours. I learned about your business. I found you on Facebook. And there's all these pictures of your son. Ten pictures in a post! Twelve. Half of them are too blurry to see straight, but it didn't matter. You were so happy. You were so proud. And I understood that. I felt like . . . this is a guy who knows how good it can be! Loving someone so damn much. Me and this guy, we're the same. He gets why family is important. But really all this came about because Gretta ran off with my daughter and destroyed my family. If that hadn't happened, we never would've met."

"Daughters," Apollo said. "You told me you had two. Was that a lie too?"

"No," William said. For the first time, his voice softened. "I had two."

Because of the moonlight, Apollo could see his face. William wept.

Apollo stood in place. His brain felt as if it had short-circuited. He had the instinct to console this man, yet he'd lied about so much. Still, he felt one thing to be completely true: this man had lost his family, and it had driven him a little insane. Apollo could identify with that much.

William slapped the mesh wall, and Apollo jumped back.

"I called in the cavalry," William said. "I'm sorry I couldn't try to help you, but that's what I was doing while they had you."

"What does that mean?" Apollo asked. "The police? The FBI?"

William ignored the question, offering something more relevant instead. "Now I'm going to pull back the very last veil, Apollo. I'm going to put every card I have face up on the table. Emma is alive. We know this. You want to find her. Cal—all these women here—they are not going to help you find her. No matter what they say, they only protect their own. But I could help you find Emma. I would travel to the ends of the earth with you."

"But . . ." Apollo said.

"But you have to help me get Gretta and Grace back first. You help me, and then I will help you, and I can be very resourceful, as you've learned."

Apollo walked closer to the window and looked out at the night sky, up at the nearly full moon as if preparing to make a wish. "What are you asking me to do?"

"Just talk to Gretta for me," William said. "They're not going to let me see her. Not while I'm still in a state to talk. But she doesn't know you. You could explain how far I've come. You could tell her I know it wasn't her fault. That she and I both lost our minds after Agnes died. That was our baby. I haven't said her name out loud in almost a year. Agnes. My sweet girl.

"I understand now that it wasn't Gretta's fault though. I want to beg for her forgiveness for all the ways I was short-tempered and quick to accuse. I want to offer her my forgiveness, if she wants it. I want her and Grace to come back home. I want my family, what's left of my family, to be whole again. I'm asking you to tell her all that."

"How do you know I'll even see her? They might come in and just shoot us both."

"You heard her. She'll call Gretta. If Gretta knows I'm here, she'll come. Maybe she really does want to see me dead, but I don't think it's that simple. It never is between people. If they take you elsewhere and you see Gretta, you tell her what I said. If Gretta forgave me, then maybe they'd let me go. I don't know, but it's the only chance I have left. You are the only chance I have left. I don't want to die without trying."

Apollo turned from the moon to look at William in the other cage. "What if I say no?"

William coughed until he choked. Eventually he recovered. "Man to man, if you don't help me, everyone is going to die on this island. Even me."

"Who's coming here?" Apollo asked.

"I won't call it off," William said. "I won't even try."

With that William walked into the far corner of his cage, where the moonlight didn't reach. He lay on the ground in darkness, rolled his coat into a pillow, and bedded down for the night.

Apollo never fell asleep.

CAL ARRIVED JUST after dawn with her twin guards. The twins looked as tired as Apollo felt—their eyes red as cinnamon hearts—but their posture remained rigid as a pair of hunting rifles. Cal opened the door of Apollo's seclusion room, and William sat up to watch. He slipped on his glasses as if, without them, he'd be underdressed.

Cal stepped into Apollo's cage. She wore the same clothes as the night before. Her gray sweater looked as if she'd slept in it. The hem of it showed traces of dirt and leaves.

"Good morning, *Pearl*," William said.

For the first time since Apollo met her, she looked startled.

"Pearl Walker," he said. "Raised off the coast of Maine. In trouble with the law for habitual shoplifting. A heavy drinker. Mother of one. Do you remember the name of your high school? Because I could tell you."

Cal pulled her gray sweater tighter to herself and looked down at the floor and breathed deeply. When she lifted her head, her cool had returned.

"I wanted to douse you in gasoline and light you on fire last night." Cal walked toward William. "But then I thought Gretta might want to do it. I sent someone in a boat to fetch her last night, right after we put you here."

William tapped the mesh wall gently, as if Cal was the animal caught inside and not him. "What about my daughter?"

"You mean the one you killed?" Cal asked. "You won't even see her in the afterlife."

William's face set into a mask of true hate. "Sorceress. Enchantress. Every word you speak is a lie."

Cal gestured for Apollo to walk out of his cage, but Apollo couldn't do anything but stare at William.

"You're saying *he* killed his daughter?"

"She's lying to you, you nitwit. She's casting a spell. That's what witches do."

"I've decided to give you one more chance," Cal said to Apollo, ignoring William.

Cal had something tucked under one arm, hidden in the folds of her sweater, but Apollo could see the way she kept one arm tight against her side. Maybe it was a gun. Maybe William told the truth and this was nothing more than a ruse to take him outside and put a few bullets into his skull. And if so, what could he do about it?

"Why?" Apollo asked. "Why give me another chance?"

"Emma told me about you, Apollo. While she stayed with us, she and I spoke quite a bit. She told me you'd come here, but I didn't believe her. I thought we'd done a pretty good job of hiding ourselves away. I told her no man could find us on our island, but here you are. Just like she said. She didn't mention this one being with you, though, so I had to think things over for the night. That's why I'm giving this second chance. You betray us again, and you won't get a third. Now come on."

She waved him out and adjusted her other arm one more time. Whatever she had there had almost slipped when she gestured. Apollo moved to the cell door. He didn't look at William.

William shouted as Cal and the guards led Apollo away, but the words—if they were words—remained unintelligible. He sounded, instead, like an animal that knows its end is near and resists the knowledge as much as the death.

Apollo Kagwa would never see William Wheeler again.

C AL DIDN'T SPEAK to Apollo until they'd left the TB Pavilion. The twin guards, as before, said nothing. Apollo kept expecting one of them to bring a mace down on his head or for Cal to reveal a pistol, raise it, and shoot. He had little to say as he anticipated his execution. As soon as they were outside again, Cal reached into the deep pocket of her sweater.

"This is for you," she said. She stopped him and turned him toward her.

"No way," Apollo said. "No way."

Cal held out a copy of a children's book. *Outside Over There*.

"How did you get this?" he asked. "I left this in my home, on my bookshelf."

She laughed. "You do know there's more than one copy of this book in the world."

Apollo took it from her and held it gingerly. He almost expected it to explode in his hands.

"I told you that Emma and I spoke. We had a lot of late nights together. She told me about your father, about this book and how much it meant."

"What does it have to do with my father?"

Apollo opened the cover as if the answer would be written there on the endpapers.

"I'm not talking about him. I'm talking about this book. This story. I want you to understand where you've found yourself."

"This island?"

"For a start," Cal said.

She took his arm and led him back toward the courtyard. She steadied him in the places where the land dipped or rose, and she pulled him when he nearly walked right into a tree. He couldn't stop staring down at the book. Confusion threatened to drown him like the rising waters of a flood.

"You were in New York when you got on Wheeler's boat, and for a time you were in the East River. You probably passed Rikers Island, maybe you went under the Whitestone Bridge or the Throgs Neck. But when you got close to us, when you approached our island, you crossed new waters, and when you beached that boat, you were on a different shore. The Amazons were said to live on the island of Themyscira, and the Yolngu people of Australia tell of Bralgu, the Island of the Dead. Magical places, where the rules of the world are different. You've crossed into such a place, Apollo."

"This is North Brother Island," he said. Ahead he heard the sounds of children now, laughter and squealing.

"It was," Cal said. "But then we arrived here and remade it."

As they stepped through the brush and into the courtyard, Apollo saw women and children out now, buzzing off in this direction or that. Young children were being led, or carried, down a path Apollo hadn't seen last night. They moved toward a small building with a series of windows facing the courtyard. Apollo watched the kids go in. Their small heads disappeared as a woman inside the building gestured for them to sit. Behind this woman, there was a blackboard on the wall.

"A schoolhouse?" Apollo said. A one-room schoolhouse.

"It's the library," Cal told him. "But it serves as their school as well. Are you hungry?"

"Yes," Apollo said. He couldn't stop watching the windows. He couldn't even see the children, but he imagined them there, sitting cross-legged, attention on the teacher. There were so many commonplace events he had expected to enjoy when Brian was born. Peeking in on his child during class. Parent-teacher conferences. Helping with homework in the evening. He hadn't understood what a luxury such drudgery would be until he lost the chance.

"We take our meals there," Cal said, gesturing to another ramshackle building.

One of the twins brought a hand to his shoulder and pushed him forward. He drifted on just so he wouldn't fall. He clutched the book tighter to his belly.

They'd reached a doorway. Cal stepped in first. Inside, women sat on the floor in small groups, plates or bowls in their laps. They noted him, every single one. More than a few of them tensed, even rose to their feet as if to rush him, but since he was being escorted by Cal and the guards, they returned to the pleasure of paying attention to one another rather than to him. To his surprise Apollo found himself scanning the faces, looking for William's wife. He didn't even know what she looked like, but he sought her out anyway. Did he plan to help William? He didn't know.

"Me and you be sisters," Cal said softly as she moved through the room, a kind of greeting perhaps. "We be the same."

The women responded, all together. "Me and you coming from the same place."

"How long was she here?" Apollo asked as Cal led him toward the one table in the room where a series of serving plates sat.

"Three months," Cal said. "On and off."

"On and off?"

"She went back to New York at least once a week. She's the one who stocked our library. She was shocked when she saw how little we had. To her, a life without books wasn't living. Even out here Emma wanted the kids to read. She couldn't stop being a librarian. The kids appreciated it. Some of the other women felt judged."

Apollo burned with hunger but had no appetite.

Cal filled a bowl with oatmeal. "This is good on a cold morning," she said.

"How did she go back and forth? I'm sure the water taxi doesn't make stops at your magic island."

"We have our own navy," Cal said. She sprinkled a spoonful of brown sugar on the oatmeal. "Navy's an exaggeration. We have a trawler and one small watercraft, a creek boat. It's built for one. You use a paddle. Emma brought books back in the creek boat."

"She knew how to use a creek boat to cross the East River?"

"There were a few spills," Cal said, leading him now to a corner where they could talk alone. "But your wife never gives up. Didn't you know that about her? She's got a will on her."

"Yeah," Apollo said. "That I knew."

Cal squatted on the ground and patted the floor for him to follow. She set the oatmeal in his lap.

He placed the book down on the ground. Instead of eating, he scanned the story.

"'When Papa was away at sea,'" Cal read aloud.

Apollo leafed through the pages. Mama sitting on the bench in the garden. Ida inside the house with the baby, playing her horn. At the window the small figures in purple robes, their faces shrouded in shadows. The goblins were sneaking in. He stopped here, pulling his hand away from the book. Cal reached out and turned the page for him.

Now Ida stayed playing her horn and looking out the window. Behind her the goblins carried her baby sister away. The child's mouth opened in a shout, the eyes wild with fear and pleading. But Ida couldn't hear her sister over the music. In the crib the creatures left a replacement. A baby, identical to Ida's little sister, wearing the same bedclothes. Except the replacement had been carved out of ice.

On the next page Ida lifted the ice child and held it close, cooing. Ida whispered to the thing, saying, "I love you." But the creature couldn't return Ida's embrace because it wasn't alive.

Cal closed the book again.

"I don't know why your father read this book to you when you were little," she said. "But I'm showing you this book because it tells the truth. You and Emma have ended up in one ugly fairy tale. Every woman on this island has been where you are now. It won't do for you to shut your eyes or pretend otherwise. You've crossed the waters, and you can't go back.

William was right about at least one thing. We are witches. But let me tell you what else is true. The man in that cage consorts with monsters."

Apollo took a moment to wonder, again, at the threat of William's cavalry.

I won't call it off. I won't even try.

POLLO ATE HIS oatmeal. Neither he nor Cal spoke for a little while, and instead the sounds of the other women filled the room. Some joked with one another, others discussed routines and repairs for the island, and here and there pairs of women sat together and whispered to one another more intimately.

"Did these women . . ." Apollo couldn't finish.

"Did we do what Emma did?" Cal set her spoon back in the bowl. "Yes. All of us."

Apollo set the bowl down. "What about the kids I saw outside?" he asked.

"Some of these women had more than one child. When they ran to me, they brought their other children with them."

"What do these kids know about what happened?"

"At the library we teach them reading and writing and arithmetic."

"But not history."

"Not that history."

"Why do they stay? Life looks pretty rugged around here."

Cal set her chin and didn't look away from Apollo, a resolute gaze. "Not all of them do. I don't demand that they stay. These women came to me bereft and confused. I offered them a place where they would be believed. Not second-guessed. Not dismissed. Here they wouldn't have their realities explained away. Do you know how few women get that simple gift? It works miracles. Not all of them want to stay but every woman leaves this place stronger than when she arrived."

Apollo rose holding the bowl, the book tucked under one arm, and for a moment he loomed over Cal. He didn't even have time to straighten up before one of the imperial guards appeared, her makeshift mace in hand.

"I'm just getting up!" Apollo shouted, agitated by the crowding. His body ached so badly from last night's beating that he couldn't imagine how they still thought of him as a threat. It had been hard enough just to get back on his feet.

Cal went onto her knees, then pushed up slowly and with exertion. In the daylight she appeared more her age. "He's fine," she said, patting the guard.

Apollo walked among the clumps of women still eating on the ground. Two basins sat on the long table, each filled with water. He did as the women did, dumping the last of his oatmeal into a nearly full bucket— collecting for compost—then washing out his bowl in the basins.

While he did this, Cal visited with the women there, saying a few words to one or another. She returned to him only to show him where they set the wet bowls out to dry. As he did this, he weighed the option of informing Cal about William's bargain, William's threat. But when she came to him, he didn't mention it.

"Can I see the kids?" Apollo asked. "Can I meet them?"

Cal gave Apollo the once-over once more. "You really want to?"

"I liked hearing the laughter," he said.

She dumped traces of oatmeal from her bowl, washed it out, and set it down to dry. "Wonders never cease," she said, more to herself than to him.

Cal brought Apollo back to the courtyard, recess in session. A few of the older children played tag while others had large plastic balls they kicked or threw around. The high point of incongruity was one girl, maybe three years old, riding a scooter on the uneven brick of the courtyard. She held the low handle of the machine, one foot on the board and the other on the ground. She couldn't keep her balance yet. She fell and she got up and she fell and she got up. When a woman came to try and help pull the scooter, the tiny girl swatted the woman back. She was going to do this herself.

Apollo listened to the children. The screeching frustration of the girl on the scooter. The monkey cries of two boys wrestling over a yellow ball. The taunting and whining, the cooing and cackling. Children. Glorious and half wild. He nearly fainted from the beauty of them.

Cal brought one arm to his back to steady him. "When I became a mother," she said, "being this close to children was enough to give my husband hives."

"Let's get closer," Apollo said.

Now a small group of women appeared from the Doctor's Cottage. They held work tools and gardening apparatus. Large burlap sacks were slung over each one's shoulders.

"The best part about setting up on this island," Cal said, "is that we can grow our own food. A kibbutz in the middle of the East River."

Apollo gestured toward the girl at the far end of the courtyard, the one whose scooter had toppled again. The three-year-old stood over the fallen scooter and hissed at it as if it was a dog in need of correction. She cried with frustration and tried to lift it herself, but it was too heavy.

Cal and Apollo walked toward her, weaving through the children who played around them. When they reached the girl, she looked up at them, squinting, then swatted at them and shuffled around so she stood between them and the scooter.

"No!" she said.

Now she reached down and grabbed the handle of the scooter and lifted it partway, but it fell back on its side.

Cal crouched down beside the girl. "You need some help," she said.

The little girl backed away from Cal and bumped right into Apollo. She turned, looked up at him, and gave a grimace. "No!" the girl shouted at him.

Cal waved Apollo down so he crouched in front of the girl, at her eye level. The girl's hair had been styled into thin, tight box braids with small, clear beads on the ends of each one.

"My name is Apollo."

She watched him curiously, then turned back to Cal, who nodded faintly. The girl looked back at Apollo, still a skeptic.

"Can I help you with the scooter?" he asked.

She looked at the unwieldy scooter, then back to him. He raised his two empty hands. With one he grabbed the handlebar of the scooter and lifted it. Instantly the girl turned from him and Cal, set one foot on the scooter, and with a kick she was off. They watched her go. She made it five feet, wobbling.

The three-year-old finally lost her footing. She flipped the scooter and flopped onto her side. It didn't look like a bad fall, and in fact, the kid just lay there on her back looking up at the morning sky as if she'd finished with riding and moved on to the leisure hour.

"Let's go get her," Cal said.

When they got there, a small hand grasped two of Apollo's fingers and tugged him. He helped her up.

"This is Gayl," Cal said.

The little girl had tired of the scooter, and now she took a step toward the library. The power of her grip told Apollo his company was required.

"I think you made a friend."

"Can I speak to Gretta?" Apollo asked.

Cal narrowed her eyes, crossed her arms. "What for?"

"You said William killed his daughter."

"He did."

Gayl took two more steps. Apollo was about to be dragged.

"Every woman here did something similar," Apollo said. "So why hold him to a different standard?"

"No. Not similar. That's wrong. What Wheeler did was evil."

"I want to hear it from her."

"You do, do you? Give a man a little breakfast, and suddenly he's giving orders."

"It's a request," Apollo said as Gayl pulled at him once more. He took three steps. "Please, Cal."

"We don't travel back and forth on the river during the day," Cal said. "Gretta will get here tonight. We'll put on the puppet show after dinner. If she'll talk with you, that'll be the time. For now, you take care of Gayl."

Off Apollo and Gayl went. Cal watched them quietly until one woman came close with urgent business.

APOLLO JOINED THE rhythm of the island. He moved from one job to the next—attending to kids or cleaning up after them—and all that time Gayl remained with him. Was he helping her or the other way around? Many of the women asked the question, playfully, and Apollo didn't mind. He met Gayl's mother. She had a five-year-old boy as well and seemed only relieved to have Apollo's help. He fed Gayl lunch, read to her from *Outside Over There*, and brought her back to her mother when she had to use the potty. Apollo felt the old push-pull return, the confidence in doing something that felt natural and necessary, the fear that he was doing it wrong, putting this vulnerable life at risk. The anxiety was even worse here on an island of women who could kill him. Together Apollo and Gayl folded laundry, Apollo doing the work and Gayl undoing it all earnestly, then peeking up at him begging to be caught. When he feigned his anger, she giggled so hard, she cried. At times Apollo heard someone else's laughter, too. It was his.

64

B Y SIX O'CLOCK dinner was served. Sippy cups to fill, spills to clean. The children were fed together in the Doctor's Cottage. Two of the women played music—guitar and a small drum—and the children sang along. They'd been taught "Diamonds and Rust," and "Umi Says," among others. The younger children were put to bed before the puppet show, but when it was time for Gayl to go, she refused. She wanted to stay up with Apollo. He pleaded to let the girl stay with him awhile longer. Gayl's mother had to laugh, but Apollo saw something else in the mother's eyes, the reflexive suspicion about a strange man wanting to spend time with her daughter. He couldn't blame her for that concern. The caution was a sign that Gayl's mother was a good parent.

But Cal indicated that this man could be trusted and the endorsement carried weight. Also, the mother's five-year-old decided to have a full-blown meltdown right then, out in the courtyard, so it was a relief to leave Gayl with Apollo for a little longer.

Take care of her for me. That's what Gayl's mother said before she pulled her son inside the Nurses' Residence. Cal called the kids to the library for the show. Apollo tucked the book into the back of his pants, and Gayl rode on his shoulders. She looked down at the older children and shouted, "I'm tall!"

Cal and Apollo stood at the back of the library as the kids bopped from one wall to another, indiscriminately pulled books from the shelves, and pushed or elbowed each other, a few explosions before settling down. Apollo tried to set Gayl on the floor among them, but she mewled in his arms, so he held on to her.

"She didn't eat much at dinner," Cal said. "I bet she's hungry."

Then Gretta Wheeler arrived, escorted by a guard.

Every grown woman in the room stiffened and turned toward her as if they were needles being drawn toward magnetic north. Apollo turned to face her only once he realized the women had grown quiet. The children continued to burble and play. Gretta came to Cal. She ignored Apollo. She gave off an anxious crackle, or was that only because of how Cal stared at her?

Gretta Wheeler's hair was pulled back severely, and she was thin in a way that suggested malnourishment. Apollo remembered the woman in the basement of Holyrood looking much the same way and even Emma had been winnowed down like this. Each had become a body nearly drained of its life essence, victim of a vampire.

"I'm sorry I had to call for you," Cal said. Normally so quick to touch others, Cal left her arms at her side. Even Cal seemed to fear Gretta, or maybe she just feared for Gretta. "Where's Grace?"

"She's with my parents. William is here? He showed up? Just like that?"

The young woman whom Apollo had seen through the windows earlier—their teacher?—clapped her hands for the kids' attention. She gestured for the boys and girls to gather for circle time.

"He came with me," Apollo said.

As soon as Gretta Wheeler turned, he regretted saying it. She raised her hands, fingers tensed, as if she might claw out his eyes.

"You're with him?" she asked.

If he hadn't been holding the girl, Apollo thought Gretta would've devoured him.

"Of course not," Cal said quietly. "We wouldn't have him out with us if that was the case."

"I'm Emma's," Apollo said. "Emma Valentine's husband." He surprised himself, trembled at the words. It was the first time in four months that he'd allied himself to Emma in any way.

I'm Emma's.

Gretta watched Apollo blankly, as if he'd spoken to her in ancient Phoenician. She had no idea who Emma was or who he was; she'd been too busy living at the center of her own horrific story to concern herself with his.

Gretta's hands fell to her sides. She waved at Apollo softly, a kind of apology. Cal brought her arm around her but didn't pull her too tight. Gretta accepted the touch but didn't lean in to the embrace.

"I keep thinking I'll be done with him," Gretta said. "But he always finds his way back into my life."

"I know," Cal said.

"He won't give up. We're his. That's what he thinks. Me and Grace. And Agnes."

She whispered the last word, the girl's name.

"Did he really—?" Apollo's question slipped out between his lips, but he squeezed them shut before he finished. It didn't matter, Gretta knew what he meant.

She looked up at him. "Kill my daughter?"

The children went quiet and looked at Gretta. No matter the circumstances children are always listening. It can be easy for adults to forget this. Apollo wondered if Cal was correct when she said the kids didn't know why their mothers brought them here. Children sniff out secrets better than the NSA. Their teacher had to clap softly and make shushing sounds to draw their attention again.

"But he said—" Apollo began.

Gretta lurched at him. "Oh yes, please tell me what he said! I came all this way just so you could explain my own life to me!"

Apollo took a step backward as Gayl shook in his arm. She looked at Gretta with suspicion. Few things are as frightening to a child as an adult about to lose control.

"Gayl looks hungry," Cal said to Apollo, moving between him and Gretta. "Why don't you take her to eat?"

Two women entered the library with the finished sets for the puppet show. The home of the parents who wished to have a child; the garden of the Enchantress; Rapunzel's tower and even the patch of thorns that would blind the prince. A third woman entered with a rickety card table that would serve as the stage. Already the children had seen the sets, the bag of puppets dangling from one guard's wrist, and went quiet at the promise of glamour.

Gretta's concentration broke, and she looked back at Cal. "He got my new address. He mailed me a book."

"A book?" Apollo whispered, but the women didn't hear him.

"I thought you were being careful," Cal said.

"It's not possible to stay off the grid all the time, Pearl. It's one thing on this island, but it's the real world out there. If you want to get an apartment, you have to have proof of who you are. That means getting a state ID. And if you want to start a bank account, then you need that ID too."

"Why do you even need a bank account?" Cal hissed.

"I live with a teenager!" Gretta shouted. The kids looked back again. "I can't have my money stuffed under the bed. You know how fast Grace would find that? She's a good girl, but she's still a sixteen-year-old."

Cal nodded wearily. The problem with the real world was that it kept intruding on you with its mundane concerns.

"A book?" Apollo said again, louder.

Gretta looked at the ground. "He ruined it. Wrote one thing across each and every page."

Gayl made a soft mewling noise and gestured to her mouth. She wriggled in Apollo's arms.

"I thought I told you to go feed that girl," Cal snapped. "Take her to the goddamn Doctor's Cottage. Gayl knows where it is. Don't you Gayl?"

The girl nodded earnestly at Cal, so serious about it she shook her shoulders as well as her head.

"You'll find food in the coolers," Cal said.

Gretta spoke over Cal. "He cleared me out. Every last penny right out of my account. You don't even need a gun to rob banks anymore, just an Internet connection. That bastard stole seventy thousand dollars from me."

Apollo felt slightly sick.

"What did he write?" Apollo asked. "In the book."

"Her name." Gretta spoke softly. "Agnes. On every page."

APOLLO WALKED TO the Doctor's Cottage with Gayl. *Stumbled* is more like it. He didn't even realize he'd taken her there. Seventy thousand dollars. As he'd been sitting in that rented boat, celebrating the biggest book sale of his life, he'd been complicit in a crime against Gretta Wheeler. Then the man had ruined every page with the name of his own daughter. Agnes. Had he really killed her? He felt so disoriented, he might as well be dying.

Apollo set Gayl down inside the dining room of the Doctor's Cottage. The girl marched toward the row of coolers that lined one wall, her shoes shuffling and scraping through the layer of dirt and detritus that covered the floor. He searched through each cooler until he found a Tupperware container with leftover macaroni and cheese. He closed the cooler and dug through a cardboard box that worked as the community utensil drawer. Plastic forks, spoons, and knives, paper plates and cups. He moved to one of the dining tables and pulled out a chair, set down the mac and cheese, a fork and spoon, then picked Gayl up. He sat her in his lap and lifted the Tupperware lid. He remained half dazed, but he could still fulfill this simple routine: feed the child. Gayl eyed the food, then looked back up at him. She waggled her head. Apollo scooped the spoon into the mac and cheese. He lifted it to her mouth.

"No!" she shouted, and slapped his hand. The mac and cheese now a splotch on the ground.

Gayl pulled at the spoon. He let go, and she turned the spoon around with two hands, gripping the handle with her left. Now she studied the Tupperware as if taking aim. She lifted the spoon and guided it toward the food. The spoon bumped the edge of the container, so Gayl lifted it again, tried again. On the second try, she landed the spoon into the mound of macaroni. She dug the tip in like a spade. When she lifted again, she sent another spray of food to the floor.

"No!" she shouted, frustration clear on her face.

"You remind me of my wife," Apollo said to her. She looked at him but did not seem interested in hearing about Emma. "My wife," he repeated to himself, trying out the term. Had she killed their son? Or was their son still alive? Cal told him he'd crossed the waters into a land of witches and monsters. Could there be hope here, too? Such a thing seemed more improbable than magic. Cal had created a jumble in his mind, but all day a voice would sometimes come to him, his own, reminding him of his mission: *Get Emma.*

When he arrived on the island, the plan had been clear: *Kill her.* But now? Was he here to harm her or help? He couldn't say. And where was she? Why hadn't she shown herself? In a moment close to panic, he checked his left hand. He gawped at his naked ring finger. He really had thrown it in the water, hadn't he? Only the red string around his middle finger remained now.

Gayl set down the plastic spoon. She tugged at the red string. When it wouldn't come loose, she pulled it up along Apollo's finger, trying to slip it off. Apollo used his other hand to snatch up the plastic spoon, scoop some macaroni onto it, and bring it to Gayl's lips. She absently took a bite. Apollo grinned, proud of himself for tricking her into eating. Then she raised her hand with a flourish. She had worked the red string loose from his finger without him even noticing.

"Baby girl?" A woman's voice came from the entrance to the Doctor's Cottage.

Before Apollo even turned his head, Gayl leaped from his lap and sprinted. "Mommy!" she called out. She practically levitated into her mother's arms.

"She's fed," Apollo said, standing up. "Well, she ate one bite at least."

"I guess that's something," Gayl's mother said, teasing. "I hope she wasn't any trouble."

"Gayl is great," Apollo said.

"Yes, she is," her mother said, looking into her daughter's eyes. "She's also up way past bedtime."

"No!" Gayl shouted, but then she yawned so wide they could've counted all her teeth.

Gayl's mother turned so she faced Apollo. "I didn't get to know Emma too well while she was here," she said. "My little ones keep me pretty busy, you understand. But she took a liking to my boy, Freddie. He's shy. Doesn't talk a lot, but he loves to read. She had her own problems to deal with, but she read to him before bedtime, each night she was here. That told me all I needed to know about her."

Mother and child walked out of the Doctor's Cottage, but in a moment they returned. Gayl's mother held her hand out. The red string lay in her palm.

Apollo took it from her with a nod. He looked at the loop for a long minute before slipping it onto his ring finger.

66

HE STEPPED OUT of the Doctor's Cottage, book tucked under one arm like a man out for a walk with the paper. He could see the library not ten yards away. Through the windows he watched Cal. She'd started her puppet show. They'd never made those frightening puppets, but it didn't matter. Apollo could see the heads of the bigger children, each of them drawn toward the puppets. Not Cal, but the show.

"Glamour," Apollo whispered.

He seemed to be the only person outside. Cal, the guards, and the children were in the library, the other women and youngest children were bedding down inside the Nurses' Residence. He stood there swaying. The courtyard took on the kind of silence New York City hasn't known for three hundred years. They weren't by the river, but Apollo could hear the sound of the waters slapping against the shoreline of North Brother Island.

As sudden as a strong wind, he felt a new current in the air. At first he mistook it for a sound, a kind of chattering suddenly filling the courtyard, but in a moment he understood it, instead, as a charge in his body. He felt as if a wave of electricity was running through his jaw. His teeth clenched tight, and his neck burned. He felt tuned into a higher frequency. He could almost sense the direction of the broadcast. Not the library or the Nurses' Residence. The Tuberculosis Pavilion.

William.

Apollo took two steps in that direction, but then spun like a top and walked back to the library. He came to the doorway and leaned in. Cal didn't look away from the children as she told the tale of Rapunzel.

The guards noted him, but it was Gretta, standing at the back, rigid and ready, who walked toward Apollo. She pushed him out of the library and squeezed his arm. "Cal may have decided to trust you," she whispered. "But that doesn't mean I do."

"Listen," Apollo said. "Please. There's something I have to tell Cal."

"You tell me," Gretta said. "Let those children enjoy ten minutes of happiness."

"It's William," Apollo said. "He made a threat."

"He makes those all the time."

"He said he'd called in the cavalry," Apollo told her. "I don't know who, but someone's coming."

Gretta let go of Apollo's arm, and her expression flattened with shock, as if she'd been slapped. "Someone's coming," she repeated. She reached a hand in the air, swatting faintly at the dark. She collected herself, turned from Apollo, and rushed back inside.

Apollo watched her skirt along the edge of the crowd, all those children listening. Gretta reached Cal, interrupted the show, leaned close, and whispered in the woman's ear. Cal lowered the puppets, just an inch, lost her smile for a moment, then caught herself and raised the puppets and resumed the story, but her eyes scanned the room until she locked eyes with one of her guards. And with that Apollo walked off.

The seclusion rooms overlooked a copse of trees at the bottom of a slight slope. The moon shone down on the top of the hill, leaving the trees in darkness, but the path quite clear. No one out there but Apollo.

He skirted along the edge of the pavilion, trying to find the window where William was being held. When he got there, he squatted and found a rock as big as a softball in the dirt. He stepped back five paces and threw the stone, and the window shattered. Now there was only the mesh of the cage between Apollo and William's cell.

From inside the cage there was no sound, no reaction. Apollo listened for something from the cage. Maybe the guards had already taken him while he'd been feeding Gayl. Maybe his body lay smoldering somewhere right now.

Apollo crept closer to the window. He tried to see inside, but the room was too dark. "William," he hissed. "William! If you're in there you answer me."

He went onto his toes to see inside. He brought his nose to the cage.

"William Wheeler!"

Finally a grunt came from inside the cage. The sound of scuffing and shuffling in the dirt. "That's not my name, so stop fucking using it."

Now a figure shambled to the window. Not a man but a shape, a shadow, grumbling with menace.

"I met your wife," Apollo said. "She said you sent her *To Kill a Mockingbird* with every page defaced."

"What do you care? You got your money, right?"

"You stole that money from her, William!"

Inside the cell the figure grumbled.

"I told you to stop calling me that. It's not my real name. I didn't know my real name either. Didn't know who I really was. Then I found the place where I belonged. Found people who understood me. I could talk to them like I never could to anyone. When I was there, I took off William Wheeler's face and found my true face underneath. Once my friends saw my true face, they gave me my true name. In fact, Apollo, you know it already, too."

"How would I know that?"

The man in the cage raised his voice and spoke as if reading an announcement. "Dinner plans tonight. A meal inspired by Baby Brian."

Apollo took a step backward. The man brought his face to the mesh barrier.

"*Boiled vegetables!*" he shouted.

"You're Kinder Garten," Apollo said.

"We!" he hissed. "We are Kinder Garten. Ten thousand men with one name."

The man in the cage jammed his fingertips through the metal webbing. In the moonlight the nails looked as ragged as claws. Apollo felt hit by a wave of confusion. He felt like a capsized ship.

"You killed your daughter," Apollo said. "That's what Gretta said."

"I made a choice!" Kinder Garten shouted back. "For my family, I made the hardest choice there is."

Apollo's jaw tightened. The electric current filled the air again. But it wasn't coming from William. The change in the air came from somewhere behind Apollo. The back of his head felt hotter by degrees. He turned.

Nothing down the hill but that copse of trees. The night cloaked them in shadows. Only the tops of the trees were vivid, truly visible. Wind off the East River caused the trees to thrash and bend. The trees stood fifty feet tall. Only after watching them directly did he realize the trees were swaying not with the wind but against it. Apollo trembled, and a feeling of disgust flooded his belly. He felt a sudden conviction that someone, something, hid among those trees and was watching him.

"Did you do what I asked?" Kinder Garten said. "Do I get my Gretta back? My Grace? Where is my family? You were supposed to bring them to me."

Apollo walked away from the man in the cage, moving along the line of the TB Pavilion, back toward the library. In fact, he started running. As he moved, he kept throwing glances back toward the trees.

"I made you a fair offer, Apollo!" Kinder Garten shouted. "This is on your head, not mine!"

Then the explosions began.

67

THE DOCTOR'S COTTAGE tore apart. A moment later two more explosions ripped through the Nurses' Residence. The sounds of destruction could be heard as far off as Rikers Island, waking the men in the units closer to the northern end of the prison. In the morning they'd swear—to fellow prisoners and guards—that they'd heard bombs on the East River. No one believed them.

Apollo hardly believed it, and he was right there running along the path back to the courtyard. How had William Wheeler—no, Apollo stopped himself—that wasn't his name. How had Kinder Garten called in artillery fire? It wasn't possible. But tell that to the buildings that had been torn to tinder, the ground that quaked beneath Apollo's feet.

Apollo heard another thunderous round go off, throaty as cannon fire, but this time he would've described it less as an explosion than as a roar. He turned back once, looking over his shoulder quickly, toward the copse of trees. Something passed overhead in the night sky—he could barely discern the size and shape. A missile? A bomb? A military drone? Then there was another explosion. In the library.

This one brought the roof down.

No screaming. No shouting. No crying. No screaming.

Apollo Kagwa ran alongside the Doctor's Cottage. The bomb had obliterated the dining table where he and Gayl ate macaroni and cheese twenty minutes ago. He sped toward the library. He didn't understand that he was listening for the screams of children and women until he didn't hear them. At least if he heard them, it would mean some of them were still alive.

He reached the library. The explosion had toppled the roof and cracked it in half, but it created an opening in an adjacent wall large enough for him to stoop and step through. He didn't want to. He wished, for just a moment, there was an adult present. Lacking one of those, he would have to do. He crouched now and stepped into the library. Broken glass scattered across the ground like glitter, brick dust floated in the air, a red mist.

A missile had hit the library, but more than half the books remained neatly on the shelves. Their spines were spattered with dirt and glass, but otherwise they seemed fine. The other books littered the floor. Among them Apollo found the first of the dead.

A pair of legs stuck out from beneath one half of the fallen ceiling. They were slim but long, clearly an adult and not a child.

"Who killed my sister?" a voice asked, hardly a whisper.

Apollo fell into a crouch as if the sky were going to fall in. Again. He turned and looked up to see Cal, shocked and disheveled. Her sweater hung half off one shoulder, her hair thrown up into spines of fright.

"I killed my sister," she said to herself. She swayed on her feet. Maybe she'd been more injured than she looked.

"She wouldn't be dead if I hadn't called her back," Cal said.

"That's Gretta?" Apollo said.

Now, out past the courtyard, a new sound. Kinder Garten. Calling out in a high-pitched yelp. Maybe they were words, but at this distance it was hard to tell. The distance was the issue though. Kinder Garten didn't sound far off, like when he'd been in the TB Pavilion. He sounded much closer. As if he'd been freed.

Cal looked to Apollo and brought three fingers to her lips. Urging him to silence, to calm. Maybe she could see he'd been on the verge of spinning into panic.

Now Apollo recognized—understood—that besides Gretta's there were no bodies on the ground. No other victims he could see. No dead children. No other dead women. Cal slapped his elbow sharply, then pointed to the hole in the wall. They slipped through and back out to the courtyard. Now Apollo found the courtyard full.

Women and children filed out of the Nurses' Residence with packs on their backs, bags in their hands, all but the youngest children carrying something. The youngest children were all being carried. More astoundingly, even the infants were silent. Had they all survived? They couldn't have. The population seemed slightly reduced, though Apollo couldn't say by how much. They moved in two columns. Their postures spoke of exhaustion and fear, but above all there remained great order. They fled in formation. A Special Forces team would've admired this level of discipline.

"I'm not a bad man!" Kinder Garten called out.

Apollo turned back, some natural reaction, the desire to shout back, to fight back, but Cal slapped him, hard, on the side of his face. He turned to her, and her face had set into a mask of dispassionate discipline. One hand had slipped into the pocket of her sweater. A knife in there? A gun? Apollo believed—knew—that if he'd spoken just then, given away their position, Cal would've taken that weapon out of her pocket and killed him. Better that than sacrifice all their lives. He turned away from Kinder Garten's voice and followed the others once again.

"Just let me explain myself!"

The Wise Ones threaded through the woods. They passed the coal storage house, moved between the foundry and the chapel. Where Apollo had seen only dense underbrush and hundred-foot trees, the Wise Ones showed him a path through the shadows. They led him, and he followed. They passed the morgue and reached the old gantry crane and ferry slip. When this island had been in operation, this was where the ferry would dock to unload or take on patients and staff.

"We're not going to swim," Apollo whispered. No one answered him.

The women and children gathered. This was the first time he'd seen the whole community out like this. They looked too vulnerable here, all exposed. Now he could count them. Nineteen women and eleven kids. That was it.

Apollo scanned for Gayl and found her quickly. She lay in her mother's arms, half asleep, nuzzling against her mother's neck. Her older brother stood at his mother's side but leaned against her hip, sleeping on his feet.

New destruction in the courtyard. More explosions, many of the old buildings back there were turning to rubble. These were the sounds of battle, thunder of war. In a way this was good. If Kinder Garten remained occupied back there, it meant he hadn't realized the Wise Ones were here, at the ferry slip.

Despite their training, a faint buzz had risen in the crowd. Busy checking bags and soothing children, who were, understandably, losing composure. A child will whine for a snack even as the world is exploding. But what could they do? Nowhere else to go. They had to wait here at the pier.

"I alone can fix this!"

Wheeler's voice caused everyone to go silent again. Even the infants stopped wriggling. Mostly. Now everyone watched the tree line. Sudden understanding: the destruction of buildings had ended, the task complete. Had it really taken so little time?

What now?

Then, behind them, a whisper played across the water.

A Pilgrim 40 Pilothouse Trawler appeared out of the darkness. One of the Wise Ones, a guard in her cloak, stood at the helm. The ship eased to the dock.

68

THE CHILDREN WERE brought on board first, but it was the older kids who were at the head of the line, seven- and eight-year-olds pulled up by three guards. The infants came next. The mothers on the pier handed their infants to the seven- and eight-year-olds, who immediately took each one to the forward master cabin, the most protected part of the ship. After the children had all gone below, the women tossed in their bags and supplies, one woman to the next, like sandbags. Last the women boarded. Two guards pulled each woman on, and in eight minutes, no more than that, the Wise Ones were ready to go.

Almost.

Apollo, Cal, and her twin imperial guards remained on the dock.

The wind picked up across the water, and the trees near the water's edge snapped and flapped. Apollo turned toward the tree line, squinted and scanned. For a moment he thought he saw a silhouette of a man . . . but a man of an unimaginable size. More likely it was only an oddly shaped hill caught by the moonlight and animated by Apollo's fear. It had to be that.

"People call us witches," Cal said quickly. She grabbed Apollo's hand. "But maybe what they're really saying is that we were women who did things that seemed impossible. You remember those old stories about mothers who could lift cars when their kids were trapped underneath? I think of it like that. When you have to save the one you love, you will become someone else, something else. You will transform. The only real magic is the things we'll do for the ones we love.

"One night I watched Emma out on the water, in her creek boat, paddling across the river, going back out to try and find her son, and I'm telling you, out on the water, that woman? She glowed."

Now Cal pulled Apollo backward, toward the trawler. The twins followed alongside. They gripped their maces so tightly, the backs of their hands were red. Apollo put his arms up to be helped onto the trawler, but the guards didn't pull him in.

"I'm sorry, Apollo," Cal said. "You're not taking this trip. My people are going east. You're not going with them." She pointed past the dock to the rocky shoreline fifty yards away, where something small had been tethered.

"That's our creek boat," Cal said. "I'm going to help you get to it." She gestured for him to shimmy alongside a ledge of dirt; from there he'd be at the rocks that sloped down toward the water.

Cal turned to her imperial guards. "You two get on board now," she said.

Neither woman moved. They stared down at her, their expressions a mask of professional cool but their eyes betrayed fear. "We're committed to you, Cal. Until the end."

Cal touched both women's faces gently. Then she squeezed their chins so tightly both women winced.

"This is not Sparta and I don't give one flying fuck about glory. Every day we stay alive is a day we beat our enemies." She let go of their chins. "I never met two stronger, smarter women than you. Who's going to need that strength, me or them?" She pointed toward the trawler where the other guards were making ready to depart.

The twins dropped their heads.

Then Cal went on her tiptoes and gave each woman a kiss on the cheek.

As the pair boarded, Cal walked to the edge of the dock. The adults and a few of the oldest children appeared at the windows of the cabins.

The moon highlighted Cal's tears, the tears of all the Wise Ones on board. She clapped one hand over her mouth to reassert her self-control.

The trawler's engine played so faintly, it could hardly be heard over the whipping winds. The boat coasted backward, and the fenders bobbled against the dock, and in a moment the trawler drifted off. Then the engine burbled louder, and the trawler pulled away. Apollo read the ship's name painted on the stern.

Merricat.

He shivered with gratitude, bone-deep relief, that they'd made it off the island. If nothing else it meant Kinder Garten's threats were at least half empty.

Cal turned to Apollo and clapped him out of his trance. "Are you still standing there?" she asked. "I thought I told you to get down there."

"Why didn't you go?" he asked. "I hope you didn't stay for me."

"Oh, please," she said. "Get over yourself." She seemed chipper when she said this.

"Then why?" Apollo asked.

"Someone had to stay here and keep them busy," Cal explained. "Until they can get some distance." She put a hand on his shoulder and urged him to move.

He still looked confused. "But once you're on the water, why would it matter?"

Cal looked back to the trees once again.

"The big one can swim," she said.

69

THEY MOVED QUICKLY but carefully along the earthen ledge, and when they reached the rocks, they scrambled down. As they descended, they saw less and less of the *Merricat*. The farther the trawler moved, the more cheerful Cal became. They weren't far from the creek boat, but still high enough that they could see the trees. And then, as casual as you please, Kinder Garten walked out from the shadows. Head to foot he was covered in brick dust. Dust in his hair and all over his clothes. His skin looked speckled and nearly red. He looked like a demon. He walked out on the ferry slip and scanned the water.

Cal crouched and Apollo crouched, too, but he wasn't used to the terrain so he fell backward, down the sloping rocks, coming to a stop at the water's edge. Cal scrambled after him.

"Apollo?" Kinder Garten called. "Could that be you? Don't tell me the bitches left you behind!"

No talking now. Cal shoved Apollo toward the creek boat. The craft was olive green, making it nearly invisible on the dark water. Cal gestured toward the boat and lifted a black aluminum paddle. He reached for it, but she swatted his hand away. She bent low and balanced the paddle half on the rocky ledge and half on the creek boat. She patted his ass, then gestured for him to sit on the paddle. When he did, she waved her hand for him to scoot himself into the little boat.

"Poor Apollo!" Kinder Garten howled. "Someone's always abandoning you."

From the sound of his voice, Kinder Garten had stalked off in the opposite direction to try and find him, the sound of Apollo's stumbling hard to trace under the echoing sky.

Apollo flopped into the creek boat. The small craft lifted four inches out of the water, enough to make Apollo fear it would capsize.

Cal brought her hand down on the edge of the boat and righted it. She leaned close. "I have to confess," she whispered. "I have to say this before you go."

"Come with me," Apollo said, grasping the sides of the creek boat as he tried to calm himself. "This thing is small, but we could try to fit."

Kinder Garten appeared at the top of the slope. He scanned the water from the rocks. He pointed. "There!" he shouted. "There!"

He sounded like a master siccing his hound on the prey. Both Cal and Apollo looked up at the man on the rocks. Farther behind him came that thunderous sound, a colossal tearing noise.

"No," Cal whispered.

The sky filled with something, it looked as large as a low flying airplane. Too big to be a man-made missile. It was a tree, going end over end through the air, out across the water.

A fucking tree.

"No," Cal begged.

The darkness hid the impact, but there was a tremendous splash. Had the boat been hit? Faintly they heard the chug of the boat's engine.

Kinder Garten clapped softly, pointed. "Again! There!"

Cal turned and reached into her sweater pocket. When her hand appeared, it held a gun, a Ruger LCR-22. She aimed it at Kinder Garten. She shot him. Even though they were outside, despite the small caliber of the gun, Apollo's eyes went out of focus from the terrific blast, the gun's report. He watched Cal but she seemed to work in slow time. The creek boat bobbled in the water, and Apollo felt his stomach seize as if he would throw up. She fired four times, and on the third pull she grazed him. Kinder Garten didn't scream. He gurgled and fell back and disappeared from view. Apollo's ear rattled and throbbed for another moment. He'd been expecting to see another tree fly out overhead, but that didn't happen. Cal's gunfire had changed the plan. She'd protected her people again.

"You know the myth of Callisto?" she asked. "She was a nymph. She had a child by Zeus, and for this she was punished by his wife Hera. Callisto was turned into a bear. Zeus suffered no consequences, of course. The baby grew up to be a great hunter, Arcas. One day Callisto saw Arcas in the woods, and recognizing her child, she wanted to hug him, to speak with him. But all Arcas saw was a great bear attacking. He was about to shoot her with an arrow when Zeus saved them both and turned them into constellations, Ursa Major and Ursa Minor. I always saw this as a happy end, as happy as those Greek stories ever get. Callisto got to spend eternity there in the heavens with her child. She could always see him. She would always know he was safe."

Cal looked out at the water then caught Apollo's eyes.

"I'm tired, and I want to see my little boy again."

She handed Apollo the paddle, sat on her butt, and with two feet she pushed him away from the rocks.

"You have to go to your son's grave," Cal said. "You have to see it for yourself so you have no doubts. You won't be any use to Emma otherwise. Then you have to find your wife." She trailed off, reached into the other pocket of her sweater, bullet shells gleaming in the moonlight.

"How am I going to track her down?" Apollo asked.

"Emma swore Brian was alive. She knew it, felt it. The last time I saw her, she said she'd finally narrowed it down."

"To what?" Apollo whispered.

Cal reloaded her pistol. "She said Brian is in the forest. I've thought about that. There's only one forest in all of New York City."

Apollo used the paddle to push off. When he'd drifted backward a few yards, he turned the boat in the water with the paddle. He looked back to see Cal climbing back up the rocks.

"What are you going to do, Cal?" he called.

She looked out at him. She appeared calm. "I'm going to show them my claws," she said. Soon she disappeared over the ridge.

"Gun!" Kinder Garten shouted. "Get her gun!"

Quickly there was some distance between Apollo and the island. The splash of the East River against his creek boat became louder.

Apollo was beginning to understand just how far he'd have to paddle—at night, in the cold—before he reached the far shore of the Bronx. He didn't look back at the island. When he paddled, he tried, as best he could, to stay quiet. Why? Cal's words came back to him.

The big one can swim.

"I am the god, Apollo," he whispered, trying to focus in this tornado of madness.

He kept on, and once North Brother Island disappeared behind him, there was only the distant shore to focus on. He picked a cluster of apartment buildings as his guiding light. He used the projects to lead him back to land.

"I am the god, Apollo."

After fifteen minutes he felt so tired that few thoughts remained, only the mechanical practice of the paddle rising and falling. He doubted he'd be able to last at this without some help, but what help could he hope for out here on the water?

Another twenty minutes, and he despaired. The Bronx seemed no closer. Still he kept on. "I am . . ."

He couldn't finish the sentence.

The shore finally became visible; it was the edge of Barretto Point Park. *You have to go to your son's grave. You have to see it for yourself so you have no doubts.* Apollo finally felt ready to know who was buried at Nassau Knolls Cemetery in Port Washington, New York.

6

BIG DIG

H OW FAST WOULD a Honda Odyssey need to be traveling in order to smash through wrought-iron cemetery gates?

Apollo Kagwa tried to do the math. He'd abandoned the creek boat at the edge of Barretto Point Park and ambled to the closest subway station, East 149th Street on the 6 line. He descended the stairs in wet jeans and boots, dog tired and half crazed with otherworldly knowledge, and even the homeless man squatting in the station looked at him with mistrust and worry. When he reached the turnstile, he reached for his wallet so he could swipe his MetroCard—a habit so ingrained that even now he couldn't stop himself—and this was when he remembered it had been lost in the waters of North Brother Island when he'd almost been drowned. Since he'd survived, maybe it was more like a baptism. Reborn now as what? Apollo hopped the turnstile, then waited on the downtown 6 calculating the amount of force required to ram a car through Nassau Knolls Cemetery's gates. He assumed he'd be going in during the night. It was doubtful they'd just let you dig up a grave while the sun was up.

But by the time he got home, it was early morning. A Wednesday. Thousands of people off to work. As New Yorkers do, they studiously avoided looking at Apollo even as they paid him their full attention. If he acted crazy and dangerous, they might switch cars, but if he only looked crazy and dangerous, they'd tolerate him. He stood the whole time because he felt he'd pass out if he sat. He reached the apartment and let himself in, took off his clothes, and it was as if he'd taken off an exoskeleton or a cast. Without the clothes his body melted. He hardly made it to the bedroom before he passed out. And when he woke, it was evening.

He felt no better rested, but he could sit up, stand up, and almost in passing he forced himself to eat. He dressed and went on the computer to reserve a Zipcar. When he discovered the Honda Odyssey was available—Suave, the same one he'd driven when he and Brian found the first edition in Riverdale—it felt like fate.

Apollo drove from Manhattan into Queens and from Queens out to Plainview, Long Island. Nassau Knolls Cemetery. Concentrate on that. He'd never been good at math, but he thought that fifty miles an hour in a 4,400-pound vehicle would tear a pair of iron gates apart.

THE FRONT ENTRANCE to Nassau Knolls Cemetery sits on Port Washington Boulevard, and while the grounds are enormous, what surrounds those grounds is still a residential neighborhood. Even more to the point, the Port Washington police department sits literally right next door to the cemetery and the Port Washington fire department is across the street. And yet Apollo Kagwa noticed none of this as he burned down Port Washington Boulevard, approaching ramming speed.

He slowed down, a bit, only when he calculated that he couldn't drive straight into the gates from Port Washington Boulevard. So he made a right on Revere Road, then turned the Odyssey around in the parking lot of a pharmacy. Now, moving west on Revere, he pressed his foot onto the gas pedal. It was eleven o'clock on a Thursday night, and the roads were empty in that baffling suburban way. He zoomed down Revere Road in an almost meditative silence. He crossed Port Washington Boulevard doing thirty-five miles an hour.

Then Patrice Green stamped his size-fifteen foot on the brakes, and the Odyssey spun out in a half circle, and the howl of the tires seemed loud enough to rouse the living and the dead. Apollo levitated in his seat. The seatbelt slapped him back down. His head spun a moment longer than the car. He bit his tongue and let go of the wheel.

"That was your plan?" Patrice asked Apollo from the passenger seat. "You're just going to bust through the gates with the police department right up the road?"

Apollo's foot had come off the gas. He looked down at it as if it had betrayed him. Patrice's big old hoof remained steady on the brake. Apollo looked back at Patrice with a catatonic air. He'd picked up the big man because he needed Patrice's help—digging up a grave would be exhausting work. But he hadn't said a thing about the tribute page. Patrice still believed Apollo didn't know who'd started the damn thing. But Apollo had a hard time playacting, kept wanting to haul off and crack his former friend in the teeth.

"I'd suggest we drive back to the parking lot and turn off the car," Patrice said.

Apollo watched Patrice for a long second.

"You hear me in there?" Patrice punched Apollo, not lightly. "I told you I'd help you," he said as calmly as he could. "You came to my place, told me and Dana a lot of shit that didn't make any fucking sense, but it didn't matter. We're your friends, do or die."

"Friends," Apollo repeated.

"Plus Dana was heated this guy took us for all that money," Patrice said. "We thought we could put a down payment on a place! But we're not going to spend money this motherfucker stole from his dead wife." Patrice rubbed the top of his head softly. "I admit I was still kind of impressed with what he pulled off. High technical skill. No question. A worthy foe."

Patrice slipped the car into park, took his foot off the brake, opened the iPad case sitting in his lap, and turned the tablet on. "Right now though you and me are two black men sitting in a minivan in the middle of the road in the middle of White Ass, Long Island, and that's bound to draw attention soon enough. I told you I'd help you, so let me help. Cool?"

"Yeah," Apollo said. "You're my friend after all."

Patrice watched Apollo thoughtfully for a few seconds. "Yeah. First thing we need to do is back up. Put the car in reverse."

Apollo nodded. He might as well have been a robot working under voice commands. Now the car coasted backward slowly.

"You'll have to steer this thing," Patrice said, looking out the back. "'Cause right now you're about to go up on the sidewalk."

Apollo looked into the rearview mirror, then the passenger mirror, then finally turned the wheel. He parked in a spot behind the pharmacy on the corner. When Patrice demanded the car keys, Apollo handed them over.

"You know, if me and Dana had kids like you once suggested, I couldn't be out here helping you right now." He grinned. "Now thank your child-free friend."

"Thank you," Apollo said stiffly.

"You're welcome."

72

THEY SAT IN the dark inside the Honda Odyssey and listened for police sirens that never came. They did hear one car cruising down Port Washington Boulevard but dismissed it, someone on their way home, that's all. But then, after a minute of silence, the same car, at least it sounded like the same car, prowled past in the other direction. Its engine had a grim, grumbling quality to it, a powerful engine, barely restrained. The pharmacy blocked their view, so they couldn't see the vehicle. Was it some random car or a police cruiser? Neither of them was going to walk out to the corner to check. They were like two fish taking shelter in a cove because a shark might be in the open water.

Patrice's iPad had gone off so he turned it on again. The lock screen showed Patrice and Dana on their wedding day. Bride and groom, in tuxedo and gown, stood below an indoor basketball hoop.

"You two got married on the court?"

"We made it work," Patrice said, looking down at the image, his face lit up by the LED screen and the memory. After a moment he swiped right, and the homescreen appeared, a familiar grid of apps. He swiped from one screen to the next.

Apollo and Patrice heard the same car for the third time, prowling Port Washington Boulevard. Apollo rolled his window down, leaned out, and this time saw the faint glow of the car's headlights as they lit up a storefront on the opposite corner. They paused there, as if the driver of the car were idling in the street. That vehicle sat on the other side of this pharmacy, and its engine grumbled and its lights played in the darkness. To Apollo's ear, it sounded—almost, nearly—like whatever he'd heard on the island that night. Whatever had been lurking in the copse of trees.

With his head out the window, he looked up at the sky as if some great object might be coming down on their car right now, flung by something impossibly strong. But the only thing visible in the sky was the moon and a sprinkle of stars. And then the car—who drove it?—trundled on again. Maybe it had just been waiting at a red light. Apollo didn't roll the window up again until the guttering of the engine passed on.

When Apollo pulled his head back in, Patrice had the Google Maps app working.

"Nassau Knolls Cemetery is almost four hundred acres," Patrice said. "Three million people buried here. It's big enough that there's got to be some part of the fencing that's easy to slip through."

Patrice had become so occupied with his Google Map, he didn't realize Apollo had swiped back his keys until they were in the ignition and the engine turned on. The Odyssey roared even as it sat in park.

"We can just drive around the perimeter," Apollo said. "You don't need to rely on computers for everything."

Patrice reached over and turned the car off. He spoke to Apollo with aggravated patience. "The two of us are not driving around slow in a suburban neighborhood at midnight. Somebody's going to call the cops on some shit like that. And I did not survive Iraq to get shot to death by some Suffolk County cop who 'feared for his life.' You feel me?"

Patrice watched Apollo now.

"Then let's get out and walk," Apollo said.

Patrice nodded. "Two black men walking through white suburbs at night. Never heard of that going bad."

Apollo gave an exasperated laugh.

"'We can be heroes,'" Patrice said. "But heroes like us don't get to make mistakes."

Patrice typed in "Nassau Knolls Cemetery."

"Street view," Patrice said, licking his lips as if he'd been given a salty treat.

"That's what I'm talking about," Patrice finally said.

He lifted the screen for Apollo to see. The image captured on a sunny afternoon. A portion of the cemetery fencing looked as if it had been torn open, a gap wide enough to fit a truck through.

"Something big did that," Apollo said softly.

"Maybe a truck or a car?" Patrice said, closing the iPad. "Big accident?"

"Maybe."

Apollo leaned out the window to listen for the prowl car. How long did he wait? He couldn't quite say. Too long, probably. Which is when he realized there might be another reason he wasn't gunning the Honda.

There are some things people aren't meant to see. Even with all he'd experienced on the island, Apollo understood that whatever lay buried in that grave existed as the farthest landmark on this new map of the spectral territories. Ultima Thule of grief. Would he go insane if he opened that casket? Would he burst into flames? Turn to stone? Despite all this, he finally turned the key. He pulled the Honda out of the parking lot and drove down Revere Road, not going too fast or too slow, nothing to cause concern among the locals.

In those old stories, the myths and fairy tales Cal had talked about, the heroes did what they did but you never knew why. In the stories, at least, they had no interior life. Their job was simply to act. Gods and gorgons allied against them, and still they bore the spear and shield. Still they walked into the deep, dark forests. But did those heroes ever feel like Apollo did now? The real people, not the characters they became. They were human beings too, after all. They must've shivered in the shadow of the world's great horrors. They must have wondered how they would ever see the quest through. And somehow they persevered. Maybe that was the point of telling those stories again and again, one generation to the next.

If they could be brave, then we might be, too.

THE MODERN GRAVE is only four feet deep, not six. In the past bodies were buried six feet deep to compensate for their eventual decomposition and, sometime after that, the casket collapsing in on itself, leaving a sinkhole. But the modern casket is much thicker and sturdier, and many have steel reinforcement, so that it produces no sinkhole. As a secondary precaution, caskets are now buried inside concrete grave liners, like a casket for the casket. This concrete vault is the other reason that being buried four feet deep is fine in the modern day. Patrice explained this as they walked through the cemetery, a dash of research done on the quick, as the two men padded across the dirt in the dark.

Patrice looked up the location of Brian Kagwa's burial plot. Nassau Knolls was so large, they could've wandered for half a day without stumbling across it. But the cemetery's website included a handy pdf.

They used the community mausoleum—a white building that looked like a banquet hall—as a kind of North Star. Brian's grave lay behind the building. There would be a road they could follow on the other side.

They weren't thirty yards into the graveyard before they heard the rumbling engine of the prowl car again. Both stopped moving and turned back toward the fence line. There were no trees here, but the moonlight was weak. They heard the car, it coasted, and soon its lights played through the fence posts like cards being run along the spokes of a bike tire. The light raked at the graveyard dirt. Apollo and Patrice didn't dare even to crouch. The car reached the big break in the fence line, and there it stopped. Apollo saw the silhouette of the car but couldn't be sure whether there were police lights on the roof. The car idled there, then they heard the mechanical hiss of a window sliding down. Could it be Kinder Garten at the wheel? How would he have known they were here?

Another moment.

Another moment.

Then, achingly slowly, the car moved on.

Once the red rear lights disappeared down the block, Patrice opened the iPad and scanned the map quickly. "The maintenance building is on the far end," he said, pointing toward the mausoleum.

The maintenance shed was a prefab beige metal building, two stories high and fifty feet long. As big as the mausoleum, but it had been tucked behind a line of trees so it disappeared in the night. Apollo was sure it was there only because of the bright yellow Caterpillar backhoe loader parked at the edge of the trees.

"I could run that backhoe," Patrice offered.

Apollo kicked at one of the enormous tires. "That probably won't make much noise at twelve-thirty at night."

Patrice simply blinked at him.

"We need the old-fashioned tools," Apollo said.

They walked the perimeter of the building. It had a rectangular shape, and on one of the longer sides sat three sets of garage doors. Apollo went along trying to lift each one, but all were locked. At the last garage door, Apollo lost his shit for about ten seconds and rattled at the door handle as if he could shake it open.

"There's going to be an alarm system," Patrice warned.

Apollo let go of the door handle and stared back at his friend. Patrice hadn't been scolding him but was thinking out loud. Patrice moved along the side of the building, but he wasn't bothering with the doors. Instead he scanned the upper corners of the building. He pointed to a corner where a gray box the size of a router had been affixed to the wall.

"Now let's say they've modernized this place in the last few years and someone convinced them to go from a wired alarm system to a wireless alarm system."

He flipped on the iPad and swiped through grid after grid of applications. He tapped an app and tapped twice more, then watched as a series of numbers appeared in a box toward the bottom of the screen.

"This is some late-nineties technology they're using. I kind of feel bad for them. They probably paid some dude more than they should have for some shit that stopped being effective fifteen years ago. They heard 'wireless alarm system' and just nodded and signed the check. Our money says, 'In God We Trust,' but technology is catching up."

He laughed at this quietly, a proud member of an upstart faith.

"Now what we're going to do is pretty simple. I'm going to use this app to send some radio noise back at the central control system. It'll be like I'm playing my radio a lot louder than the alarm system's radio. When we push open this door, that radio signal will die out, but my radio will be playing so loud that the system won't be able to tell that its radio has gone quiet."

Patrice tapped once on his screen, and a small blue circle in the upper-right corner throbbed. He set the iPad face up on the ground. Then he threw his hip against the door, and after one pathetic squawk, the perimeter was breached. Sure enough, the night's silence remained.

Had there actually been a working alarm system at all? Apollo couldn't say. But he skirted his way around the little tablet on the ground anyway just to be sure he wouldn't interrupt its wizardry. He followed Patrice inside. The iPad stayed outside standing guard.

PATRICE CARRIED THE flat blade shovel, the crowbar, and the ax. Apollo had taken only one tool from the maintenance building, a mattock, heavy as the shovel and ax combined. A four-foot wooden handle topped by a two-headed metal device. One end sharp like a pick, and the other was called an adze. The adze looked like an ax head but instead of being vertical, it was horizontal, like a weapon out of the Dark Ages, something for smashing through armor. It was made to dig through hard-packed dirt like the kind they were likely to find here in winter. Apollo had the iPad tucked under his free arm.

Apollo scanned the rows of gravesites as they moved. Brian Kagwa had a grave marker instead of a tombstone. Twelfth row, and nine grave markers in. There it was. He felt compressed, all out of breath, seeing the name. Brian.

Brian.

"Are we really going to do this?"

Apollo didn't understand it had been him asking the question until Patrice responded. "We don't have to, my man. We can get back in the whip right now."

Apollo nodded absently. That's what they should do. Sure. Right. He stared at the plot and practically heard his nerves playing like cello strings in the night. "You gotta give me a little help," he whispered. He wasn't sure what he was asking for.

Patrice dropped the tools and slipped the iPad free. After a few taps, he read from the screen. "I found instructions. Okay, remove the sod using a flat blade shovel." He looked at Apollo. "I don't know how to do some shit like that. Maybe I can find a video."

"Military man," Apollo said.

"I could defuse a roadside bomb if you had one," he offered.

Apollo dropped the mattock and pulled the shovel from Patrice. He placed the thin edge of the shovel to the ground, then pressed down with his right foot until it sank into the dirt. After the head of the shovel went about two-thirds deep, he pulled the handle back, causing a crunching noise like a paper bag being crumpled. He slipped the shovel out, moved one step to the right, and did the same again. Within twenty minutes he'd pulled up the whole top layer of sod over the grave. It was easy to pick up the clumps and toss them aside—they looked like used tea bags in the dark. By the time he'd finished, his arms pulsed with fire. Too cold out to really sweat, but his face went clammy. His breathing had grown so loud, he sounded like a panting dog. When he finished, he found Patrice gawking.

"Where'd you learn to do that shit, city boy?" Patrice asked.

"Me and Emma used to watch those home improvement shows," Apollo explained between gasps.

Patrice nodded. "Me and Dana watch those, too."

Apollo tossed the shovel away. "Now hand me that thing."

Patrice gave Apollo the mattock. Neither of them knew what it was called. It certainly had never been used on the home improvement shows, but Apollo intuited its method. He turned the adze end of the head so it faced the rectangle of dirt he'd uncovered, the soil so dark, it looked like a pool of black water. When Apollo stepped in, Patrice expected him to sink.

Apollo raised the mattock and brought it down hard into the earth.

"We can take turns," Patrice offered.

Apollo nodded. "When I can't lift my arms anymore, we'll switch."

"You need light?" Patrice asked. "I got this app. One of mine. I mean I wrote it myself. It's called Daylight."

"Maybe you could save it till we get deeper down," Apollo said. He didn't notice the pride in Patrice's voice. He had his own work to do. Patrice nodded softly, embarrassed by how much he'd been fishing for praise.

Apollo brought the mattock down. The adze sank into the dirt, satisfyingly deep, but it sent an electric shock up through Apollo's arms, right into his shoulders. Hard earth. He'd be tired sooner than he thought. He looked at Patrice and felt so grateful for his friend. This feeling was followed by the desire—the need—to ask Patrice why he started that Facebook page. And why he didn't tell Apollo.

For a moment he had the worst thought of all: What if Patrice was on Kinder Garten's side? What if he was one of those ten thousand men? It seemed impossible—he knew Patrice, didn't he?—but by now he also knew he couldn't trust his own judgment. Maybe the man driving that car had made plans with Patrice and right now Apollo was digging his own grave. Patrice, or someone else, might just shoot him in the head and leave his body in the hole he'd dug. Nothing for it, though. If Patrice was going to betray him, he'd just have to deal with it then. For now he raised the mattock and brought it down again. Dirt sprayed back up into his face, coating his skin, causing an itch along his neck.

"It's one in the morning," Patrice said. "This better be over by five."

Apollo wiped at his face, scratched his neck, put both hands on the mattock's handle, and raised it again.

FOUR FEET DOESN'T seem deep, but it took them one and a half hours to clear half that much. Patrice and Apollo had changed places twice already. As one broke up dirt with the mattock, the other, standing outside the hole, used the shovel to clear the soil. Both of them looked as if they'd run a marathon inside a coal chute, dirt on their clothes, on their hands, in their hair, in their ears. Each man alternated between digging with his jacket on until he was so sweaty his shirt stuck to his skin, then slipping the coat off in order to dry out and within minutes getting the shivers all over.

By three in the morning, they were three and a half feet down. Patrice sat on the rim of the grave. Apollo remained in the hole. He couldn't lift the mattock again, so he dropped it. His stomach shrank with hunger, and his rib cage burned from his heavy breathing.

"I know," Apollo said. "I know about you and the Baby Brian page."

Patrice shifted where he sat. Dirt fell from his perch down into the hole. "I told you I joined it when we took the train out to Long Island. I didn't hide that from you, not on purpose."

"But you didn't tell me the rest," Apollo said, leaning back against the dirt for fear he'd collapse. "You didn't tell me you'd started the page. Why would you do that? If you're my boy, why would you?"

"Start it? You mean like I'm the administrator for that shit? I wouldn't do you like that. I wouldn't."

"The day I went out to the island, you left a message on the board. Green Hair Harry, that's you."

Patrice opened the iPad, shaking his head as he did it. He opened the Facebook app. Apollo watched him as he tapped his way toward the tribute page.

"Why keep playing?" Apollo asked. "Just say fuck it, let's have it out."

Patrice's eyes scanned left to right. Apollo watched him reading, then a second later Patrice's eyes grew wider as reading turned to deeper comprehension.

"That's not me," Patrice said. "That's not. When you left our place, me and Dana just sat there in straight-up shock for like half an hour. I couldn't believe Kim would do you like that. My dude, I'm telling you this, we went straight to bed like we were holing up in a cave or something. Couldn't fall asleep for hours. And I damn sure didn't get on the computer to type you messages."

Patrice looked both angry and panicked. He looked at the screen again.

"Just check out the time when the post went up. It's like ten minutes after you left. I swear to you, on my moms, I did not get on that computer for the rest of the night."

Apollo bent and gripped the mattock. He hardly had the strength to stand up again, but somehow he found the power to heft the tool. "Who else could know I was going?"

"This dude knew," Patrice said, eyes on the mattock's blade. "William knew."

"It was you and me and Dana in that basement. He didn't know I was coming, not for sure, until I showed up in the Bronx."

Apollo and Patrice remained in this standoff for thirty seconds that felt like three years.

Then Patrice sat up straight as if he'd been stabbed, shut off the iPad, and closed the cover. "What if he was there too?" he said softly.

"How?"

"Titan," Patrice whispered. "If he hacked Titan, he could turn on my camera, my mic, control all of it remotely if he wanted. He could've been watching us the whole time." He set the iPad down in the dirt and watched it cautiously.

"But how would he do that?" Apollo asked. "How would he even find your computer out of all the computers in the world?"

Patrice pointed at Apollo's pocket. "He sent you that video of Emma. You sent it to me. I ran it on my computer. It would be that easy for him to hop from your phone to my computer. I gotta warn Dana," he said, taking out his phone. But before dialing, he froze up and turned it off. He opened the back of the phone and slipped its SIM card out. For good measure, he crushed it with the bottom of the ax.

"My phone and computer are synced," Patrice said. "He knows exactly where we are right now."

"He's not the NSA," Apollo said.

"Could've fooled me," Patrice said. He gestured for the mattock now and slid into the hole. "I want to get back to my wife. Let's hurry."

Apollo climbed out, barely strong enough to make it that far. He pulled the mattock up with him. Patrice clutched the shovel. So little light fell in the open grave that its bottom couldn't be seen. They might as well have been digging into the underworld.

B Y FOUR-THIRTY, APOLLO took over again. Patrice lay by the open grave, so exhausted he looked as if he'd fallen asleep. The dirt was down to inches. Though Patrice offered to switch with Apollo, Apollo didn't reply. His body hurt so badly, it had gone cold. The aches in his arms and shoulders, his lower back and his knees—he would pay for all of them later, but he'd become exhausted in a way that made him invulnerable. Willpower was all he used to dig now.

Then to Apollo's great surprise, the sun rose behind him. But it came much too quickly and in the wrong place. From the west a blinding light appeared, so powerful Apollo dropped his shovel and covered his eyes.

Patrice said, "I thought you needed help seeing."

The beam of brightness came from Patrice's iPad. The screen glowed like molten gold. Apollo couldn't even make out Patrice behind the pad, so his voice became disembodied and divine.

"I bring you Daylight," Patrice said.

Apollo looked back down into the grave. He could see everything now. The shovel had fallen at an angle; his shoes and pants were so matted with dirt, they looked soggy. And below him, he clearly saw a shape, an outline. The casket? Could he really have reached it? He'd started to fear there would be no end to the dig. Apollo went down on one knee and patted the earth.

Then Patrice's iPad beeped three times, and right after that, the light died out.

"Eats up a lot of battery power," Patrice said. "Even a full charge only gets you four minutes. It works on tablets and phones."

"It helped," Apollo said. He tapped the head of the shovel against the dirt. Almost there.

The shovel dug into the dirt, and a dull thump played in the graveyard. Apollo brought the shovel down again. Once more a solid thump.

Apollo bent forward and brushed at the dirt until a flat gray surface appeared.

Beside him, above him, Patrice perked up. Apollo went to his knees, wildly brushing with his hands. But then this horrible choking noise rose out from the hole, a sob of turmoil. Apollo raised a hand and slapped at the buried thing.

"It's not the casket," Apollo said. He sounded undone, almost unraveling.

"Tell me what you see," Patrice said.

"It's concrete!" Apollo pushed himself onto his knees and cleared more of the dirt. A flat block of concrete, like a panel of sidewalk.

"That's the grave liner," Patrice said. "There's two kinds, solid concrete and sectional panels. The panels are cheaper, easier to break through. Which one do you think your mom paid for?"

How early would the Nassau Knolls maintenance crews arrive? This was the question. How long before the sun rose just enough for a neighbor to open her second-floor bedroom curtains, peer out at the day, and see two black men at an open grave?

Apollo used the shovel to push himself onto his feet. How long would it take to chop through it? And how loud would that noise be?

"Drop me down that thing," Apollo said to Patrice. "The one I was using."

A large silhouette moved, and a moment later the mattock fell into the grave. Its head landed on the sharper end, the one shaped like a pick. The thing made a loud popping noise when it landed and sank right into the concrete, like a thumbtack going into a bulletin board. Apollo pulled at the mattock, but it was stuck. He crouched and leaned back and wrenched the tool out, and when he did, a sound like ice cubes being cracked out of a tray played in the hole.

Apollo tamped at the concrete liner with one foot and felt it waver. He brought the mattock down to another terrific chorus of cracking concrete.

Four blows with the mattock, and the sectional liner turned to dust. And there lay a child's casket. White. The decorative hardware—handle rod brackets, caps, stamped metal corners—all antique nickel.

Apollo crouched and ran his hands along either side of the casket, searching for the groove between the lid and the base. He couldn't bear the idea of chopping through the top of the casket. He just couldn't do it. He found the space and slipped the pick end of the mattock inside. When he wrenched it open, the locking system groaned and finally came apart with an almost wet snap, like a tooth being torn out of a jaw.

He pulled at the small lid. Halfway up it caught, and he dropped the mattock, used two hands to pull it the rest of the way. He heaved and bent low in the posture of a supplicant. The dawn light reached along the top of the gravesite though it remained darker down in the hole. And finally, for the first time in four months, Apollo saw his child.

The mortician had done his best, but Brian Kagwa's face still bore the burn marks. The skull showed through at the top, gray as grief. His tiny body had been wrapped in a light blue blanket. In the chaos of opening the casket, dirt and stones fell onto the pillow, across the blanket, across the body. Apollo looked down on his son, once sealed away clean but now soiled.

"Look what I did to my boy," Apollo whispered.

He'd been wrong to think Cal and Emma had been anything but insane. They'd convinced him not to follow common sense. Maybe he hadn't wanted to be sensible. Better to believe in monsters than that your child is dead. He closed the lid of the casket, then opened it once again. He couldn't bear the thought of his baby boy lying there with dirt on his face, pebbles in his hair. The least he could do—the very least—was to wipe his son's face clean.

He touched the baby's forehead, and with that, he broke the spell.

THORNS.

His fingers caught on a knot of them.

That's how it felt. Sharp enough to tear skin. So surprising he pulled back, and only after the seconds of shock passed did he realize his ring finger was bleeding. The tip had been cut when he caressed his dead child.

Apollo steadied himself, and when he clutched at the body again, he made sure to touch only the blue blanket it had been buried in. Inside the grave the world remained lightless, but above him Apollo found the glow of the rising sun. He lifted the body from the casket, lighter than he remembered and smaller, too. Through the fabric of the blanket, he felt a knotty mass, as if he held a wasp's nest instead of a baby. He'd become so used to the smell of dirt after hours digging this hole that he could smell nothing else.

Above him, at the surface, Patrice coughed and said, "That's foul."

He looked over his shoulder. Patrice looked more frightened than him. He wondered at the sight he must've made just then. His skin dirtied all over—his face and neck, his back and stomach, his hands—everything was coated in earth, entirely soiled. And he was carrying—what? He rose up from his knees and brought the baby higher. And in the dawn light, he saw what he held.

It looked like clotted hair. The stuff you'd fish out of the bathtub drain in a house that had been abandoned, overtaken by the elements, matted and gnarled. What made it monstrous was the size, as big as a six-month-old. Pounds and pounds of hair—fur?—looped and twined so tightly, it looked more like barbed wire.

How had he mistaken this for a child?

For his child?

He held it but felt a rising impulse to throw it back down into the dirt, to clean his hands with holy water. He retched, stooping forward, nearly dropping the thing. He looked down at this bundle and retched again. Despite the blanket, his skin itched with repulsion.

"What the fuck."

Patrice staggered back from the grave. It was too much to see. Inadvertently he stood on another grave, that of a woman named Catherine Linton.

The Scottish called it glamer.

Glamour.

An illusion to make something appear different than it really is.

This was what he'd been feeding and changing and hugging and holding? This was what he sang to at night when Emma wouldn't do it anymore? This was what he took to the park with all the other dads so early in the morning? He thought of Ida, holding her false sister, a child made entirely of ice, loving it as if it was alive.

He found he couldn't drop the thing, but at the same time he wanted—he needed—for it to be far from him. He extended his arms. Now the blanket fell away from the body so it draped backward over his hands. Fully exposed, top to bottom, it really did look like a wasp's nest, gray, and the hair so tightly ground together it looked woven. There was more mingled within the layers of hair. He'd thought he'd cut his finger on a thorn, but that was wrong. Now he could see it. Jutting out, here and there, were fragments of teeth and splinters of bone and shards of fingernails.

"Emma," he whispered. "I should have believed."

Then he felt something new through the blanket. A tremor.

Movement.

In the light Apollo saw, deep inside the little form, something moving. He watched the face, or the place where the face should've been. There were two concave grooves, like eye sockets smoothed into soft clay. Below that a thin line ran, a mouth.

A mouth.

And below that, where the chest would be, deeper inside, Apollo saw a small mass, a lump. A heart? Faintly, it beat.

He watched in quiet terror. He wished to unsee this. He shivered and felt his legs going weak. And then, to make it worse, the heart did more than beat—it *moved*. The lump shuttled, faintly, higher. And then again. It was climbing, wriggling like a maggot. It reached the thin line of the mouth, and then the mouth parted. There was no other way to say it; the thing bucked, one grand exhalation, as if unearthing it finally allowed it to breathe.

But it hadn't been a heart he'd seen inside the little body. Instead that inhuman mouth spewed a mass of water bugs, at least a dozen, each one as big as a silver dollar. They wiggled across the blanket and reached Apollo's arms. They crawled up his arms, scrambling toward his neck, his face.

Apollo howled. The sound of an animal, not a man. He dropped the body. The blue blanket floated to the far end of the grave, draped back over the casket. He slapped at the roaches on his arms. One made it to his neck. He felt its bristled legs skitter as it reached his cheek. He nearly tore his own skin away just to get it off.

Meanwhile the body, the baby, landed at an angle. It seemed to be sitting up, watching him. He still felt the bug on his skin. Overwhelming disgust filled him with the instinct to destroy. Apollo found the mattock and brought it down on the casket. It sounded like he was chopping wood.

In minutes he'd destroyed the casket and turned the rest of the sectional liner to dust. At a quarter past five in the morning, an early sun rose in an especially clear morning sky. Birds chirped. The night had fallen away, and down in the grave Apollo raised the mattock one last time, aiming for the creature.

But something about its posture was so unsettling to him. Or to be more precise, so familiar. At this angle it might've been a child strapped into a booster seat and pulled up to the kitchen table. In fact, it had been that child, and Apollo had fed him—fed it—spoonful after spoonful of applesauce or yogurt or sweet potatoes he'd roasted and pureed.

He set the mattock back down. Despite the revulsion he felt, he picked the thing up again. Without the blanket, the rough surface of the body threatened to cut him again so he was forced to hold it tenderly.

He focused on its face, the sunken suggestion of its eyes, the thin line of the mouth that hadn't quite closed again. This gave it the suggestion of a sleeping child, and Apollo couldn't stop himself from wanting to soothe it. Not a conscious reaction but something primal. He cradled the figure with one forearm and gently held the back of the head with his right hand. With his left, he touched the spot where the eyebrows would've been.

He traced his finger down. Once he had seen his son's face here. He tapped the place where the nose would've been, where it had been. A nose he'd loved. How many times had he kissed it? A thousand times a week. He brought his finger to the mouth. He used to tap Brian's lips trying to predict when the teeth would appear. He rested his fingers there.

And the body moved again. The mouth. The maw. It opened and closed, opened and closed stiffly, like a puppet's jaw. Then he heard a straining sound, like an empty Styrofoam cup being squeezed and released, the hinges of the dry jaw creaking. Apollo feared more roaches would stream out, but that didn't happen, so he held on to the body. The mouth stretched and shut. Not hard to see what it was doing. It was trying to feed.

Drops of his blood quivered on those inhuman lips, the blood from his cut finger.

Nothing else about the body suggested life. Only the mouth became animated. Not really alive, but impossible to think of it as truly dead. An automaton. Fueled by blood and belief.

As it suckled blood from his finger, the creaking sound came in a rhythm, squeeze and release, squeeze and release. Apollo pulled his finger from the mouth, and in an instant the jaw stopped working. It lay as still as before.

"Something made you and then left you behind," he whispered.

Patrice's voice came to him from outside the grave. "This is way past late, Apollo. We have to go."

Apollo crouched and found the blue blanket. He wrapped the body in it again. He'd done a lot of damage to the casket, but—best he could—he returned the body to its resting place. Once it was in the shattered remains of the casket, once it had been returned to the shadows of the grave, its glamour returned. It appeared to be a child again. His child again. In the dark it became Brian Kagwa.

He checked to see if the red string had been cut loose by the thorns, but its knot held.

"You deserved better than you got," Apollo said. "I'm sorry if you felt any pain."

Apollo closed the lid of the coffin as best it would go. He tossed the mattock out of the grave, then the flat head shovel. Patrice extended a hand, and Apollo took it. Apollo climbed out of the grave. He went into a pocket and gave the Zipcar card to Patrice. He told Patrice to go on and get the minivan, he'd be out soon.

Apollo used the shovel to throw dirt down onto the casket. He couldn't fill the grave—he didn't have the time, and his body didn't have the power—but he wouldn't leave the grave with the body exposed.

After that Apollo took up the mattock and moved to the brass grave marker. He brought the adze down into the dirt, and it sank deep with the first blow. He used the handle like a lever and pulled back until the grave marker buckled. He moved six inches and did the same again. When he wrenched back, this time the top half of the grave marker lifted from the dirt.

The marker had been attached to a granite block, common practice. In order to remove the marker, Apollo would have to take the block as well. Since this had been a baby's grave, the block was small. In three minutes Apollo pulled it free. The sounds of roots tearing loose and soil cracking played alongside his labored grunting. He dropped the mattock. So close to collapse, it seemed impossible to do anything more than breathe. And yet with a stoop, he lifted the grave marker with its granite backing. It must've weighed thirty pounds. His body didn't know how it could handle the weight, but there was no room for discussion. This wasn't the grave of Brian Kagwa, so why would his father leave the marker there?

Apollo moved toward the fence. He hefted the grave marker under one arm and dragged the mattock behind him with the other. The Odyssey idled in the street, Patrice at the wheel. When Apollo appeared at the fence, Patrice startled as if he was seeing Death by daylight. Apollo opened the side door of the car and plopped the grave marker down as if it was a bag of fertilizer. He dropped the mattock onto the floor. Then he got in. Patrice looked back at the marker and the mattock.

"We can't explain that stuff if we get pulled over," Patrice said. "You understand that, right?"

"Then don't get pulled over," Apollo said.

Patrice put the car in motion.

Port Washington became Munsey Park, then Manhasset, then Great Neck and onward in the journey out of Long Island and back to New York City. Apollo felt a kind of calm that might also be called certainty. The magic of the world had been revealed. All the deceptions were gone. To believe in only the practical, the rational, the realistic was a kind of glamour as well. But he couldn't enjoy the illusion of order anymore. Monsters aren't real until you meet one.

Well, Apollo had met a monster. He and Emma and Brian, they'd all met it. Apollo wasn't thinking about the thing in the grave. Or even the thing that spawned it. He meant the man who'd pretended to be his friend, the former William Wheeler. He'd met his enemy. He knew its true name.

7

KINDERGARTEN

78

B RIAN WEST WAS at the front door.

Apollo reached his hand in the air and turned all three locks.

It wasn't Brian West yet.

The man knelt and pulled off his blue skin.

Brian West called Lillian Kagwa's name.

Gargamel and Azrael wanted to destroy the Smurfs.

Hot water ran in the bathroom, and the apartment filled with steam.

Gargamel and Azrael hid in the woods.

The Smurfs suspected nothing.

Brian West picked up his son.

Brian West carried Apollo into the bathroom.

"You're coming with me," he said.

He took off Apollo's clothes.

79

APOLLO SLEPT, ON and off, for two days and two nights. It might be a stretch to call it sleep. More like a little coma. He woke in starts but couldn't muster the mindfulness to do more than roll over and fall back asleep again. He felt so groggy, it seemed like he'd been dosed. The last two days had been an uncut drug, an overdose of the improbable.

Patrice had driven him home, helped him upstairs, where he stumbled and flopped onto the mattress. Apollo remembered none of this. He had sat in the back of the minivan cradling a grave marker bearing his son's name and awakened in his bed. Outside he saw morning light. He thought he'd only shut his eyes for ten minutes. When he tried to rise, his body still felt sore, so bruised he might've turned purple. He staggered to the kitchen. He stood at the sink and stared into the glass-faced kitchen cabinets but could make out only a hazy vision of himself. He and Emma had brought the cabinets home from IKEA by train. Two boxes per trip because that was all he could carry. Akurum wall cabinets in Lidi white. Each cost $115 before taxes. Ridiculous the kind of stuff that comes to mind. Insane to imagine they'd once fought over the choice as if nothing mattered more.

He needed water; he needed food. He filled a glass from the tap, then drank three more. He turned to find the grave marker on the kitchen table, laid out like a placemat. The mattock was propped by the front door. What about the book? He tensed so tightly, he nearly threw his back out. He scanned the kitchen, the living room, went to the front door and opened it. He returned to the bedroom, his bed. No book. No book. He'd had it tucked under one arm, hadn't he? Had slipped it into the back of his pants while he held Gayl.

The book. He focused on that. He'd lost the one Cal gave him, but he had another one here. His father's copy. He went into Brian's room and pulled it from the shelf.

Outside Over There.

He returned to the kitchen and slid the grave marker aside so he'd have room to read. Then, before he sat, he pawed through the pantry and found a box of table crackers. They were stale, but that didn't matter. He would force himself to eat something.

" 'When Papa was away at sea,' " Apollo read.

On the next page Apollo stopped to examine the image of Mama, a young white woman with long brown hair. She wore a faded red dress with a white ruffled collar. She stared into the middle distance.

At what?

At nothing. Her look was one of a woman lost. Bereft. Depressed. In this story, the father might've been off on a ship, but the mother hardly counted as present either. Apollo brought a finger to the illustration now. Her vacant eyes; her downturned mouth. He traced her slumped shoulders. Hadn't he looked across his kitchen table at Emma and seen this same woman?

On the next page the scene of Ida playing music for her sister, the goblins sneaking in through the window. Then the goblins made off with the human child, leaving its replacement behind. Next Ida picked up the child and held it, hugged it. The page after that showed the ice child half melted and dropped to the floor. Finally Ida had realized the fraud.

His finger rested on two words. "The changeling." There it was in the crib, in Ida's arms, disintegrating on the floor.

The changeling.

Apollo couldn't keep reading because the words on the page blurred. This happened because his hands were shaking. He had to lay the book flat. He heard the sound of dirt being cleared with shovel and mattock, the hours of night he'd been down in that hole.

"No one was watching the baby," he said in the empty apartment.

But then he turned and looked at the chair to his right. The one where Emma used to sit. He could almost make out her image, a ghostly silhouette. He touched the ragged red string with his thumb, turned it on his ring finger.

"One person was watching," Apollo said.

She said Brian is in the forest.

There's only one forest in all of New York City.

H E PACKED A suitcase because he didn't know when he would be back. He couldn't be sure he'd ever be back. He found the small suitcase they'd kept under the bed, the one they'd planned to use if Emma went into labor and the home birth didn't work. Their hospital bag. Emma had unpacked most of it long ago, of course, the nightgown and extra toiletries, slippers and socks, snacks and drinks, all those things had been returned to their drawers or consumed. The only stuff left in it was a pack of bendy straws for sipping liquids during labor and a bottle of massage oil. To save space, Emma had slipped both into a pouch on the side. Apollo didn't realize they were there when he pulled it out. So now both the straws and the oil would be making the trip with him.

The only forest in New York City is located in Queens, in the neighborhood of Forest Hills.

He went to the closet in Brian's room, dug through bags and boxes that he and Emma had filled, and found a change of clothes for his wife. He hardly paid attention to the items, just pants, blouse, sweater, panties, socks. He found a pair of pajamas for Brian, a onesie with footies, a red and green holiday-themed kind of thing, baby becomes an elf. But when Apollo held it up, he realized that if Brian was alive, he wouldn't fit these clothes anymore. He'd be ten months old now. This idea struck him with a cold sadness. So chilling he had to grab some size-one pajamas quickly and jam them into the bottom of the bag and just get out of that room.

In the living room he packed the mattock, then set Emma and Brian's clothes down on top of it. He closed the lid and lifted it. With the mattock inside, the suitcase felt heavy with violence.

Instinctively he checked his coat for his wallet, but it had been lost. No ATM card, no credit cards, no driver's license. He had ceased to exist in any modern sense. Or more precisely, he had lost access to nearly his entire modern existence. The only totem left was his phone.

In the kitchen there were cracker crumbs on the bronze grave marker. Beside the grave marker lay his father's book. Apollo opened the suitcase one more time. He packed the book and the grave marker. For a moment he pawed through the contents: a mattock, some clothes, a children's book, and a gravestone. This was how you packed for a trip to another world, not another borough.

Off he went.

IT SNOWED IN Queens. Apollo left the train station—Forest Hills–71st Avenue—and as he climbed the stairs to the sidewalk, he felt the flakes against his face. The stairwell was so crowded—rush hour in full effect—that he nearly lost his grip on his suitcase twice just from all the jostling. He stopped at the top of the stairs, his arms tired from hauling the bag, but he wasn't given any time to get his wind back because there were five hundred more men and women right behind him, and didn't they all have things to do? Trying to stand in place would've been like turning his back on a cyclone. He was tossed and nearly turned over. He scurried against the nearest storefront, a Chase bank. The evening sky turned as dark as shale, and the snow came down. The thick flakes clung to umbrellas and hats, the roofs of cars and buses.

The snow continued to fall and traffic backed up on 71st Avenue. A white family had hailed a livery cab, and now the mother was loading a gaggle of children into the backseat. The father folded the stroller with expertise and walked to the back of the cab, knocking on the trunk. Both mother and father looked haggard and angry, and Apollo felt his throat tighten with envy.

Those crackers hadn't filled him up much. Neither had four cups of water. Down the block he saw a Starbucks sign. He'd lost his wallet—all his money—but he might still get something in his belly. He had the Starbucks app on his phone. Enough on his account for a meal he could take with him into the forest. If they had sandwiches, he could even leave a trail of breadcrumbs so he and Emma and Brian might find their way out.

It was a cramped little Starbucks branch, long and narrow. The store had the look of a sunken living room. Enter, then climb down three stairs. There were two small tables with two chairs at each. The tables had been pushed together, and somehow nine teenagers had fit themselves into those four seats. Seven o'clock, most people returning home from work, but still a long line.

"Welcome to Starbucks. May I take your order?"

He couldn't see the barista yet, the line ran that long. He scanned the small fridge unit where they kept sandwiches and salads, juices and milks and waters. He figured he'd clear them out, or at least as much as he could carry. He could also just grab it and run. He was in a fucking hurry, after all. The thought of committing the crime—even one so minor—caused a memory flare. He was on parole. He opened his phone and checked for recent calls. There were a few. He recognized Lillian's number. There had been six from a 212 caller that could've been his PO. None had left messages. What if he swiped those sandwiches and got caught? Hard to flee when you're hauling a suitcase. And what was inside it? Holy shit, if he was found to be a shoplifting parole violator with a digging tool and a grave marker? Why in holy hell had he brought those things? His rational mind scolded his magical thinking. He resigned himself to wait on line patiently. He'd even say sir or ma'am to the barista just to be safe.

Then this wild-looking old white man, standing five places ahead in line, leaned into the fridge unit and scooped up all the remaining food. Just like that. Those awful prepackaged sandwiches cradled in one arm, and the slightly less awful prepackaged salads in the other. He cleared the damn thing out. The old man reached the register and dropped the gathered food across the counter.

"I better get you a bag or two," the barista said.

"Oh?" the old man said. "Do you think so, *Louise*? I thought I'd carry all this on my head."

The barista ignored the words, registering only a weary fluttering in her eyes. When she brought two paper bags from under the counter, the old man leaned forward and snatched them from her. The woman didn't even respond, only scanned each item and handed it over.

The old man leaned backward and squinted at the other customers. He looked like an old Viking gone to pasture, but a hint of the berserker still remained. Despite his age, the tall old man fairly throbbed with vitality, slim, and the skin of his face was tight against his cheeks. He had a thinning beard, and his hair, visible in wisps underneath his wool cap, looked like white lines of electricity.

"How much?" he demanded. "How much?"

"It's right there!" a man behind him on line snapped, pointing at the register's display.

The old man looked at the other customer and slapped the counter. "Do you know there was a time when a man might be told the price to pay? Instead of having to read it off a screen!"

"Weren't dinosaurs alive then, too?" the man asked.

The old Viking frantically patted at his waist as if he were reaching for a gun, or a battle-ax, and seemed mystified when he found no weapon there. The man who'd made the dinosaur snap waved the old man off wearily.

The old man took his bags of Starbucks food, beaten but unbowed. He muttered to himself as he walked, head down. He slammed past the table crowded with teenagers. To Apollo's surprise, they said nothing. Their phones held their attention.

"When Papa was away at sea," the man grumbled as he plowed through the store and continued to mutter as he moved.

Apollo had been scanning the counter. What would he do for food now? They had small packs of nuts or cookies by the register. He could fill up on those, he supposed. He felt a vague buzzing along his jawline, as if a fly were coming too close to his ear. He scratched at his chin, but that didn't fix it.

Apollo spun around.

The old man.

The old Viking paused at the door, as if collecting himself before stepping out into a storm. The whole time he spoke the lines from that children's book in a tortured growl, and Apollo listened along like a child.

The old man walked out the door, into the night. Apollo would've sprinted toward the door and tackled the man if he hadn't been wheeling that heavy suitcase. When he got out the front door, he saw the shape of the old man already two blocks away.

Apollo followed.

82

I T'S DIFFICULT TO follow a man when you're pulling a squeaky suitcase. Apollo tried to carry it instead, but between the mattock and the
gravestone, he couldn't heft it for long. The old man moved south-
west down 71st Avenue, and Apollo kept his distance, trailing by a
block in the hopes he would not be heard as they entered the tony section
of the neighborhood, Forest Hills Gardens.

Seventy-first Avenue became Continental Avenue, and the sidewalks
blossomed with trees, and Tudor brick homes lined the road, which had
hardly any traffic. Just like that, a walk of three blocks, and Apollo entered
one of the wealthiest neighborhoods in New York City. Two blocks ahead,
barely visible in the dim light of the cast-iron streetlamps, was the old Viking, striding on. He and Apollo were the only human beings to be seen,
and the grand Tudors watched both with solemn caution.

They passed Slocum Crescent and Olive Place, Groton Street and
Harrow Street. The sun set, and Apollo followed the man through the
deepening night. Ingram Street, Juno Street, Loubet Street, and Manse.
The old man never looked back, never turned his head as he crossed the
street, and never seemed to tire, though he had to be thirty years older
than Apollo.

Finally they crossed Metropolitan Avenue. Goodbye Tudor brick and
hello detached colonial one-family; the end of brick facades and the rise

of aluminum siding. This lasted all the way to Union Turnpike, and still the old man traveled on as if he was leading a tour through the descending class structure of Queens.

It really felt, to Apollo, as if they'd tripped into another region, another world. Block after block of single-family homes, sidewalks lined with aging cars and rusty SUVs, gas stations and corner stores, and then they reached the Northern Forest, the northeastern edge of Forest Park, more than five hundred acres of wilderness right there in the borough of Queens. If they'd come to a towering city of silver and gold, it would've seemed no less strange. The old man crossed the street to walk along the perimeter of the park. Apollo thought maybe the old guy had finally figured out he was being followed and planned to sprint into the woods, lose Apollo inside, but maybe that wouldn't matter. He'd led Apollo to where he wanted to be.

The old Viking reached a corner and went around it. Apollo broke into a jog, pulling the suitcase behind him, creaky wheels be damned.

Apollo turned the corner expecting the old man to appear right there and confront him, but the old man was far ahead. He stood before a stairway that led up into the grounds of the park. There were two streetlamps at the base of the stairs, so Apollo saw quite clearly as the old man climbed to the top of the stairs. But instead of disappearing into the trees and underbrush, the old man went down on his knees, his head bowed. He set the bags of Starbucks food at the top of the stairs. He stood and watched the tree line. Because of the streetlamps, Apollo could see the man's profile. His lips were moving, but was he speaking to someone or simply muttering to himself? Hard to say.

Finally the old man turned and walked back down the stairs. The way he held the railing made him appear tired or drunk. Apollo thought the old man might return the way he'd come, so he picked up the suitcase and crossed the street and hid himself in the shadows. He propped the suitcase against the back wall of a brick garage and settled himself on the luggage, a makeshift chair. The old man watched the top of the stairs, the border of trees, the brown bags emblazoned with the Starbucks logo. Eventually he turned and strolled away. Apollo meant to keep following, but he couldn't do it.

A police car appeared at the corner.

It came down Park Lane South as casual as a puma. Just as the car reached Apollo, the driver threw on those red and blue lights, though he didn't use the siren. Apollo had been concentrating so directly on the bags of food at the top of the stairs that when the lights popped on, he fell right off the suitcase and sprawled on the sidewalk.

The officer in the passenger seat rolled down his window and leaned out to watch Apollo. He surveyed Apollo for about twenty seconds before he spoke.

"Bad place for a nap, my man."

Apollo pushed himself up onto his knees. The cop in the driver's seat watched him carefully.

"That was fast," Apollo said.

The cop pointed at the houses behind Apollo. "This part of Forest Hills is still called Little Norway. You were never going to blend in."

"Even at night?"

"Especially at night," the driver said.

Patrice had been right. Heroes like him didn't get to make mistakes.

Apollo set his hands on the ground to get himself up on his feet, but the cop at the passenger window said, "Why don't you stay there on the ground for a minute."

"It's cold," Apollo said.

"It's winter," the cop said.

The driver opened his door and came around. Then the cop on the passenger side stepped out. He walked closer to Apollo, put out one hand, and waved for Apollo to stand.

"Where do you live?" the cop asked.

The driver looked behind them, into the park, then back at Apollo. He didn't seem to notice the bag of food at the top of the stairs. To him, it must've seemed like any other piece of garbage. His radio beeped and chattered, but he ignored it. The red and blue lights continued to glow and gave the moment a dizzying quality.

"Manhattan," Apollo said. He left his hands at his sides but still far enough from his pockets that neither cop might have reason to get shook. This would go worse for Apollo if they got scared. More importantly, he realized, if they called his name in, they'd find out he violated his parole. He hadn't been to the therapy session and, even worse, hadn't gone in to see his PO. Any urge he might have to argue hid itself away deep inside. The only point was to avoid being hauled back to jail. And getting shot to death. The two were his top priority just now.

"You came all the way to Forest Hills, from Manhattan. With a suitcase. Just to lie on the sidewalk in Little Norway?"

"That's one long trip," the driver said, and he let out a quiet, incredulous laugh.

Then behind them both, at the top of the stairs, something stepped out of the woods. Someone.

Emma Valentine.

His wife stood at the top of the stairs.

But it wasn't her. Not exactly. A witch. That's what he saw.

He wouldn't ever have thought the gaunt figure was the woman he'd married. It was the coat he recognized, the knee-length maroon down puffer coat she'd been wearing in the video from the night she escaped. The coat was torn and dirty, and the same could be said about Emma. She looked as thin and tough as the limb of a tree. But also—really and truly—she glowed.

As she stepped out of the woods, she seemed to walk in a cloud, an actual nimbus of blue energy. She cast off a color almost as bright as the blue police lights flashing on the patrol car; it was as if she wore sparks of electricity.

Emma Valentine stepped out of the woods and picked up the bags of Starbucks food. Then she turned and walked back into the deeper darkness and disappeared.

And that was that.

"Seriously, chief," the cop closer to Apollo said. "If you need shelter space, we can point you the right way, but you can't be lurking around people's houses."

"Gives people the creeps," the other cop said.

"No, sir," Apollo muttered. "I mean, yes, sir. She was glowing. She was . . ."

It took a clap on the shoulder from one of the cops to bring Apollo back to himself. That was Emma. Was she living in the park? And why had the old man brought food to her?

Now he looked at the officers with clarity. "I don't need a shelter or anything," he said. "I just got confused. I'll go back home. I'll catch the bus."

"You got money?" the cop asked, arm still on his shoulder. It would be easy for the man to tighten his grip and force Apollo into the back of the patrol car.

"I can—"

But before he finished floating some lie, the cop walked back to the patrol car. "We got any more of those MetroCards?" he asked his partner.

"Look in the pack," the driver said, and while his partner leaned into the car, he came around the front, closer to Apollo, hand floating near his hip, his holstered pistol.

"Got it." He returned to Apollo. "This has twenty dollars on it. This is a gift from the NYPD."

The MetroCard lay inside a clear plastic sleeve. The cop tore it open and handed the card to Apollo.

"You can catch the Q11 or the Q21 right over on Woodhaven Boulevard," the cop said.

"Thank you," Apollo said. He accepted the MetroCard, but then he just stood there. If the cops drove off, he could still rush up the stairs right now and hope, maybe, to find her.

"I tell you what," the driver said. "We'll give you a ride to the bus stop right now."

The other went back to the patrol car and opened a back door. "You don't have to thank us," he said. "But you do have to accept."

He climbed in, and the lights were turned off. As the car approached the bus stop on Woodhaven Boulevard, the officer on the passenger side spoke without turning his head.

"We love driving down Park Lane South. It's one of our favorite streets. We'll be driving down it most of the night. We don't expect to be seeing you there again."

They reached the bus stop, and one cop let Apollo out. Apollo wheeled the suitcase onto the sidewalk.

The driver rolled down his window. "It's going to be a while for that bus," he said. "But you need to be on it. Don't let us see you out here again. It'll be a bad night for you if we do."

Apollo didn't respond because no response was required. The cops drove off, and he stayed at the stop until their car went well out of view. He wasn't returning to Washington Heights, but no doubt those cops had been telling the truth. They would be patrolling the perimeter of the grounds all night. He needed to shelter until morning.

THE FOREST PARK Visitors Center sat only thirty yards behind him, just inside the park, and beside it a smaller brick structure, the public bathrooms. Apollo waited at the bus stop for fifteen minutes. No bus, no cops, no one around but him. Finally he hurried through the front gates into the park. He shut his eyes as he crossed from the sidewalk to the concrete path leading to the bathrooms, expecting the cops to jump him, but they didn't.

He reached the bathroom. There were two doors, one on either side of the small brick hut, the men's room and the women's. Heavy black doors showed chipped paint and faint names or symbols, many pictures of tits and dicks, etched into the surface. Both doors were locked, large padlocks hanging from looped handles, but Apollo had brought along the right tool. He laid the suitcase flat, unzipped it and took out the mattock. If he slid the flat mattock blade between the door and the frame, he could force the door open quickly. Now the only question was which bathroom he wanted to hide inside: the women's or the men's? If he had to guess which side would be cleaner, there really was no question.

He popped the lock of the ladies' room door with two sharp yanks. The metal door shrieked loudly each time. So loud Apollo felt sure the cops would arrive or a denizen of Little Norway would call them in. Some "concerned citizen's" anonymous phone call had killed many a black man before him. But the bathrooms were far enough inside the park and flanked by trees.

Apollo pushed the bathroom door open. There were no windows, so the room remained murky. He stepped inside and let his eyes adjust. Two stalls, one sink, enough floor space for him to set his suitcase flat. So cold here that the bathroom didn't even stink, or maybe his nose had just gone numb. He stepped outside once more. Why not just go looking for Emma now? He took four steps in the direction of the forest but stopped at the sight of all that territory, the shrouded dark. Would Emma welcome him? Would she even give him a chance to admit the mistakes he'd made? The woman who'd stepped out of those woods hardly seemed human, and he was the man who hadn't believed in her. What might she do to him if he stumbled across her in the woods well after midnight?

Finding her in daylight seemed safer. No shame in admitting it, he felt afraid. Also, the park spanned hundreds of acres. Wandering that much land late at night, in the midst of winter, was a surefire way to end up frozen dead in the maze of trees. No thanks, Jack. He returned to the bathroom. The darkness inside the ladies' room would become total as soon as Apollo shut the door. He welcomed this idea. Like bedding down inside a cocoon.

Apollo still couldn't quite believe what he'd seen. All these months, and there stood Emma. The last time they'd seen each other, they were the exhausted parents of an infant, estranged man and wife. What were they now?

Apollo needed to talk all this through with someone. Wanted to explain what the old man had done: setting the food at the top of the stairs like an offering. And when Emma appeared, she'd scooped up the bag quickly, as if she'd been expecting to find it.

He took out his cellphone and dialed a number.

"You shouldn't be using your old phone," Patrice said as soon as he picked up. His mouth pulled away from the phone. "It's Apollo."

"I don't have a choice," Apollo said. "I can't outthink this dude every minute."

Patrice huffed into the mouthpiece. "Yeah. You plan for one thing, and he'll just switch to another. You want to hear something wild? I came back home and did a complete flush of the computer. Found his finger-prints all over my files. Do you know this dude took back the money he paid us? We can't even do the right thing with the cash. Cleared it right out of our account. This motherfucker is as good as the Russians."

"So he knows everything?" Apollo asked.

"No one knows everything," Patrice said. "But he knows more than we'd like."

Apollo straightened up, his back tight against the cold wall of the women's bathroom inside Forest Hills Park.

"Where are you at now?" Patrice asked.

Instinctively, Apollo formed the words—*Forest Park*—but caught him-self. He'd made this call so he could say he'd seen Emma, but that too seemed imprudent now. What was the only way to keep a secret in the modern world? Never type it on a keyboard; never utter it over a phone.

When Apollo didn't answer Patrice let it go.

"Are you and Dana okay?"

Now Patrice spoke quietly, sounding winded, or wounded. "Dana has to sign in at her job at the start of her shifts," he said. "Normal procedure. But she got there yesterday, and they told her they had no record of her being employed by them at all. Obviously they know she works there, but right now, officially, according to their records, Dana Green has *never* worked for them. I mean, this motherfucker wiped her out completely. And for what? Because she's married to me? Because I'm helping you? They're treating it like a computer error, but how much damage is this guy going to do? One angry man with a computer—that's all it takes any-more."

He sounded pained.

"124 86th Road," Patrice said.

"What's that?" Apollo asked.

"That's about the only piece of help I can offer you. 124 86th Road. That's in Forest Hills. Can you get out there tonight?"

Apollo leaned forward into a crouch, as if Patrice—or someone else—might suddenly see him there. He decided to play pretend. "Why go out there?" he asked. "What's in Forest Hills?"

"You remember when that motherfucker took us on his boat? He said he only had one boat signed up for that stupid app of his. I took a look behind the wall and found out who the boat was registered to. Jorgen Knudsen. The address is 124 86th Road. Wheeler probably stole access to the boat just like he stole his wife's money, but at least if you talk to Knudsen, he might have some kind of clue to finding William."

"I saw—" Apollo began, but hesitated.

"1-2-4, that's the house number." Patrice's voice played weak and tinny in the air, but it brought him back. "86th Road. Forest Hills. Jorgen Knudsen. Go find that guy. Don't think about anything else. I'm hanging up now. Just in case. We love you. Good luck."

OVERCAST MORNING. The snow hadn't stuck, so the park sagged everywhere, as if a damp blanket had been cast over the land. The limbs of the bare trees hung low, and those that still had leaves hung even lower. Great swaths of grass lay matted. The single concrete road that wormed through the middle of Forest Park had been soaked so dark, it looked freshly laid. Apollo left the bathroom with the suitcase and went to find Emma.

He tried the Carousel and then the George Seuffert, Sr., Bandshell, which looked like the kinds of places someone might hide to protect against the elements. Did Emma need such protection? The woman he'd seen last night seemed to generate her own weather system. Apollo walked until midday but never caught sight of Emma. For all he knew, they were separated by little more than a few dozen trees. When you were inside the thickest parts of the Northern Forest, it was possible to forget you were in one of the most densely populated cities on the planet in the twenty-first century. It could be a hundred years in the past, a thousand or more. Apollo wandered in the wilderness, and who knew what else was in there, too.

Eventually he had to give in and give up, and by noon he'd left the forest and found the sidewalks surrounding the park. Now he and his suitcase made their way toward 86th Road.

Little Norway. Apollo had seen this area only in the dark and learned the name only from the cops who'd stopped him. What did he expect to see now? What he got would've been familiar almost anywhere in the borough. One-family homes with aluminum siding walls; midpriced sedans and minivans parked on streets and in driveways; small front lawns behind chain-link fencing and satin window treatments in every room. Little Norway could've been Little Ecuador or Little Korea or Little Ghana. The flags might differ, but the stages were the same.

Apollo stopped at the address Patrice gave him. He found a three-story house, one of the largest and oldest on the block. No car in the driveway. The windows were all blocked by yellowing blinds. Apollo brought his suitcase up a small flight of stairs, right to the front door, no bell, so he knocked. No answer, so he kept knocking, but eventually he gave up. When he turned to the street, he saw a neighbor watching him from the house across the way. Man or woman, young or old, he couldn't say. The window treatments hid the details. How soon before more cops were called? Apollo descended the stairs and wheeled his suitcase down the block. He'd spent half a day in the park looking for Emma; now he'd have to do the same hunting for the person who lived here. If he couldn't just sit on the steps, he'd make a circuit around the block. How long could it take before Jorgen Knudsen returned?

It turned out to be hours. By the time the old Viking showed up, the sun was going down. Apollo's knees hurt. He hadn't had anything to eat or drink since yesterday. As a result, he felt so starved he thought he was hallucinating when that white-haired codger appeared on the block. He carried two large white plastic bags, both heavy with goods. Moving slowly. When he passed under a streetlamp, Apollo could see the man muttering as he walked.

Apollo stopped at the far corner of 86th Road, right in the middle of the street. A woman had to beep three times to get him out of the way. The old man looked up when he heard the car horn, and there stood Apollo Kagwa, but the guy didn't seem to notice. Instead he resumed that hobbled march until he reached the three-story house, climbed the stairs, unlocked his front door, and went inside.

Apollo counted to one hundred before he moved up the block. When he reached the house, he actually gasped. The old man had left the front door wide open, the light above the front entrance turned on.

Apollo almost took the stairs. Almost. He set his foot on the first one but stopped himself before he tried the second. He watched the open front door. He looked both ways. Many of the other houses on the block showed lights on the first floors, a few on the second. People were home, but no one seemed to be watching him at this moment. And yet he hesitated to simply walk inside. He looked behind him but didn't see anyone peeking out from behind the curtains there.

Apollo walked around the side of the house and down the open driveway. Houses like this always had more than one entrance. He found a second door along the side. He assumed this one led down to the basement, but this door had no handle, no lock either. After only a second standing there, a light flared on above his head. He leaped backward, letting the suitcase fall, scanning in all directions. He stood in place, and after another moment, the light snuffed out. Apollo stepped to the door again, and the light, on a motion sensor, flipped on again. Apollo pressed at the door once, but it was barred from the inside. He stepped back, and the driveway returned to darkness.

He picked up the suitcase handle and went farther along the house, all the way around the back, and here he found a third door. It opened with a turn of the handle. Apollo left his suitcase outside. He didn't want to worry about running out with it if things came to that. Inside he found a short set of stairs that led up into a kitchen.

Two plastic bags sat on the kitchen counter. A large pot sat on a burner, the flame turned high, but the water inside still felt cold. Apollo stood quietly in the large, outdated kitchen. There were two open doorways out of the kitchen, leading to the rest of the first floor. One opened onto a dining room, and the other a hallway. He moved toward the hallway and leaned out. From here it was a straight path to the front door. The front door remained open. He stood there a moment listening for the old man but heard nothing.

He moved to the other doorway and entered the dining room. There was a large dining table covered with mail and newspapers, circulars, all still in their rubber bands, a mound of the stuff, some spilling onto the floor. Apollo moved around the far side of the table, trying to keep silent, step softly.

As he moved alongside the table, he found the old man. He stood with his back to Apollo. He waited at the threshold of the front door, hidden right behind it. In his left hand he held a large boning knife.

Apollo scanned the table for some kind of weapon, or at least something he could use as defense. He touched his hand to the nearest rolled-up newspaper, and just as he lifted it, the old man turned.

Apollo raised the newspaper like a club.

The old man pointed his knife at Apollo. "I'm going to tell you a story about a little boy," he said.

THE OLD MAN spoke as he and Apollo faced each other in that dining room. One man poised with a boning knife, the other with a roll of newspaper. A standoff on the blue shag carpeting.

"There once was a farmer who had three sons," the old man began. "His farm was so badly off that none of them ever had enough to eat. A large, good forest sat right nearby, and the oldest brother went off one day to chop wood. He hoped to get enough wood to pay off their father's debts and finally have some money of their own. But he returned before even an hour's time, and he would not speak of what had happened. He had no wood with him.

"The second son was sent next. He snatched the family's ax from his older brother and marched off into the woods. But he returned even sooner than his older brother. This time he returned not only without wood but also without the family's ax! The old farmer was distraught. Only his youngest son remained, and he was just a boy.

"But the youngest, Askeladden, didn't even wait for the sun to rise before going out to the woods. The moon lit the sky, and the boy left without telling his father, or his brothers, that he was going. He entered the woods as quietly as he could, and in no time he found the family's ax. It was still stuck in a shaggy fir tree, right where the middle brother had left it. And just below that was a mark in the fir tree where the oldest brother had swung the same ax. Curious.

"Askeladden then heard something moving through the trees. The ground shook and the tops of the trees shivered as something enormous came closer. The boy needed to hide, but the forest floor offered no such places. If he could reach the upper branches of this fir tree, he thought, he could disappear in its leaves. But the limbs were too high up. Then he remembered the ax. He was still small enough that he could climb onto the handle and use it like a stair without shaking it loose. From the place on the handle, he could jump and reach the lowest branch.

"He climbed almost to the top of the fir tree, and there he hid. The cuts his brothers made had caused sap to leak from the tree, but Askeladden didn't realize it until he'd stopped climbing. His hands and feet were wet with the stuff, strong scent of wood and resin. He tried to wipe it off, but very quickly he had to be still.

"Out of the woods came an enormous troll. Six stories high, with shoulders as wide as a bull. It was hideous and smelled of swamp rot. It growled and coughed. When it bumped the fir tree, poor Askeladden was almost thrown to his death. The troll sniffed the air. If the sap hadn't been on the boy's hands and feet, the troll would've smelled him right away. They can track the scent of human flesh like a shark tracks blood. But still it knew something was wrong. Hadn't there been two other boys in its woods not long before? It pulled a face of rage.

"'Who dares come into my woods?' the troll howled. 'I will eat his bones!'

"Askeladden had an idea. He shouted, 'My head is right there on the ground! Why don't you just try and crack my skull!'

"The troll bent low and found a stone on the ground, the size of a boy. 'I have you!' he shouted, and bit down hard, but immediately he howled. 'My teeth! You have broken my teeth with your thick skull! I will do better with your other bones instead.' The troll became so angry, it could hardly think.

This time the boy shouted, 'I have no bones! I am made of wood, you stupid troll!'

"'Stupid, am I?' shouted the troll. 'Then I will chop you to pieces!'

"'But where will you find an ax, you buffoon?' taunted Askeladden.

"'There is one here!' the troll bellowed. 'And I will chop down this whole forest to find you!'

"The troll had fallen into a fury, and not being very bright, he began chopping at every tree nearby. Finally that fir tree was the only one left in all the wood. All the rest had been chopped into small pieces.

"'Now I have you!' the troll called. He raised his ax to fell the last tree, but his chopping had taken all night, and now it was morning. As the troll raised the ax, the sun finally rose, and that troll was turned to stone by the daylight.

"Askeladden climbed down. He tried to push the stone troll over because he wanted his father's ax. But eventually he gave up. It was too big and heavy to budge. But what did it matter? The boy realized that with all the wood the troll had chopped, his father would be a rich man and more than able to afford a new one. And they lived happily ever after."

The old man cleared his throat. He waggled the knife so the tip of the blade seemed to be sniffing the air.

"Why did I tell you that story?" the old man asked. "What did I want you to hear?" He paused here a moment and watched Apollo.

"I have no fucking idea," Apollo said eventually.

"My father told it to me. And his father told him. On and on like that. We're from Norway originally, and we brought the tale with us. There are a lot of stories about that boy, Askeladden. He always beats the monsters and comes away with some treasure. It's nice stuff to hear when you're a pup."

The old man waved to take in the run-down living room, worn carpet, frayed curtains, and cluttered dining table with room enough for only one.

"But now I think I hate those fairy tales." He raised his hands in a gesture of peace, as if used to being argued with. "Not really the tales, but how they end. Three words that ruin everything. 'Happily ever after.'" He stuck his tongue out as if tasting something bitter as bile.

"'Happily ever after,'" he repeated. "Even when they don't say it in the story, those three words are there. Take my story, just as an example. Will Askeladden's father become truly wealthy and have enough money to send all three sons to university or only one or two? How does he decide? The youngest beat the troll, but the oldest boy is still firstborn and deserves the spoils, no? What about when father dies? Did he leave a will? Will there be an equitable distribution of his assets? If not, will the sons all retain legal counsel and spend the next twenty years in court haggling over the estate?" The old man laughed bitterly. "'Happily ever after' won't prepare you for that!

"Personally," he continued, "I always thought it was there to shut the child up. It's bedtime, and you've just told this incredible story, and a child, as children do, wants to know more. Did they throw a party for Askeladden when he came home? Did the brothers and the father go out to the woods to see where the troll had turned to stone? Did Askeladden ever marry? If so, what was she like? And did they have children of their own? What were they called, all of them?

"This is what the children would be saying, should be saying, after a tale like that, but by then it's already late and you've been up all day working, and now you just want to go to sleep, and in fact this child is starting to really get on your nerves with all these questions. Always more questions! So you lean close and say, 'What happened next? They lived happily.' 'For how long?' your beautiful babies ask. 'Forever,' you say. 'Now go to sleep!'"

The old man sighed.

"And your lovely, stupid child believes you. Then he grows up and tells the same lie to his daughters. And she tells them to her sons. Then, finally, it has to be true, because why else would my good, caring family have passed it on for so very long? Do you know how much harm 'happily ever after' has done to mankind? I wish they said something else at the end of those stories instead. 'They tried to be happy.' Or 'Eternal happiness is a fruitless pursuit.' What do you think?"

"You're definitely Norwegian," Apollo said.

He lowered the knife. "Why don't we go into the kitchen?" he said. "The water is probably boiling, and I'm making a meal for her."

"No more Starbucks?" Apollo asked.

The old man dropped his head. "Normally I cook her food myself, but yesterday morning she told me exactly where to go and when to go there.

Isn't that funny? Never once has that happened before, but then snap, just like that, she sends me there."

"I know," Apollo said. "I saw you."

"Wouldn't it be funny if—" he began. "I mean, if she'd known that you'd be there."

The old man, Jorgen Knudsen, swept his free hand over his wild, white hair.

"Forgive me, I've been drinking," he said.

"Today?"

"Every day." His eyes fluttered with weariness.

Apollo looked toward the kitchen, where he could hear the water roiling. "What are you making?" he asked.

"*Smalahove*," he said. "It's Norwegian. Just like my story. Let me show you." He gestured toward the kitchen with the blade.

Apollo waved the newspaper. "You go first."

86

THE WATER HAD indeed come to a boil. The old man set the boning knife on the counter and turned to the plastic bags on the small kitchen table. He reached into one but kept his gaze on Apollo. He pulled something large out of the bag. It was wrapped in wax paper. He set it on the counter. It was as big as a bowling ball but oval shaped. The old man folded the empty plastic bag neatly and opened a cupboard under the sink where he had a stack of the exact same plastic bags, also folded. He added the new one, then shut the door and returned to the kitchen table. He unfolded the wax paper, that snapping sound as it came flat.

A sheep's head lay on the table.

Apollo audibly gagged.

The old man laughed quietly and wagged a finger at Apollo. "You can't be disgusted," he said. "This is a tradition from my home country, and we must never judge anyone's traditions! Be politically correct, or I will protest you. No judging. Just acceptance. Well, here it is. Accept it."

Now he slapped a hand on the side of the sheep's head. It made a wet squelch and spun a few degrees so that its mouth pointed directly at Apollo. Its lower teeth, a row of small, discolored pegs, jutted out past the slightly open lips. The skin and fleece had been removed, so the head shone a reddish-pink under the kitchen lights. It still had its eyes. Each looked like a globe of black jelly set into the puttied red flesh.

The old man grabbed it by the snout and in one motion lifted it, brought it to the pot of boiling water, and dropped it in. Small amounts of scalding water flew out of the pot, some of it landing on the old man's forearm, but if it hurt he showed no sign. He simply turned back to Apollo and clapped, a proud chef. He scanned the countertop and grabbed a novelty kitchen timer that was made to look like a fluffy white sheep.

"If I don't use the timer, I'll forget the head is boiling," the old man said. He held up the display screen, which was set in the center of the sheep's belly. "I let it go three and a half hours so the meat isn't too tough or too soft."

Apollo nodded because he simply couldn't keep up. The open front door, the old man hiding in wait with a knife, the tale of Askeladden and the troll, and now a sheep's head boiling in a pot. And he thought the island had been as wild as things would get?

"My wife," Apollo said, the words like a lifeline. He raised his free hand to show the red string on his finger. "I don't care about all this other shit. I just have to find Emma."

"You must approach her with caution," the old man said as he set the timer on the counter. "There are ways such things must be done." He pointed at the pot. "With an offering."

The old man walked to the fridge, opened it, and reached inside. He pulled out a bag of potatoes. He walked back to the counter and dropped them with a thump. He returned to the fridge once more and revealed a green bottle with no label.

"That's a strange wedding ring," the old man said, pointing at Apollo's left hand. "Is hers made of barbed wire?"

He took a coffee mug out of the sink, opened the green bottle, and poured a clear liquid in. He set the bottle down.

"It took you months to finally show up," he said. "I thought you'd get here sooner."

This hit Apollo so hard, he dropped the rolled-up newspaper on the table. "You know about my wife and son, don't you."

"I do."

From a cabinet by the sink, he took out an eight-ounce bottle of Ensure. He poured the chalky white drink into the mug that held the clear liquor. He swished the cup to mix the two. He took a gulp. His top lip showed a faint cream mustache.

"You can help me then."

He took a second gulp from the coffee mug, then turned away from Apollo. He picked up a potato and peeled it over the kitchen sink. "Do I want to help you?" he asked.

"You're helping my wife," Apollo said.

The old man finished with the first potato and got to work peeling the second. The old man looked out of the window above the sink, into the modest paved yard behind his home. Up the slope of the block, he could see the trees of Forest Park.

"Ever since your wife appeared, I haven't had a night's rest," he said. "All my life I've slept well. Even as a baby, my mother told me. But now it's one hundred and twenty days without a good night's rest." He dropped the second peeled potato onto the counter with a *thunk*. "And it's all because of your wife."

He looked over his shoulder at Apollo. "Will you prepare the cabbage?"

Apollo watched him, stupefied.

"You have to core it first." He pointed at the second supermarket bag impatiently, a grandfather supervising his grandson for the afternoon.

When Apollo still didn't move, the old man took out the cabbage and brought it to the table on a cutting board. Apollo would've argued more, but there on the board he'd also set out a large utility knife with a serrated blade. Better than rolled-up newspaper as far as weapons went. The old man watched Apollo calmly. Apollo pulled the board to himself and picked up the knife. The old man then turned his back to Apollo and went under the counter for a smaller pot in which to boil the potatoes. The enormous pot with the sheep's head continued to burble and roil.

"Jorgen Knudsen," Apollo said, picking up the knife.

For the first time, the old man went rigid. He turned from the cupboard and stared at Apollo. But in a moment he recovered his weary whimsy. It might have been that the liquor kicked in.

"Joe," he said. "Here in the United States everyone calls me Joe. In America your name must be convenient or it must be changed."

Jorgen rose slowly, filled the pot with water.

"So I'm guessing you know William Wheeler," Apollo said.

Jorgen took another pull from the coffee mug, then refilled it with liquor and Ensure. "Is that what he's calling himself?" He said nothing more. He drank instead.

Apollo cut the cabbage into quarters, then used the knife to slice out the wedge of cabbage core. Jorgen set the small pot on another burner, and then there was the sound of the *tick tick tick* as the pilot light caught, and the halo of blue flame appeared. When he looked at Apollo, he seemed pleased.

"Now chop the cabbage very fine." He put out his hands for the bits of core, and Apollo handed them to him. Instead of going to the trash bin, he pulled a small pail from under the sink. He dropped the bits of core inside. He caught Apollo staring. "You do compost, don't you?"

Apollo brought the knife down into the first section of cabbage, chopping it into fine strips. When Brian had first been born, Emma hadn't been able to cook anything, of course, and it had fallen to Apollo to prepare foods from his admittedly limited repertoire. Now he felt himself transported back to that sensation of preparation and responsibility. He was making a meal for Emma.

Because Apollo lost himself in the work, it took a few moments before he realized Jorgen had started speaking to himself, under his breath. He removed a third pot from a cupboard. He came to the kitchen table and swept in the cabbage Apollo had chopped and returned to the counter. He found a bag of flour and poured some in, estimating the proper amount with practiced ease. He finished with another gulp from the mug.

He recited lines from *Outside Over There* as he dropped salt and caraway seeds in with the cabbage.

Apollo joined him. Word for word.

This stopped Jorgen's patter. "Why did you say that?" he snapped.

"I thought we'd recite it together."

"You know it?" he asked. "What is it? A song?"

"A book," Apollo said. "A fairy tale."

He snorted. "Of course."

"My father used to read it to me when I was a baby."

"That book exactly? Have you ever wondered why?"

Apollo tapped the tip of the blade against the table. "Yes, but I don't know."

Jorgen turned from the oven. He gulped down the rest of the potion in his mug, then bumped the side of the cup against his forehead. "I hear her in here, day and night. Even right now, as we are speaking. Your wife. She repeats and repeats the words from that book, and I can't drown it out no matter what I try. I can't get any sleep because of it. She's torturing me." He pulled the mug away from his face and peered in. "I don't know how she's doing it. Do you?"

"She's a witch," Apollo said, and he almost sounded proud. He finished chopping.

Jorgen reached across the table for the cutting board, but Apollo held on to the knife. "You're scared of Emma," he said.

"Yes," Jorgen said. "I am."

He looked at the cutting board in his hand with some surprise. He set it back in front of Apollo as if there were more work to be done. He looked back at the timer. Three hours before the sheep's head would be ready.

"I hear her voice," Jorgen said. "And at night, from my bedroom, I see her out there. Walking in the woods. I see her blue light. A witch. Yes. Did you know that's who you'd married?"

Jorgen didn't leave time for a response. He brought one hand to the collar of his shirt. He undid the top two buttons and pulled back the fabric. A bright red vertical scar appeared near the base of his throat, hardly healed.

"I did this two months ago. I hit a vein, but not the artery. I bled a lot but only gave myself a real sore throat. The doctors prescribed the Ensure because I can't eat solid food. I add the liquor to wash it down. That's a family prescription. It's called Brennivín. Went to the ICU, but I was back home in four days. I couldn't even sleep while I was in Jamaica Hospital.

Not even with the sedatives. I heard her all that time, even there. I know she will never forgive me."

Now Jorgen slipped into the seat across from Apollo.

"You stole our son." The words so low, they hardly registered.

"No," Jorgen said. "Not me. I'm too old." He looked up at the ceiling. "But when I was younger, yes, I did my service."

"Service," Apollo repeated. The word singed his tongue.

Jorgen set both hands flat on the tabletop. The man had been so commanding as he prepared the meal. Sitting like this, though, across the table in a kitchen with linoleum floors and cheap particleboard cupboards, he settled into his age and his drunkenness and his tortured feelings. He seemed to decline right in front of Apollo.

"I want you to see the living room," he said. "No point in trying to avoid it anymore." He looked at the pots on the oven and nodded faintly. "She won't appear without an offering so there's no point in rushing."

He set his hands on the table and pushed himself up.

Apollo slid out from his seat and peeked into the boiling pot. The sheep's head had shifted so it grinned right up at him. He followed Jorgen out of the kitchen. He held the utility knife.

87

ORGEN LED APOLLO out of the kitchen and across the hallway. The old man opened the door to a den and stepped in. He waved for Apollo to follow. Jorgen's den had a rectangular shape, as long as the kitchen and dining room combined. The floor had that hideous blue shag carpeting too, and the walls were painted a very faint yellow. It was an almost nauseating combination of colors. Add to that how much hotter this room felt. The dining room had been chilly and the kitchen warm because of the oven, but this room practically boiled. Bad enough that Apollo had to undo his jacket and take off his knit cap. He felt like that sheep's skull, dropped into a pot.

There were three space heaters on the floor, in a row along one of the walls, all three on the highest setting. They were the kind Patrice and Dana had used in their basement apartment, the kind Apollo recognized from his childhood. They looked like enormous toaster ovens. Each had a grillwork facade and behind it coils that ran bright orange. If they were left on for hours, they tended to rattle and give off a static buzzing. The three space heaters in the den were doing exactly that now—rattling and buzzing. Jorgen had been running them a long time.

The den was divided in half—lengthwise—by two tall black Japanese folding wall panels. The shitty, black lacquered kind, the type sold in only the bleakest of neighborhoods. Eight panels all together, a series of outstretched cherry blossom designs. With both fully extended, Apollo couldn't see what hid on the other side of the den. On this side: the three space heaters on the ground, Jorgen, and a small handful of framed pictures hung on the wall, hovering a few feet above the heaters. Apollo couldn't make out the images from here in the doorway.

Jorgen walked closer to those framed pictures, but Apollo stayed still. He felt a whiff of cool air and looked to his right. Down the long hallway he saw the front door of Jorgen's home. It remained wide open. Winter air free to sneak inside. Apollo had the urge to walk down there and shut the door, but then Jorgen began talking.

"The first immigrant to have an impact on Queens was the Laurentide ice sheet, twenty thousand years ago," Jorgen said. "The northern hemisphere was in an ice age, and a glacier in Labrador—we call it Canada now—spread itself across a border that had yet to be drawn up."

Jorgen beckoned for Apollo, but still Apollo didn't move any closer. He scanned the room again, those Japanese screens, wondering if someone, something might be hiding on the other side. Meanwhile this old man wanted to talk about glaciers.

"The ice sheet reached Wisconsin, then Michigan," Jorgen continued. "Central Indiana, Illinois. Nothing could stop it. It moved rock and split the earth. When the glacier reached New York, the ice sheet was one thousand feet thick, almost as tall as the Empire State Building. When it finally stopped moving, it lay here, across what we would eventually call New York City, for the next twenty-five hundred years. Eventually the world warmed up again, and that glacier melted away.

"But by then it had done something miraculous. It had moved enough stone and earth to make a great barrier between the land and the sea. It pushed the Atlantic Ocean back. If it wasn't for that glacier, all of Queens and Brooklyn would still be underwater today. We'd be underwater right now. All that thanks to one Canadian."

Jorgen grinned at Apollo and waved for him once more. He gestured to the photos hung on the wall.

Apollo finally approached. But since he wasn't a fool he peeked behind the Japanese panels. No one there. Only the same blue shag carpet on the ground. There were no space heaters on that side. The long wall showed many more framed photos, all hung up. A hundred pictures, maybe more. It put Apollo in mind of a family album. Instead of collecting them in a book, they were spread across this wall. He could see they were pictures of people, but before he could focus, Jorgen came for him.

"Please, Apollo." Jorgen touched his arm.

Apollo turned. How had the old man come so close so quickly? It was this damn shag carpeting, muffling sound.

Apollo came back around the Japanese panels. Only as he did this did Apollo realize something strange about the den. There weren't any windows. How was that possible, in a one-family house that stood on a detached plot? The dining room had windows that faced out onto the street. The kitchen looked out onto the small backyard. But this den faced only inward.

Jorgen brought Apollo back to the framed photos on this wall, the ones hanging right above those three space heaters. The machines sent heat along Apollo's legs.

"I told you about the first immigrant," Jorgen said. "Now let me tell you about some more recent ones." He raised one hand and tapped at the largest picture here, a framed rendering of a ship at sea.

"On July 5, 1825, fifty-two Norwegians sailed out of the city of Stavanger in a sloop they named *Restoration*. Many on board were Quakers seeking religious freedom in America. The *Restoration* was the first organized group of Norwegian immigrants to come to these shores since the times of the Vikings. It is the Norwegian *Mayflower*.

"Their ship, this sloop, was a very small vessel for such a journey. Only fifty-four feet long and sixteen feet wide. It took them fourteen weeks to make the crossing. They arrived in New York harbor on October 9, 1825. Not one passenger died. In fact, the newspaper reported that there was even a birth. One girl, born on board. This was without hospitals or painkillers or any of that. The old way."

The space heaters buzzed now, all three at once, so it seemed as if some large, metallic insect had landed in the windowless den. Apollo could feel sweat beading on his neck and chin.

"Their journey became national news. Because they'd made the trip in a sloop, the newspapers called the Norwegians the Sloopers. The question that most fascinated the public was how on earth these people had made it across the Atlantic on this tiny ship. It seemed improbable. Impossible. Even most of the people on board didn't know the truth.

"Their leader, Lars Larsen, spoke only of their desire for religious freedom. He spoke of the singular goodness and liberty of the United States. He said all the right things. The Sloopers were granted access. They became Americans. Soon the most important question about them was no longer asked: How had they made this impossible trip? How had they crossed the Atlantic? I can tell you. They had help."

For an instant, Apollo felt himself back on North Brother Island and Cal there with him as they watched the trawler chugging out to open waters.

"The big one can swim," he muttered.

"Yes, he can," Jorgen said, watching Apollo with a look of surprise.

Now Jorgen pointed to another sketch. People this time. Far fewer than fifty-three. Only three in fact. Two women and one man.

"The Sloopers settled around here too, but it didn't last long. Most soon followed Lars Larsen and his family. They moved upstate, to Orleans County. It became the first Norwegian colony in America since Leiv Eriksson reached these shores in the year one thousand."

"Leif Eriksson?" Apollo corrected, a holdover of whatever he'd learned in some elementary school class.

"I suppose," Jorgen said.

Jorgen looked back at the sketch. "These three did not go on," he said. "Instead they remained here in Queens. Still mostly farmland then. Little Norway, as this neighborhood came to be called. These three started it. This sketch was made about eight months after they arrived in America."

Jorgen tapped the glass, the man's face, beardless and thin. The ink drawing hardly qualified as a sketch, but still the eyes were vivid, much too large, which made it seem as if the man were staring at Apollo and Jorgen across time, seeing them even now.

"That's my ancestor, Nils. My great-great-great-grandfather."

He tapped the first of the two women, also thin, and taller than Nils. Her hands were crossed in front of her. Her hair was hidden under a scarf.

"This is my great-great-great-grandmother, Petra."

Last he tapped the third woman. Small, wearing a shawl over her dress. Her mouth had been drawn in so faintly, she seemed to have none. Her eyes were tiny, hardly there. Her shoulders soft and slumped. It was as if the woman were turning into a phantom, fading away.

"And this is Anna Sofie. Nils's first wife."

"He married them both?"

"Well." Jorgen smiled. "Not at the same time."

"All three of them were on the sloop?" Apollo asked.

"Oh yes," Jorgen said. "Nils and Anna Sofie had been married four years when they boarded the *Restoration*. They were not Quakers, but they were ready to try their fortunes in a new place. It's possible Nils had to escape the country, I can't say. The ship's captain offered work to men who agreed to crew the ship. Nils bargained for Anna Sofie's passage. She was already pregnant. Anna Sofie is the one who gave birth on the trip."

"A girl, you said. What was her name?"

Jorgen's hand lowered from the frame. "Agnes Knudsdatter."

"Agnes?" Apollo whispered. He recovered his composure. "If she was born on the ship, how come she's not in the picture?"

Jorgen pursed his lips. "Agnes was dead by then. Anna Sofie never really recovered from the loss. My father remarried Petra eventually."

Apollo looked at Anna Sofie's faded face again. Now she seemed erased by grief. "What about Anna Sofie?" he asked. "She stuck around here after the divorce?" The room felt intolerably hot. Apollo sweated in front of the heaters.

"She went off into the forest."

"The forest? What for?"

"She wanted to find her daughter. She knew Agnes was somewhere out there."

"What about Nils?" Apollo asked, looking away from the rendering, facing Jorgen. "Did Nils help look? Did he try?"

Jorgen raised his hands. "Well no, of course not."

"But he was her father," Apollo said.

"He's the one who took Agnes into the woods in the first place," Jorgen said. "And he's the one who left her out there. In the cave."

88

JORGEN SAID SOMETHING more and gestured toward the Japanese screens, but Apollo couldn't hear him. His ears had plugged, and Jorgen's words were little more than a vibration against his skull. Instead he found himself staring at the utility knife in his left hand. It had been the casual tone of the words. *He's the one who left her out there. In the cave.* The knife began to rise, as slowly as a helium balloon.

Jorgen placed his hand on Apollo's, the one that held the blade. He pressed the hand back down. It settled by Apollo's side for now.

"Have you noticed that the stories about the first colonists in America are always about how they think the Devil is living out in the woods?"

Jorgen peeked down at the knife quickly, with little more than a glance, and when the knife didn't rise again, he stopped holding Apollo's wrist.

"I'm talking about the Puritans, I guess. They came to North America and swore monsters were waiting to get them in this savage land. But maybe it was the other way around. Maybe those Puritans brought monsters with them. Unloaded them from their ships right alongside the cargo. That's what my people did. My great-great-great-grandfather. He brought a monster with him. It emigrated to America just like him."

"Did the others on the ship know? The Sloopers?"

Jorgen patted his belly. "No. I don't think so. They put their faith in their crew and their God, but Nils put his faith in something older. They all have him to thank for making a safe crossing to America even if none of those pious sorts ever would. People can choose ignorance, can't they? Life is easier in blinders. In my old age now I have time to wonder about such things though. Even if you choose to ignore the truth, the truth still changes you."

Jorgen pointed at the Japanese panels again and walked around them, disappeared on the other side. Apollo looked at the knife, then at the rendering of those three people—Nils, Petra, and Anna Sofie. The heaters clattered and snapped, the heat so strong by now it felt as if they were trying to chase him away.

Then, on the other side of the panels, Jorgen raised a hand and waved to Apollo, a big goofy gesture like when you're meeting a relative at the airport and you want them to see you at Arrivals. Apollo walked around the Japanese panels and joined Jorgen.

The old Viking stood before the long wall where well over one hundred framed photos hung. This side of the den felt significantly cooler. No heaters on the ground. Jorgen tapped at a picture frame when Apollo joined him. Hardly more than an outline, really. A child. Its eyes were closed and its mouth tight, as if it was whistling, wisps of hair splayed out over both ears.

"Agnes," he said. "My father drew this likeness much later, from memory."

Jorgen took his hand away from the sketch, then brushed at the edges of the frame.

That baby had been abandoned in the woods—in a cave—by her own father? It was too much to contemplate. Apollo looked away from the sketch to the walls, the mystery of the windowless den. Now he could see there had been windows once but the walls had been altered. The windows hadn't been covered. They'd been removed. This wall had been re-framed, but the job still showed. The places where the new framing had been set stood out slightly from the rest of the wall so there was a faint up-and-down effect, like the difference between the black keys and white keys on a piano. This variation in the wall made the framed photos seem to undulate, some pitching forward and others rolling back, an effect like watching waves. From here he had an easier time identifying the subjects. Children. All of them were portraits of kids. A sea of small faces.

"Why did Nils bring the monster over?"

"He had to leave Norway, and he needed to bring his wife with him. He loved her, I expect, and didn't want to start his new life without her. But when he saw the ship those naïve Quakers planned to sail, he immediately held doubts. The sloop was too small. He had to think of his family. So he brought insurance. But it came at a price. The Sloopers made it to New York and scurried away upstate. But Nils and Anna Sofie and Petra Mikkelsdatter stayed here in Queens. There was no park here, it was farmland. Thousands of acres of forest and greens. In our homeland these things are creatures of the natural world. Forests and mountains are where they make their lairs. Queens was a perfect place for it to settle. By 1898 the land for the park, as you see it now, was bought, and they began to design it. Golf courses, hiking paths, on and on. But it's hilly country, still lots of pockets. Lots of caves. Lots of places for something large to hide. *Jotunn. Trolde.* That's how we say it in Norwegian."

Apollo's eyes met Jorgen's now.

"Nils would be its caretaker. That was part of the deal he struck in Norway. Making sure it was appeased. It demanded only one thing. A child. That had been the bargain. So one night, when he couldn't put it off any longer, Nils Knudsen took his daughter Agnes out into the woods, and to the cave of the beast he delivered her."

89

THE PICTURE FRAMES ran left to right like a time line, one that began at the upper left end of this long wall and ran to the right. When the limit of the wall was reached, it started again, one row lower. Sketches and charcoal renderings, then the almost shocking leap into clarity that was the daguerreotype, then black-and-white photos led to the early, grainy color stock. All of them infants. None older than a year. The magnitude of this collected horror made Apollo feel as if the skin had been peeled back from his face.

"All these kids," Apollo finally said. "You fed them to it?"

"No," Jorgen said firmly. "That's not accurate. It tries to raise them. You see? It tries to be a good—"

"Father," Apollo said, but the word sounded spoiled in his mouth.

Jorgen raised his arms and shrugged faintly. "It tries, but it fails. When it fails, it feeds. Then we must try again. That was our pact."

"Our," Apollo repeated.

"The men of the Knudsen line," Jorgen said.

"What about its own babies? Couldn't it raise those?"

"Those things?" Jorgen cleared his throat as if he was about to spit. "They're too ugly to love."

Apollo might just have fallen backward, paralyzed by this tableau, this horror history. What was this? An education of a kind. Jorgen Knudsen had taken Apollo Kagwa to school.

"Nils learned it was difficult to ask a mother to hand over her own child, you see. Anna Sofie cracked. She disappeared into the woods to look for her daughter and never came out."

"Then maybe she found Agnes," Apollo said. "Found Agnes and ran like hell because her husband couldn't be trusted."

Jorgen gave Apollo a thin smile. "Isn't it pretty to think so?"

Apollo nearly sank at the words.

"Nils married Petra quickly and had seven children with her. But he never took them into the woods. He'd learned his lesson. And I like to believe it was too hard for him to make such a sacrifice again. He wasn't evil, no matter what you might think. All seven of his children told stories of his kindness."

Apollo switched the utility knife from his left hand to his right as he moved toward Jorgen. His hands wanted to use the blade again. But he stopped and looked at the pictures of those victims once more. These other boys and girls—black and brown, yellow, white, and red—a roster as varied as the general assembly of the United Nations.

"If he didn't sacrifice his own kids," Apollo said, "whose children did he use?"

"Queens has many immigrants," Jorgen said. "Immigrants have many children. It was a different time. You can't judge him by the standards of today. Men like him, men with the temperament to make tough choices and see them through, made this country thrive."

"You really believe that?" Apollo asked.

"No one wants to learn their history," Jorgen said firmly. "Not all of it. We want our parents to provide but don't want to know what they had to sacrifice to do it. No nation was ever built with kindness."

From the other side of the Japanese panels, the three heaters squawked and rattled. It sounded like tinny laughter just then.

"How do you find them?" Apollo asked. "How do you choose?"

Jorgen ran a hand over his nose and down to his chin.

"When I was in service, I could be searching for hours. Days. In the eighties I drove everywhere in my white van. It was really too much. But eventually I would find a candidate. A boy or girl without protection. A baby that no one is watching. The castoffs. They have a look to them. I learned to recognize it instantly."

He shook his head at Apollo as if Apollo might offer sympathy.

"But now you hardly have to leave the house," Jorgen said. "All a man needs these days is an Internet connection."

"What the hell are you talking about?"

"In folktales a vampire couldn't enter your home unless you invited him in. Without your consent the beast could never cross your threshold. Well, what do you think your computer is? Your phone? You live inside those devices so those devices are your homes. But at least a home, a physical building, has a door you can shut, windows you can latch. Technology has no locked doors.

"People share everything now," Jorgen said in a marveled hush. "They share which playgrounds they visit with their children and at what times. They share when they've hired a babysitter. They share photos of the schools their children attend. They're so proud of their children. They can't help themselves. They want to share it all. But who are they sharing it with? Do they really know what they've invited into their homes? I promise they don't."

He extended a finger and wagged it at Apollo.

"And you, I know you. One of these special new fathers. You're going to document every moment, every breath of your child's life. You take videos of them while they're sleeping and slap them on the computer before the baby wakes up. You think you're being so loving. You'll be a better father than the one who raised you! Or the one who was never there at all. But let me tell you what I see instead. The neediness of it. The begging to be applauded. As if the praise of a thousand strangers would ever make up for the fact that you didn't feel loved enough as a child. Oh, you poor thing. You were begging to be devoured. Maybe it's you your child needed to be protected from. You leave a trail of breadcrumbs any wolf could follow, then act shocked when the wolf is outside your door. So concerned about being the perfect father, you don't even notice your child has been snatched away! Replaced in the night by the offspring of a troll, a changeling whose beauty is only a projection of your own vanity."

Jorgen clapped his hands.

"Shall we go check on the sheep's head?"

90

APOLLO PRACTICALLY CHASED Jorgen down. A short sprint from the den into the hall. The old man went to the kitchen, and Apollo followed.

"Why not say no?" Apollo asked. "That was Nils's fucking daughter. Why not refuse!"

Before checking on the sheep's head, Jorgen poured himself more to drink. He'd finished off the bottle of Brennivín, but no worries, he had more. He took a new bottle from the cabinet as well as another Ensure. After he'd made the mixture and swigged it, he checked the timer. Almost done.

"He tried that," Jorgen said, leaning back against the sink. "That's the first thing he did."

Apollo pointed the blade at Jorgen. "And?"

Jorgen raised the mug and waved it from side to side. "That beast destroyed everything. I told you the Sloopers settled here for a short time? Well, that's why they packed up for Orleans County."

"So then they did know," Apollo said. "If it destroyed their homes."

"Do you know what those people said?" Jorgen asked. "Until they all passed on, do you know what those people said happened to their property here in Little Norway?" He closed his eyes and raised the mug high. "It was an act of God." He laughed bitterly.

He drank slowly, but Apollo caught his eyes dancing over Apollo's shoulder, down the hallway, toward that open front door. Apollo spun, expecting to find himself under attack. But no one was there. He turned back to Jorgen, who had finished the drink and held the mug tightly in two hands. The old man looked worn down, tapped out. His lips were shut tight but quivered with exhaustion.

"Why have you told me all this?" Apollo finally asked. "What's the point? Confession?"

The lids danced on their pots. Jorgen turned off the fire under the potatoes and the cabbage. Only the pot with the sheep's head rattled on.

"Why do you think I did it?" Jorgen asked. He opened another cupboard, above the fridge, and pulled down a silver serving tray.

"You feel guilty," Apollo said. "For what you've done. For what the men in your family have done. And you should."

Jorgen went back into the cupboard for the serving tray's matching domed lid.

"You're right about the guilt. I can't deny that." He set down the lid and tapped his scarred throat, proof of his previous suicide attempt. "I wouldn't have done this otherwise. But let me ask you, and think about your answer, what would you do for your child?"

"I'd do anything," Apollo said. "There's no end to what I'd do."

Jorgen wagged a finger. "Exactly. Exactly. This is what a good father must say. This is what a good father must do. The same for me as it is for you."

Jorgen looked to the bottle of Brennivín again but could hardly raise a hand. The old man must've been drunker than he seemed. Instead of reaching for the bottle, he simply swayed in its direction, then gave up on the effort.

"My son saw what was left of the Knudsen line. Just me, this house, and all the debt associated with it. But he had a wife and two daughters of his own. A good job, working with computers, but it hardly made him enough. There was a time in this country when a man like him could be sure his children would do better than he had done. Once that was the birthright of every white man in America. But not anymore. Suddenly men like my son were being passed over in the name of things like 'fairness' and 'balance.' Where's the justice in that?"

Apollo approached Jorgen Knudsen. "He's your boy," Apollo whispered.

"He believed that the troll wasn't our burden but our blessing. That we had to go back to the old ways, before we abandoned our traditions. When we were great. He thought maybe things had been going wrong from the moment Nils refused to sacrifice one of Petra's children. The troll brought us to these shores, and it could save us again. That's what he believed. We could channel that monster's power into our own deliverance. That was our right, our heritage. That's why we came to America! That's why we worked so hard. But to do that, we had to return to our origins with whole hearts. So he took it upon himself to honor the pact, as it was meant to be. He did exactly as Nils had done one hundred and ninety years ago. I admired his fortitude."

"He left Agnes in the forest. In a cave."

Jorgen slapped the countertop. "But his wife couldn't understand his vision. She didn't appreciate his courage, she scorned it. She left him. And took Grace with her. He loved them so much, he would sacrifice his own child—and Gretta abandoned him! That broke him. I saw it. My son lost his mind. I've been taking care of him ever since."

Jorgen slipped down from where he'd been leaning against the sink. Fell right on his butt. Instead of trying to stand again, he went slack there on the floor.

"Did you really think I left the front door open for you?" Jorgen asked, his eyes focused on the blade rather than on Apollo. "Did you believe I told you all this history simply to unburden myself?

"If the front door is open and the front light left on, my son knows to run," Jorgen said. "What you took as a confession was my way of giving him time to flee." He looked up at Apollo. "It's what any good father would do. I've done all I can. Now give that blade to me."

Apollo went down on a knee. "You can have it."

Apollo brought the blade to Jorgen's neck and thrust. Instinctively, Apollo's eyes fluttered shut. He heard the old man's choking, astonished cough. When he opened his eyes again, the man's throat threw out gouts of blood. Apollo blinked furiously but was blinded. His face felt scalded. Jorgen's blood clogged Apollo's nose and clotted his left ear; it cloaked his eyes. Apollo felt absolute disgust spread across his skin like a coating of mud. It threatened to suffocate him.

On the counter the kitchen timer beeped. It sounded as loud as a tornado siren. The old man's legs kicked underneath Apollo and nearly sent him over. The only way to stay upright was to lean into the knife so it pressed deeper into Jorgen Knudsen's throat. Apollo felt it lodge into something sturdy that was either the wooden drawer face or the old man's spine. The pot with the sheep's head jumped and shook, and it seemed as if the whole house was giving off the old man's death rattle.

Apollo fell back from the body. He rubbed the sleeves of his shirt over his face just to clear the blood from his eyes. There was Jorgen Knudsen, back against the kitchen cupboards, and his eyes were gone back in his head. A house without its lights on, that's what Jorgen's body looked like now.

The alarm continued to sound, and its cry brought Apollo back to himself. He looked at the alarm, then at the large pot with the fire still going high beneath it. He turned off the flames.

"The sheep is ready," Apollo said.

APOLLO KAGWA LEFT 124 86th Road under cover of night. He carried, in two hands, a large serving plate covered by a domed lid. The potatoes and the cabbage had been boiled for as long as the sheep's head, three hours, and were ruined. In both pots the water had long boiled away, and the rest left behind was scorched. Only the sheep's head came out whole. Its flesh had gone from yellowish red to an overall darkish gray, and its eyes hardened until they looked like marbles. Apollo took the sheep's head out of the boiling water with his bare hands and set it on the tray. His hands turned a bright red, nearly purple, but if there was any pain, his mind couldn't register it. His body still throbbed in the aftermath of the murder he'd just done. The water in the big pot turned a murky maroon from the blood on his fingers.

He set the head on the serving tray and covered it. Jorgen said he brought meals to Emma, whether Starbucks or homemade, as a kind of offering. Would Apollo have to do the same? Would this sheep's head be enough? There was just so much Apollo still didn't know. He shouldn't have killed the old man until he'd learned all the steps, but he hadn't been able to help himself once Jorgen explained how he'd played Apollo and why. *It's what any good father would do.* Kinder Garten had been living in this home; maybe he'd even come to the front door, seen his dad's signal, and escaped. And while that happened, Apollo had been in the windowless den, talking about the past at the expense of the present.

Apollo washed his face and his neck in the sink. It hardly cleaned him off. On the second floor he found a bathroom that had a large, claw-foot tub. He showered himself clean. He went upstairs and found Jorgen's bedroom. Or was this Kinder Garten's room? In a dresser he found slacks and a shirt, socks and a tee. He dressed himself and came back down to the kitchen. He hadn't been wearing his coat and cap when he killed Jorgen Knudsen, so those were still clean.

He covered the sheep's head with the lid. He took the bottle of Brennivín and swigged it. Three gulps, and he felt steadier. Took it with him, jutting out of his coat pocket, the serving tray carried with two hands. Out back he found his suitcase. He'd forgotten it was even there. He set the tray on the top of the suitcase and pulled the suitcase along by its handle.

Apollo returned to the staircase by the park, where Jorgen had set out the bags of food the night before. He climbed to the top and set down the serving plate, lid on. He thought better of crossing the street and trying to hide in the shadows there. Whoever had called the police on him might just do it again. This time he figured it was better to walk into the park.

He lifted the suitcase and led with it, using it to push at the wall of brush. Just three feet into the wooded area, the streets of Queens were scrubbed away. The sudden quiet overwhelmed him like a rogue wave. Not silence, but quiet. The limber creak of trees bending in strong wind, the dried leaves underfoot making a sound like crackers being chewed, the smell of winter air, which is expansive, it hollows out the nostrils. He touched at the red string as a Catholic might caress a rosary. He turned it around and around on his ring finger.

Then the last sound, playing at a register below the others, so regular Apollo mistook it for running water, a babbling brook. But they were words. The woods themselves seemed to be whispering. Not to him, not for him, but all around him. He had entered the woods of a witch and made an offering.

And now the witch appeared.

APOLLO SEEMED TO be standing inside a thunderstorm. He shielded his eyes. He had stumbled into view of a blue cosmos between the rows of winter trees. He saw his wife—she appeared at the center of the rippling lights, the clouds of cobalt smoke, but the distance between him and her appeared insurmountable. Freezing wind pulled at his coat. His ears rang louder than when Cal had fired shots from her gun. The air itself smelled burned, and the scorch of lightning strikes dazzled his eyes. Emma Valentine wore this terrible weather like a cloak.

Then she moved toward the staircase landing and the trees parted before her. She didn't raise her arms and move the branches; they parted for her. Apollo witnessed this. She stepped onto the landing and hardly seemed to bend. The serving plate, lid still on, rose into the air and landed on her outstretched hand.

He heard the words from the children's book. They played on her lips but hardly seemed to come from her. He heard it in echo, sound bouncing across the dirt and up the tree limbs and even pebbling against the concrete staircase, swirling in the night sky.

She stepped back between the trees and turned in the direction she'd come from, her back to him. The metal lid scraped faintly as it trembled with movement. She moved away from him. She was leaving. She hadn't even noticed him.

"Em," he said.

His throat hurt, dried out. The air burned the inside of his mouth.

"Emma," he tried again. "It's me."

She walked away. Not a moment's hesitation. A path led deeper into the Northern Forest, and she seemed to glide upon it. He followed her, trying to think of what else he could say. The only reason he held on to the suitcase—dragging it behind him in the dirt—was because his right hand had stiffened so badly that he couldn't let it go.

The path wound first up a low slope of tulip trees and red oaks, a handful of black walnut. As the climb became steeper, the hills taller, there were tall black oak, black birch, and pignut hickory trees. The black birch gave off the smell of wintergreen. The witch led him deeper into her forest. He followed her blue light.

The path became less and less clear. The trodden dirt gave way to grass and moss and fungi underfoot. Earthworms, millipedes, and sow bugs lived below the forest floor. Apollo could almost sense them down there, feel them far underfoot. The Northern Forest was home to moles and shrews, gray squirrels and cottontail rabbits, chipmunks and raccoons. The moles and shrews survived the winters in the subsurface tunnels that ran throughout the park. Worlds upon worlds upon worlds hid here.

As Emma reached the top of a sharp slope Apollo called out again. "You were right all along, Emma."

No response. No acknowledgment.

"It wasn't a baby."

Just like that she turned to him for the first time, looking down the sloping hill. Her eyes appeared so dark, she actually looked blind, blinded. She didn't open her mouth, but around them the entire Northern Forest rose into a shout.

"The goblins were real!" Apollo shouted. "I couldn't see them."

In that moment the cloud of energy, electricity, that surrounded her parted, and she became a thin woman wearing a ragged maroon puffer coat holding a pewter serving tray. In the moonlight he saw her cracked lips and puffy, yellowing eyes. She became a portrait of anguish.

The forest fell into true silence.

"Emma," Apollo said.

She looked down at her hands and marveled at the serving plate she carried, as if this was the first time she'd even noticed it there. She went down into a crouch and set it on the forest floor, its thin layer of snow. She pawed at the ground, hands grubbing through the leaves.

"It's Apollo."

Emma Valentine stood. She had something in her right hand. She cocked her arm back, grunted once, and threw a stone the size of a softball. It hit Apollo right above the knee. A cold, sharp stab ran up his thigh. He went down like a chopped tree.

She lifted the tray.

She turned away.

She went over the other side of the hill.

Apollo lay in the dirt looking up at the canopy of trees. His leg throbbed so badly, he felt as if it would swell and burst through his pants. He lay there gasping, then pushed himself over onto his stomach. He couldn't stand, not yet, but he could crawl, drag himself through the underbrush and snow. He left the suitcase where it had fallen beside him and mounted the top of the hill.

The hill fell sharply, and the forest became even denser down below. Apollo crawled until he could walk. When he could walk, he rose again. In the Northern Forest there were two layers of trees, the tallest and oldest, and below that the second canopy of newer growth, younger trees. Even though their branches were bare, they crowded together and blocked out the moonlight. He was on the path, faint as it was, but couldn't be sure to stay on it in the dark. The solution waited in his coat pocket. His cellphone. It held a full charge. The small screen glowed. No signal, but what did that matter? The only person he needed to reach was already here. He held the phone out in front of him like a torch. He found Emma's footprints in the snow.

Apollo followed the path.

THE LAND FLATTENED again, and the trees spread out slightly, and the undergrowth became more tamped down. He'd reached a clearing, the forest floor so trampled it had gone smooth. The trees that ringed the clearing tilted at angles as if they'd been bumped aside by something as large as a truck or a tank.

"*Jotunn*." Apollo remembered Jorgen's voice. "*Trolde*. That's how we say it in Norwegian."

Apollo stood in the clearing, under the moonlight. He could see clearly so he turned off his phone. Emma's footsteps continued back into the woods, so he went that way, too.

Onward like that for another fifteen minutes that felt like two hours because of the cold and the ache above his knee. She'd pegged him hard and hadn't hesitated. What had he been expecting, hugs and heartfelt kisses? Maybe so. Maybe so. But reconciliation never came easy, not with the things that mattered.

The tree cover here became sparse, and moonlight made the snow on the ground glow. The path grew wider and split in two. Two paths curled away from each other in either direction like a pair of enormous ram's horns. Easy to see which one Emma had taken. Partway down the path to the left, the pewter lid lay on its side. In the dark, under the moonlight, it looked like polished silver. When Apollo reached it, he picked it up. Instinctively he held it in front of him like a shield, scant protection. And on he went, around the curve.

The cleared land opened even wider, like marching into a bowl. The word that came to him right away was *quarry* though really the space wasn't quite that huge or deep. Still, compared to the rest of the densely packed Northern Forest, this pit of stones seemed as wide as the Grand Canyon. There were rings and rings of gray stone and rubble leading toward the bottom of the pit. At the very bottom he saw a gaping black cave opening. Emma Valentine sat at the lip of the pit, peering down at the cave, her back to him.

Apollo stopped moving and watched the cave, too. He'd been cold for a while now, but a new kind of frigidness froze him at the core. It had been one thing to hear Jorgen spin a story but was another to see the cave, for the tale to turn true.

"Agnes," he whispered.

"You're supposed to save the eye for last," Emma said.

She didn't look up at him, but her words drew his attention back. Apollo waited there with the serving lid still in front of him. What would stop Emma from picking up another one of the thousands of stones all around her and strafing it at him? Her aim had been excellent. Maybe this time she'd get him in the head. He moved toward her cautiously even though no storm of blue magic swirled around her now. He moved closer.

Emma watched the cave. She sat hunched forward there on the stones. She creaked forward and back faintly. Apollo realized she was eating. The serving plate with the sheep's head balanced on her lap. He reached her side. He stood, and she stayed cross-legged on the ground.

"The old man once said the eye is like the dessert," Emma whispered. "Or maybe I heard him think it. Anyway, he told me to save the eye for last. But I don't take orders from him."

Emma stiffened her thumb and pointer finger and dug them into the sheep's eye socket with expertise. The eyeball plucked out without a sound. Apollo reached out to stop her hand, but when he moved, he dropped the domed lid, and it bashed to the ground, then went end over end down the sloping curve of the pit, and the clangs echoed in the darkness. He scrambled two steps down the slope to catch the lid, but the stones were loose so he only slipped and fell on his side. The bottle of Brennivín in his coat pocket made a dull thump, then its shape went flatter, and he knew it had broken open. The fumes rose and overwhelmed him, he swam in a cloud of spiced gasoline. He got on his feet to escape the odor, but it had soaked into his coat and his pants so he carried it with him.

Meanwhile, casually, Emma tossed the first of the sheep's eyes into her mouth. It looked as if she was sucking on an enormous lozenge. She closed her lips and pursed them. She didn't stop staring at the cave opening even as Apollo caused all this chaos. Apollo gagged as he watched Emma eat the eye. And finally she pursed her lips and spat out a small stone bit, like an olive pit, and it plinked across the rocks below her. The last of the eye went downhill as Apollo scrambled back up.

Emma dug two fingers into the meat around the now-empty eye socket and pulled at a hunk of flesh. She slipped it into her mouth. She swallowed, almost without chewing. She remained vigilant in her view of the cave.

Apollo looked down into the pit. The serving lid had come to a stop not twenty feet from the cave mouth. He crawled up until he could sit next to Emma. She didn't seem bothered by the Brennivín stink. Perhaps she was beyond caring.

"I've been searching for you," Apollo said.

She took up another portion of meat, swallowed it without expression. "Well, this is where I've been."

"Not the only place you've been," Apollo said. "I've been to the island. I met Cal."

Apollo watched his wife's profile. Her eyes were glassy with weariness. Her hair had grown tangled and long.

"When's the last time you had any rest?" he asked. "Where do you sleep?"

She reached for one last pull of meat that remained around the eye socket, but Apollo touched the back of her hand, and she dropped the meat and pulled her hand back to her lap. She looked up at her husband.

"I never sleep," she said. "Sleep is the cousin of death." She pointed at the mouth of the cave. "I keep watch through the night so Brian will stay safe."

He wanted to reach out and hold her hand. More than that, he wanted to cradle her in his lap. Let her rest her heavy head.

"When I was eight months pregnant," Emma said, "this woman came up to me on the street. She had this big smile on as soon as she saw me but I didn't know her. She stopped me and told me once the baby was born, I'd never have a life without stress again. She said I'd never have a good night's rest once I was a mother. She seemed so happy to say it to me. Like she thought the anxiety was a badge of honor. I wanted to scratch out her eyes."

Apollo kept his hands flat on his thighs. No quick movements, voice calm. "When I first saw you in the woods you were glowing," he said. "You had a blue light all around you. But when I spoke to you, it went away."

"Is it still there?" she asked.

"No," he said. "I can't see it anymore."

"'You're what's wrong with our family,'" Emma said. "'You. Are. The. Problem. Go take another pill.' Those were the last words you said to me."

Apollo lowered his head. "I—"

She spoke over him. "That's the first time you took my light from me."

"You could rest tonight," Apollo said. "I'll stay awake."

She looked at the cave, then at her husband. She brought two fingers to the sheep's head but didn't pick at it. Her finger, he noticed, trembled. "You're sure?" she asked.

"Yes," he said.

"Go down and look at the stones," she said. "When you're ready, you go down there and really look."

With that Emma's puffer coat seemed to deflate, as if she'd slipped right out of it. That's how small she shrank. She brought the arms of the coat together across her belly and lowered her head until the hood covered her face. It was like watching a pill bug curl in on itself.

"Apollo," she said, her voice muffled through the material.

"Yes."

"If this turns out to be a trick. If you're working with those men and try to betray me—"

"I'm not," he said. "I won't."

She wasn't asking for reassurance, though. She spoke almost with nonchalance.

"If this turns out to be a trick, I will take you with me to hell," Emma said.

94

APOLLO FINALLY BELIEVED Emma had fallen asleep when her wheezing became regular and deep. In sleep she sounded like someone going through a prolonged asthma attack. If she looked exhausted, she sounded truly unhealthy. The fact that she was alive at all seemed like an act of will beyond comprehension.

Eventually the rhythm of her snoring worked on him like a sleep aid. If he stayed there next to her, listening to her, he might be drawn down into the same deep slumber. So finally he stood and went down the slope of loose stone. Ten feet down, and he looked back at Emma. He couldn't see her face, only her shape, but he felt safer knowing she was there. Already he felt a little happier because he wasn't doing this alone.

When Apollo turned back toward the bottom, he focused on the domed serving lid rather than the rocks. Twenty feet farther down lay the entrance to the cave. Was this really the same one from Jorgen's story? Where a baby named Agnes had been abandoned by her own father? Twice. And what of all those other children whose pictures hung on the wall? He felt dizzy at the idea, a soul-deep nausea. To find such a place in the middle of Queens. To find it anywhere on earth.

In order to avoid the cave and the rocks, Apollo made for the serving lid. He lowered his ass almost to the ground so he could scoot forward without risking another spill. When he reached the lid, it felt like an accomplishment. So much so that he turned and held it up toward Emma, like a child trying to impress. But doing that meant he looked away from the cave, and the sudden feeling of terror that hit him felt hot as sunlight against the back of his head. He looked to the cave mouth and after a moment realized it wasn't only fear making him feel warm but an actual burst of hot air. It felt as if the cave itself had breathed on him. Or something deeper within it.

Impossible to move. Impossible to flee. The heat of the hot wind melted the snow around him in a ragged half circle. Farther up the little valley it remained winter, but a warmer season started here. The nearby stones, once lost under a layer of snow, now lay exposed.

Apollo lifted the serving lid again, like a shield, and now he found a stick partially upright on the ground. This was what had snagged the serving tray. A piece of a tree branch maybe, as close as he could find to a weapon. He pulled it up from the stones and held it out, as high as his makeshift shield.

"Apollo."

This was Emma's voice, coming from behind him. At least that's what he thought. Because he couldn't see her face, couldn't see her lips moving, it felt as if she were speaking to him inside his head.

"Look at what's in your hand," she said.

Apollo raised the stick so he could see it in the moonlight. Hard and off-white, almost gray. The top part of it had two knobby bulbs at the tip, and the bottom had a single, more prominent knob. Not a stick or a piece of broken branch.

It was a bone.

He held a bone in his hand. But it was small. A child's leg bone. A child's femur. When Apollo realized this, he dropped it with a start, and it clacked onto the stones.

The stones.

Now Apollo went on one knee. His ears filled with a kind of hissing, like steam playing from a radiator, but this was only the sound of his confusion and disgust. He dropped the serving lid and didn't even hear the noise it made when it landed. He grabbed at a large, rounded stone with his right hand. He turned it over.

It was a child's skull.

It had a hole the size of a silver dollar in it, right above the left ear. Apollo's hand pulsed with a painful spasm, but he couldn't drop the skull, couldn't look away from the hole. He felt rage, roiling like bile, in his throat. He turned and took a step toward the cave.

"You go in there now, and you won't survive," Emma said.

She'd come out of her cocoon, risen from her crouch. She stood at the top of the valley of bones and spoke with the assurance of a prophet.

Apollo moved backward, and the bones beneath his boots chucked and clattered. He still held the skull. It felt cruel to drop it on the ground again. He decided it was the skull of Agnes. The first Agnes. Agnes Knudsdatter, the first abandoned child in Queens.

Apollo sat beside Emma in the cold. He placed the serving lid back on the tray, hiding the sheep's head. The skull of Agnes remained in his lap, but when he looked down at it now, it resembled only a large, gray rock again. Apollo almost laughed, but he felt too weak. The world is full of glamour, especially when it obscures the suffering of the weak.

"So we stay here till morning," Apollo said.

"When the sun is up, it sleeps."

"And you're sure Brian is still in there?" Apollo asked. He couldn't make himself say the second question—*And that he's still alive?*

But Emma understood him. She brought one hand to her belly. "A mother knows," she whispered.

"What do you do during the day, while it's asleep?" Apollo asked.

"I walk," she said.

For the first time, Apollo risked bringing his hand closer to Emma. He pressed it, lightly, against the small of her back.

"In the morning I want you to come with me," Apollo said. "I know a house nearby where we can rest. No one there can bother us now."

Emma didn't answer him. Didn't lean into his touch or otherwise appear relieved, but she didn't shrug his hand away either. Apollo kept it there, and they sat together until dawn.

95

EMMA AND APOLLO stood over the body of Jorgen Knudsen.

It had actually surprised Apollo to return to this house and find the old Viking still dead on the kitchen floor, utility knife still stuck in his throat. He'd been anticipating, in some way that wasn't conscious, returning to find Jorgen up and pouring himself another of his Ensure cocktails. No matter how much the old man deserved killing, such a thing still costs. Seeing the body, the blood already dried on his clothes, the floor, even droplets of it on the ceiling and the table where Apollo cut cabbage, made Apollo blink wildly, as if he'd never washed Jorgen's blood from his face. He would probably always feel the stain of it, until his last day.

Nevertheless this much reality still held. Dead was dead. Jorgen Knudsen lived no more.

The only surprise here was Emma. She stared at the body and tapped her throat. "I made him do that," she said.

Maybe Apollo didn't expect shock really—think of all she'd experienced so far—but she discussed Jorgen's wound, his death, so casually, like a bit of home improvement. A tasteful choice for the backsplash above the kitchen counters.

"I wouldn't let him sleep," Emma said without passion. "I wouldn't give him any peace. Every night I slipped inside his head and made him listen."

They'd retrieved the suitcase on the way back to Jorgen's house. Taken the same path she'd led him on the night before but in reverse, the suitcase lying right there in the underbrush like the last piece of luggage at a baggage carousel. He'd scooped it up and pulled it along with them, but at this point it had been too heavy. Though he'd been loath to do it in front of Emma, Apollo unzipped the case and slipped out the grave marker. She watched him but didn't speak about it. He set the grave marker there in the woods, and this felt appropriate. The changeling had been born nearby—where better to commemorate its passing? To this day, there's a bronze grave marker with the name "Brian Kagwa" hidden in Forest Park.

Meanwhile Emma and Apollo returned to Jorgen's kitchen.

"He showed up with food every night," she said. "He thought he could appease me. You know how much sheep's head I've eaten? Last night I'd had enough. I made him bring me Starbucks."

"That's the reason?" Apollo asked. "You just wanted a different meal?"

Emma watched him quietly for a moment and pursed her lips, a look that verged on playful. "Why else would I do it?" she asked. She kicked at one of Jorgen's limp legs. "You don't know the things this man has done in his life," she said to Apollo.

"He told me some of it."

She tapped her temple. "I saw it. All of it."

"Let's go upstairs," Apollo said.

Emma looked at the ceiling then back at him, wary but ready. "What's up there?"

"A bathroom. A tub."

Apollo ran the water. He tried to unzip her coat, but the zipper had frozen or rusted up by her neck long ago. He left her in the bathroom and went down to the kitchen and found scissors in a drawer. He stepped carefully over Jorgen's body so he wouldn't slip in the blood. Upstairs he cut the old coat off her. The puffy fabric fell from her stiff as a beetle's shell.

Emma had always been a small woman, but without the coat she appeared whittled down to a pine needle's width. Strangely, this didn't make her seem weak. Imagine the coat falling away to reveal a single plutonium rod underneath.

The clothes, on the other hand, had nearly bonded with her skin. He tried to pull at the sleeves of her wool sweater, and they crumbled between his fingers. Her jeans were nothing more than long strips of denim that came off in faded blue ribbons when he tugged at them. Her socks couldn't be slipped off her feet. They would have to come off when she stepped into the tub, so rotten they'd dissolve in the water.

He turned off the faucet. It was only when he leaned close, right up against her skin, that her smell overpowered the Brennivín coating his skin. She smelled so tart from dried sweat and a longtime lack of soap that Apollo's eyes hurt when he leaned into her and picked her up.

"Ready for the water?" Apollo asked, but Emma didn't answer. She stared at the bathroom mirror and, maybe for the first time in four months, saw her reflection. She couldn't look away from it.

"Who is that?" she whispered.

He leaned over the tub and let her down. The water turned to a murky, almost greenish sludge seconds after she was immersed. Months of filth floated off her body. Apollo lifted the plunger and let the water drain, then refilled the tub. It took three refills before the water stopped turning dirty. Then Apollo found a cloth and a bar of soap and washed Emma's body.

They were in the bathroom for two hours.

When they finished, Emma couldn't really stand. It was as if the bath had also scraped away some armor she'd constructed, an exoskeleton. He carried her into the largest bedroom, what he assumed had been Jorgen's bedroom, though the bed clearly hadn't been slept in. No indent in the sheets or the pillows. Emma had been keeping the old man awake for a long time. Maybe he'd stopped coming into this room at all. This wasn't the room where Apollo found the clean wardrobe. This meant he was wearing Kinder Garten's clothes.

He pulled back the covers and laid Emma on the bed. There were two space heaters in this bedroom, neither one turned on, so the room felt chilly. He spun each one's black dial. Late morning light curled in through two windows at the head of the bed and clarified just how gray, how bloodless, Emma's skin had become. She looked like a body that had been dug out of the ice. Cleaning her up actually made Emma look worse. As a witch, she had been imperious; she walked in a blue cloud of power, a being for whom the trees parted and the woods whispered. The woman on the mattress now nearly got lost in the bedsheets. She should've been hooked up to an IV and put on bed rest for six weeks. She hadn't spoken once since Apollo ran the bath. Emma appeared more lost than she'd been out in the forest. Had he done more harm than good by bringing her back?

Apollo pulled the covers over her and returned to the first floor. There were clothes in the suitcase—he'd brought a change for Emma and for Brian—and he thought maybe seeing the clothes would return her focus. He didn't know what else to do. In the kitchen he found Jorgen's body once more, but being alone with it again, he had to steady himself against the counter. This was when he felt the powerful cold throughout the house. He stepped into the hall. That damn front door had been open all night. He walked down the hall. The whole first floor felt frigid, the place gone as silent as a tomb. He shut the front door and turned off the porch light.

He dragged the suitcase up the stairs and unpacked nearly everything, even the mattock. He showed her the clothes he'd picked for her, but her eyes remained focused on the ceiling, unfocused, dazed.

Apollo checked the small zippered side pockets of the suitcase, the faint bulge suggesting something he'd overlooked. He found the packet of bendy straws and the bottle of massage oil. The last of the labor kit. Apollo took up the faintly yellow liquid and shook it, unscrewed the cap, and smelled. Pure almond oil. Emma had packed this suitcase over a year ago, so it was as though she'd packed this small gift for herself.

He pulled the covers away from Emma and poured a dollop of the almond oil into one hand. He moved to the bottom of the bed and brought two hands around Emma's right foot. He squeezed her foot and rubbed the almond oil across the skin until it soaked in. The skin looked no richer or softer, no less gray. He poured more oil into his hand and rubbed it into the bottom of the same foot, pressing at the heel and running his thumb all the way up to the toes. When he finished with the first foot, he moved on to the other and continued upward across her legs and along her sides.

When he'd finished, she rolled onto her side, facing him, but still didn't say a word. Apollo brought the blanket up to the bridge of her nose. Her hair had tightened into its curls as it dried. The two of them stayed in a moody silence for ten minutes or ten years.

"I should've believed you," Apollo eventually said.

Two fingers appeared at the top of the sheet and pulled the fabric down below her chin. "I wouldn't have believed you either," she said. "If it had been the other way around."

Apollo tapped her fingers gently. "We're together now," he said.

She nodded quietly, then locked her gaze with his as she pulled the bedsheets back for him to see her. Her skin shone like burnished brass now. She held the sheet open for him.

He hadn't felt this nervous since he'd been fifteen. When he took off his clothes the scent of Brennivín filled the room, as if the odor had seeped through his clothes and into his skin. But in the moment it hardly mattered. He slipped in beside Emma, and she dropped the sheet around them both.

So long since they'd even kissed each other. He'd forgotten the goodness of her lips. The soft slope of her long, narrow throat. He climbed on top of her, and to his happy surprise, she wrestled him for the position. She laughed with him when her forehead bumped his chin. She humped against his thigh and climbed higher along him. They made love until they fucked. They fucked until they were spent.

When they finished, they came to rest with their heads near a window so the sunlight bathed both their faces. A comfortable silence, they lingered in it, this short reprieve.

Emma rested a hand on Apollo's chest and patted it twice. She rose on an elbow and kissed his shoulder. He raised his left arm and brought his hand to her ribs, but before he could touch them, she grabbed his wrist. She turned his hand so she could see his ring finger.

"Did you make a wish with this?" she asked.

"I did. But I'm ashamed of it now."

"Why don't you wear it until you can put your real ring back on?"

Apollo lowered his hand. "I threw the ring into the East River."

She clapped a hand to his chin and squeezed a little too tightly. "You're going to have a real hard time finding it there."

Apollo laughed. "You'd make me do it, too."

She brought her nose to his rib cage, sniffing theatrically. "Smells like you've already been there."

"It was Jorgen's favorite cologne," Apollo said.

"Go take a bath," she said. "I need to sleep just a little before it becomes night."

Apollo slipped out of bed and pulled the covers over her. He did need a bath, but there were even more important things that needed to be done. He picked through his pile of clothes and found the phone in his coat pocket. Emma had already fallen asleep.

He went downstairs with the phone. When Emma woke up, they were going back into the forest and, this time, marching into that cave. Maybe he'd give her the knife that had killed Jorgen, and he could heft the mattock. But suppose they never made it back out? Anna Sofie hadn't, and neither had all those children. Who knew how many other bodies had been lost down there? He didn't want to disappear without saying goodbye to his mother. He turned on the phone and dialed Lillian.

"M OM," HE SAID when Lillian picked up.

"Apollo? Apollo." She whispered when she spoke because it was either that or choke up and say nothing.

"How are you?"

"Happy to hear your voice," she said.

Upstairs Emma slept. Apollo walked to the front door and almost opened it casually, as if this were their home, and he'd called for a weekly check-in with his mother.

"Things have gotten pretty wild," Apollo said, the line a true achievement in understatement.

"I left you alone," Lillian said quickly. "I left you alone, and that's when things went bad."

Apollo leaned against the door. He'd only meant to say goodbye, but now he shut his eyes as if Lillian were about to tell him a bedtime story.

"The last time we talked, you were so angry at me. I understood why, but I've been thinking and thinking about everything you said, everything I said. There's so much I never explained. I guess I hoped I would never have to."

"What does that mean?"

"You were so young," Lillian said softly. "I prayed you'd just forget."

"Then I started having the nightmares."

She sighed on the line. "Yes. And even then I pretended that's all they were."

"But why? I'm not accusing you of anything, I'm just asking. What was the point of pretending my dad didn't come back for me?"

A longer silence now, so long Apollo thought she'd hung up the line. He pulled the phone from his ear, but the battery still had plenty of power, and the two of them hadn't been disconnected.

"I got to know that lawyer, Mr. Blackwood, once I'd been at the job for a few years. We didn't become friends, but if you work with people long enough, you're going to have a few conversations. At some point he told me why he'd been so hard on me in the beginning, forcing me to come work on Saturdays.

"And do you know he had a whole story about how he was trying to help me? The firm was going to be letting go of staff, and as the newest hired, I'd be the first one fired. But if I'd learned enough about how the firm worked, proved myself a hard worker by coming in on weekends, they'd probably consider me valuable enough to keep. That's what he said. Maybe that was true, but it certainly wasn't the only reason that man forced me to come to the firm on Saturdays. I knew it, and I thought he knew it, too.

"But by the third or fourth time he told me this story, I realized he did believe his version. If you asked him if he'd ever pressured me for a date he'd swear it never happened. That fact had left his mind. He'd done me a favor, and look, five years later I still worked at the firm and even had two promotions. He was trying to tell me how grateful I should be! I'm not saying he lied. Not exactly. But his story was more flattering to himself, so with some time and distance, that's the story he chose to believe. I'm realizing that by telling you nothing about your father, I might have been doing the same thing. Not just for myself but for him."

"Just tell me what happened," Apollo said. He stood straight now and began to pace, but Jorgen Knudsen's kitchen lay directly ahead, and in that kitchen lay a man he had killed. He didn't want to hear this story while staring at a dead man. He stopped moving and braced himself against the door that led to the den.

"I came home from work at one," Lillian began. "I'd brought some

McDonald's for us. I felt guilty, and you liked the French fries. But when I reached home, the front door wasn't locked. Already that was very strange. I heard the bath running. I panicked. Dropped all my things. I thought you'd gotten yourself in there, and what if you drowned or something? I ran to the bathroom and opened the door and saw the ugliest thing I've ever known."

She stopped talking. It even sounded like she'd stopped breathing.

"Brian had you . . . I can't say it, Apollo."

"I want to hear it," Apollo told her, though he wasn't quite sure.

"He had taken off your clothes, and he had you in the tub."

"I thought you said the water was hot. Steaming."

"It was," she said. "He had his hands on your chest, and he had you under the water, and you were kicking and crying because the water was burning your skin."

Apollo's hand slipped and he slid down to the floor. "What?"

"Your father tried to kill you," Lillian said. "And when I came home, he planned to kill me. Then himself."

"Why?" Apollo whispered.

"I told you. I wanted a divorce. I was leaving him and taking you with me. Your father had a terrible childhood. His mother and father were awful people. He wanted a family so badly. He wanted to make up for everything he'd missed. He'd been telling himself stories about how it would be since he was twelve years old. But twelve-year-olds don't understand adulthood. Even when he became a man, he still thought like a child. He couldn't change, couldn't adapt. I served him with divorce papers, but he had other plans."

Apollo sat with his back against the door. "But I always thought—" he said. "The stuff in the box. The book."

"Your father lived in terror that he'd lose you. That's what the whole book is about. When he was young, he didn't have an Ida who could come save him. He always felt like the goblins had stolen him and raised him and no one came to bring him back. That's why he had it, why he wanted to read it to you. He was always going to come for you. He loved you with all his heart and he tried to take your life. I'm sorry, Apollo, but both those things are true."

She cleared her throat. Her voice became the steadiest it had been this whole call.

"You have the right to think whatever you like about him, and about me, but at least you'll know it all. That's the only way to understand anything."

Apollo pressed his free hand over his eyes. "I'm amazed anyone survives childhood," he said.

"Apollo, you hear me? I want you to know that no matter who your father became, you're not him. I'm proud of the man you turned out to be."

He looked up at the ceiling, rested his head against the den's door. "I spent my whole life chasing him," he said. "But you're the one who was always there."

"I was where I wanted to be," she whispered.

"What happened to him?" Apollo asked. "I mean after you found us. I'm sure he wouldn't just apologize and walk away."

"You think a man is going to hurt my child and I'll just see him to the door?"

"Did you call the cops?" Apollo asked.

"No," she said. "They weren't needed. I stepped into that bathroom, and I saw my son in danger and I . . . turned into something else." She went silent.

"Where is he now? Do you have any idea?"

"I know exactly where Brian West is," Lillian said. "He's where I left him."

Apollo held the phone to his ear, expecting her to reveal more, but instead she said, "You sound tired. Are you eating? Do you want to come over and I'll make you dinner?"

He laughed hoarsely. "I'll eat something soon," he said. "But I do want to come over, very soon."

Apollo began to form the words—*Emma is here with me*—but before he could say them, he realized how cold the first floor felt, even here by the den's door. He told his mother he had to go, hung up, and opened the door. The room looked exactly as it had a day ago, but that didn't mean the room was unchanged. He walked inside, shivering.

The space heaters weren't on.

No heat. No sparking, sputtering, rattling clatter.

He stooped in front of them. All three were cool to the touch. Maybe a fuse had blown. But when he turned the dials, each one lit up and hummed. The fuses were fine. That meant last night someone had come into this house and turned the heaters off.

97

APOLLO KNELT IN front of the space heaters, and Emma stood behind him. She'd pulled the top sheet off the bed as she came down the stairs behind him, and now she coiled it around one shoulder and draped it over the other so it looked as if she wore an off-white sari.

"If they turned this off, then they must've seen Jorgen, right?"

It seemed impossible someone would miss a seventy-year-old man with a knife lodged in his throat.

"He's in the kitchen," Emma said. "And down on the floor. So maybe not."

"But the blood," Apollo said.

She put a hand on the back of Apollo's neck and the touch soothed him. "If they didn't come in through the back, they might not even know he was there."

"But that would mean Kinder Garten came in here just to turn off the space heaters," Apollo said. "Why would he do that?"

"What?"

Apollo waved an arm. "William Wheeler, I mean."

"And who's William Wheeler?" Emma asked.

Apollo actually laughed when she said this, like maybe she'd just been fucking with him. But of course, how would she know? Good God, the man at the center of all their misery might as well be a phantom to her. An avatar on a screen and nothing more.

"He's the man who sent those texts to your phone, then made them disappear."

"Oh," she said. "I didn't imagine it."

Apollo explained as much as he could, as quickly as he could, right there in the den. How Kinder Garten had even infiltrated Patrice's machine, hidden inside the hard drive, lurking.

"He's a troll, too," Emma said.

Her face tightened with anger, and she threw one arm out. She needed to strike something just then, and the only opportune targets were the Japanese panels in the middle of the room. She hit one, and when it fell, the other panel fell, too. They landed with two muted thumps because of the shag carpeting, but they raked the far wall and brought down twenty or thirty of the children's portraits hanging there.

Emma pointed. "What is all this?" she asked. Though she had been haunting Jorgen's head, she hadn't ever been in his home.

Apollo didn't know where to begin, so he walked to the far end of the room and pointed at the small ink rendering. "This is Agnes Knudsdatter," he began. "She was the first. I don't know the names of most of these other kids, but Kinder Garten's daughter must be here. Her name was Agnes, too."

She stepped closer to the wall. She brought a hand to her mouth and scanned every face. Then she looked down and saw the frames that had fallen. She bent and picked up two, hung them back on the wall, then dropped her hands.

"All those mothers," she whispered. "This is an evil home."

Emma went to the space heaters and turned all three back on. Once their coils glowed orange, she tipped each one over, facedown on the shag carpeting.

"That's going to start a fire," Apollo said.

"I hope so," she said.

Jorgen's home stood alone on its lot, driveways between it and the houses on either side. Room enough, he hoped, to prevent a blaze from spreading before the fire department would arrive. Quickly they moved through the rest of the first floor, shutting all the windows. They used the months—years—worth of newspapers and circulars on the dining room table like kindling, crowding the papers around the space heaters, then placing more around the two rooms so the fire would spread. Then back to the den.

She pointed at the suitcase. "Show me the clothes you brought me," she said.

Apollo set them out on the carpet as Emma undid the sheet she wore. After dressing she raided a closet in the hall and found a heavy parka with a fur-lined hood. She had to fold each sleeve up twice, and the bottom of the parka came down just past her knees. Now she wore Jorgen's clothes, and Apollo wore William's. They had become the Knudsens, burning down the ancestral home.

Already the carpet beneath them stank as it singed. The first traces of smoke could be seen in the den. Now the suitcase had nearly emptied. The only things left were the mattock and Brian's outfit. Apollo took the former, Emma the latter. They left the den and walked through the kitchen. Jorgen's body remained pinned to the cabinet like a butterfly in a display.

"When this house goes up in flames, he's going to get a Viking funeral," Apollo said.

"Better than he deserves," Emma said.

Apollo set down the mattock and leaned close to the body one last time, but he wasn't planning some sentimental goodbye. His fingerprints were on the handle of the knife. The house might burn, but who knew what might survive? At the very least he should take the murder weapon. He grabbed it and tugged, but the tip had lodged deep. Apollo had to plant a foot against the dead man's chest to yank it free. Jorgen's body flopped down on its side making a dull thud. Emma had already gone out the back entrance.

Apollo and Emma walked alongside the house. From the street no one would guess at the arson inside. Not yet. Meanwhile the interior of Jorgen Knudsen's home had already filled with fog. Shutting the windows, slipping a few of the circulars under the front door, had helped to turn the place into a smoke box. The lack of windows in the den meant even a nosy neighbor wouldn't see the flames until they spread. By then it would be too late to save the place.

They were halfway down the drive when they were bathed in light, bright as a brilliant idea. The motion sensor had done its job again, capturing them. But this time Apollo didn't flee or freeze up. In the middle of the day, the light wouldn't even be noticeable to people across the street, or even on the other side of the alleyway. He and Emma stopped at that curious door. No handle. No locks.

"Look at that," Emma said.

At hip level, a faint handprint.

"That's blood," Apollo said.

Emma pressed at the door, but it didn't move. "What's down there?" she asked.

"I never got in," he said.

"If the old man kept pictures in his den, what do you think he might be hiding in the basement?"

She didn't speak again but pointed at the mattock in his left hand. He lifted it and slipped the adze end in between the door and the frame. He looked across the street and behind him. No neighbors watching. He pulled back, and the wood squawked loudly. He didn't hesitate, moving the adze lower and yanking again. A third time, lower, and the door lifted off its hinges and fell back. Apollo pushed it farther so they could get inside.

A long staircase led down into the basement. They remained there at the threshold, silent, and heard the faintest tapping sound. Another moment, and they heard it again.

"I'm going to activate subject twelve. You guys will like this one."

A man's voice.

Apollo recognized it.

He gestured down with the mattock. As they descended, they felt heat from the floorboards above their heads.

98

ABOILER, A WASHING machine and dryer; six cans of paint so old their lids had oxidized; an air mattress with a comforter heaped in a pile on top; one thin pillow, and two garbage bags containing a jumble of clothes fit for a stocky, middle-aged man; a black ergonomic office chair, a computer desk and computer system exactly, perfectly the same as the one Patrice had built in his basement apartment; and an iPad propped up beside one of the monitors. The iPad showed a photo of an infant cradled in a man's hands.

And Kinder Garten was down here, too.

He sat in the office chair, staring at the middle screen of his rig, a pair of giant headphones on his ears. Droplets of blood stained the floor beneath his seat.

"This is the place in Charleston," William said, as if answering someone's question. He laughed softly. "No, I will not give you the address. Only paid subscribers get platinum access."

Apollo and Emma watched this man in a choked silence.

Kinder Garten had slipped a camera into the home of a family in Charleston, South Carolina. Five people—a father, two grandparents, and two teenage girls—flitted around an expansive kitchen, preparing breakfast. And he watched them from here in Queens.

Not only had Kinder Garten found a way inside their home, it seemed like the camera wasn't even well hidden. The perspective suggested something right at counter level. The kind of thing at least one of the people in that kitchen should see, but all five appeared oblivious. Worse was the moment when the grandfather came right up to the camera, leaned close, and looked into the lens with no apparent concern. He raised one finger and typed slowly, occasionally looking up at the camera.

This was when Apollo and Emma realized what was going on. "It's their laptop," Apollo said. "He turned their own laptop into his camera."

Both of them tensed now, waiting for Kinder Garten to hear them, but with those headphones on, the man had no idea they were there. He'd turned his computer station into a kind of sensory deprivation tank.

With a sting, Apollo realized Kinder Garten must've done the same thing with Patrice's computer. Apollo, Dana, and Patrice had been in the basement playing the video of Emma's escape while Kinder Garten, quiet as you please, watched them. He felt weariness weigh down his eyelids. You could never outthink these guys.

Now Apollo noticed the other screens, the ones that weren't spying inside some middle-class kitchen. On each there were four smaller boxes, and in each smaller box a man sat at a desk. Each face was captured in the greenish reflective light of his computer screen. Each man wore headphones just like Kinder Garten's. Each had a small microphone arm extending from the right ear cup. They could've been a crew of online buddies playing a videogame, but instead of pillaging a dungeon or fighting some simulated war, they were invading a family's home together, a bit of harmless fun.

"I don't think I can stay up that long," Kinder Garten said. "Come on, man, we've been at it for, like, eight hours! I'm crashing."

Apollo and Emma stood immobilized.

"No," Kinder Garten said. "The mother's in Chicago. She's staying at the Renaissance Blackstone Hotel. Two more nights."

Quiet for a moment, he leaned forward as one of the men in one of the small boxes spoke. Apollo watched the lips move.

"Yup," Kinder Garten said. "The dad is a true beta cuck. The mom is fugly, but the girl's all right for now. But you just know if the mom looks like that, the girls are going to turn just as fat when they grow up."

Emma snatched the mattock from Apollo. "That's enough," she said.

She swung the mattock at Kinder Garten sideways, more like a bat, so the sharp ends of the head weren't aimed at his flesh. She wasn't being gentle, the mattock just turned out to be heavier than she'd expected. It connected at shoulder level, sending Kinder Garten out of his chair. He fell sideways, and the chair came down with him.

A puddle spread out on the basement floor when he landed. The chair had been collecting his spilled blood. It was as if a jar of raspberry jam had been shattered. His headphones flew off. The man actually yipped like a puppy. He looked up to find Emma standing there, and Apollo right behind her.

"Fuck," he said, but he didn't move. He couldn't. The right side of his sweatshirt showed dark with dried blood.

Emma, realizing her mistake from the first swing, turned the mattock so the pick end faced Kinder Garten. She leaned back and raised the weapon.

"No, no, no," he shouted. "I can help."

Emma brought the mattock down. The pick end pierced Kinder Garten's collar, and now the man screeched, small and shrill like a bat. The tip of the pick lodged just above his clavicle. His legs thrashed. Apollo flinched, remembering Jorgen's last moments in the kitchen upstairs. Emma pressed one foot to Kinder Garten's chest and cracked the mattock free.

Kinder Garten's eyes swam in his head and found Apollo. "Please," he pleaded. "Control your wife."

Emma raised the mattock again and brought the pick down. This time it landed in his chest, the sharp edge sank in about an inch, lodged in the pectoralis major. "You don't beg him," she said. "You beg me."

Kinder Garten nodded. He tried to raise his arms and bring his hands together beseechingly, but they were trembling too much. Besides, there was still the matter of having a mattock stuck in him.

"Please," Kinder Garten said. "I know I've done you wrong, but please don't kill me." He panted before he could speak again. "I have a daughter of my own. And she just lost her mother."

Emma placed a foot on his collarbone and pressed hard as he spat and choked and howled, while she wrenched the mattock free again. Blood seeped out of this wound.

Apollo touched her arm. "I didn't know you were going to do that."

"I didn't know either," she said.

Apollo reached for the mattock, but she wouldn't let it go. He didn't fight for it, he just stooped closer to Kinder Garten. "Your father is dead," he said. He meant to hurt him.

"I know," Kinder Garten said. "I saw him."

"And you just left him there?" Apollo asked.

Kinder Garten brought one hand to his sweatshirt, pressing against the second wound, the larger one.

"He's been suicidal for months. I came upstairs to get something to eat, and then he's just there on the kitchen floor. I figured he'd finally gone through with it all the way." He blew out a breath. "It was kind of a relief, honestly."

Apollo almost fell over.

Even Emma seemed shocked. "Damn," she said.

"I mean, I was going to call the cops eventually, but I was in the middle of something down here. So I came back to it. It's not like he was going anywhere, right?"

"But why'd you leave the front door open?" Emma asked.

Now Kinder Garten shifted, trying to raise himself. "I came in through the back. Was the front door open? But he would only do that if . . . he was trying to warn me you were here," Kinder Garten said softly. "Did you two kill my dad?"

Apollo looked up at Emma then back to Kinder Garten. "We did," he said.

Kinder Garten nodded. "Well . . . thanks."

Apollo, to his own surprise, jabbed a finger directly into the hole in Kinder Garten's chest. This made the man pop upright. The pain would've made him jump right to his feet if Emma hadn't stepped on one of his ankles.

"He tried to protect you," Apollo said.

Kinder Garten sighed. "You know what's worse than being abandoned? Being raised by a man like him."

"He did what any good father would do."

"You sound like him!" Kinder Garten shouted. "A good father protects his children. If that moron had put some money aside, if he'd planned for the future in any way instead of taking his fortunes for granted, then I wouldn't have had to do what was necessary." He lost his breath for a moment. "I wouldn't have had to make such a big sacrifice."

Behind them, on the computer table, the iPad scrolled through photos, all of them of the same small child, various moments from the first six months of her life.

"Why didn't any of you ever kill it?" Emma said. "That's what I don't understand."

"You can't kill it," Kinder Garten said. "Come on."

"Why?" Emma snapped.

Kinder Garten shook his head. "You don't understand. I don't blame you. I mean you weren't raised . . . like us. You can't change history. All you can do is make the best of what you've inherited. So that's what I did."

"By taking my son?" Emma asked. She pressed her weight onto his ankle.

Kinder Garten raised a hand, pleading. "He's alive," he said. "You understand he's alive, right?"

"How do you know?" Apollo asked.

He gestured with his chin. "Bring me to the computer, and I'll show you."

Emma took her foot off his ankle, and Apollo grabbed Kinder Garten by the arm to lift him. If it hurt to be raised so quickly, neither Apollo nor Emma seemed concerned.

"Why's it so hot?" Kinder Garten asked, looking up. The beams above his head were starting to spit smoke.

"We set your house on fire," Emma told him.

Kinder Garten adjusted his chair, though this was difficult. It seemed like his right arm was losing movement. The whole thing hung loosely from the shoulder. The wound to the chest had brought up more blood. He touched at his ribs—the large patch of dried blood, an older wound lay there.

When Kinder Garten returned to the computer, the family on the middle screen were at their kitchen table, eating breakfast, basic morning business down in Charleston. They were completely unaware of the vulture in the room.

Kinder Garten shut off the remote camera feed from the family in South Carolina. Meanwhile the men on the other screens, the ones who'd also been watching the remote feed from their locations, now gawped openly at the scene in Jorgen Knudsen's basement. Eight men leaned forward, every mouth hanging open. They could see Kinder Garten had company, that he'd been injured. Were they concerned for their friend, or had they decided this might be an even better show?

"I'm going to activate subject zero," Kinder Garten said, as if addressing the men on the screen instead of the couple in the basement. Maybe it was easier to do all this if he continued to think of the child by his designation rather than his name.

"Brian," Apollo said.

Kinder Garten nodded faintly. The middle screen went black, but a small numerical counter appeared at the bottom right of the screen.

"There's nothing there," Emma said.

"Let me move the camera," Kinder Garten said.

He tapped at two keys on the keyboard, and the image on the screen swiveled side to side. Now Apollo understood they were looking at an underground scene, packed earth and stone.

"It's the cave," Apollo said. "You put a camera in that cave."

"I told you," Kinder Garten said. "All you can do is make the best of what you've inherited."

"So what did you do?" Emma asked, leaning forward, squinting at the hazy screen.

"I monetized it," Kinder Garten said, clearly proud. "My father did his service for free, but that was never how it was supposed to work. The pact was that we, the Knudsen men, would make the ultimate sacrifice. But in return, we would prosper. My father failed to make the proper sacrifice and received no blessing. He kept the troll from rampaging, but that didn't pay my goddamn mortgage, let me tell you.

"So I spread the word on certain specialized boards. For a monthly subscription, you log on to the camera anytime you want and watch the proceedings. These men are watching all of you all the time. No act is unknown to them. If people put a little electrical tape over the cameras on their laptops, we could never see. A little thing like that is all it would take, but most of you don't think that far ahead. In Apple we trust. For guys like this you need to offer a special treat, a mystery, something they've never seen. That's worth more. The only thing worth anything. I don't have a big pool yet, but I think word will spread. Subject zero has been our beta test. I'm hoping to set things up so I can take payment in bitcoins. Harder to trace."

Kinder Garten slumped back in his chair.

"Honestly, things could be better. I've only got one camera down there. I couldn't risk being in there long enough to place more than one. What I want to get is a 35-millimeter full-frame CMOS sensor camera for full HD video capture. Then we'd be able to see everything. Of course, what they're really waiting for is the finale. That's what I advertised anyway."

He looked up at Apollo, then at Emma, grinning, the excitement of a promising start-up company acting like a painkiller.

"You promised they'd get to watch the troll eat our child," Apollo said.

Then his face dropped. "I'm sorry," Kinder Garten said. "In the past it didn't take this long though. It tries to raise the children, but it's terrible at it. What it wants to feed them, they can't always eat. Or it forgets its own strength. But it's been different with Brian. I can't say why, exactly."

"It's like he's being protected," Apollo said, looking to Emma. She hadn't looked away from the screen.

Kinder Garten peered up at the ceiling. Impossible to ignore the smoke slipping between the floorboards now. A black cloud formed above their heads.

Then Kinder Garten raised his good arm. "But let me show you!" he said. "I have proof he's okay. I've got pictures of him." He reached for the iPad, tapped in his code, and carried on.

"You'll see," he muttered.

He opened the photo gallery and swiped from one file to the next.

"You'll see."

But before he could find the image, Emma stepped back and raised the mattock. She swung sideways, with better aim this time. The pick lodged in the side of Kinder Garten's head, right above the left ear.

The power of the attack sent Kinder Garten over just like before, but this time when he landed, the force of the fall tore the mattock from his head. When it pulled free, it took a portion of his skull with it. Kinder Garten thrashed on the ground, and the side of his head bled wildly.

Apollo and Emma watched him from a distance. They could see his brain. It looked like uncooked, gamey meat. It pulsed in time with his heartbeat. He seemed lost in shock, but then his eyes shifted toward Apollo.

Kinder Garten bled and choked and cried, and even though the house above them had broken into flames, even though the whine of a fire engine could be heard in the distance, even though they had to get back up the stairs and escape, they couldn't go yet.

They couldn't move as Kinder Garten's blood pooled on the ground. It reached the iPad, face up in its case. It reached their shoes and soaked the soles. His eyes lolled back in his head until only the whites could be seen.

His hand tapped at the ground three more times and went still.

A POLLO BENT AND pulled at the iPad, watching the body. Its eyes stared up at the ceiling. The protective cover had been soaked through with blood, but when he slipped the device out, it was fine. When he looked at the other monitors, five of the eight men remained in their seats, watching with a nearly catatonic glassiness. What would this show offer next? Apollo pushed both monitors off the desk, and they fell backward and cracked on the floor.

Curiosity overcame Apollo. There was one thing he had to see, a question he needed answered. They pulled at Kinder Garten's sweatshirt, lifting the right side.

"I think Cal must've hit him at least once," Apollo said.

But when he lifted the shirt high enough, the wound didn't look made by a bullet. Instead the flesh hung loose, and the skin appeared to have three long parallel tears.

"Good for you, Cal," Emma said.

The heat above became powerful enough to make both of them sweat. More smoke curled down into the basement through the floorboards. Soon it would fill the space. The sound of wood cracking, crackling, played through the basement.

The heat turned oppressive, and the smoke now obscured the exposed beams in the ceiling. Apollo and Emma covered their mouths. Outside they heard the sirens. No doubt the neighbors were out in force. Apollo and Emma weren't going to be escaping via the driveway anymore.

They scanned the basement. An old blue washing machine and dryer set sat side by side. There was a supply closet containing a threadbare broom and two nearly toothless rakes, a shovel with a splintered handle, and worn-down work gloves.

Because it was an unfinished basement, the ceiling showed the wood-work and floorboards of the first floor, and even piping was visible, running from the kitchen connections and the bathrooms, leading to a boiler tucked into the far corner of the basement. The large upright cylinder looked like a missile. Pipes ran from its top and up into the ceiling.

"Why did they have so many space heaters if they had this big boiler down in the basement?" Apollo asked, staring at the machine.

"The pipes are cut," Emma said, pointing to the ceiling. "All of them."

Kinder Garten's blood appeared in their peripheral vision. The pool had found the level of the ground, slightest of angles, and begun rolling downward. It turned into a tributary, searching for its confluence. It ran toward Apollo and Emma, and for only a moment Apollo imagined the man's blood sought them out. Instead it found its way to the boiler, rolling underneath it. From below the boiler, as they moved closer, they heard a faint, dribbling sound.

Apollo set down the iPad. He and Emma moved to one side of the boiler and pressed their hands to it. Together they pushed, and the boiler rocked slightly. It was like trying to upend a fridge or a grandfather clock. Push again, and the boiler tipped. When it fell to the ground, it clattered and cracked.

And below it they found a large hole cut in the concrete. Kinder Garten's blood dribbled into that darkness. The hole, not even or neat, looked as if someone had spent many nights here, chipping and chopping. The work did not seem recent.

They looked into the portal. Hard to even say how far down they would fall. Firemen barked to each other on the street. The floorboards above Apollo and Emma were burned black by now.

She sat and scooted to the hole, but before she dropped through, Apollo stopped her.

"Wait," he said. "We need one more thing." He took out his phone, turned it on.

"You're making a fucking phone call?" Emma said.

He reached for the iPad and opened it again. He swiped, and a series of apps appeared.

On the other end of the line Patrice picked up. "You're still alive then," he said, sounding relieved. "Your mom came by here this morning, looking for you. She's real worried. Did you call her? She said you sounded off."

"Patrice, you have to shut up. I won't be able to call you again."

"Tell me," he said.

"Do you have Daylight up in the App Store?"

"You saw it yourself," Patrice said. "Biggest bug is that you still only get one use out of it. Drains so much battery power."

Emma sat at the edge of the hole, looking like a woman hanging her feet off a pier.

"I need it," Apollo said.

Patrice sighed on the phone. "Well, it's there," he said. "It costs $3.99. I can change the price so it's free, then you just download it."

When Patrice said that, a new idea came to Apollo. One so good it actually made him laugh, even in the midst of all this. "I do want you to change the price. Is there a maximum you can charge?"

"It's supposed to be $999.99, but there's an easy way around that."

"Can you do it now?"

"This is me," Patrice said. "Of course I can. How much?"

"Seventy thousand dollars," Apollo said.

The laughter on the other end of the line came so loudly, even Emma heard it before Apollo hung up.

By the time he found the app in the App Store, the price had been changed. He tapped to purchase. He squatted beside Emma, and together they watched the download bar progress.

"But what's the point if we can only use it once?" Emma asked. "The park is half a mile north of here."

"The old man told me a story," Apollo said. "Do you know what kills trolls?"

"Daylight," she said.

The house above rumbled, a thunderous crash, so loud it seemed possible a wall had collapsed. Soon the second floor might come down on the first, and then the first would be driven down into the basement.

Emma looked back to where the stairs had been. Hard to say if they were still there, through the black smoke.

Emma gripped Apollo's hand, and he lowered her into the hole. Not as deep as they'd feared. He handed the iPad down next. The Knudsen line, and their centuries of service, had come to its end. By evening, there'd be nothing left of them but scorched wood and bones.

8

THE WILDNESS

APOLLO EXPECTED EMMA to make magic. He climbed down into the dark alongside her, the passageway walls of compacted earth tight around them, hardly wide enough for one person, let alone two, the path ahead a long dark gullet, and above them a house on fire.

Though they were standing chest to chest, it was so dark he couldn't see her face. His eyes hadn't yet adjusted. He wanted to reach out and touch her cheeks or her nose to be sure this was really her.

"What are you waiting for?" Emma asked.

"I'm waiting for you," Apollo said. "Your light."

"You said we could use this only once," she said, tapping him with the iPad.

"Not that. I'm talking about, you know, that light I saw in the forest. It floated all around you. It was like a cloud."

Emma remained quiet. He couldn't see her face to read any expression.

"You controlled Jorgen's dreams," Apollo said, sounding exasperated and desperate. "The trees parted for you. Don't tell me you don't know what I'm talking about!"

Emma finally spoke. "I'm not saying that. I'm saying I was on my own and keeping Brian alive, keeping myself alive, working on Jorgen day and night, and it was killing me, Apollo. You saw me, didn't you? I wasn't able to do it because I was so powerful, I was able to do it because I had no other choice. I had to do it alone, so I did. But now I don't have to do it alone. At least I hope I don't. We could be stronger together, but that means you have to help me. Can you do that? Will you?"

Apollo nodded. They moved forward.

The passageway became even tighter, the roof coming down at an angle so they had to lower their heads. It felt like a funnel, a chute, the same as one might use on a cow, or a pig, in a slaughterhouse.

"Don't be mad at my sister," Emma whispered. "Please."

"You're thinking about that right now?"

Both spoke in hushed voices, though it sounded louder down here.

"Please, Apollo. It seems ridiculous to you, but it matters to me."

"Kim lied to me," he said. "I put a check in her hand, and she didn't blink."

Here Apollo stopped moving. Their eyes had adjusted enough that he could make out her outline behind him.

"Why did she believe you?" he asked. "What did you say that convinced her?"

"She didn't believe me," Emma said. "But she's my sister. She wasn't betraying you, Apollo. She was protecting me."

They scrambled forward in the dark.

The passageway finally opened into a large space, an earthen amphitheater, a series of ringed ridges that fed down to a broad floor of flattened earth. Kinder Garten had shown them the camera. Were those other men watching Apollo and Emma now?

They moved down the ringed levels, shallow as stairs. As they approached the floor of the amphitheater, Apollo felt Emma's eyes as surely as a touch. He felt himself shiver with the desire to tell her about Brian West. The dream that was not a dream, but a memory. Kinder Garten had clung to his belief that he'd cared for his family, that he'd done something so horrific as an act of love. Did Brian West feel the same when he'd plunged his only child into steaming hot water, when he held him under? He must have; against all common sense he must have. When Apollo had become impatient with Emma, when he'd become cruel, how had he justified it to himself? He was trying to focus on Brian, to be the kind of father he'd never had. What lengths will people stretch to believe they're still good?

Apollo scanned the higher ridges of the arena. The darkness hid everything more than two feet away, the effect more disconcerting in this open space. In time their eyes would adjust to the dark, but just now they felt nearly blind. In the tunnel they'd been cramped, but out here a tank might be sitting at arm's length, and they wouldn't realize its main gun was pointed at them until it fired. Hands outstretched, skitching forward in small increments, legs slightly bent as if expecting a blow. They moved forward until they reached the far end of the arena's stone wall, then pawed alongside it to traverse the space. Because of the shadows, because of the almost hypnotizing rhythm of their feet on the loose dirt, they felt dizzy as they moved.

Then Apollo bumped into something. When he hit it with his foot, there was a low, hollow thump. Emma went down on a knee.

A large gray polyethylene storage box.

The lid still on.

Apollo and Emma pulled the top off, trying to stay quiet, both breathing so heavily, they sounded like winded dogs.

A small body lay in there, on its side. Naked.

They knelt there waiting, listening, and then they heard it, faint but regular: the child's breathing. Without the lid, it echoed in the chamber.

Emma choked with shock—it sounded like she was retching. She dropped the iPad and reached into the storage box. The bottom of the bin showed layers of dead leaves and dirt, a makeshift mattress. She lifted the body and there he was. Sleeping beauty.

Brian.

He looked big for six months old, but that's because he was ten months old.

Being lifted, being held, caused the boy's breathing to change; a long, low gurgle escaped those lips. His skin felt cold to the touch. His eyelids fluttered open. Emma leaned close to see them. The baby yawned and squinted his eyes.

But even after the child woke, the echoing steady breathing in the chamber didn't change.

It went on as it had been, rhythmic and deep, not an echo, Apollo realized, but a matched pattern, something else breathing in sync beside the child. But now even that sound stopped, and all around them came a low rumble, like a bowling ball rolling on wood.

They'd thought the storage box had been sitting beside a portion of the amphitheater wall, but now the wall moved. The wall rolled like an alligator spinning its prey in the water. Apollo and Emma were still on their knees. There, in the dark, an eye as large as a manhole cover opened.

Jotunn.

Trolde.

Troll.

AHOT, DANK WIND blew out from the hole in the wall, a gas
that stank of dirt. In the cave's chill, the creature's exhalation
became a cloud of fog that filled the floor. Apollo and Emma
went back on their asses. Emma held tight to Brian as she
fell. Brian squirmed in her arms but could hardly wriggle in her grip. She
would not let him go again.

A shape emerged from the hole, but in the darkness and cover of the
cloud, its particulars were tough to see. Its dimensions were clear though.
An arm as thick as a tree stump moved above their heads. Emma fled
awkwardly, stumbling off. Apollo looked up and felt as if he'd been caught
before a great, yawning door and he had let this thing in.

Another breath, another cloud filled the dark amphitheater. The arm
hung in the air a moment, then its tip trembled and stretched, an enormous fist opening. Hard to call the digits fingers—there were either too
many or too few. Apollo couldn't get his bearings for the fog. But in a moment he smelled its body, a stink like rotten milk, and he nearly went sick
right there. He looked to his left to find Emma and Brian weren't there.
That, at least, relieved him.

The fingers on the misshapen hand showed great nails at the tips. The
troll slammed the fingers down into the dirt. The thumb landed right in
the middle of the open storage bin. If Brian had still been inside, he

would've been impaled. Emma yelped nearby. Brian, hearing her, reached up and found her chin.

With the nails dug into the dirt, the troll pulled its body out of the hole where it had been sleeping. It rose to its full height, the body unfurling until it stood as tall as the sail of a sloop. Its mouth opened wide, and it breathed a third breath, deeper than the others. Once more Apollo found himself swimming in that mist. It snorted heavily through its nostrils twice. He felt the moisture dapple across his scalp and forehead like dew. He couldn't move, and worse still, he felt a sick wave of something like nostalgia. To his horror, he almost called out Brian West's name.

The troll pulled its thick nails out of the dirt. It slapped the storage bin, one quick touch, and the container flipped end over end, landing about a foot away. The air filled with dead leaves and dirt. Apollo threw up an arm to shield his eyes. When the bin landed, its thump echoed, and the troll moved fast, a massive shape loping forward on short, thick legs, something simian about it, even more so when it bent to the ground, sniffing closer and closer to the bin.

Apollo turned on his feet to try and track Emma, but his shoes scuffed the dirt louder than he would've expected. Or maybe there weren't any other sounds to compete.

Before Apollo could move, the creature's eyes were on him. Nothing to do. No time to run, nowhere to hide. Two strides, and it came near. The troll stooped so close now, Apollo could reach out and touch it. From here he saw its greenish skin with collected dead leaves and clots of dirt; tiny bones—from squirrels or birds—were embedded in its flesh like pins in a pincushion. It snorted and breathed again, and this time Apollo's whole face went wet with moisture, but he stifled the impulse to retch. Its enormous eyes faced Apollo, and they were flat, off-white disks. The troll couldn't see him because the troll was almost blind. No wonder it relied on its nose. Its nostrils were recessed like a bat's.

It sniffed the air around Apollo. Sniffed again, and finally a great rip appeared in its face, somewhere below the nose. Its teeth were as large and jagged as its nails. But the creature didn't tear into Apollo; instead it yawned and blew another wave of fetid breath. The pair of them lost in the cloud. When Apollo blinked, he could almost hear water running nearby. It sniffed near him one more time, then turned away.

What saved me? he asked himself.

Now that it had moved, Apollo could see where it had been sleeping, not a nook but the mouth of a tunnel. A different quality of darkness lay at the far end of that passage. Moonlight. He saw moonlight out there. And small stones running up a slope. The park, the outside world—their escape lay fifty feet ahead.

The troll brought a hand tight around the bin, crushing it. It scanned the amphitheater, and its mouth opened, its belly expanded, filling with air. Now it produced a howl like a nightmare from some distant age. Nearby, Emma had been trying to make her way back the way they'd come. Jorgen's house might be burning, but it wasn't a fucking monster on the hunt. She wasn't thinking clearly, but it was the best idea she could form. And yet when she heard that howl—like standing with your ear to a foghorn—she collapsed into a crouch just as Apollo did. She saw the iPad lay a foot from where she went down.

The only one not thrown by the bellowing, in fact, was the baby. Emma's arms couldn't keep hold of him because she'd stretched out to grab the iPad. She couldn't hold on to both, not with one wriggling to break free. Brian rolled himself into the dirt, then did the most shocking thing Apollo and Emma had yet seen.

He walked.

And where was he walking?

Back toward the troll.

Only three steps, arms out in the dark, but it was enough for Emma to feel wounded, nearly mortally. Should she run after Brian, or was there a better strategy? She activated the iPad, and when the screen lit up, she became bathed in the light of the home screen.

The troll sensed the change in the gloom. It turned in her direction. Brian turned back toward her too, then threw one arm over his eyes, unaccustomed to the glow. He squeaked, a cry of distress. Both Emma and Apollo tried not to notice how close in tone this cry sounded to the troll's bellow. Emma didn't look up. She had to work. She found the app and turned the screen so it faced the others. She stood and held the device higher, hoping to spare her son's eyes. She tapped the icon once, and the chamber flared.

Brian screeched like a tiny primate and fell forward on his face, flailing with surprise that seemed like pain. The troll stumbled too, slumping backward and making that foghorn sound.

But it didn't turn to stone.

The fucking app did not win the day. In a moment that thing would find its balance and be all over them. They needed a new plan.

Emma rose and ran to the center of the chamber. "The sun is rising!" she shouted.

Apollo understood her idea immediately, intuitively. If the troll feared the sun, then it might run from the light. If he could get it outside, Emma and Brian would be able to slip out, too. He ran for the tunnel. He looked over his shoulder and shouted, "The sun is rising!"

The troll shivered with confusion. First its head darted toward the sound of Apollo's voice, but then it looked upward, throwing an arm out as if it could bat away the threat.

"The sun is rising!" Apollo shouted again, his voice trailing down the long throat of the tunnel.

The troll spun left, then right, unsure, confused. The battery life of the iPad was nearly depleted, but for the moment Emma wielded a shining star. Apollo escaped the passageway and into the open night.

The troll turned, determined to follow, but then it sniffed the air once again and reached back one enormous hand. Its fingers found the child and plucked him up and with a single gulp the troll swallowed Brian Kagwa.

102

POLLO SCRAMBLED UP the hill of bones, and now that he was out of the cave, free from the cloistered air down there, he could smell himself. He carried with him a cloud of spiced gasoline. The bath he'd taken in the old man's Brennivín remained in full effect. Maybe that's what had saved him down in the darkness. The troll hadn't been able to smell his flesh. But this would only be a moment of grace—in seconds that troll would be up the hill, and then what?

Why did I tell you that story? What did I want you to hear?

Jorgen's voice sounded so loud in his head that he expected it to echo through the woods. The words so surprising, so unexpected Apollo could hardly register what they meant. Then there was no time for parsing out the meaning because a sound played from the tunnel, a long low rumbling roar, and a moment later an arm emerged from the cave mouth, the tips of the enormous hand baring those jagged nails. The nails slammed into the stones—the children's bones—and sent them flying in all directions. The beast dragged itself out of the passageway, into the open air. It stood more than three stories tall.

Apollo stiffened at the top of the hill. How could he defeat such a thing?

Why did I tell you that story? What did I want you to hear?

The troll lumbered up the hill. It moved with such gracelessness that Apollo wondered if it might be wounded. Had Emma hurt it before it got out here? As it clambered up the hill toward him, it made faint coughing sounds, sputtering, as if something was caught in its throat.

Apollo took three steps back, but where would he go? The Northern Forest surrounded him. Even though the modern world was less than a half mile away, he might as well be in some German wood a thousand years ago.

Something silver shined in the moonlight and caught Apollo's attention. The serving lid still there, right where he and Emma had left it. And if the lid was still there, then the sheep's head would be, too.

Why did I tell you that story? What did I want you to hear?

Apollo rose to his feet and lifted the lid of the serving tray. The sheep's head's remaining eye watched him. Apollo picked up the head and held it in front of him, balanced in one open palm. In the other hand he held the lid. The troll might not be able to smell him because of the Brennivín, but this boiled flesh might tempt.

The troll's head jutted forward like a hound's. A moment of stillness, then the thing sniffed the air, snorting. It croaked again, but the gagging soon passed. Apollo held the sheep's head out and watched as the troll sniffed a second time. It squeezed its enormous eyes shut and cocked its head, listening for a sound.

"I'm right here, you goddamn troll!" Apollo shouted. "But you're too stupid to catch me!"

With that, Apollo turned and ran, holding the sheep's head high and the serving lid in his other hand. Like Askeladden, he sprinted deeper into the Northern Forest, the troll tearing after him through the trees.

Apollo scurried like a wild rabbit, weaving through the thickest stands of trees, places even the troll couldn't penetrate. He hid inside while the creature stalked in circles, bellowing and bashing at the branches, stopping occasionally to stoop forward and paw at its throat, slapping at an irritant, then righting itself.

He used such moments to dart out again, aiming for the next copse of thick trees, pursued again by the predator, then hiding inside and shivering with adrenaline and fear. They moved like this as the night passed, and Apollo hardly felt the cold, hardly registered fatigue. There were moments, when he wasn't running, that he swore he heard Emma's voice on the wind, calling out to him. But he knew that if the troll was here with him, then Emma and Brian had escaped. This idea fueled him, fired his courage.

Apollo remained tucked inside a circle of pignut hickory trees. The troll soon appeared. It heaved loudly now, and its mouth dripped a jelly as green as its skin. The troll spat this out and coughed loudly, sounding like a car engine that wouldn't turn over. It sniffed at the trees, bumped the side of its head against the hickory, testing them. Nearly dawn now. When the sun rose, it would turn to stone, and that would be the end of it.

Not twenty yards from here Apollo saw the large clearing he'd come across when he'd followed Emma the day before. Apollo rose to his feet and bolted. When he reached the open ground, he set down the sheep's head and the lid. He placed the head so it was cradled in the lid, face up and exposed, easily scented. Apollo ran straight on from there, back into the trees on the other side of the clearing. He found a scarlet oak with branches low enough to scale. It hadn't lost all its leaves, so he disappeared among them when he climbed.

"My head is right there on the ground!" Apollo shouted. "Why don't you just try and crack my skull!"

The trees at the far edge of the clearing didn't part—they shattered. The troll swept them aside with a renewed fury. It entered the clearing so quickly, it seemed to be flying. As it moved, it lowered its head, its jaws expanding, teeth plowing through the dirt and snow, inhaling all of it, just to get that sheep's head. It clamped its teeth down, and in a moment there was a metallic clank that made even Apollo's mouth clench. The troll threw its head back, bringing one hand to its mouth in shock, spitting out what it couldn't swallow. The lid, cracked and bent, hit a tree trunk and the clang echoed.

Now the troll thrashed in the clearing. It fell into frenzy. It threw out its arms, digging its nails into tree trunks and pulling them right up out of the earth, torn roots dangling down like veins. It tossed those trees into the air, then tore up more. The troll lost itself in its ferocity, mindless, thoughtless. Apollo watched it from his perch in the tree. He couldn't shout taunts at it, couldn't make jokes or jabs, because he felt small and terrified. The troll created such chaos that it flung one tree right up into the air, and it tumbled right back down on its head. The beast fell on its back pinned beneath a large hickory tree. It heaved there, on its back, panting and undone. The sky had gone from black to purple. The troll kicked its legs to try and escape, but it had nearly no fight left.

"Apollo! Apollo!"

He leaped down from his hiding place. It was Emma's voice. Quite close.

She came into the clearing through the gap in the trees the troll had caused. Her hands were in the air, waving back and forth.

"Where's Brian?" Apollo shouted.

Emma didn't hesitate—she clambered onto the troll's belly. "He ate him! All this time I've been trying to catch up. He ate Brian."

She stomped on its heaving gut. It opened its mouth but could only throw its head back. Was it defeated or was it gloating? The threat of sunlight lingered near the horizon.

Apollo ran to Emma. In his coat pocket was the knife he'd pulled from Jorgen's throat. He brought it out now and plunged it into the troll's flesh, up near the top of the belly. He sank it in until even the handle disappeared. The creature thrashed now, and the tree on its chest buckled. Apollo pulled the blade downward, splitting the creature's skin apart.

He pulled down until his shoulders burned. He cut, and the belly opened wider before them. A dark green liquid the consistency of mud pooled out. A smell of sewer water filled their nostrils, and neither noticed or cared.

The troll's legs kicked more frantically. The pitch of its foghorn bellow went higher, and its arms slapped at the tree trunk until the hickory went up at an angle, like a seesaw, and flipped over.

Apollo found the belly sack but didn't dare plunge a knife inside for fear of hitting their son. He dug in with his hands, and Emma did, too. They tore at the sack, the texture of a hot water balloon.

The stomach split open, and a thinner yellowing liquid sprayed out and soaked their faces, their clothes. It meant nothing to them. They hardly noticed.

And inside they found their son, tucked into a ball and still wriggling. Swallowed whole and thus still alive. They pulled him out into the world.

Brian Kagwa, the only child ever born twice.

They fell away from the troll's body, crawling as quickly as their weary bodies could manage. The sun rose, and daylight—true daylight—found them all. The troll trembled, and its body stiffened, and its sickly greenish color drained. It made one last sound, a whimper that almost sounded like relief, and darkened as it turned to stone. A moment later the large shape broke apart. Now it looked like a mound of boulders, nothing more. To any passerby, it would look like a small hill there in the Northern Forest.

Emma didn't wait. She rose on her unsteady legs, cradling Brian close to her chest, and started for the woods, the path they'd taken a night ago.

Apollo lingered. He approached the stones, skirting around until he found the largest one, what had been the troll's head. He could still make out the soft depression of those great blind eyes. He brushed each one with a finger. He leaned close to the stone and pressed his forehead to it. He felt as if he was finally burying what had been haunting him since he was a child. A funeral not for his father but his fatherlessness. Let that monster rest.

APOLLO FOUND HIS way to the path where he saw a set of footprints. Emma's tread, but deeper than when he'd trailed her before, the extra weight of their child in her arms. He followed and found them, Emma hunched over and moving slowly. She had her coat unzipped and the boy tucked inside, his body against hers. This was the parka they'd taken from Jorgen's house; it was so big it had plenty of room for both of them. She'd done her best to clean off his face, but his hair remained matted a muddy green. Apollo and Emma looked even worse.

Brian Kagwa, ten months old, squinted at the sky, at the canopy of bare tree limbs. He didn't look frightened or wounded, not even shocked. Instead, it seemed as if he was thawing in the daylight. Neither Apollo nor Emma spoke to him or to each other. Brian didn't move his head much, but his eyes scrolled left to right from one tree to the next. When a bird on a tree chirped or cawed, Brian stared at it and pursed his lips as if to answer back.

Finally they left the woods and reached the paved parts of the park. They passed the Carousel and the George Seuffert, Sr., Bandshell. Strange to see these places again. Apollo hadn't expected he'd be back this way, he hadn't truly believed he'd come out of this alive. Soon they reached the bathroom where he'd spent the night. The door to the ladies' room hadn't been fixed, only pulled shut; a few strips of emergency tape were easily pulled down.

The sinks worked, and they washed Brian's hair out, cleaned his face. They each did a little dabbing, at least to clear out their ears and eyebrows, swish their mouths. Apollo realized the red string had come off his finger. Who could say when? Maybe when his hands were inside the troll's belly, pulling Brian free. Maybe it lay in the center of a stone in the Northern Forest. That seemed improbable enough to be true.

"We have to get Brian to a hospital," Apollo finally said as they left the bathroom. They still looked rough, a feral family, but at least they didn't have bits of troll guts stuck between their teeth.

Emma didn't answer. She hadn't looked away from Brian yet.

"I wanted to call Kim in," she said tentatively. "She's still his doctor. And it's going to be pretty remarkable if we just show up at a hospital. Kim would be discreet."

Apollo watched her as they made a few steps but finally laughed quietly. "Well, I know she can keep a secret."

Apollo couldn't be aware of this yet, but Kim had never cashed that check he gave her. Instead she'd slipped it under his apartment door days ago, two words written on the face: I'M SORRY.

"Maybe someone will pick us up," she said, gesturing ahead to Woodhaven Boulevard.

No surprise, but they were the only people on foot at this hour. The early morning traffic clocked at speeds of fifty miles an hour. The only thing that could stop these drivers was a red light, and even that might only slow them to about thirty-five. Nobody would be giving some random hitchhiking family a lift. Especially not with the way they looked.

Apollo couldn't call 911. He had no cellphone power left, and there were no working pay phones on the street. No yellow or even green taxis were out here, and even livery cabs were a rare occurrence. Some would suggest running out into the street to hail a passing car, but such suggestions would never be made by anyone familiar with the drivers in Queens. Imagine slaying trolls and then being killed by a hit-and-run driver.

"We have to wait on the Q11," Apollo said.

The bus stop had a bench. Emma nodded and sat, cradling Brian against her belly. She raised her free hand and extended a finger, brought it close to Brian's face. The move looked so tentative. Brian Kagwa was the only living thing that made Emma Valentine tremble. Finally she brought her finger to the boy's chin. She touched him gently there and rubbed the skin. She put her finger to his lips.

She pointed into the partly open mouth. "He has teeth," she said softly.

They both shivered with the pleasure of seeing them. Followed by a throbbing sadness in the rib cage. They'd come in while they weren't around. Had he cried as he was teething? Had there been anyone to soothe him?

Apollo slipped a hand inside the parka and held one of Brian's feet. He squeezed, and the toes wriggled. Apollo closed his eyes and grinned.

Apollo saw the days and months and years to come playing against the screen of his eyelids. He saw Apollo and Emma wrangling Brian into learning how to use the potty; waking often each night, for many nights, when it was time for him to graduate to sleeping without a diaper; sneaking vegetables into his diet and coaxing him to kindergarten; the tedium of doing homework with him; the intimidation when his homework became too complicated for them to understand; cleaning him up after his first real fight; the first time he stole money from them; the first time they noticed; the faults the boy would find with each of them; the age when he learned to think of his father as a failure; the age when he told his father so; all this—and worse—was going to happen in the years to come, and thank God, thank God, thank God.

Apollo felt dizzy with appreciation. He leaned into Emma as he squeezed Brian's other foot. They both sobbed at the bus stop.

Brian caught sight of an airplane and watched it thread across the sky.

"There's something I always wanted to ask you," Apollo eventually said. "What was your third wish?"

For the first time since they'd left the cave, Emma looked at Apollo instead of Brian. "My first wish was to meet a good man. My second was to have a healthy child."

"Yes."

"And my third wish was for a life full of adventure."

Some time passed, but neither of them counted how long. It was still early morning. Then Emma leaned forward slightly and gestured with her chin. Down the long stretch of Woodhaven Boulevard, they could see a bus, still a few minutes away.

It occurred to Apollo that the driver could give them a hard time if they didn't have the fare. It sounded impossible, but who could say? They were a family trying to get home, but who knew what the driver might see? Maybe he wouldn't extend a bit of charity to a trio like them.

Brian and Emma had been exposed to the elements for months—they needed to get on that bus and reach the care of a professional. That incoming Q11 took on the aspect of a lifeboat. Apollo found himself concocting all sorts of speeches to try to explain why they had no money to pay the fare but then remembered how he'd ended up at this bus stop the night before. The MetroCard was still in his pocket. He slipped it out and showed Emma.

"A gift from the NYPD," he said.

The Q11 approached, its interior lights blazing. At this hour it was the brightest thing in the world. It might as well be a chariot pulling the sun across the sky. Nothing less would do for Emma, Brian, and Apollo. They stood as it slowed.

"And they lived happily ever after," Apollo whispered.

Emma leaned into him. "Today," she said. "And they lived happily today."

"Is that enough?" he asked, looking at Brian, looking at her.

"That's everything, my love."